I
Remember
Valentine

I
Remember
Valentine

Liz Hamlin

 E. P. DUTTON · NEW YORK

Lyrics on page 175 to "My Melancholy Baby" printed by permission of the copyright owners Jerry Vogel Music Co., Inc., New York City, and Shapiro Bernstein & Co., New York City.

Copyright © 1987 by Liz Hamlin

All rights reserved. Printed in the U.S.A.

PUBLISHER'S NOTE: This novel is a work of fiction. Names, characters, places, and incidents are either the product of the author's imagination or are used fictitiously, and any resemblance to actual persons, living or dead, events, or locales is entirely coincidental.

No part of this publication may be reproduced or transmitted in any form or by any means, electronic or mechanical, including photocopy, recording, or any information storage and retrieval system now known or to be invented, without permission in writing from the publisher, except by a reviewer who wishes to quote brief passages in connection with a review written for inclusion in a magazine, newspaper, or broadcast.

Published in the United States by E. P. Dutton,
a division of NAL Penguin Inc.,
2 Park Avenue, New York, N.Y. 10016.

Library of Congress Cataloging-in-Publication Data
Hamlin, Liz.
I remember Valentine.
I. Title.
PS3558.A446I2   1987   813'.54   86–24193

ISBN: 0-525-24524-3

Published simultaneously in Canada by
Fitzhenry & Whiteside Limited, Toronto

COBE

Designed by Steven N. Stathakis

10 9 8 7 6 5 4 3 2 1

First Edition

To Bobbie

I
Remember
Valentine

1

I was eleven years, three months, and four days old when I moved out of the world of the breasts and into the world of the tits. The year was 1936—the same year that Valentine Hart became my Best Friend.

Before our destinies coupled, when Valentine and I first came face to face on a narrow stairway in a low-rent flat, I'd had less important friends—girls amazingly like myself whose very sameness confined our friendships to the small-letter category. Girls who were shiny clean, remarkably uniform. Girls who made good grades in school and never said dirty words. Girls who were proper little ladies skipping sedately over clipped green lawns, always being careful to keep their stiffly starched skirts decently in place so as not to embarrass themselves or society by accidentally baring their snugly covered backsides.

We were sociable, civilized creatures who slept over at each other's houses and giggled ourselves to sleep in neat, frilly bedrooms and arose clear-eyed in the morning to share nourishing breakfasts served by conscientious mothers in spotless kitchens. We were small, synchronized echoes of each other as we marched through childhood in perfect step, accepting without question our parents' supremacy in the pecking order of family life.

The rules were never ambiguous, having been distinctly developed and defined by our parents, who were also remarkably similar to each other. My mother's friends were replicas of my mother; they visited frequently to exchange recipes and advice, and to play bridge or Parcheesi, while my friends and I pushed wicker buggies quietly around card tables set up in prim parlors in the winter and on trim lawns in the summer. My father's friends fit the contours of my father's mold: they met for golf at the country club on sunny Saturday mornings and occasionally—but rarely, for my father and his friends were not given to taking risks—spent an evening playing poker. For limited stakes.

All of us inhabited a space so remote in philosophy and so foreign in concept from the space occupied by Valentine and Lacey and Big and Black and Broken—the Hart family I was soon to meet—that we could have been residing in two different galaxies instead of in two different sections of a small Ohio Valley town.

Having serenely waltzed through eleven predictable years, I had no reason to think that the orderly cadence of my life would ever become discordant, and I was totally unprepared for the shock my parents gave me early in the January of 1936.

Until then, I had been swaddled in such a protective cocoon to insulate me from reality that the word *Depression*, which appeared daily on the front page of the *Marietta Times*, had no meaning to me. Although I was an excellent

2

reader for my age, I hardly noticed the word, casually bypassing it on my way to the comic page to follow the adventures of Dick Tracy and Tillie the Toiler.

Nor was the Depression mentioned often in conversation by my parents or their friends. On the rare occasions when they did acknowledge its existence, they did so with the well-bred distaste with which they would have admitted the existence of any other social disease. Like syphilis and gonorrhea, the Depression simply did not infect the people in our antiseptic world, even though it was filling the minds and emptying the stomachs of millions outside our sphere. Until it harmed me personally, the Depression remained as foreign as the blue shape of Germany, the green shape of Spain, and the purple shape of a hard-to-spell country named Czechoslovakia—shapes that we were expected to locate and identify on the maps in our geography book, and that we forgot as rapidly as we passed the tests covering them.

But suddenly, overnight, the Depression became as real to me as the swing on our shady front porch, the dollhouse in our spacious backyard, the dotted swiss canopy over my brass bed. Had I been as tuned in to my environment as Valentine Hart was to hers, I would have been better prepared for the bad news my parents gave me after the Christmas of 1935 was packed away. There had certainly been indications of change—changes I could have analyzed had I been as streetwise as Valentine, had my two immaculate little ears been pressed to the ground to detect the overt rumbles that should have warned me a personal earthquake was soon going to crack the serene crust of my life and rearrange and shatter its pattern.

For there *had been* indications of change—visual and conversational straws in the wind, barometers to suggest that the atmosphere was charged. My mother's winter boots, for instance, which were resoled rather than replaced when they began to show signs of wear. And my mother lugging the L. C. Smith typewriter down from the attic and practicing typing instead of joining my father in front of the Atwater-Kent to listen to Lowell Thomas.

And my mother's coat. For as long as I could remember, buying a new winter coat had been an annual ceremony for my mother, one that began early in autumn as she sipped tea and leafed through women's magazines, studying the styles currently in vogue, then making the traditional late-September shopping trip to town, always taking with her one of her friends with a daughter my age. The two women joyfully scanned racks of coats while we two children stood politely by in quiet anguish awaiting our trip to the dime store, where we would be treated to lunch and a small shopping expedition of our own. I should have been alerted when, in the autumn of 1935, I casually mentioned the anticipated shopping spree and my mother quickly changed the subject.

There had been other straws in the economic wind that would soon blow me into Valentine Hart's erratic world. I was not sent to camp during the dog days of 1935 as I had been every other summer since I was old enough to understand and follow camp rules. I was disappointed when my mother, who had a dread that I would be exposed to polio in the town swimming pool or the cooling waters of the Muskingum River, told me that there would be no swimming for me that summer, since I could not go to camp and she would not let me go to the pool or the river. Being an accepting, obedient child I cried when my friends left for camp, but I did not challenge my mother.

There were also subtle changes in my father's routine. He cut down on cigarettes, stubbing out his cherished Chesterfields when they were partially smoked and relighting them later. And as time passed, rolling his own Bugler cigarettes. And shining his shoes himself instead of tipping Joey, the black boy who swept the barbershop, to put a gleam on them. And not renewing his membership in the country club, explaining to his golfing pals that he was too busy with his job as assistant bank manager to join them on Saturday mornings. Ironic that he used being busy on the job as his excuse, since the deplorable truth was that there was virtually no work for an assistant manager in a bank that had little need even for tellers.

Although none of the summer and autumn signs of change alerted me to the possibility that the smoothly flowing waters of my life were about to turn turbulent, the Christmas of 1935 did awaken small stirrings of curiosity. I was puzzled when I listened to my parents turn down invitations to holiday parties, which were as traditional as the Christmas tree itself, murmuring inexpert apologies of being committed to attend other parties—then staying home. I was confused by their hesitancy when I asked for money to buy their Christmas gifts and my mother rapidly left the room while my father told me that neither he nor my mother could think of a thing they wanted for Christmas that year. I was old enough not to believe in Santa Claus, but not old enough not to believe in my father. I did not question his answer.

There were packages under the tree for me that Christmas. Heroically—and probably foolishly—my parents managed to make Christmas as merry for me as it was for my friends. But when the holiday ended and the New Year began, they faced the inevitable. They told me in words impossible to misinterpret that due to the Depression, my father had been demoted from assistant bank manager to teller, and his salary had been cut. There was a possibility that if the Depression worsened, even the teller's job would be eliminated. We would have to move away from Washington Street. There was no way we could continue to pay the rent on our large house. Suddenly the Depression became more alive than "Little Orphan Annie" and "Dick Tracy."

"Because of this terrible Depression," my mother said, "we will have to move, and move very quickly."

I bombarded her with questions. Why? Where? When?

"Because we already owe the landlord three months' back rent. He can't afford to carry us any longer. He has his own bills to pay. I've been looking for a place we can afford, and I've found one in a reasonably decent neighborhood. I rented a flat on Fourth Street."

Flat? Flat? The word confused me. The only flats I knew were the black fat symbols our music teacher taught us to draw on our wide-lined music paper. I had never cared much for those flats. Compared to the friendly, open-faced sharps, the flats represented to me the dark side of music.

"What's a flat?"

"It's an apartment." My mother's doleful tone told me that there was something not quite desirable about a flat or an apartment, and I tried to think of what I knew about apartments. They did not have yards with elm trees to support rope swings. Apartments offered no cool thick grass to run through to chase fireflies on hot July nights, no space to build snowmen on cold January days, no yellow dandelions to hold under a friend's chin to see if she liked butter.

"I won't have a yard to play in," I wailed.

My mother offered a crumb of consolation. "On nice afternoons you can walk home from school with your friends and play in their yards."

The next day, that small bit of comfort was taken from me when I was summoned to the principal's office. My mother sat in a straight chair opposite his desk, like a chastised child. She was crying. I cried too when the principal explained to me what he had just explained to my mother. The flat on Fourth Street was outside the Washington Street School district. When we moved to the flat, I would have to transfer to Marion Street School.

"We're sorry to lose you," he assured me. "You're a fine student. But we can't make an exception for you, or

6

we'd have to make exceptions for everyone. We'll send your records to your new school and they'll be there when you enter after the midwinter break."

I was insulted by this second rearrangement of my life, and I was terrified. I belonged in the school I'd attended for six years with students who were healthy, clean, polite. I should not be forced to go to a school where the boys and girls were dirty, shabby, too skinny or too fat, had no manners, and yelled dirty words at ball games and track meets.

When I got home that afternoon, I discarded any pretense of being civilized. I kicked, screamed, and cried just like any spoiled child would when grown-ups are not being reasonable. I vowed that I would not move to a flat, would not leave my school. I threatened to lock myself in my room and never come out again. I told my mother that if she and my father wanted to move, they could forget about me because I would not go with them. I threw myself facedown on my soft pillow and kicked my feet against my shiny brass bed and accused my mother of not loving me. I was encouraged when she began to cry; I thought I was winning the battle, until the door opened and my father came into my bedroom. He was a quiet, unobtrusive man who rarely asserted himself, never raised his voice. That afternoon he assumed a role unfamiliar to me. He ordered my mother to leave the room and to close the door. When we were alone he rolled a cigarette and smoked while he stood by the window and looked down at the snow-covered lawn. He waited until I ran out of tears and threats, and then he spoke quietly and without sentiment. I didn't believe him that afternoon, but before another week passed I learned that he had told me the cruel truth.

"You might as well stop crying. Tears won't change a thing. You have to take this move in stride and try to make it easier on your mother, not harder. She feels as bad as you do. Worse, because she feels so guilty about making

7

you unhappy. She shouldn't feel that way, but she does. It's not her fault, and it's not mine. The Depression did this to us."

There was that hateful word again.

"And as long as the Depression continues, we have to learn to live with it. The first thing we must do is move. Even if we could afford the rent here, which we can't, your life wouldn't stay the same. You can't buy the clothes your girlfriends buy. You won't be able to give parties, or go to them. We can't afford to buy gifts. It will take every cent I make to feed us and keep a roof over our heads. And more besides. Your mother plans to look for a job as soon as we get settled in the flat. That's why she's been brushing up on her typing. Her life will be changing too, just like yours. There's nothing we can do about those changes until the Depression ends. We just have to hang on and make the best of it. You're old enough and smart enough to face the truth and I'm going to tell it to you. Since the word got around that I've been demoted at the bank, our old friends don't call us very often. They're uncomfortable around us. They pity us, they're embarrassed for us, and they're scared of being too close to someone who's been hit by the Depression. As if hard times, like measles or the mumps, might be contagious, passed on to them. You'll find your girlfriends won't be quite as friendly with you when you move away. You'll have to make new friends in your new school. You can kick and cry and make your mother feel worse than she does, or you can accept what's happening and make the best of it. It's entirely up to you, but either way, you're going to move to the flat and you're going to go to Marion Street School and that's that."

It was the only long speech I ever heard him make. I made no more threats about staying behind when they moved. I tried not to cry around my mother. My surrender did not extend to helping her get ready for the move, however, and while she packed, I gazed out of my bedroom

8

window and worried about the kids in Marion Street School. I knew they were a tough group. I had watched them at interschool ball games and track meets and I, along with my friends, had always been politely disdainful of them, judging them to be our inferiors in all aspects other than their constant ability to emerge as winners, even though they looked like losers. Their teeth were usually bad and sometimes missing. Their hair was unkempt. Their clothes were patched and shabby. Yet an inner grit enabled them consistently to outscore us in ball games, outrun us in track meets, and outshout us in the bleachers. Though most of them were shorter and smaller than I was, they made me uneasy, and I was frightened by the thought of trying to form friendships with them.

As for my old friends, unfortunately my father's prediction about them was right. When they heard that I was going to transfer to Marion Street School, they tolerated me until we moved, but occasionally I caught them looking at me as if I was someone they had just met and whispering behind their hands. There were no more party invitations for me, no more sleeping over. Until my last day in the neighborhood I secretly hoped that they would surprise me with a farewell party, but they didn't. Like the well-bred little mannequins they were, they did not embarrass me or themselves with a formal good-bye. The girl who was my current best friend did shove a brightly wrapped bottle of Blue Waltz perfume toward me as we parted at my gate on my last day in Washington Street School, and I promised her that I would never, never use it and that I would keep it forever in remembrance of our undying friendship.

Within a month of making that promise, I helped Valentine douse the perfume on Black's only sweater in revenge for his putting turpentine on the cat's tail.

We moved on the first day of my midwinter break. On Valentine's Day. I tersely rejected my parents' invita-

9

tion to go to the flat with them the night before we moved in, and listened half-heartedly when they returned from checking to see if the utilities in the flat were functioning.

"It won't be so bad," my mother said. "With a bit of cleaning it will be quite presentable. It's in much better shape than the flat across the hall."

She snared my interest. "Do you mean we'll be living with another family?"

"No. The two flats are separate. Each has three rooms and a bath. The only thing we'll share with the other occupants is the hallway and the stairway. I arranged with the landlord to move in tomorrow, and the other family is scheduled to move in the following day, so we will make efficient use of the one stairway."

My mother's efficiency had not yet collided with Lacey Hart's philosophy. Their opposite concepts met head-on when my mother and I turned the corner into Fourth Street on moving day and beheld what appeared to be a completely disorganized rummage sale on the sidewalk in front of the flat. A dilapidated sofa was piled high with lamps topped by torn shades, stained pillows, a three-legged footstool, and a haphazard collection of *True Confessions* and Street and Smith *Love Story* magazines. The only suggestion of order was the big feed and grain calendar nailed to the wall of the building, securely out of the snow and slush. Four bright red *X*s were marked over four early February dates. My mother looked at the calendar and fidgeted. I was to learn later that the only element of time that concerned Lacey Hart was the four days of each month when she would know whether there was another little Hart on its way.

My mother drove past the crowded sidewalk and parked well up the street, leaving room for the moving van to unload. As we walked toward the flat I studied the conglomeration spilling over the curb. A small wooden icebox with its door hanging by one rusty hinge leaned against a lamppost. The icebox door swung open in the brisk wind, disclosing a stained interior and an ice card with one corner missing. I learned later that Broken Hart had eaten it. On top of the icebox was a scratched guitar, and on top of the guitar was a Crosley radio covered with a layer of dust so thick even the February wind couldn't dislodge it. Directly in front of the door leading into the flat, blocking the moving men's path, was a potty-chair with most of its red paint peeled off. Beneath the chair was a discolored enamel pot with its handle missing.

As the moving men reached down to push the potty-chair aside, the door of the flat flew open and I saw Lacey Hart for the first time. There was a lot of Lacey to see.

Lacey's face was wide, round. She had incredibly beautiful white skin and pink cheeks that looked so soft I wanted to reach up and touch them. Lacey's big cornflower blue eyes were trimmed in the longest, darkest, thickest eyelashes I had ever seen—even in Maybelline ads. Lacey's bright red hair tumbled to her shoulders and teased her forehead and caroused around her ears as it danced to the tune of the February breeze.

I was only fleetingly aware of Lacey Hart's hair and skin and eyes and the rest of her glorious face, because I, like the moving men and my mother, was mesmerized by the great big bare tit which Lacey was holding in her hand as casually as my mother was holding her purse.

I had never before seen a bare tit.

Standing by Lacey's side, clinging to her leg and grabbing upward toward the great big bare tit was a queer little creature with a lamb-leg dripping from its squashed nose. Its lips were shiny with slobber, and an out-to-lunch stare was in its squinted eyes. Its body was as lopsided as its face. One leg was shorter than the other, and one arm hung at half-mast and flopped like a flag in a stiff breeze.

As my mother and the moving men and I stared, Lacey spoke. "Hey guys, hand me up that potty-chair. Poor little

11

Broken's going to pee his pants if we don't get that thing up here soon."

Her voice was fascinating. It boomed. In its own way it was as big as the tit at which everyone but my mother was still staring. My mother had stiffly turned her back and was intently studying the other side of the street. Lacey waited for a moment for the moving men to quit looking and start moving and then she strengthened her request.

"For Pete's sake, what are you guys staring at? Ain't you ever seen a tit before? Get the lead out. Carry that potty-chair and the pot upstairs before Broken turns on his water works and gets icicles on his legs. Here, Broken," she turned from the men and directed her attention toward the queer little creature hanging on her leg and inching his misshapen mouth up toward her bare tit. "Have another suck while these big galoots get the lead out of their ass."

She bent down and stuck her big brown nipple in the small creature's mouth. As she bent over her loose wrapper fell open and the moving men and I were treated to the sight of the other tit. It was just as impressive as the one she was feeding to what I could now see was a little boy.

The sight of the other tit seemed to break the spell the first tit had cast on the moving men. They closed their gaping mouths and got their eyes back down to normal size and obediently reached for the potty and the chair, falling over themselves and each other to see which of them could be of quickest service. They finally compromised, one carrying the pot and the other the chair, and they followed Lacey's round backside—fluid and rhythmic as it bounced up the stairs. When I started to follow Lacey and the men, my mother grabbed my arm.

"Wait here," she ordered, and she called coldly and clearly up the stairs to the moving men, "I'd like for you to start carrying our things in, please."

"Sure, lady. Be right down," came the answer. My

mother propelled me up the stairs ahead of her and unlocked the door to our flat. While she inserted the rusty key in the tight lock and struggled to open the door, I popped across the small landing and stared into Lacey Hart's kitchen. I watched her move the boy from her tit long enough to open the kitchen window and reach out into the leftover snow to bring in two bottles of cold beer and hand one to each of the moving men before she stuffed her big brown nipple back into the child's groping mouth again. While the men opened the bottles she shoved the potty-chair through a door, which I assumed led to the bathroom, and disappeared for a moment, obviously putting the potty-chair to its intended use.

By the time my mother succeeded in opening our door and entering our kitchen, Lacey was back in hers. Her tit was tucked inside her flowered wrapper. She deposited the child in a corner of the kitchen and spoke gently. "Stand right here, Broken, while Momma starts to unpack."

The men tipped up their beer bottles and drained them, then went downstairs to begin portaging our furniture into our flat. My mother left the haven of her kitchen for Lacey's, where she tapped ceremoniously on the door—an unnecessarily polite gesture, since the door was wide open and Lacey was well aware of my mother's presence.

"Come on in," Lacey invited.

But my mother said, "No, thank you. I just came to clear up a point. I thought my day to move in was today, and that you wouldn't be moving in until tomorrow. I don't understand why we both got here on the same day. It's going to complicate things considerably, with both of us trying to move our belongings up one stairwell at the same time."

"Oh, it won't make any difference," Lacey assured my mother, tossing that beautiful red mop of hair back and turning the full force of her big blue eyes toward us. "My stuff can sit out on the sidewalk until Big and the kids get here. By then the movers will have your things upstairs. Don't worry about it."

"I'm not *worried*," my mother said coldly. "I'm *curious*. How did it happen that you're moving in today? The landlord assured me you wouldn't be here until tomorrow. Or at least I thought he did. Did I misunderstand?"

Lacey laughed, and her laugh was even more glorious than her voice.

"Hell, no, honey," she said. "The landlord doesn't know I'm moving in today. I didn't bother to tell him. I put one over on him, that's all. Now let's forget about it. How about a cup of hot coffee?" She shoved the one chair that had made it upstairs toward my mother. "Sit your fanny down. Take it easy for a while."

"No thanks."

My mother's refusal was as frosty as the windowpane. She took my elbow and propelled me out of the room.

We weren't aware then of Lacey's personal pride and pleasure in outdoing landlords. As Valentine later explained, one of Lacey's chief joys in the battle of living was to outmaneuver a landlord. To Lacey, every landlord was her own personal Mount Everest, to be conquered simply because he existed. Nothing made her happier than to do a landlord out of his rent; she had a track record for outrunning landlords that would put Jesse Owens to shame. One of her most practiced and successful techniques was to promise a trusting landlord that she would pay him on the last day of the month, then skip on to another gullible landlord, where hopefully she would be able to pay just enough to lull him into believing her story that the balance would come to *him* before the month ended, and then, right under the deadline, rapidly pack up her brood and skip out, hopefully owing the landlord something . . . anything, just so long as she bested him. Although Lacey usually preferred to amble through life using as little energy as possible, she was magnificently energetic when it came

14

to plotting nomadic journeys from one FOR RENT sign to another, leaving a trail of frustrated landlords eating her dust.

It was Lacey's propensity for besting her new landlord that placed the Harts' belongings, Lacey's tits, and the peculiar little boy in my mother's path at the precise time my mother was relocating us and our possessions. The result was inevitable. After the movers departed and my mother and I brought up the boxes from our car, Lacey bounced down the stairs a few times to carry up her guitar and radio and the big calendar, calling to my mother and me that she would leave the rest of her things for Big—whoever he was—and the kids to handle. Each time Lacey and my mother met on the narrow stairway, my mother drew back against the roughly plastered wall and muttered polite monosyllables in response to Lacey's constant chatter. I never took my eyes off Lacey.

I had never seen anybody like her before, and I had certainly never heard anyone use the words she was tossing around so easily. Nor had I ever seen tits before. I knew, of course, that women had *breasts*, but the women in my mother's world kept those breasts securely brassiered, snugly covered, made them look as flat as possible, and certainly never let even the suggestion of a nipple show through a blouse or sweater. I had never seen my mother unclothed, not even partially, nor had I ever seen my father's naked body. Lacey's big bouncy tits with their huge flamboyant nipples were a revelation to me, and I spent quite a few moments that day overtly studying my mother's trim flat blouse and wondering what her breasts looked like. Odd that even then I thought of Lacey as having tits, and my mother as having breasts. Already, in one short afternoon, my life had taken on a new dimension. I was beginning to inhabit two totally different worlds—the world of tits and the world of breasts.

My mother and I devoted the next two hours to unpacking the boxes we had carried upstairs and arranging the furniture.

With the radio turned up to let us listen to our daily serials as we moved from living room to kitchen to bedroom to closets to cupboards, we did not hear much from the flat next door other than doors slamming and heavy footsteps periodically marching up and down the stairs. Occasionally a loud voice drifted up to us but the words were indistinct. By midafternoon the soothing syrup of unpacking familiar belongings and turning the once-bare flat into a small but attractive apartment had perked us up considerably and prepared my mother to pick up the reins of her usual daily routine.

"Put on your coat," she suggested late in the afternoon, "and we'll walk up to the grocery store and get something special for supper tonight. It will do us good to get out in the fresh air for a bit."

We dressed warmly and left the flat, my mother carefully locking the door behind us and trying the doorknob twice to be sure it was secure. Obviously she was not going to chance our weird neighbors sneaking into our flat in our absence. As we stood on the upstairs landing and my mother opened her purse to put her key in its inside pocket, another odd figure climbed the stairs and advanced toward us, hopping up two steps at a time, whistling "Ain't We Got Fun," and swinging a basket filled with dingy towels and ragged washcloths, nearly colliding with me when she reached the top of the stairs.

For the first time I came face to face with Valentine Hart.

She was small—much shorter than I was, although we learned later that we were within months of being the same age. She was dirty. There was no other word for it. Valentine Hart was dirty. Her hair was the shade of Lacey's, with a layer of grime dimming its red lights to a dull, unattractive off-auburn. It was shaggy, unevenly cut. Even though the February day was bitterly cold, she wore no gloves, and her hands were crusted with the same shade of dirt that colored her hair. Her nails were bitten to the quick. One frayed shoestring flopped from scuffed shoes with heels so run down they had run out—they were no longer there, forcing her to stand tip-tilted, suggesting that she was apt to topple over backward any second. When I looked at her thin legs I thought she, like her queer little brother Broken, was deformed, or was perhaps the unfortunate victim of a horrible disfiguring disease. Huge bumps protruded like buckeyes beneath her black cotton stockings. Closer scrutiny revealed that the bumps were probably made by long underwear hastily and improperly wrapped around the skinny legs beneath the stockings. Later, after we became Best Friends, I taught her how to wrap the underwear smoothly, one fold at a time, so the bumps would not be there. That lesson in dressing was a revelation to Valentine, who all her life had assumed that long underwear and bumpy stockings just naturally went together, like Amos 'n' Andy and Popeye and Swee' Pea. In eleven years of mothering, Lacey just hadn't got around to showing Valentine how to cope with long underwear.

When Valentine reached the top step, she and I stood staring at each other, taking each other's measure. Lacey .popped out into the hallway.

"Hi, Valentine."

Her daughter casually tossed, "Hi, yourself, Lacey," back at her.

The lopsided little creature was hanging on Lacey's leg, reaching up for Lacey's tit. Lacey pulled the tit out of the loose wrapper and hoisted him up to it and stuck it in his mouth. Valentine ignored the feeding process, but my mother turned bright red.

"Do you think you should do that right here in the hallway?" she asked indignantly.

And Lacey replied with a good-natured, "Hell, no. I

17

ought to do it where I can sit down. The little bugger nearly bites my nipple off when he tries to suck on it standing up."

My mother marched stiffly down the stairs and out into the fresh air.

When we returned from our short walk to the grocery store we saw and heard from Lacey again. Her tousled head was hanging out of the upstairs window and she was shouting to a taller male version of Valentine. He stood on the sidewalk gripping a skinny black cat and rubbing it with a chunk of ice. The cat squirmed and howled and the boy rubbed more vigorously.

"Let that cat go, you mean little bastard," Lacey shouted. "Get your backside up here and help me straighten up before Big gets home."

She pulled her head back inside and the boy thumbed his nose toward the empty window and rubbed the ice harder against the cat. The downstairs door of the flat suddenly exploded open and Valentine appeared, flying faster than the February wind toward the boy and the cat, and delivered a hard sock to the boy's nose, freeing the half-frozen cat who wisely took off for warmer pastures.

My mother screamed at witnessing violence so closely and her scream brought Lacey to the downstairs door. Lacey plowed through the snow and grabbed Valentine under one arm and the boy under the other and dragged them inside, shaking them as she pulled them along. My mother and I followed, carefully stepping around the drops of blood that were coming from the boy's nose. With impartial firmness, Lacey deposited both her burdens on the landing and shoved Valentine toward the kitchen.

"Get in there and put Broken on the pot," she ordered. "And hurry up about it. If he dirties his pants, I'll rub your nose in it."

My mother's gasp, "Oh my God," was more a prayer than a profanity.

Lacey turned to the boy they called Black and lowered

her face to his, putting her beautiful soft nose close to his bloody one. "If I ever catch you tormenting that cat again I'll beat the holy shit right out of you myself," she threatened.

"What the heck you getting so steamed up about? Black cats are bad luck and it's good luck to rub ice on them."

"Try it again and you'll see what kind of luck it is," Lacey promised. "Now get in there and clear the junk off the table. Big will be here any minute."

Before my mother retreated to the haven of our flat, she asked Lacey, "How many children do you have? Is there another one we haven't met yet?" Her question sounded like an accusation, and Lacey answered defensively.

"No, there *ain't* another one you haven't met. Big is my husband, the father of my kids. I have three kids, but I only got caught twice. Valentine and Black are twins. Little Broken came along by accident when Big couldn't find his rubbers one time when we moved and things weren't unpacked yet and Big just couldn't wait. You know how men are."

My mother groaned, put her hands over my ears, and shoved me into our flat. I was irritated with her for removing me from the scene of the action. In just a few short hours my life on Fourth Street had taken on a fascinating sheen, and I was beginning to think that perhaps leaving Washington Street had not signaled the end of the world after all.

I was an unwilling captive of respectability for the next hour until my mother, exhausted by the traumas and tasks of her unusual day, sat down to listen to "The Romance of Helen Trent" and fell asleep in her chair. I waited a minute or two, then I tiptoed out of the flat and went over to Lacey's kitchen, where the door, as usual, was wide open. Lacey's door, like her heart, was rarely closed. I was to learn that there was nothing and nobody who was not

19

important in Lacey's world. She had a zest for living that fed on people and events. Her first approach to people was to like them and to go on liking them unless they wounded or betrayed her or little Broken, then she would turn like a fiery tigress and cage them out of her life and, if necessary, give them a couple of claw marks to remind them that she and Broken were not to be attacked. She did not carry that same protectiveness over to Big or Valentine or Black, assuming, I suppose, that they were tough enough to handle most situations themselves.

When she saw me standing in the doorway she kicked a rickety stool toward me. "Come on in, honey, and set a spell. Valentine, get this kid a cup of coffee."

Again I was enthralled. I was rarely permitted coffee at home and the few times I was, the cup was half-filled with milk. The cup Valentine handed me held hot black steaming coffee, and it smelled as good and as strong as Lacey looked.

"Have a chocolate drop."

Lacey reached into her wrapper pocket and pulled out a piece of candy and handed it to me, then searched out another piece and put it in Broken's mouth. After he ate it she said, "Time for a nap, baby," and again I saw her tits. This time I could study them without my mother interfering. Lacey sat on a crooked rocker, cradled Broken in her arms, pulled loose her wrapper, and out came those tits. Pineapple shaped, watermelon-sized, white mounds with huge brown nipples that were soft and flexible until she fingered one of them slightly and it came to a big brown sharp point, which she shoved into Broken's drooling mouth and let him suck on for a moment or two until his heavy eyelids drooped completely closed. Then she gently arose and carried him over to the corner of the kitchen and laid him down on her discarded coat.

"He'll sleep now," she said. "He hasn't had a nap today because he's been sort of upset with all this confusion going on. He's three years old and I took him off the tit over a year ago and there's not any milk left in them but he still likes them so I just let him have a pull or two when he's upset and he goes right to sleep. It's better for him than letting him suck his thumb, because if he sucks his thumb his teeth won't grow in straight."

I was intrigued by her lesson in child care, and bewildered about why she cared if his teeth grew in straight when nothing else about his twisted little body had symmetry.

The last and largest member of the Hart household arrived while I was propped on my stool, talking to Valentine and watching Lacey. Big Hart suited his name. He was tall, broad-shouldered, muscular. He towered over Lacey as she greeted him at the kitchen door with a huge kiss and a hug that looked like she really meant it, and not at all like the small pecks my mother and father exchanged automatically when they greeted each other. Big's hands were as busy as his lips while they kissed, one squeezing Lacey's round backside, the other reaching inside her wrapper. I wondered what it would feel like to touch those magnificent mounds that Big was fondling. Valentine appeared not to notice Lacey and Big. She talked to me, telling me about the school and the kids and the teachers, but I was picking up only part of her conversation. The message coming through from Lacey and Big was so overpoweringly sensuous that it muted Valentine's.

Watching Big feel Lacey's top and bottom, my own body felt little stirrings it had not known before. I liked the sensations, and wondered how I could make them happen again. I knew the odd pounding and pulsing had something to do with what Big was doing to Lacey, but unfortunately I had little time to analyze the connection. My mother's frantic call from the hallway jerked me out of my reverie and off the lopsided stool, and I scooted rapidly out of the land of the tits and circumvented the lecture I sensed I was about to receive. I made my lip tremble and I lowered my head so my mother wouldn't see my eyes, which were full of excitement put there by the Hart family, and tried to look sad.

"I got lonesome," I lied, "for my old friends. You were asleep so I went next door to be with a girl my own age."

Not such a big lie, at that. An effective half-truth it was, one that brought my mother instantly to heel. She didn't scold me, but while we ate our evening meal, she put sharp words to her thoughts about our strange new neighbors.

"They're simply awful," she told my father. "I had no idea when I rented this place that such common people would move into the flat next door. The woman's language is outrageous, and the least said about the way she dresses, the better. The youngest child is obviously an idiot, and the older children are dirty and disrespectful. As for the father, I just got a glimpse of him, but from what I saw, he looks as disreputable as the rest of the family."

"Valentine's nice," I ventured.

"Nonsense," my mother corrected me. "There's nothing nice about that hoyden, and I want you to stay completely away from her. And from all the rest of them. Do you understand?"

I felt tears in my throat, and I didn't know what to do with them. I nodded and swallowed hard and poked at the green beans on my plate.

"Let's not be so quick to make a rule like that." My father's intervention amazed me; it was not like my parents to disagree about anything. "I don't think we should forbid her to associate with the girl next door, at least not until she makes other friends. Things are different for all of us today. A different roof over our heads, a different neighborhood, a different school. Until we get back to where we once were, we're going to have to live with what we have. Whether we like it or not, we'll be sharing this building with the people next door. We'd better get along with them the best we can."

Bolstered by my father's unusual disagreement with one of my mother's opinions, I repeated, "I like Valentine. And at least she's someone my own age that I can talk to."

My mother sighed. "Apparently we are going to have to make some adjustments in our way of thinking. I suppose we can start, for the time at least, with that girl next door. So until you make some really nice friends in your new school, I guess we'll just have to let you associate with that peculiar Valentine person. But I don't want you to have anything to do with that twin brother of hers. He has a mean streak in him a mile long. And also, I think the less you see of that woman next door, the better off you'll be."

"Good." My father pushed back his chair and walked around the table and patted me on the head and touched my mother's shoulder, indications that the meal and the deal had ended compatibly.

It was easy to promise to keep Black Hart at a distance. I didn't like him any better than my mother did. I was smart enough not to tell her that Lacey Hart fascinated me. I didn't press my luck; I settled for permission to associate with Valentine.

By eight-thirty all activity in our flat was ended. The rooms were in order. The only remaining evidence of our relocation was a change in our sleeping arrangements. My mother gave me the only bedroom, optimistically commenting that perhaps some of my former friends might want to sleep over. The leather couch that opened into a full-sized bed in the den in our old home and had been so convenient for guests was now in our living room. By early evening it was open, covered with clean white sheets and a down comforter and two big pillows, and my mother and father were asleep on it. The large sliding doors between the living room and my bedroom were closed, shutting us into our separate child and adult worlds.

I learned later that Lacey's sleeping arrangements were more informal. All the Harts shared the one bedroom, which held a double bed for Lacey and Big, a small cot for Valentine, and a larger cot that supposedly was shared by Broken and Black, although Broken usually spent most of the night in bed with Lacey and Big. Broken hated to let go of Lacey, even in sleep.

I was wide awake, still dressed, and sitting forlornly on the edge of my bed when I heard a sharp thud against my icy window. At first I thought it was the sound of ice dropping from the eaves. When the thud, thud rhythmically persisted, I went over to the window. Through the frosty glass I saw Valentine standing in the snow-covered alley. Her arm was raised to toss another hard snowball. I opened the window.

"What do you want?"

"It's Black's and my birthday. Lacey baked us a cake and she wants you to come over and have a piece. Can you?"

"Yes."

I slipped quietly out of the flat, carefully avoiding the creaky boards in the hallway.

Life was in full swing in Lacey's flat. The radio was blaring, tuned to a Wheeling station, the nasal twang of Ernest Tubbs adding to the general chaos.

Big and Lacey were in charge of festivities, Big's dark brown eyes dancing a duet with Lacey's bright blue eyes whenever they met. Big and Lacey were dispensing justice, merriment, hospitality, commands, and cake.

"Sit here," Big boomed, and shoved the rickety stool toward me.

"Get your goddamned finger out of that icing," he

shouted at Black, who was standing between the cake and the rest of us with his back turned, obviously hoping that his furtive swipes at the icing around the cake were unnoticed.

"Get the matches," Big told Valentine, his voice softened.

He waited patiently while Valentine searched for the matches and when she found them beneath a gray frazzled dishtowel plopped in the middle of the table, Big handed the matchbox to Lacey, who was sprawled inelegantly but comfortably in the one overstuffed chair in the room, with Broken nestled on her lap.

"You want to light the candles, Lacey?" Big asked.

"Naw," she said, "you do it, Big. You know you get a kick out of it."

As Lacey moved Broken from one side of her lap to the other so she could watch the candlelighting ceremony, her loose wrapper flopped open and again I caught a glimpse of her tits and her two huge brown nipples. Valentine and Black didn't seem to notice them but Big and I did, and I watched hypnotized as Big crossed the room and stood behind Lacey's chair and bent his dark head down to her bright red tousled one and she tipped her face up and their lips came together and his big hairy hand touched her throat and then rapidly slid down to her bare tit. He cupped it and squeezed it, and although at first his kiss and his touch had seemed casual, even as young and inexperienced as I was at that time, I began to sense a charge in the atmosphere, and a change in their positions. Lacey sat up straighter. Her body reached up toward Big. His hand tightened around her tit and his fingers touched the light brown nipple and caressed it. Suddenly their contact was no longer casual.

"Holy shit," Big breathed, and "Sweet Jesus Christ," Lacey whispered. Broken, sensing Lacey's brief emotional

25

withdrawal from him, reached his small twisted fingers up for Lacey's other nipple and found it and stuck it in his mouth.

For several moments the room was quiet except for Ernest Tubbs in the background. Big's and Lacey's lips met. I don't think she was aware of Broken's mouth on her other nipple. Meanwhile Black made good use of his time and their preoccupation and scooped another fingerful of icing from around the cake and licked his fingers. Seeing him, Valentine seized the *True Confessions* magazine, which had dropped from Lacey's hand, rolled it into a paper club, and sneaked up behind Black and swatted him hard on the head. Black yelped, grabbed his head, and ran after Valentine, who quickly scurried behind Big, using him as a buffer between herself and Black. She stuck her tongue out at Black before she jabbed Big in the ribs and said, tolerantly but firmly, "For Christ's sake, Big, finish your feel and let's light those candles before Black licks *all* the icing off the cake. Can't you and Lacey wait until *this* party's over before you start one of your own?"

The spell was broken. Big slowly removed his fingers from Lacey's nipple and Lacey lowered her body back into the chair and absentmindedly reached down and removed her other nipple from Broken's mouth and I relaxed. I don't know what I had expected to happen next between Lacey and Big, but again I found a secret part of my own body feeling the same excitement it had felt earlier that day when Big and Lacey fondled each other.

The birthday party was totally unlike any other I had ever attended. There were no dainty little pleated paper cups filled with colored sugar candies, no crepe paper streamers, no silly hats, no balloons. But there *were* two clumsily wrapped packages, one with Black's name scrawled on it in bold black crayon, and one with Valentine's scribbled in bright red crayon.

Valentine carefully unwrapped her gift and went into verbal ecstasies over the book of American poetry. Black tore into his package and gleefully traveled around the cluttered room, aiming his water-filled Junior G-man gun at everything and everyone. He boasted that he could aim straight enough to shoot out the candles on the cake, but decided not to make good his boast when Big threatened to beat the holy crap out of him if he ruined the cake Lacey had worked on so hard.

While Lacey strummed "Happy Birthday to You" on her old guitar, Big and I sang, and Valentine and Black joined forces for a rare moment to blow out the candle flames with one puff.

"That's good luck," Lacey said. "Blowing out all the candles at once means your wish will come true."

"Then I'll get to see Miriam Hopkins in *Becky Sharp* when it comes to the Hippodrome next week," Valentine said.

"And I'll get to catch that black cat that got away from me this morning and put turpentine on its ass," Black predicted. "I saw a kid do that once to a cat and it was a real kick. The cat damned near flew over the house."

Lacey got up from her chair and with Broken tucked under her arm she cut the cake in generous pieces and passed them around on a cracked plate. When Valentine saw me looking for a fork, she said, "Eat it with your fingers. It tastes better that way."

She was right; it did.

"Yeah, and it saves washing dishes, too," Lacey added.

We washed the cake down with lemonade and then Lacey put Broken to bed and sat down to play her guitar. We sang while she picked out a few verses of "Casey Jones" and "The Little Red Caboose Behind the Train" and "That Silver-Haired Daddy of Mine" and "She'll Be Coming 'Round the Mountain When She Comes." We were relaxed, easy

27

together until Lacey played the first few chords of "I Can't Give You Anything but Love, Baby," and again the atmosphere changed, became charged with emotion.

Big stood behind Lacey's chair. His fingers found her throat and slid down to her bare tit. The room zinged with excitement. At first Valentine looked a little piqued, but then she sighed and said, "Oh, what the heck, I guess it's bedtime anyway."

I got up from my stool and thanked everybody for the good time. I don't think Big and Lacey heard me, and if Black did, he ignored me. Valentine walked out into the hall with me and sat down on the top stairstep.

"I'm going to sit here for a while and give Lacey and Big a chance to Do It and get it out of their system," she said. "Want to sit with me?"

"I *want* to, but I don't dare to. My mother might wake up and I'd better be in bed if she comes in to check on me. What do you mean," I asked, "you're going to give Big and Lacey a chance to do what?"

"Are you kidding?" Valentine looked incredulous. "You mean you don't know what they've been building up to doing all evening?"

"No. I don't know. Tell me."

Valentine leaned her head against the wall and closed her eyes. "Are you sure you're eleven years old?" she asked.

"Eleven years, three months, and four days."

"Good grief. For being so old, you sure are dumb. I'll tell you about it some other time. Maybe tomorrow."

She closed her eyes and ended the conversation. I returned to my bedroom and lay awake and wondered what I would hear from Valentine the next day.

2

I was awakened early the next morning by a reverberating concert coming from Lacey's kitchen. The sounds intrigued me, and I lay in bed and tried to separate instruments from words. Lacey spoke.

"Get your backside off that stool, Black, and warm Big's jacket. It's cold enough to freeze the balls off a brass monkey. Valentine, get your nose out of that book and find a plate for Big's eggs. Hey, Big, the coffee's ready. I poured you a cup."

Pans collided, cupboard doors slammed. Silverware clinked, and plates rattled. The Big Ben beside my bed told me that although it was not yet seven o'clock, life was in full swing next door. In our flat, the only indication that a world existed outside my unfamiliar bedroom was the smell of coffee perking. The uncanny silence told me that my parents planned to let me sleep late. Were they protecting me from a long lonely day, or did they think I needed the rest after our busy move? I didn't know, but I did know that they were again wrapping me in a loving cocoon, dooming me to be a caterpillar when I wanted to fly wild and free with Valentine and taste the exotic flavors of her world again.

I knew better than to let my mother suspect that I was eager to get out of bed and go next door. I lay in bed until I heard my father tell my mother good-bye, and then I arose, put on my fuzzy slippers and my cozy robe, and pattered into the kitchen, plotting how to manipulate my mother into letting me spend the day with Valentine. I was spared the trouble.

My mother hung a newly ironed white blouse on a hanger with her good wool suit and talked while she poured my orange juice.

"I should have spoken with you about this sooner," she said, "but I wanted to get us settled first. I'm applying for a job this morning. I have an interview with an insurance office downtown and I have to be there within the hour. There are several other applicants for the job, and the company will spend the day interviewing us and giving us a typing test and weeding out the people they don't want. I won't be home until late this afternoon. Do you think you can get along all right by yourself today?"

I nodded. I knew I wouldn't be by myself any longer than it would take her to get dressed and depart. I read the comics until she kissed me good-bye. As soon as I heard the downstairs door close I scooted across the hall where Lacey's kitchen door was wide open.

Lacey still wore the same loose wrapper she had worn the day before. Broken was on her lap and she was reading aloud a story from a *True Confessions* magazine. Valentine sat at the cluttered table drawing on a paper bag that bore greasy evidence of having been used as an impromptu napkin during the noisy breakfast I had listened to earlier.

She was as swift with her crayon as she was in all her movements, and the Betty Boops she sketched between the grease spots were quite good. She looked up and grinned at me, divided the brown bag and the black crayon in half, and we sat quietly together drawing Betty Boops and listening to Lacey read.

The story concerned a woman who discovered her husband was having an affair with his secretary, who was a brazen vamp. The betrayed wife was a saint whose many virtues included that of forgiving the wandering husband. At the happy conclusion, which put the repentant husband back in the loving arms of his understanding wife and sent the vixenly secretary out of town and into disgrace, Valentine and Lacey indulged in what I would in time recognize as a frequent—and often fiery—literary, philosophical, and moral critique.

Valentine plopped down her crayon and launched the discussion.

"That wife must have been a real dodo bird. In the first place, she should have suspected that her husband was up to something when he didn't come home for a week. In the second place, she should have kicked his ass right out the door when he did come home and never let him in again."

Lacey let the magazine slide to the floor and shifted Broken to the other side of her lap. "Oh no, Valentine. The wife did the right thing. That's what love is all about. Being forgiving and taking a man back even when he's done you wrong."

"Why?" Valentine asked. Lacey momentarily looked nonplussed, but she thought hard and came up with a reply, if not an explanation. "Just because."

Valentine snorted. "Crap. That's just plain crap, Lacey, and you know it. The man made a fool out of his wife and out of that stupid secretary too. If the secretary had the sense God gave a goose she'd have known a respectable businessman with a house and a wife and a car and two kids wouldn't give up all that just to get into her pants— not when he didn't have any trouble getting in them to start with. In fact, I feel sorrier for that stupid secretary than I do for the man's wife. Sounds to me like the wife came out on the winning end, and the secretary got left with the dirty end of the stick. The man got his piece of ass, the wife got to keep everything she already had, and the dumb secretary had to leave town and find a new job."

"Served her right," Lacey declared. "She shouldn't have messed around with a married man. Served her right for trying to trap him."

"*Trap* him?" Valentine snorted again. "Ye gods, Lacey, it didn't sound to me like he was very hard to catch. He was a goner the first time he knocked at her apartment door and she met him with that black lace negligee on. He sure didn't waste time working. It says right there in the story that they didn't even take the report out of the file folder for a whole week."

"Well, anyway, the secretary shouldn't have tempted the man, and the wife was right to take him back." Lacey's verdict sounded pretty final. Valentine stretched and yawned. "It's stuffy in here. Let's go outside." But she shot one last question at Lacey.

"What would *you* do, Lacey, if you ever found out that Big was messing around with another woman? Would you take him back like that dumb wife in the story did?"

Lacey seriously pondered the question before she gave a reasonable answer.

"Yeh. I probably would. But first I'd go find the other woman and beat the shit out of her and then I'd kick Big so hard right where it hurts the most that he'd behave himself for a long, long time because he couldn't do anything else. Then I'd take him back."

"Good thinking, Lacey." Their philosophies had meshed

and the literary discussion ended compatibly, as most of their disagreements did in those days.

Valentine and I spent the day together, getting to know each other. I was fascinated by her explanations of their unusual names. It turned out that the name on Broken's birth certificate was Douglas Fairbanks Hart, but after Lacey got a real good look at him she immediately nicknamed him Broken, and Broken had been his name ever since.

"Broken's all messed up because when Lacey got caught she tried to get rid of him with a coat hanger and something went wrong," Valentine said. She may as well have been speaking in tongues. Nothing she had just said made sense to me, although I had a vague feeling that she was referring to what she had casually mentioned the night before about Lacey and Big "doing it."

"I don't understand. What do you mean about Lacey getting caught?"

"She got knocked up. In the family way. Was going to have a baby. That's what 'got caught' means."

"Oh." That much at least was clear. I moved on to the next puzzler.

"What do you mean about the coat hanger? I don't understand."

Again I earned an incredulous look from Valentine.

"How old did you say you are?"

"Eleven years, three months, and *five* days, now. One day older than I was last night when you asked me."

"Yeh. And one day dumber. Ye gods, you sure haven't learned much in eleven years, three months, and five days. I knew all about getting caught and getting rid of kids since I was old enough to understand English. Lacey and her friends are always talking about it."

"Tell *me* about it," I urged, "so I won't go on being dumb."

33

"Okay. She and Big had too good a time the night before he left for Washington. She wasn't careful and neither was Big, so she got caught. She found out for sure right after Big got back from the Bonus March. He was so down in the dumps from being shot at by the same army he had fought in during the war that she didn't have the heart to tell him there was another problem on the way. Big was out of work for quite a while and Lacey didn't think it was fair to bring a kid into the world if she wasn't sure there'd be enough money to take care of it, so she didn't tell Big she had got caught. She waited till all of us were out of the house and then she straightened out a coat hanger and rammed it up her front end and tried to pry Broken loose. But Big had rammed Broken up there real good, and Lacey didn't have any luck getting rid of him, so when Broken was born he was all messed up. That's why Lacey makes over him so much. Lets him have everything he wants. She says it's her fault he's like he is and says she'll spend every minute for the rest of her life making up to him for what she did to him before he was born."

"Oh. Well, what about Black? Is that *his* real name?"

"Ye gods, no. His real name is Rudolf Valentino Hart. He was called that until he was about three months old but then one day when Lacey was nursing him he bit down so hard on her nipple that without a tooth in his head, he darn near bit her nipple off, and Lacey decided right then and there that any male who didn't know any better than that how to handle a woman's tit sure didn't deserve to be named after Rudolf Valentino, so she nicknamed him Black and that's what he's been called ever since."

"What about you? Is your name really Valentine?"

"Yeh. Big named me. He says I'm his gift of love from Lacey."

"What about Lacey? Is that her real name?"

"Almost. It's really Lucy, but when Big first met her

he began to call her Lacey, because he says she's as rare and pretty as a piece of Irish lace."

"What's Big's real name?"

"It's Eugene, but don't ever call him that," Valentine warned. "He beat the crap out of a guy once who did. Lacey says his nickname is just right for him, because he's big in all the places that matter. I guess she means he's big-hearted, among other things."

"What other things?" I asked, but I didn't get an answer to that one right away. I heard the door open downstairs and the drum-drum of my mother's high heels clicking on the stairs. I jumped off my stool and hastened toward my own flat. I bumped into my mother in the hallway and stiffened myself for a lecture I expected—and didn't get. She looked triumphant. She proudly carried a package wrapped in brown butcher paper. "I got the job. Tonight we eat steak, just like old times. Tomorrow it's back to hamburger, but tonight we celebrate. I start work at eight tomorrow morning. Work from eight to five. Five and a half days a week. That means eight dollars more coming in each Saturday. Reason enough for a celebration."

"Can I ask Valentine over for supper?" I expected her to say no, but again she surprised me.

"All right. Just this once. But don't make a practice of it." She hummed as she went into the bathroom to change into a house dress. I skipped across the hall to give Valentine the invitation—which she flatly refused.

"Nope," she said, "if I eat at your place, your mother will expect me to be cleaned up and act polite, and that's too much trouble to go to just for a piece of steak. I've got a better idea. You come over here this evening and let me fill you in on things you ought to know about the kids and the teachers before tomorrow."

My mother, relieved yet insulted by Valentine's rejection of an invitation to a decent meal, didn't take kindly to my suggestion that I spend the evening with Valentine.

"You've seen enough of that bunch for one day," she said.

My father intervened. "There's no use pretending that there won't be differences between the old school and the new one. There are cultural and social walls between them that will be difficult to scale. If Valentine Hart can give her a boost over those walls it will be all to the good."

My mother looked wounded, but she didn't argue. After I helped straighten our kitchen, I joined Valentine.

"I'm really scared about going to school tomorrow," I said. Lacey offered comfort. "No need to be. Not with Valentine on your side. She knows the ropes. There isn't a kid in that school who would dare to pick on a friend of Valentine's. Next to Black, she's the toughest kid there. It'll work out okay. Just wait and see."

Valentine added her assurance to Lacey's. "Lacey's right. I'll pass the word tomorrow that I'll beat the holy crap out of anyone who tries to give you a bad time. By recess there won't be a kid in the place who'll dare to say boo to you. Just stick close to me and you'll get along swell."

Despite their encouraging words, I cried myself to sleep that night.

I was overjoyed when I awoke the next morning to a world so snow-filled that I couldn't see across the narrow alley by my bedroom window. Flakes tumbled in thick white sheets outside, making a thicker curtain than the muslin on the inside. As I gleefully watched them fall, my mother stuck her head in my bedroom to deliver the welcome message that she had just heard the local radio station verify what I was anticipating—school would be closed for the day. A scarf was around my mother's head; she was wrapped in her last winter's coat, wore her last winter's boots.

My heart danced. "I'm sorry you have to go out on

such a bad day," I lied, impatient for her to leave so I could rejoin Lacey and Valentine.

"Businesses can't close for the weather, like schools do," she said. "It won't be so bad. I'm taking along a sandwich for lunch so once I get there I won't go out again until quitting time. Think you can make lunch for yourself?"

"Oh, sure. Don't worry about me. I'll be fine."

Within minutes I was in Lacey's kitchen where life was perking as hard as the coffee and moving as fast as the snowflakes hurling themselves against the window. Big had already left for the day to work with the highway crew to keep the snow-covered roads passable. Black was preparing to go outside to challenge the elements and the cat. Before he left, he and Valentine exchanged verbal blows, Black staunchly defending himself against Valentine's angry accusation that he had stolen the newspaper from her boots to put in his.

"You're crazy as a bedbug," he hooted. "I put this newspaper in my boots a week ago when the old fart on the radio said it was going to snow and it didn't. And it's been there ever since."

"You're a goddamned snotty-nosed liar," Valentine yelled, and turned to Lacey for verification. "Isn't he a goddamned snotty-nosed liar, Lacey? Isn't he?"

Lacey turned from the window where she had been holding a disinterested Broken up to see the falling snow and rendered judgment.

"I think you're wrong this time, Valentine. I don't think Black took the paper out of your boots. I grant that he's a mean little bastard, but I've got this much to say about him, he isn't a liar. If he says he didn't take the paper, he didn't. So shut up about it and let him get the heck out of here so I can get back to reading to little Broken."

37

Black stuck his tongue out at Valentine, and when Lacey turned back to the window, he thumbed his nose in her direction. Valentine leaped across the room and swatted him on the head. Instantly they were wrapped around each other like big pretzels and were wrestling on the floor, first Valentine on top, then Black. Lacey turned from the window and propped Broken in a chair. "Sit there a minute, doll-baby, until I get these two brats straightened out."

She swooped down, skillfully evading the writhing arms and legs and flying fists, and collared Black with one hand and Valentine with the other. She held them apart at arm's length, shaking them both impartially, clutching them firmly until they calmed down and their flailing arms paused and their clenched fists opened. She gave them each another hard shake to make sure she had got her point across and to ensure their surrender before she loosened her grip and returned to Broken. I assumed they'd take up their battle where they had left off, but obviously Lacey wasn't worried about a return engagement. Black went back over to the chair where he'd been sitting getting ready to put his boots on, and Valentine sat down at the kitchen table and glowered at him. I perched tentatively on the edge of my stool, ready to hop out of the way if round two began, but apparently Lacey had temporarily shaken the violence out of them. Black put on his boots, fastened their buckles, and turned to leave.

Valentine screamed at him as he went out the door, "I hope you get lost in the blizzard, you little fuckhead, and never get found."

"Don't talk dirty," Lacey casually advised, and snuggled Broken against her.

"Let's go over to my flat," I suggested. "My parents are gone for the day and we can have the place to ourselves."

"Good idea," Lacey said. "That'll give me a chance for a little peace and quiet."

"Okay," Valentine agreed. "I can't go outside. That little fuckhead took the only newspaper in the house and my boots have holes in them."

We went over to my flat and I taught Valentine how to make cocoa with evaporated milk while she told me about sex. Although there was no school, I learned a lot that day. My education began when I asked, "What's a fuckhead?"

"It's the worst thing I could think of at the time to call Black."

"What does it mean?"

"Nothing, really. Why do you want to know?"

"I've seen the first part of the word scribbled on the sidewalk." I couldn't bring myself to say the word, not even to Valentine. I knew that it was an ugly word and meant something bad, but I also knew better than to ask my parents to define it.

"Do you mean to tell me you don't know what *fuck* means?"

Again I earned Valentine's incredulous look.

"No."

"Ye gods. I thought you were a smart kid. You told me you get A's and B's in school and you have your own library card and you read newspapers. I thought you were smart."

"I am, but I'm not smart enough to know what that word means. I know it's a bad word, but I don't know *why* it's a bad word. So tell me."

"Holy Jesus." Valentine sat on the neatly folded leather couch and began my education.

"*Fuck* means when a man sticks his thing in a woman."

"Sticks what thing where?" I was beginning to get a glimmer, but the full light of understanding had not yet dawned. I was aware that there was an anatomical difference between men and women, my knowledge being based primarily on my parents' strict rule that I was never to enter the bathroom when my father was using it, nor go into their bedroom without knocking first, and on the vague but stern warnings my mother had given me from the time I was old enough to go outside alone that I mustn't ever let any of the boys in the neighborhood pull down my panties. Having no brothers, and living in a world where diapers were changed in private, I had never seen firsthand this "thing" that Valentine was telling me a man puts in a woman.

"Ye gods," Valentine said. "You mean you've never seen a naked man?"

I shook my head. "Not even a naked boy?" When I shook my head again, she persisted, "Not even a naked *baby* boy?" Again I shook my head. "Holy Christ," she groaned. "Didn't any of your mother's friends have boy babies that needed their diapers changed?"

"Oh, sure, but their mothers changed them in private."

"Ye gods. Lacey would run her legs off up to the kneecaps if she left the room to change Broken every time he dirties his pants. She says he's as full of shit as a country goose. Oh well, since you don't know anything about anything at all, I guess we might as well begin at the beginning. Get me a pencil and a piece of paper."

I supplied her with fresh white notebook paper and a sharpened pencil. She spit on the pencil and drew a picture, talking as she sketched.

"See, here's a guy's stomach . . . side view. And here's his balls." At the bottom of the stomach she drew two round circles suspended from the bottom line of his side view. "Some people call them nuts." She filled in the two round balls with quick circular motions like the ones I had studied in the Palmer Method Penmanship Book when I was learning to write in cursive letters. She added a couple of lines to form a shape resembling a limp worm connected to the round circles.

40

"That's his thing," she said, "and that's how it looks when it ain't doing it. It just sort of hangs there most of the time. It's handy when he has to pee because he doesn't have to sit down. He just pulls it out and aims it."

I was fascinated, but still puzzled. "Is that all there is to it? That's his thing?"

"Oh, there's a lot more to it than that. That's just the way it looks when it isn't doing anything but hanging there. When he gets in the mood to fuck, it changes shape. It gets great big and long and hard." She quickly sketched over the limp loose outline, bringing it out to the margin of the paper, making it wide and bumpy and big.

"That's what it looks like when he's getting ready to shove it in a woman. It gets big and stiff and hard as a rock and that's so he won't have to waste time trying to tuck it in her. He can just ram it in and get right down to screwing in a hurry. I saw Big's once when he was getting ready to shove it in Lacey. They thought I was asleep, but I wasn't. I was watching them. And I tell you, his thing was as big as a horse's. I don't know where he found room to put it all. But then Lacey *is* a good-sized person. When they were fastened together they looked like a couple of freight cars hooked up. Sounded like it, too, when they really got going good."

"Do all men have a thing that gets big and hard?" I asked. "Even my father?"

"Well, if they don't, they're in trouble. And if your father didn't have one, you wouldn't be sitting here right now."

"What about boys? Do they have the same thing?"

"Well . . . maybe not as big. Every once in a while I see Black's. Sometimes he gets dirty pictures from the kids at school and brings them home and takes them into the bathroom. Once I peeked through the keyhole and saw him with his pants down. He was looking at the pictures and playing with his thing and it was twice as big as when

41

he uses it to pee with. But not anywhere as large as Big's. Black was hopping around like a frog on a lily pond and making funny noises. Just when he was having a real good time, I jerked the bathroom door open and screamed for Lacey and she came and caught him red-handed."

"What did she do to him?"

"She really gave him hell. Told him he'd better quit doing it or his brain would go bad and he'd grow hair on the palms of his hands and get pimples on his face and everyone would know by looking at him what he'd been up to. I don't think he believed her though, because the next week I caught him doing the same thing again, but that time I didn't tell Lacey. I thought, what the heck, I'd like for his brain to go bad and I'd love for him to get hair on the palms of his hands and a face full of pimples. So now when he plays with his thing I just don't say a word about it."

"I wonder what it feels like," I said, "to have a man's thing inside you."

"I can't imagine," Valentine admitted, "but it must feel good or Lacey wouldn't sound so happy when Big does it to her. Sometimes I wish I had a thing like a man has so I could fool around with it and find out what the fuss is all about. Well, anyway, that's what *fuck* means—a man's thing gets big and he sticks it in where a woman pees and he jumps around until something squirts out of it and then it goes limp again until the next time. By the way, I guess you know that's how a baby gets inside a woman."

"No. I didn't know. I know they're in a woman's stomach, but I never knew how they got in or out."

"Simple," Valentine said. "They come out the same way they went in. But the difference is, when they get put in, they're just a bunch of gooey stuff the man squirts in, but when they come out nine months later they're big. Black weighed six pounds when he was born. I was smaller."

"Good grief. It must hurt something awful when it comes out."

"It sure does," Valentine agreed. "I heard Lacey screaming when Broken was being born. Black and I were in the other room and we heard the whole thing. It took Broken all day to get out and poor old Lacey screamed the whole time. I figured he'd given her so much trouble she'd beat the shit out of him when he finally did come out, but two minutes after he was born she was slobbering all over him, cooing at him and kissing and hugging him and she hasn't stopped since. I heard her and Big talking later that night when she tried to tell him what the pain felt like. She told him to try to imagine what it would feel like to shit a five-pound watermelon and that's what it feels like to have a baby, only worse."

"My goodness gracious," I gasped. "No wonder my mother only had me. I can't imagine why any woman has a baby if it hurts that bad."

"I asked Lacey about that," Valentine said, "and she told me that when I get older and fall in love I'll understand. She said that when you're making love it feels so good you just don't worry about making babies."

"I can't imagine it," I said. "I just can't imagine it."

And I couldn't. Regardless of Valentine's graphic lesson in anatomy and sexual urges, I couldn't imagine my own parents indulging in such primitive practices. On the other hand, it wasn't at all difficult for me to imagine Big and Lacey doing it. It seemed right for them.

"Can I sleep over at your house some night and pretend to be asleep and watch them?" I asked.

"Yeh. They don't do it every night, but they do it a lot. We'll pick a night when they've been feeling each other up during the day . . . like they did yesterday."

The snow continued to fall for the rest of that day and was still coming down when I went to sleep that night.

I awoke the next morning to a silent, muffled world. Even the noise from Lacey's kitchen seemed softer, absorbed by the deep drifts that insulated the flats from sound. Although the snowfall had ended, the roads and streets were still impassable and the schools remained closed for another day. I could hardly believe my good luck . . . another day of reprieve. I got up early and ate breakfast with my mother and again pretended to be sorry that she had to bundle up and plow through the snow to go to her job. As soon as she was out of the house I started over to Lacey's kitchen, but Valentine stopped me in the hall. "Let's go back to your place. I have a swell idea."

"What is it?" We sat down at the kitchen table and, while I made hot cocoa, Valentine outlined her plan.

"Black and I decided last night that you need a dictionary."

"I already have one. I got it for Christmas last year."

"Not like the one we're going to make for you. I began to think last night while I was laying in bed about how dumb you are about the kind of words you have to know how to say if you want to fit in with the kids at school. I woke Black up and told him how dumb you are and he said we should put together a dictionary that will smarten you up."

I learned as time went by that although they usually fought like cats and dogs, there were times when Valentine and Black did join forces, especially in areas where they both knew Lacey and Big would unite against them. As I listened to Valentine's plan I had no doubt that Lacey and Big wouldn't approve of it.

"Black and I figure you need a four-letter word dictionary since four-letter words are what you're going to hear the most of at school. So. I'm going to tell Lacey that you are going to help Black and me with our homework and that we want the kitchen to ourselves. Black says he'll help make the dictionary, but he turned thumbs down on

44

telling the lie to Lacey. He's really proud that he never lies. Not even when we wish he would. Like the time he broke a window at school and wouldn't lie his way out of it even when Big asked him to, and Big had to pay for it. Black says he ain't going to lie for anyone, so *I* told Lacey the lie and she says she and Broken will go into the living room to read the *True Confessions* stories and leave us alone. Come on over and let's get started."

True to her word, Lacey stayed out of our way for the morning. We kept our voices low as we worked on the dictionary. I did make a few shaky statements about already having a good vocabulary and always making A in Language, but Black sneered and Valentine scoffed.

"Yeh? Well the words you used at your old school are the words that kids use when they wouldn't say shit if they had a mouthful. They won't do you a darned bit of good at our school."

"My mother will wring my neck if she hears me use dirty words," I objected.

And Valentine logically advised, "Then don't say them where she'll hear them."

"Let's get started," Black growled. "I ain't got all day to sit here with you two nitwits. I got better things to do. Come on, now. Shut up and start thinking of dirty four-letter words that start with *A*."

We had trouble with that one, so we left a space for later inspiration and went on to *B*. When Black dictated "butt," Valentine objected. "Don't put that down. Everybody but a dumb bunny knows there's only three letters in but."

"Like hell," Black snarled. "The kind of butt you sit on has four letters. It's another word for your ass. Write it," he ordered me, and I did. "And you quit calling me a dumb bunny," he said to Valentine, "or you can stick this whole idea right up your butt and I'll go outside and have some fun doing something else."

45

"Yeh. Like chasing that poor cat," Valentine muttered.

The letter *C* was easy, although I didn't understand a couple of words. "We'll explain them later," Valentine said. "First let's write them down."

The letters *D* and *H* offered no challenge, although Black and Valentine agreed that "damn" and "hell" weren't really that bad. The letter *F* was a bonanza, and after Valentine's earlier lesson I felt quite proud of myself when I volunteered the first word.

"Fuck," I said.

Black's eyes popped open; he looked as if he was really seeing me for the first time.

"That's swell," he congratulated me. "I didn't think you had it in you."

The letter *I* stopped us cold; *J* gave us some trouble, and we finally compromised by accepting Black's offering of "jerk off," including it with the justification that the second part of the word didn't count. I didn't know what it meant but I obediently wrote it down after Valentine told me it was an important word because in case I saw somebody I didn't like jerking off, I'd know how to tell the teacher. We had a slight argument about the letter *K*, with Valentine insisting that "kiss" wasn't a dirty word, and Black insisting that there were certain kinds of kisses on certain parts of the body that deserved to be in the dictionary. Since we couldn't think of another word for *K*, we finally did write "kiss" on our list. *L*, *M*, *N*, and *O* earned empty spaces for later ideas, but we had a good time with the letter *P*. Black brought forth a couple of biological functions starting with *P* that made Valentine pinch her nose and giggle while I wrote the words. When we came to *Q*, Black wanted us to include the word "queer," but we insisted on keeping the words consistently four lettered, and Black was furious. There was a heated disagreement between him and Valentine, so heated it nearly brought our entire effort to a quick end. Black was angry at having the

46

word rejected, insisting that it was an important word for school kids to recognize so they'd know enough to punch the shit out of anyone who tried something queer with them. He reached over and grabbed my list and threatened to rip it into pieces, so, knowing full well that Black was a mean little bastard but that he never lied about what he did or planned to do, Valentine reached a rapid compromise. "We'll leave 'queer' in but we'll spell it with only one *e*."

"Rump" was a rather tame word for the *R* section, but it was all any of us could come up with at the time. *S* presented no problem, nor did *T*, although there again were a couple of entries I would have to have explained to me later.

The last few letters of the alphabet defeated us. *U* through *Z* held little hope for obscenities. We were tiring of our endeavor by then anyway, so Valentine folded the paper and gave it to me and told me to study it whenever I had a chance, and she'd go over the meanings with me a little at a time.

I hid it between my mattress and the bedsprings for weeks and suffered agonies every time my mother cleaned my room or made my bed, but she never found it. I faithfully memorized the words and their meanings, and within a month I was familiar enough with them to let Valentine and Black give me a verbal test one evening when we again had Lacey's kitchen to ourselves. While she and Big sat in the living room and listened to the clutter fall out of Fibber McGee's closet, I took the test. Valentine proudly gave me an A, but Black awarded only a C, telling me that even though I had memorized the words and their meanings, I didn't say them right, didn't have the proper expression in my voice or on my face.

"You've got to let them roll off your tongue as easy as pee off a prick. Every time you say a dirty word you squint your eyes and let the word sneak out of the side of

47

your mouth. You won't get an A from me until you do it right."

I never did get an A from Black.

True to her word, Valentine was my protector at school. When the streets were cleared and passable, and the snowflakes surrendered to a bright blue February sky cheered by a yellow sun that radiated brilliance, if not warmth, the inevitable happened. I entered my new school.

The teacher assigned me to the only vacant seat in the room. Fortunately, it was close enough to Valentine for us to whisper occasionally and pass notes constantly. Valentine stayed by my side at recess and at lunch, and quickly and competently handled the only crisis that occurred when a fat homely girl came running up to me and jerked my ribbon from my hair and tried to run away with it. She jeered at me while she blundered across the playground, yelling back insults about teacher's pet and stuck-up brat. Valentine let her get a few feet away, then propelled her thin little body through the air like an angry ferret, caught up with the fat girl, and threw her to the pavement and sat on her chest, pulled both her ears, and spit in her face. She jerked the ribbon from the girl's clutched fist, jumped off her as quickly as she had jumped on, and brought the ribbon back to me before the girl was up from the pavement. Valentine shoved the ribbon at me without taking time to speak, raced back to straddle the sobbing girl, and made a fist and shook it over her broad nose.

"If you ever bother my friend again I'll beat the holy piss out of you. Understand?" She helped the girl indicate agreement by grabbing the girl's ears and lifting her head off the pavement and dropping it down again. As quickly as she had attacked, Valentine jumped to her feet and said to me and her admiring audience, "Let's play jacks."

The incident was ended, and the teachers at the far end of the playground were no wiser. Ended, that is, until the recess bell rang to summon us back into the school.

When our teacher went to the front of the two groups to be sure the boys were in their line and we girls in ours, Valentine quickly slid out of line, stepped back a couple of spaces to where the fat girl stood, face tear-streaked but otherwise not showing any evidence that could be held against her or Valentine. Valentine sidled into line behind the girl and grabbed the girl's fat arm, twisting the flesh until a look of agony covered the girl's face.

Valentine released her arm with a whispered promise.

"If you ever bother my friend again, I'll pinch your fuckin' arm till it bleeds. Understand?"

She didn't have to help the girl signal agreement that time; the bobbed head voluntarily nodded assent and Valentine swiftly reentered her place in line, looking completely innocent when the teacher checked us.

On the way home that afternoon I asked, "Valentine, why did you pinch that girl after you'd already beat up on her?"

"That's the best way to win a fight and keep it won. First you punch the hell out of the person, then you let them think the fight's over with, and then, whammy, when they're off guard you give them another good pinch or swat or kick. That way you keep the shit scared out of them for a long time because they never know when you'll come back after them again."

"Gee, I never would have thought of that."

Valentine groaned. "Ye gods, you've sure got a lot to learn about how to get along in this world. It's a good thing you met me before you got much older and lots dumber."

As usual, Valentine called the shots correctly. Although I never formed any deep friendships with the other girls at the new school, I made no enemies; at least I broke even.

3

The February snows turned to slush, the March winds blew, and April arrived. By then Valentine and I had indeed become Best Friends, with Valentine as dependent on my friendship as I was on hers. In retrospect I know now that I must have been as fascinating to her as she was to me. We were so different. I was neat. I knew and used proper grammar. My fingernails were clean and tapered, my hands soft and white. My hair was shiny and I dressed it up with pretty ribbons. I wore a clean dress or skirt and blouse to school each day. I had my own library card, a privilege that Valentine, who loved to read much more than I did, had to relinquish when Broken wet on the library's copy of *Little Women*, soaking it from cover to cover. Valentine had always had her trials with her library books, having a constant contest with Black to see if she could locate and erase the dirty words he delighted in scrawling at random throughout the books. She managed to keep one step ahead of Black, and she never dreamed it would be Broken who would be her nemesis in the reading world. The day she got home from school and found the pee-soaked *Little Women*, she screamed at Lacey, why in the hell didn't Lacey pay more attention to what was going on right under her nose, and then she scowled at Broken, which called for an inordinate amount of courage since Lacey was sure to attack anyone who criticized her deformed little cub.

Valentine wasted no more time on recriminations; she seized the dripping book and raced the three blocks to the public library with the wet pages flopping in the breeze. Breathless, but determined to straighten out the matter before it got worse, she exploded through the doors of the library, slapped the wet book down on the librarian's desk where evil-smelling wet spots quickly appeared, and said to the librarian, Mrs. Sturgiss:

"Here's *Little Women*. Broken pissed on it. I wasn't home and I didn't have a thing to do with it and I'm sorry it happened and if you want me to come in after school and work to pay for the damages I'll do it and that's all I have to say."

Unfortunately, Mrs. Sturgiss had more to say. She promptly demanded the return of Valentine's library card. After we became Best Friends, my card became Valentine's passport to worlds she could move into only between the covers of a book. She and I worked out a foolproof system to let her have the books she wanted. She would go into the library a few minutes before I did, amble through the tall aisles and slyly pull out her choices just a trifle and then leave. I would enter immediately, talk to Mrs. Sturgiss, who was much impressed by my spotless dress, my clean fingernails, and what she thought were my literary choices. Choices that I would select by locating the books Valentine had pulled out before I got there. We were a complement

51

to each other, my Best Friend and I. She had grit; I had class. She was the performer; I was her audience. She was the teacher; I was her student. She found in me a serenity, a refuge from her wild, vivid, alive-and-kicking family. I found in her a rage to live, to feel, to communicate, to care.

Even Black wasn't too terrible to me. Most of the time he ignored me, which, coming from Black, was almost a compliment, since when he really disliked someone he could be unbelievably creative.

For instance, Mr. Hunt, our principal, was one unfortunate man who dared to tread on Black's rocky path, having insisted even when Black denied it, that Black had stolen a dime from the desk of another boy in Black's classroom. The incident happened late in March, and it did somewhat enliven an otherwise boring month. Big and Lacey were summoned to school to listen to the principal's charge. After giving them a summation of Black's supposed crime, the principal was amazed to hear both Big and Lacey leap hard to Black's defense.

They listened stoically to the principal's charges, and when he finished talking, Lacey said quite agreeably, "I don't blame you for thinking Black did it. He's a mean little bastard. But I know he didn't take the dime or he would have admitted it. He ain't a liar. If he says he didn't steal that dime, he didn't."

"That's right," Big agreed. "Black don't tell lies. He's a little devil, that's for sure. He cusses, sometimes steals, torments animals, jacks off in the bathroom after he looks at dirty pictures, eats more than his share of the food if we don't keep an eye on him, and about once a week tries to beat the shit out of his sister. But he don't tell lies. And that's that. If he says he didn't take that kid's dime, he didn't."

Being presented with such a long and disheartening list of Black's bad habits, it was no wonder Mr. Hunt found it impossible to believe the one truth told in Black's favor, that Black did not tell lies. Mr. Hunt didn't believe Lacey and Big any more than he believed Black, and he sentenced Black to receive five whacks on his bottom while the entire school watched. From that day on, Mr. Hunt was in jeopardy.

Black did not cry during the whacking, and he said no more about it other than to repeat one more time to Mr. Hunt, after the whacking was completed and the classes were still seated in the auditorium where they had been spectators to his punishment, "I did not take that money."

Anyone who knew Black would have known that the episode wouldn't be ended until Black had his revenge. It was not long in coming.

A few weeks later a story circulated around the school that our principal had his eye on Black's teacher. Black did not start the story, but he did use it. Black, holding both his teacher and his principal equally guilty of publicly shaming him, quietly sneaked back into the school one afternoon after dismissal and hid in the cloakroom to wait for developments. The word was going around the school that Mr. Hunt and Black's teacher got together every afternoon, and not to check papers.

Unfortunately for Black's plan to catch the two of them in a compromising position, the eraser dust lingering in the air made Black sneeze and the principal found him and collared him and sentenced him to ten public whacks instead of five.

With the doubling of the punishment, Black's desire for revenge tripled. He became craftier and more determined.

He left little notes around town about Mr. Hunt's extracurricular activities, and on the dust on Mr. Hunt's black Ford he wrote in large, easily readable letters, "Hunt hunts cunt."

Thanks to my four-letter word dictionary, I deci-

53

phered that remark without the aid of Valentine. Mr. Hunt drove around town for a couple of days with his reputation following him before someone pointed out to him the words on the back of his car. Although every kid in school either knew or suspected that it had been Black's revengeful finger that had scrawled the indictment and Mr. Hunt handed down the dictum that there would be no recess for any of us for two weeks unless the guilty party came forth, none of us told on Black. Our fear of what would happen to a stool pigeon far outweighed our dismay at losing our recesses.

As the April evenings grew warmer and daylight lingered, Black hatched another glorious plan for revenge against the man who twice had publicly humiliated him, once for something he hadn't done, and once for something he hadn't been able to carry through. He began to haunt Mr. Hunt's neighborhood. Early one April evening, just after darkness had dropped a discreet curtain over prohibited activities, Black loitered on the corner of Mr. Hunt's street and watched Mr. Hunt kiss his wife and three children good-bye, doff his hat, and climb into his Ford and rumble toward the school building a couple of blocks away. By taking a preplanned shortcut and jumping over a few fences, Black got to school before the principal arrived, and was tucked safely between a tree and the school building when Mr. Hunt's Ford puffed into the deserted schoolyard and Black's teacher slipped out of the building. She and Mr. Hunt climbed into the rumble seat and, as Black told Valentine and me later, "Fucked the hell out of each other."

Black remained discreetly hidden until he was sure their connection was absolute. His teacher's legs, stockings rolled down around her knees, were flailing wildly around Mr. Hunt's portly body, and her cotton panties were hanging forgotten over the back of the rumble seat.

Black shot out of the shadows. "RECESS!" he yelled,

54

as he grabbed the cotton panties. "Let's play tag. You're it, Hunt."

Black stood nearby and watched Mr. Hunt dismount from the coupling while frantically trying to pull his trousers up and the teacher's skirt down to cover her bare bottom.

Black waved the cotton panties toward the rumble seat and stayed long enough to let the sweaty, panting occupants see who he was and what he was waving. Then he turned and strolled jauntily out of the schoolyard, whistling "Who's Afraid of the Big Bad Wolf?"

When he got home he motioned for Valentine and me to come downstairs and the three of us sat on the trunk of the big old elm on the corner and he regaled us with his story. We rolled on the ground and laughed until we cried. Everyone but Black and Valentine and I were amazed when Black made the honor roll and Mr. Hunt and Black's teacher sent a nicely penned note home to Big and Lacey to ask their forgiveness for their hasty misjudgment of Black, and to assure them that Black was indeed not a liar and had not stolen the dime.

In return for which Black stuck the teacher's white cotton panties into a brown bag from the A&P and left it on his teacher's desk the day before Easter vacation.

For me, that spring was glorious. I was having my first taste of freedom, with my mother working every weekday and until noon on Saturdays. I was having new adventures with Valentine, experiencing my first exposure to the pure pleasure of living. I was becoming increasingly aware of my own body as I listened to Valentine's and Lacey's hearty exchanges about love and sex and birth and bodies. An awareness was stirring way down deep in me, just as spring was stirring under the moss.

April had begun wetter than usual and was a little too cool to bring out the flowers, but a warm and sunny May compensated and violets and dandelions were thick in the

Lutheran churchyard at the far end of the street. Every Saturday morning in May, Valentine and I journeyed to the churchyard and gathered violets, returning to the flat to make them into small bouquets tied in bright yellow yarn. We walked around town and peddled the bouquets for a penny apiece.

One lovely morning we walked several blocks with our violets, engrossed in conversation. Before I was consciously aware of being there, I found myself turning the corner into Washington Street, the street on which I had lived every day of my life until that year. I was back in the neighborhood that I had a few months earlier declared I would rather die than leave. Strangely, nothing stirred in me as I walked past my old home and saw a girl my age sitting up in my treehouse in the cherry tree in the backyard. I noticed without rancor that the white organdy tieback curtains that had been in my bedroom window had been replaced by yellow plaid drapes. Halfway down the block I came face to face with two girls who a year earlier had been my best friends. They smiled vaguely and spoke to me as if they were having difficulty remembering just where I had fit into their smug lives. I saw them smirk when they looked at Valentine's dirty feet, which were bare now that warm weather had come and she had given up wearing her only pair of shoes on weekends. I saw the girls turn up their noses when they looked at Valentine's skirt, which had been handed down from one of Lacey's friends and was skimpy and unevenly hemmed and spotted. Suddenly I was filled with the same kind of anger that Valentine had known when the fat girl at school had tormented me. I, who had never resorted to using my fists or my tongue as weapons, wanted to grab those two girls by their neat little pigtails and curse them and smash their stuckup noses flat, but I had neither the nerve to try it nor the skill to accomplish it, so I silently fumed.

I was delighted when Valentine, always attuned to my

thoughts before I put them into words, seeing the patronizing smirk on the two clean faces, shouted, "What's wrong with you two fuckheads? You look like you think your shit don't stink."

Their eyes widened, their mouths gaped, and they turned and fled up the quiet street. Valentine and I linked arms and, with our violets firmly clutched in our hands, we left my old neighborhood.

I was glad to see the last of it.

4

The violets gave way to roses, and soon June and summer were in town. Valentine and I devoted equal time to studying for our school finals and to planning what to do with our summer. We were very organized in making our summertime plans; we borrowed Lacey's big feed and grain calendar that hung by one rusty nail over the kitchen stove and prepared to make good use of the unmarked June, July, and August dates. There were only four marks on the calendar when we requisitioned it; the marks in May were identical to the ones I had seen on it in February when we moved into the flat. Recalling my mother's obvious embarrassment when she first saw Lacey's calendar, I asked Valentine what the mysterious red Xs represented.

"Oh," she answered casually, "those are the days Lacey's supposed to fall off the roof this month."

I was dumbfounded. I knew that Lacey was a lively, daring creature, but I found it impossible to believe that as much as she disliked physical activity she would deliberately plan in advance to fall off a roof.

"Isn't that dangerous?" I asked. "Won't it hurt?"

"It'll hurt her a lot more if she doesn't." Seeing my puzzled frown Valentine asked the question I was becoming accustomed to hearing: "How old did you say you are? Ye gods, you've sure got a lot to learn." Her lesson about the big red Xs was fascinating. "It's called other things besides falling off the roof. Some people call it the curse, but Lacey says it sure as heck isn't a curse when it comes to her. It's a blessing. But then she says it isn't really a blessing, either, because it means she and Big can't mess around in bed for the next few days. Lacey says the High-Muckety-Mucks call it having a period, and Big says that that makes sense because it puts an end to his fun in bed until it's over. Some people get really silly and say things like 'my cousin's coming to visit.' Lacey says that People Who Wouldn't Say Shit if They Had a Mouthful call it 'that time of the month.' That's probably what your mother calls it."

"I don't know," I admitted. "I never heard her call it anything."

"That's because she's the kind of Person Who Wouldn't Say Shit if She Had a Mouthful. So don't let on to her that I told you about it. Pretty soon she'll have to tell you herself and when she does, act like you're surprised."

A month or so later, when my mother did have her mother-daughter talk with me, she did refer to it as "that time of the month." Valentine had been right again.

Valentine and I blue-penciled our own important dates on the big calendar, leaving Lacey's bright red Xs on her four days and claiming the other spaces for ourselves. By the last day of school we had filled all the squares in June and July and were working on August. We blue-marked a week to search for photographs of Richard Arlen. We set aside time to hit a tennis ball against the deserted school building, seeing ourselves as serious threats to Helen Hunt Jacobs. We anticipated walking down to the Muskingum to wade out from the small rocky beach into the river. Free tap dancing lessons would be ours at the Betsy Mills Club. By autumn we would be able to outdance Ruby Keeler.

On the day school closed, Valentine and I were ecstatic. We put our heads together right after supper and decided in a short discussion to go to bed immediately so we could get up early the next morning to begin to enjoy our freedom. As usual in Valentine's hectic life, nothing went as planned. We did go to bed early, and we did arise early. But we did not know when we told each other good-night and good morning that Lacey too had made plans for the day, and that her plans were destined not only to change our calendar-marked activities, but ultimately to change our lives.

We were strolling the brick sidewalks leading to town by nine in the morning. We walked down to the Muskingum and watched a tug push its cargo upriver and speculated about its destination. We ambled over to the small park to watch the caretaker scrape the pigeon-splattered benches in readiness for the Fife and Drum Corps' first concert of the season. We roamed over to the Hippodrome to read the marquee. We scouted around town searching for discarded Tootsie Roll wrappers to enter in a contest being sponsored by a neighborhood store. A giant Tootsie Roll would be awarded to the person who found the most Tootsie Roll wrappers within a month. Valentine already had collected quite a few, which she prudently stored in the trunk in my bedroom, knowing that Black, who was also in the contest, would never dare to steal anything from my flat. My mother's cool scorn toward him inhibited Black much more effectively than Lacey's loud threats or Big's hot anger. Black simply did not know how to deal with anyone who looked right through him as if he didn't exist.

By four o'clock we had accumulated three wrappers to add to our inventory, and we headed back for the flat. Valentine wanted to be home before Big; one of the pleasures in her life was to watch for him to appear on the horizon, then run to meet him, hair and skirt flying in the wind, heart and arms reaching out for Big, who would swoop her up on his shoulders and proudly carry her home. His Valentine, his gift of love from Lacey. Valentine was small, and Big was large, so even though Valentine was rapidly moving out of childhood, the feat was physically possible. My mother thought it was disgraceful and said that Valentine was too old for such behavior, and that if she insisted on pursuing it, the least she could do was put on some decent underwear. Whenever I watched Valentine run to meet Big to be piggybacked home, I envied her and pitied myself. I was tall for my age, and my father was a small man. Even had we shared the unconventional relationship enjoyed by Big and Valentine, my father would have had a difficult time transporting me home on his shoulders. One evening, wanting to be like Valentine, I watched for my father's car to turn the corner. When it did, I ran down the street to meet him and waved him over to the curb and jumped on the running board and held on for dear life while he slowly drove homeward. My attempt at deformalizing our relationship resulted in a stern lecture from my mother about the dangers of riding on a running board and a gentler but still firm reminder from my father that it was all right just for that one time, but it would not be advisable to do it again.

When Valentine and I got home from our tour through town, Lacey's flat was uncommonly quiet. No soap opera blasted through the rooms; no comforting creak came from Lacey's dilapidated rocker.

"Where's Lacey?" I asked, and Valentine told me that Lacey had mentioned earlier that she might go to town that afternoon. Lacey's visits to town were infrequent; it was difficult for her to maneuver the uneven brick sidewalks with Broken's misshapen arms clinging to her neck, his drool wetting her shoulder when he became too weary or too disinterested to walk and had to be carried. Broken was Lacey's beloved albatross, and she would never have considered leaving him in home port.

Lacey's journey into town that day was prompted by her desire to pick up a copy of the *Columbus Examiner*, a weekly tabloid that, although published in Columbus, often contained gossip about Marietta's High-Muckety-Mucks.

"High-Muckety-Mucks" was one of the three classifications in which Lacey filed citizens of our small town. In her own way, Lacey honored a caste system as rigid and well-defined as India's. To Lacey, Ohio Valley society was divided into three distinct categories: the High Muckety-Mucks; People Just Like Us; and People Who Wouldn't Say Shit if They Had a Mouthful. Being a lifelong resident of Marietta, and having either worked or lived in practically every part of town, Lacey prided herself on knowing something about everyone worth knowing about, and she assigned the citizenry to their proper caste according to criteria based upon a combination of geographic, religious, economic, and social factors.

The High Muckety-Mucks either lived on Harmar Hill at present or had lived there in the past. They were urbane, well-to-do, and educated. Their names frequently appeared on the society pages of the *Marietta Times*, but never in divorce listings or on police blotters. They usually attended the Presbyterian Church, although occasionally a few of them strayed toward Unitarianism. Lacey forgave them that transgression, charitably assuming that they did so because they had been overeducated. People Just Like Us included Lacey's legion of women friends, Big's pals, friendly neighbors the Harts had left in their dust on their numerous safaris from one home to another, and just about anyone else who would come through Lacey's open door and accept Lacey and her family as they were. To Lacey, I was People Just Like Us, even though I had once lived in a high-class neighborhood and still attended the Presbyterian Sunday School. I was never quite sure how Lacey classified my father, but I had no doubt where she had filed my mother the first day they met, and Lacey was right; my mother Wouldn't Say Shit if She Had a Mouthful.

Lacey's impromptu trip into town had a dual purpose that day. In addition to buying the hot-off-the-press *Columbus Examiner*, she wanted to pick up the new *True Confessions*. Lacey adored the magazine and never threw one away. They were scattered throughout her flat. I spent almost as much time reading them as she did. Their story titles intrigued me. "I Betrayed My Husband on Our Wedding Night" and "What My Wife Didn't Know about My Past" and "Why Didn't My Mother Tell Me Before My Husband Showed Me?" My father's Zane Grey books and my mother's *Saturday Evening Post*s couldn't hold a candle to Lacey's *True Confessions*.

Valentine told me that Lacey had had a real fight with herself that morning about whether she should go to town. Money was rare and dear in the Harts' household, and whenever a spare nickel or penny did come along, it was usually dropped into an empty can in which Big stored his dream that someday he would save enough money to make a down payment on a house. Just as Lacey found joy in outmaneuvering landlords, Big found pleasure in dreaming that the day would come when he would have no more to do with landlords.

Obviously Lacey's longing for new reading material had outweighed Big's dream; the can sat on the table with its lid half off—a sure sign that it was empty, or Lacey would have hidden it from Black.

While Valentine and I were storing the Tootsie Roll wrappers in my trunk, we heard Lacey on the stairs. We joined her over a cup of hot coffee.

"Did you kids have a good time today?" Lacey propped Broken in her rocker and unbuttoned her blouse and pulled off her brassiere. Her huge tits flopped loose. She rubbed them and sighed, "It sure feels swell to get that harness off." I watched, fascinated as I always was and always would be by Lacey's big white tits. She massaged them for a moment and then slipped them back inside her blouse.

"Yeh," Valentine said, "we had a swell day, and we've got another one planned for tomorrow."

Lacey blew on her hot coffee and then dropped a bombshell that exploded my summer into bits and pieces. "Good, I'm glad you kids had fun today, because I've got something else in mind for Valentine for tomorrow. I heard today about a job you can get, Valentine. It's a swell chance for you to make some money."

Valentine yawned and dismissed the thought. "Thanks for nothing, I ain't a bit interested in getting a job, Lacey. I got too many other things to do."

"Yeh?" Lacey sounded as disinterested in Valentine's lack of interest as Valentine had sounded toward Lacey's news.

The dialogue paused, brought to a momentary standstill, but I knew the two of them well enough by then to know that the conversation had not really ended. Each was busy thinking, biding time, considering how best to outwait and outwit the other. Lacey nuzzled Broken's neck and wiped the perpetual lamb-leg from his nose and cooed to him. Valentine ambled casually over to the window and leaned on the splintery sill and pretended to have a great interest in the trash cans in the alley. I perched on my stool and put my hands behind my back and crossed my fingers, crossed my ankles, and if I'd known how, I would

64

have crossed my eyes for good luck. For Valentine and our summer. The impasse lasted for minutes, during which I sent silently fervent messages through the kitchen to Valentine not to speak first. I had witnessed enough of the Valentine–Lacey standoffs to know that whoever weakened and spoke first usually lost the contest. Unfortunately, Valentine did not receive my telegraphed message. She turned from the window and I had an ominous sense of foreboding that our summertime plans were about to fly right out of the window that Valentine had been using as her waiting room for Lacey's surrender.

Valentine spoke to me, not to Lacey. "What time did we decide to go hit the tennis ball against the school tomorrow?" I opened my mouth to reply, but Lacey beat me to it.

"Well, it had better be after six o'clock in the evening, because you won't be home till then. Mrs. Grey works until five and by the time she drives out to Sycamore Lane and you walk home, it'll be at least six o'clock. That's okay, though. There's still plenty of daylight left. You'll have time to play."

"What in the holy hell are you jabbering about?" Valentine scowled at Lacey and Lacey snapped back.

"I'm not jabbering. I'm telling you about the job I got for you today. I ran into a friend at the five-and-dime, and she told me that a woman named Mrs. Grey that works at Monkey Ward's in the hosiery department needs someone to stay at her house while she works. Needs someone dependable to take care of her three-year-old kid and look after her crippled husband. I stopped in to talk to her and I told her how good you are and she said she'd give you a try for a couple of days and if you're as good as I say, she'll keep you on all summer. Six days a week. And you get to eat your breakfast and noon meal there. She'll give you four dollars for the week if you do the job right. It's a good deal and we're lucky she said she'd give you a try. I guess I did a pretty good job of selling you to her."

"Oh yeah? Well thanks for nothing, Lacey. Don't do me any more favors like that. And you might have done a good job of selling *me* to *her*, but you sure as heck didn't do a good job of selling the *job* to *me*. Nobody but a nitwit would waste a perfectly good summer taking care of a three-year-old brat and a broken-down old cripple. So forget about it, Lacey. Just forget about it."

Lacey continued talking as if she hadn't heard a word of Valentine's protest. Valentine moved over behind Lacey and thumbed her nose at Lacey's back.

"You'll be doing light housekeeping," Lacey said. "Taking care of the kid, giving him his meals, making him take a nap, and sort of fetching and carrying for the woman's husband. She says he gets around good in his wheelchair and can do most things for himself, but there's a few things he needs help with, and now that the kid is old enough to get around and get into things, she has to have someone there to watch him. The older woman that has been doing it got sick and had to leave."

"She probably died of boredom," Valentine sneered. "A job like that would make me sick too. In fact, I want to puke when I even think about it. So I *ain't going to think about it*. And that's that." Valentine stuck out her tongue.

Lacey was stone-deaf to Valentine's proclamation.

"The Grey family were High-Muckety-Mucks. They lived on Harmar Hill most of their lives. I recall seeing their name on the society pages a few years ago. They were always taking trips and giving parties, or going to them. But when Mr. Grey had a bad auto accident they lost all their money and had to sell their house on Harmar Hill. Mrs. Grey went to work at Monkey Ward's. And now they live outside of town—on Sycamore Lane."

"Yeh." Sarcasm dripped from Valentine's one point

of agreement with Lacey. "You said a mouthful there, Lacey. Sycamore Lane *is* outside of town. It's on the edge of nowhere. I walked out there one day looking for Tootsie Roll wrappers and that road is one hell of a mess. There's only a couple of houses on it and it's dead as a doornail. No siree, Lacey, old girl, I ain't about to waste my summer out on the edge of nowhere taking care of a brat and a cripple. Nothing doing and that's final. So put that in your pipe and smoke it."

My sense of doom deepened. I had the uneasy sensation that every time Valentine said "and that's final," our summertime plans became less and less final. I knew by then that Valentine had lost the skirmish, and Lacey made certain in the next few minutes that Valentine knew it too.

She carefully lifted Broken off her lap and propped him securely in the arm of the chair before she went over to Valentine and bent down until her nose and her eyes met Valentine's nose and eyes.

"I've heard enough from you, young lady," she said in an iron voice. Whenever Lacey referred to Valentine as being anything as unlikely as a young lady, whatever game they were playing against each other was ended and Lacey was the victor. Always.

"You're going to be out on Sycamore Lane at eight-thirty tomorrow morning and you're going to do your job right and you're going to keep on doing it right all summer long and there's no ifs, ands, or buts about it. And that, young lady, *is* FINAL."

"HORSE SHIT!" Valentine shouted on her way out of the room. She slammed the door. I remained to do something I hadn't done before: I challenged Lacey. By then I loved her, and I felt that I had the right to ask a woman I loved why she had ruined my summer.

"Why is it *Valentine* that has to go to work? Why can't Black?"

Lacey groaned. "Oh, my. I can see you don't know much about the reputation Black has around town or you wouldn't ask that question. Black can't get a job. That's all there is to it. Anyone dumb enough to hire Black wouldn't be smart enough to have the money to pay him. So Valentine can stick out her tongue and finger her nose and yell till her tonsils hurt, but the plain fact of the matter is, she's going to be on Sycamore Lane at eight-thirty sharp tomorrow morning, come hell or high water, and she's going to be out there every day this summer except Sundays, and that's final."

Lacey opened the *Columbus Examiner* and read the headline to Broken, who promptly fell asleep. Valentine stomped back up the stairs, jerked open the door, and again stuck her tongue out at Lacey, thumbed her nose, and signaled for me to come out in the hall.

Lacey placidly continued reading her newspaper.

My summer had ended before it had begun.

The angry clop, clop, clop of Valentine's footsteps going down the stairs early the next morning echoed my frustration as I lay in bed and heard my summertime fun going out the door—banished by Lacey, a woman I adored. The dull day ahead didn't deserve my presence. I stuck my head beneath the sheet to close out the daylight and the day itself, and I kept it there until my mother tapped on the door and called me to come eat breakfast with her. I didn't mention my crisis to her as she poured Wheaties and passed milk and sugar. I felt she would be relieved that Valentine and I would not be together so much during the summer holiday, and I feared that she would be insensitive enough to say so. I shoved the Breakfast of Champions past the lump that had been in my throat since I awoke, and I stayed calm until my mother dropped a light kiss on my forehead, told me to have a nice day, and high-heeled it out of the flat.

Then I cried.

Tears didn't help.

I enlisted the aid of the radio. I suffered through soap opera agonies alone, not going over to share them with Lacey. My anger toward her was still warm, and I didn't want to chance saying something that I might later regret.

As the day wore on and I remained in solitary confinement with nothing to do but think, I reluctantly faced the truth that Lacey's logic made sense. The Harts did need money, nobody would hire Black, Big was busy every day at one job or another, there was no way in the world that Lacey could leave Broken, and nobody would hire Lacey with her ugly little opossum clinging to her.

Lonely and immobile, I commiserated with "Our Gal Sunday" and "Ma Perkins" and "Helen Trent," and found their problems about money and family and love insignificant compared to my own tragedy.

Late in the afternoon I gave up on the soap operas and went downstairs and sat on the front stoop and watched for Big, just as I had done with Valentine so many afternoons. When he appeared, I went back upstairs and cried some more, and then held a cold, wet washcloth against my face so that my mother, who would be home soon, wouldn't know I had spent the day suffering. She arrived promptly at 5:30, as usual, and by the time Valentine arrived our meal was over and our kitchen straightened. I had been listening for Valentine's returning footsteps. They were unexpectedly light, dancing, keeping the beat of the song she whistled as she came up the stairs—"Don't Give Up the Ship."

"Hi, Big. Hi, Lacey." She sounded exuberant. My heart sang. Obviously the miserable day had had a happy ending. She had found a way to get fired on her very first day on the job. Valentine was smart, smart, smart. She had saved our summer.

69

I hurried over to hear first-hand how Valentine had outwitted Lacey. When I joined them in the kitchen, it was easy to see that Big and Lacey weren't upset by whatever trick Valentine had pulled to rejoin the ranks of the un-employed. As usual, everyone was talking at once, and nobody sounded angry. Obviously Valentine's dismissal had been accepted as just another hurdle that the Harts would clear and then forget on their hectic race through life.

I arrived in time to hear Big and Valentine collaborate in saying a grace appropriate for the soupbeans, ham-hocks, onions, and cornbread Lacey was scattering around the table. They put their heads together and chanted their thanks while Lacey ladled bean soup into mismatched, cracked bowls.

"Beans, beans, a musical fruit, the more you eat, the more you toot, the more you toot, the better you feel, so LET'S HAVE BEANS AT EVERY MEAL!"

I adored the benediction, so much more colorful than the stiff verbal thank-you notes that my parents and I dispatched to God at mealtimes.

"Have some beans," Lacey offered. I sat on my stool and shared their supper and watched Lacey sneak pieces of hamhock from her plate to Broken's while Big chopped off hunks of his soggy meat for Valentine. Nobody but Black looked out for Black.

The summer evening was still light when supper ended and the dishes were stacked on the already full sink waiting for Lacey to get around to washing them. Lacey hoarded water; she never got out the dishpan until every dish from the cupboard had been used. Then she heated water and peeled slivers of Octagon soap and attacked the mis-matched spoons, crippled knives, and forks with missing teeth. Lacey hoarded time like she hoarded water. She didn't waste time in such unessential activities as drying dishes. The pots and plates and silverware sat on the drainboard for days. Occasionally, in the middle of a conversation or while reading to Broken, Lacey ambled over to the sink to stash away a few clean dishes to make room for newly soiled ones. I admired Lacey's system and often wished my mother were as sensible as Lacey.

"How did you manage to get fired?" I asked Valentine when we were outside in the summer dusk. "Come on, Valentine, tell me the truth. How did you do it?"

"What makes you think I got fired?" Valentine looked as puzzled as she sounded.

"The way you came home this evening. You bounced upstairs whistling. And you aren't mad like you were when you left this morning. So I figured you'd thought of a way to outfox Lacey."

"Oh no, I didn't get fired. In fact, I don't want to get fired. I like it over there. The woman's a real pain in the ass, and the kid is a little brat, but Mr. Grey is awfully nice. And so is Gretchen, his dog. Mr. Grey says tomorrow he'll show me how to teach Gretchen a trick. I had a swell day. In fact, I can't wait to get back over there tomorrow."

"That's nice," I lied. I hadn't wanted Valentine to enjoy her day. I wished she had been lonesome, miserable, sad. But I understood her pleasure in the dog. Even a second-hand pet would be enough to make Valentine have a good day. She had always wanted a dog, but Lacey's food budget couldn't handle another mouth to feed, and even Lacey's big heart couldn't open far enough to allow an animal into her crowded nest.

"What are the people like?" I asked, again hoping for the worst and again not getting it.

"The woman looks like Carole Lombard, except she looks like she's mad at something all the time. She's blond, like Jean Harlow, but her lips aren't big and wet like Jean's. She never smiles. Her eyes are dark brown and they look like they don't like anything they see. She's tall, like Lacey,

71

but not round like Lacey. Her tits are as flat as a pancake. She's built sort of like your mother."

"Oh. What's the man like?"

"He looks just like Leslie Howard. He says funny things to make me laugh. He smells good. He has beautiful hands. His nails are long and clean. He played the piano for me today, and it was just like watching a movie, only better, because he let me choose the songs. His eyes are brown too, like hers, but his are soft and they twinkle, and hers are hard and cold."

"What about the little boy?"

Valentine made a face. "He's spoiled rotten. Mrs. Pain-in-the-Ass gives him anything he wants. Mr. Grey just ignores him. The brat takes a long nap every afternoon so he can stay up late and give Mrs. Pain-in-the-Ass more time to spoil him. I'll have a couple of hours each afternoon to be alone with Mr. Grey. I can put up with the kid the rest of the time. It's worth it to be with Mr. Grey. He's different from anyone else I ever knew. You'll see what I mean when you meet him."

"When will that be?"

"As soon as I prove to Mrs. Pain-in-the-Ass that I'm a good worker. Would you like to come over and spend the day with me sometime?"

Do birds fly? Do fish swim? Was Daddy Warbucks rich?

Even though it was dusk, sunshine returned to my day.

"Let's go hit the tennis ball against the school building before it gets dark." We skipped through our evening.

Every evening for the next two weeks I met the people of Sycamore Lane through Valentine's second-hand introductions. By the time I met them face to face, my opinion about each of them was already formed, sculptured by Valentine.

If Valentine said the man looked exactly like Leslie

Howard—he did. If Valentine said the boy was a spoiled brat—he was. If Valentine said the woman was a pain-in-the-ass, she was a pain-in-the-ass.

"Be sure to set your alarm to get up early tomorrow," Valentine cautioned me when she told me she had requested and received permission from Mrs. Grey for me to go to Sycamore Lane. "She says you can only stay until Tommy wakes up, but that should give us an hour together. He sleeps late. Mrs. Pain-in-the-Ass won't leave until we get there and she gets mad as heck if I'm late. She's always standing on the porch tapping her foot and looking mean, ready to jump into her old car and leave the minute she finishes giving me my orders for the day. She punches a time clock at the store and she gets docked if she's late."

Valentine's well-meant reminder about getting up early was unnecessary. With my bedroom adjoining Lacey's kitchen, I couldn't have overslept if I'd wanted to. The early-morning cacophony of shouted orders and clattering pans and silverware were better than an alarm clock and would have awakened me even if the excitement of anticipating a visit to Sycamore Lane hadn't.

I was out of bed, dressed, and over in Lacey's flat while Lacey was still stirring the cornmeal mush, cooking Braille-fashion, never taking her eyes off the magazine she held in her hand. I took my customary seat on the stool and waited impatiently to be on my way with Valentine. Lacey dished the mush, Valentine ate it quickly and added the empty bowl to the pyramid of dirty dishes in the sink, and we left, unpursued by any foolish do's and don'ts from Lacey, who had returned to her magazine.

"Bye, Lacey," Valentine said, and "Bye, Valentine," Lacey answered, and we were on our way to Sycamore Lane.

When we reached the sidewalk, trouble erupted. Lacey

73

had leaned out of the window to check on Black's early-morning activities, and she saw him creeping into the alleyway, clutching the squirming cat by the scruff of its skinny neck.

"Put that cat down right this minute, you mean little bastard," Lacey shouted, "or I'll beat your ass off."

Black wasn't impressed, knowing that Lacey's threats were always more verbal than physical. Both he and Lacey tacitly understood that Lacey's maternal responsibility toward Black and her societal duty toward the cat had been fulfilled by her shouted command. The cat didn't have the same understanding. It hissed and clawed at Black who tightened his hold and squeezed harder. Lacey withdrew back into the flat. Black twisted the cat's neck with one hand and thumbed his nose toward the empty window with the other. Although Valentine herself often thumbed her nose at Lacey, for some reason she decided that morning to be indignant on Lacey's behalf.

Trouble was on its way.

I saw it coming when Valentine strutted over to Black, and stood on tiptoe to bring them nose to nose.

"I saw you thumb your nose at Lacey. You ought to be ashamed of yourself. You know what that means."

"Shit, yes," Black hooted. "It means kiss my ass."

He brought his free hand up between his nose and Valentine's and gave her the same salute he had given Lacey. Valentine lowered herself from her tiptoes and punched him hard in the belly. He yelped and bent over and grabbed his belly but didn't loosen his hold on the cat.

Valentine kicked Black's shin while he was doubled over.

"If you thumb your nose at Lacey again I'll tell Big and he'll beat the crap out of you."

Having survived the first attack, Black straightened up and hit Valentine with words that at the time didn't make sense to me. But, as Lacey constantly said, Black was

74

a smart little bastard. I know now that Black had sensed straws in the wind that I did not see until it was too late.

"Fat chance," he snarled. "You know damned well you ain't going to tell Big anything that might start a ruckus. You're so stuck up since you went to work for the High-Muckety-Mucks that you ain't got the balls to start a good fight. You got your nose up in the air these days just like that crip you work for. So don't give me that shit about telling Big anything."

"Lacey's right. You *are* a mean little bastard."

Realizing he had touched a raw nerve, Black drilled again. "I might be mean, but I sure ain't stupid. And that's what Old Crip is. Stupid. Just plain stupid. If he hadn't been so stupid he'd have kept both hands on the steering wheel and he wouldn't be stuck in a wheelchair now."

"You shut your fuckin' mouth or I'll knock your fuckin' teeth right down your fuckin' neck," Valentine shouted. I moved away from ringside.

Black was delighted. Joy was in every movement as he danced around Valentine, making verbal jabs.

"Be careful, Miss High-and-Mighty. Be careful how you talk around here. You might slip up someday out there with the High-Muckety-Mucks and talk dirty and Old Crip will find out just what kind of kid you *really* are."

Valentine's scarlet face told Black he had won that round, so he didn't wait for the bell—he punched again.

"Crip, crip, crip," he jeered, prancing around Valentine in a wide circle. "Crip, crip, crip, rhymes with drip, drip, drip. Old Crip is a Big Drip."

Valentine was on top of him before he could escape. Her small fists beat both Black and the cat, which was still struggling to get loose from Black's clutches. By the time Lacey heard the racket and got downstairs to separate the fighters, the cat had clawed its way to freedom, fled the field of battle, and was crouched trembling in the crook of the top branch of the nearest tree.

Black didn't come out of the contest as well as the cat. Either the cat or Valentine left a wide ugly scratch across Black's face. Blood mixed with dirt on his chin. Black treasured the scratch for days, making it last by picking the scab whenever it threatened to heal. Black enjoyed displaying scars of combat, his only marks of honor.

Lacey sat Broken on the stoop safely out of harm's way before she attacked the combatants with impartial fierceness. She shook Valentine loose from Black, grabbed Black and slapped him hard, then, seeing blood on his face, lifted the hem of her housecoat, spit on it, and rubbed it over the scratch.

"Get out of here," she barked at Valentine while she held Black back. "Get out of here right now, young lady, and get to work. You're going to be late, and if you lose that job just because you've been fooling around here you'll be in more trouble than you know how to handle. Now get."

"Well I'll be goddamned." Indignation dripped from Valentine's every word. "That's the last time I'll stick up for you, Lacey. From now on Black can say anything about you he wants to and I won't do a damned thing about it. So there."

"Good." Lacey picked up Broken and shoved Black toward the stairs. "Get up there and put some iodine on that cut." Black went upstairs, but I doubt if he followed Lacey's prescription for first aid. Black wouldn't have wanted the wound to heal too soon, and Lacey would have forgotten about it by the time she and Broken reached the top of the stairs and the *True Confessions* story. Lacey never let small crises interfere with the larger events in her life.

"You took an awful chance, jumping on Black like that," I warned Valentine as we ran toward Sycamore Lane, hurrying to make up for the time we'd lost in the military engagement. "If Lacey hadn't come down in time, Black would have really beat up on you. He's bigger than you are."

"So what? I'm faster than he is. If that mean little bastard ever calls Mr. Grey a cripple again, I'll kick him so hard his balls will bounce up and black both his eyes."

Even then I didn't realize what was happening, but as I said, Black was always two hops ahead of the rest of us when it came to figuring things out.

"What did he mean about Mr. Grey not keeping his hands on the steering wheel?"

"I don't know and I don't care. He's a mean little bastard and that's that. Now let's forget about him."

"Suits me. Tell me about the dog you've been taking care of."

"Her name is Gretchen. She's a Doberman. She's real friendly. You can help me feed her this morning. When I told Mr. Grey that I'd never had a dog of my own, he told me I could have half of Gretchen, and he offered me the half that eats."

"If they're so hard up, how can they afford to feed a dog?"

"Mr. Grey says that keeping Gretchen is sort of like having a policeman around the place. He says that a Doberman is a real smart dog. Some of them are killers. Gretchen isn't; she's as gentle as a kitten. But Mr. Grey says just looking at her is enough to scare away anyone who might be thinking about stealing from a man in a wheelchair."

It was true that the Depression had moved more people than me and my family out of their homes. Many of those displaced persons were roaming the highways, taking whatever they could find to keep themselves alive until prosperity came around the corner.

"What does Gretchen look like?"

"She's black and brown. Has long legs and short hair. Mr. Grey says that a Doberman is one of the smartest dogs there are. Some of them can be real mean, but not Gretchen. He has had her since she was eight weeks old and she's been trained to be real gentle. Mr. Grey says she wouldn't hurt a fly."

5

We heard the courthouse clock strike one time before we reached the edge of town. "Oh, no," Valentine groaned, "We're in trouble. It's eight-thirty. Run faster."

We were breathless as we turned into Sycamore Lane. Tall thick sycamore trees with reddish brown trunks and olive green branches bordered both sides of the road. Their creamy tops towered high above us, and their broad leaves mingled to form a dark green canopy that shadowed our path even on that brightly sunlit June morning. Valentine cursed when she stubbed her bare toe on a rock, but she didn't stop running.

Debris cluttered a deep ditch on the left of the lane, dumped there by townspeople determined to cling to precious pennies that in more prosperous times would have gone to the garbage collector. Much of the trash was camouflaged by weeds. Wildflowers climbed a fence that leaned backward in some places and veered forward in others, looking as if it had been there as long as the land itself, and throughout time had learned to conform to its contours.

Blackberry bushes formed a bee-filled barrier to the right of the lane.

The road was a curious combination of nature's wild beauty and mankind's deliberate wretchedness. No sign of habitation, no echo of life, came from any of the three shabby houses that were on the road. Two of the shacks huddled side by side as if to share their misery; they were separated only by a narrow gully. The third house kept to itself farther up the hill, standing aloof against the sky, which swooped down to skim the shaggy hilltop. Valentine pointed uphill toward the third house.

"That's where Crazy Gurney and his mother live."

Everyone in Marietta knew Crazy Gurney and his mother. The old woman was a common sight on the downtown streets and alleyways as she followed Crazy around while he leaped ahead of her and scavenged for old bottles or discarded toys and anything else that caught his fancy or might bring in a few pennies. Not even Lacey, who usually knew such things, had much information about the Gurneys' background. Nobody knew who his father was or Crazy's real name or how he and his peculiar mother had become part of the staid Ohio Valley town. No one knew how old Crazy and his mother were; it was impossible to guess. Although the woman appeared ancient, she moved along in her son's shadow with the agility of youth. She had to keep pace with Crazy or he would be sent back to the asylum. The story around town was that his release from the institution had been made in exchange for his mother's promise that she would keep watch over him. He had been released to be her helper; she had been charged with the responsibility of constant vigilance over him, to be sure he would never be out of her sight, would never again get in the same kind of trouble that had sent him to the institution. He had been accused of bothering a young girl, and although nobody—not even Lacey—knew for sure what *had* or *had not* occurred, everyone agreed that it was a good thing Crazy had been sent to Athens, since he had been transported out of town in the sheriff's car just two hops ahead of the girl's father who, along with half a dozen other men, had purchased a hank of rope and had set out to find Crazy and a tree with a good strong limb. Crazy had remained in the asylum until the girl and her family moved out of the valley, and then he was released in custody of his mother.

In time, the legend of Crazy Gurney lost its drama, and now he and his mother were just two eccentric characters, always alone together. Nobody spoke to them; nobody harassed them. Like the Ohio and Muskingum Rivers, they were part of Marietta, yet separate from it. Crazy was free to follow his erratic route through town and occasionally contributed to our childhood entertainment when we huddled together and told ghost stories featuring Crazy Gurney as the villain. Like the other children in town, I too had been warned by my parents to stay away from him. They'd not gone into detail about why I should avoid him; they'd simply told me he was "bad."

Knowing I was running up the street on which he lived, I asked Valentine, "What did Crazy Gurney do that was so bad?"

"Lacey says he grabbed a girl and pulled down her pants and tried to shove his thing in her. But she got away from him before he could really do it."

"Aren't you scared to be on the same street with him?"

"No. He never gets two feet away from his mother. I don't pay any attention to him. Anyway, Mr. Grey wouldn't let him hurt me."

"How could he stop him?"

81

My question remained unanswered as we hurried up an uneven path and climbed rotting steps to come face to face, as Valentine had predicted, with an angry blond woman who stood rigidly on the porch, impatiently tapping her foot.

"You're five minutes late, Valentine." The snap to the woman's words was mirrored in her hard cold eyes. "I can't afford to be docked, and neither can you. I punch a time clock, and if I'm late I lose money. You must learn to be prompt on your job so I can be prompt on mine."

"Yes'm."

I blinked, astonished. That humble mutter certainly hadn't come from the Valentine I knew. Not the Valentine who had just fought with Black and told Lacey off. What metamorphosis had taken place between Fourth Street and Sycamore Lane?

"Your duties for today are on the notepad on the table. You have a busy day ahead of you, so you'd better get started."

The woman's direct look at me said that Valentine would not have time to waste with a visitor. I turned to leave, but Valentine backed down the steps and put out her hand to stop me.

"See to it that you aren't late again." The woman's departing order was crisp.

"Yes'm." Valentine's meek agreement was accompanied by a swift dart of her tongue toward the woman's stiff back. I relaxed. This was the Valentine I knew.

Mrs. Grey clip-clipped down the rough walk, high heels punctuating her rapid departure, leaving exclamation marks in her wake. She contrasted oddly with her surroundings. The paint remaining on the house was chipped, peeling. The gutters were rusty, filled with leftover leaves from many autumns. The porch was lopsided, and the steps leading to the porch were worn, tilted. But the woman wore a spotless white blouse, with not a wrinkle in it. Her dark skirt was neatly pressed; the wide black patent belt encircling her narrow waist was shiny, and the kick pleat in her skirt was well-behaved. Her black patent pumps were as shiny as the belt, and their heels were rubber tipped, straight. Her pale blond hair, pulled tightly back from her face and gathered in a tight bun on the back of her head, was as disciplined as her clothes. Her skin, like her hair, was light and smooth, unblemished. Everything about the woman was controlled, rigid. Earlier in the spring, with Valentine's encouragement, I had confiscated a small sample of face mask that had come through the mail to my mother, and Valentine had smoothed it over my face. Looking at Mrs. Grey, I was reminded of how my face had felt beneath the dried mask, and how it had been impossible to talk or smile, even though I wanted to. I was relieved when the old Ford in the weed-covered driveway carried the woman around the corner and out of sight. She had been an icy intrusion on a warm June morning.

I followed Valentine into a kitchen that, like the woman who had just left, contrasted strangely with the outside of the house. The kitchen was immaculate; it was pretty. Oilcloth on the table matched red and white gingham curtains that blew gently in the breeze coming through the window above the sink, which was old but spotless. Its mismatched faucets gleamed, caught reflections of the sun and tossed them to the ceiling. Valentine picked up the notepad and scornfully reviewed her duties for the day.

"Dust the living room. Empty the ice pan. Order fifteen pounds of ice. Bathe Tommy before his nap. Dress him in his plaid sunsuit. Cook four stalks of rhubarb. Run the Bissell in the living room. Take good care of Tommy."

Valentine crumpled the paper and tossed it into the wastebasket. "Same old crap, day after day. As if I don't have enough sense to do it without being told. That woman is a pain-in-the-ass. Come on." She pulled me toward the back door. "Let's go out and say hi to Mr. Grey and feed

Gretchen before the brat wakes up. He ought to sleep for another hour. He never goes to bed until *she* does. That's why she makes him take a nap every afternoon. So he can stay up all evening with her. It gives her more time to spoil him. Let's go out while we have a chance. Once the brat gets up, the day's shot."

I met Mr. Grey for the first time on a peaceful sunlit June morning. My first impression was that he resembled Franchot Tone more than Leslie Howard, but we did agree that he definitely was a High-Muckety-Muck, in the truest sense of the word. He looked, smelled, and talked like a gentleman.

His short-sleeved shirt was as crisp and wrinkle-free as his wife's blouse and skirt. His shiny hair was combed neat and flat. The fresh scent of after-shave lotion teased my nose. I was impressed; my father had had to give up after-shave lotion several months earlier.

When Mr. Grey held out his hand to shake mine, I marveled at his immaculately manicured nails. Though the summer sun was rapidly heating the yard, a light blanket was over his lap. The shoes that showed beneath the blanket did not look like Depression shoes—that not uncommon combination of cardboard soles, scuffed toes, rundown heels, knotted shoelaces. Like the after-shave lotion and the perfect nails, those shoes separated him from most men who were struggling with hard times.

I have forgotten his greeting to me, but I remember what he said to Valentine as he held out to her a four-leaf clover still wet with dew.

"I found this just for you, Valentine. By evening it will be dry and you can press it in a book and remember years from now that on a June morning once long ago a man gave you all the luck he could hold in his hand."

Valentine reverently put the clover in her blouse pocket.

"He talks just like the movies," she said as we went into the kitchen.

"Yes. It sounded like he'd rehearsed those lines."
Valentine frowned.

I rephrased my thought. "I meant to say it sounds like he's said those words before."

Valentine frowned again and I changed the subject.

"Let's feed Gretchen."

I stayed on Sycamore Lane for an hour. Gretchen immediately made friends with me, and at Mr. Grey's bidding she held out her big paw to shake my hand. I prudently decided not to mention Gretchen to my mother. I could easily predict her reaction to the thought that I might transport fleas or ticks into our sterile flat.

I helped Valentine push the Bissell carpet sweeper through the living room. The room was pretty, again a contrast to the dreary outside of the house. The two long windows that looked out at the dusty road sparkled. They were dressed in lace curtains with brightly hued butterflies made from felt and pipestem cleaners clinging to the curtains. The sofa and its matching armchair looked as unused as Mrs. Grey's face. Their stiff mohair covers cautioned me not to muss them if I dared to sit on them.

Fringed lampshades perched on the two slim floor lamps, one by the sofa, one by the armchair. Highly polished end tables threw back a warm glow from the sunshine coming through the lace curtains. An upright piano occupied a position of honor in one corner. Looking at the tidy room, it was easy to understand Valentine's eagerness to exchange the flat for Sycamore Lane. Although I myself found Lacey's haphazard housekeeping interesting, I had my own neat living room to return to when things got too hectic in Lacey's flat. In Lacey's living room, a couch that had been severely wounded by time and people was joined by a tubercular chair that wheezed and spat its gray insides on anyone foolhardy enough to sit on it. The linoleum on Lacey's living room floor had long since lost its pattern and was a montage of black spots, where the original flooring had worn through, and mysterious conglomerations of various substances that had been spilled and forgotten and coated with either mud or dust, according to the weather and the season. The carpet in this house on Sycamore Lane was covered with dark red cabbage roses climbing off-white trellises and moss green leaves leading methodically from flower to flower.

"Valentine." A small voice called from the bedroom at the back of the house. Valentine grimaced and put away the Bissell.

"The brat's awake. Let's get him before he has a fit."

I followed her into the bedroom where a small boy was climbing out of a narrow white iron bed.

"Hi, Tommy," I said. "I think I'd better go home now, Valentine."

"Yeh."

She took the child's hand and walked to the front porch with me. Before I left I pointed to the house across the gully.

"Who lives over there?"

"Kathy Flint. Her husband hauls produce to the markets. He owns a truck. She's out on the road with him now, but Mr. Grey says she'll be home soon. He says he knows I'll like her a lot."

I hummed and skipped on my way home. Through Valentine, another dimension had been added to my life.

I too was now part of Sycamore Lane.

I was waiting for Valentine on the stoop when she got home. I was curious about a room I hadn't seen.

"Where do Mr. and Mrs. Grey sleep?"

"In the bedroom behind Tommy's. I don't have to clean it. Mrs. Pain-in-the-Ass makes the twin beds before she leaves."

"She and her husband don't sleep together?"

"Ye gods, no. Who'd want to sleep with her? She's so cold she'd freeze the balls off any man dumb enough to get in bed with her. And anyway, Mr. Grey wouldn't want to get that close to her. He never touches her. Never kisses her when she leaves or when she comes home. In fact, they hardly speak to each other at all. I bet if he was able to walk, he'd walk out on her. He's so much fun when she's gone, but the minute she comes home he gets real quiet and never says a word unless he has to."

"She's sort of pretty," I ventured. "Like you said, she does resemble Carole Lombard and Jean Harlow, except whenever you see a picture of them they're laughing or crying, and Mrs. Grey doesn't look like she could do either one. She looks like all the feeling is frozen out of her. But I bet if she'd warm up a little bit she'd be a real knockout."

"Yeh," Valentine snapped. "And I bet if the fox hadn't stopped to shit it would have caught the rabbit."

I recognized the tone, if not the message, in Valentine's retort. I had displeased her. I quickly hopped to safer ground—mollified her by telling a little white lie. I compromised with the truth, as I was rapidly learning to do.

"You're right about something else, too. Mr. Grey *does* look exactly like Leslie Howard. He looks a little bit like Franchot Tone, but *exactly* like Leslie Howard."

6

An unexpected treat came my way late in June when my aunt who lived on a farm near Nelsonville invited me to be her guest for a week. My mother wasn't happy with the invitation, and predicted dire catastrophes for a city girl going to a farm without her parents. My father came to my rescue by reminding my mother that his sister had successfully reared her own two children into adulthood, and that considering she had seen them safely through years of those hazards that my mother predicted, it was probable that she could guide me through one week. My father's logic, added to my clever reminder that summer camp was again unaffordable, brought a reluctant agreement that I could go to the farm for one week—and not a day longer.

Valentine was ecstatic when she heard that my aunt

owned a horse. She totally disregarded my statement that the swaybacked workhorse was older than I was and immediately wove a movie plot around the humble animal.

"If you really try, you can teach that horse to jump fences," she insisted. "Then, when your dad gets his old job back and has more money, he can buy you a horse and you can take riding lessons and someday an agent from Hollywood will come to Marietta and he'll see you on the horse and he'll sign you up for the movies and you'll be rich and famous."

My brain told me that the workhorse's chance of jumping a fence and mine of jumping into stardom were just about as remote as the chance that an agent from Hollywood would ever come to Marietta; but my heart, as usual, responded to Valentine's dreams, and I left for the farm determined to turn the tired old mare into a racehorse. The mare didn't share Valentine's illusions of glory; she balked at my urging her toward a fame she didn't desire. Every morning I mounted her and she sauntered across the fields, placidly halting to chomp the tall grass that bordered the fence. She remained completely disinterested in running or jumping over fences. Real life rarely followed Valentine's scenarios.

Nevertheless, the week was fun. The Ohio Valley early tomatoes were beginning to form on the thick vines, and the young corn held much promise. The cherry trees were heavy with fruit, and vegetables were on the table every day. Bessie, the farm cow, was much more cooperative than the horse, and obediently did her duty in providing fresh warm milk. I returned home two shades darker, three pounds heavier, and sore-hipped from my daily bouts with the mare.

I was home only a few minutes when Valentine burst into the flat. As usual, she didn't accept my story that the horse didn't measure up to expectations and assured me

89

that when I went back to the farm again the horse would remember what I had taught her and would do my bidding. By the time Valentine finished talking, she had almost persuaded me that sooner or later I'd be Hollywood bound—on horseback.

She had news about her week, too. "Kathy Flint came home. Her husband only stayed a couple of days, and then he left, but she says she's not going to go with him anymore. She says she's never again going to go away from Sycamore Lane because she'd rather be there than anyplace else in the world."

"What is she like?"

"She's real small for a grown-up woman. She's not much taller than you are. She has freckles across her nose. Her eyes are bright blue."

"She sounds like the descriptions of the heroines in Lacey's love stories," I observed.

Valentine chose to ignore the comparison.

"She usually wears shorts and a halter. She never gets all fancied up in high heels like Mrs. Pain-in-the-Ass does."

"Does Kathy work?"

Valentine ignored my question.

"Her hair is light brown and shiny, and it curls up around her face. She has a cute little nose. Mr. Grey teases her. He tells her that her nose turns up to catch the sunshine and turn it into pretty freckles."

"Mr. Grey sure knows how to say nice things," I said. "I wonder if he gets them out of books?"

Valentine frowned. "Of course not. He says nice things about Kathy because he's in love with her."

That caught and held my attention. I sat back to enjoy another of Valentine's plots. "How do you know? Did he tell you so?"

"No. He didn't have to. I can tell by the way he looks at her."

"Do you think Kathy loves him?"

"Of course she does." Valentine was positive. "Everybody loves Mr. Grey."

"His wife doesn't," I said.

Valentine made a face. "Mrs. Pain-in-the-Ass doesn't love anyone but herself and that little brat."

"Why doesn't she love her husband?"

Valentine shrugged. "For Pete's sake, how would I know? I don't know, and what's more, I don't care."

I met Kathy Flint the next day. As Valentine had said, she was built like a young girl; her cotton halter was flat in front and I thought to myself that she didn't belong in Lacey's world of the tits, nor in my mother's world of the breasts. She belonged to my world, and Valentine's.

When she crossed the gully early that morning to sit beside Mr. Grey's wheelchair, her curly hair blew like tiny flags in the breeze. As the two of them sat together, nothing touched but their eyes, but watching them look at each other, I knew that Valentine was right. They definitely were in love. Just as surely as there were good women and bad women in Lacey's love stories, there were good women and bad women in life. And Kathy Flint was a good woman—a childlike, adoring woman who sat in the grass and snapped polebeans she had gathered from her small garden and looked up at Mr. Grey while she worked.

I saw him touch her just once that morning. He put his hand gently on her head and smoothed her curls. She moved closer to his wheelchair and leaned her head against his knee.

Later in the morning, after Tommy awoke and Kathy returned to her yard, the blanket slid off Mr. Grey's lap and Valentine went over to pick it up. As she stooped down, Mr. Grey patted her head, and Valentine responded like Kathy to his touch.

I was puzzled. What was it about the man's touch that made Kathy and Valentine look so proud and yet so humble? I had a desire to know for myself, and when the newspaper slid from his lap I knelt beside him and very slowly put the pages in order, giving him time to work his magic on me. He didn't touch me.

7

As June closed in on July, the novelty of summer vacation palled. I tried to shorten the long and empty hours between Valentine's departure and return by spending more time with her on Sycamore Lane. Neither Mrs. Grey nor my mother would have permitted me to be with Valentine all day, every day, but I did manage to spend several midday hours with her after both women were safely out of the way. I was getting to know Tommy better, and the better I knew him the more I agreed with Valentine that he was a spoiled little brat. Fortunately, Valentine's lifetime of surviving Black's tricks had taught her tricks of her own, and we used them mercilessly on Tommy.

With Kathy's return home, Mr. Grey asked Valentine to keep Tommy occupied in the front yard while he and Kathy were together in the backyard.

"I enjoy talking with Kathy, but when Tommy's with us he monopolizes the conversation." Valentine pretended to believe him, but she told me she knew the real reason for his request.

"When people are in love they like to be alone with each other."

The big lopsided wooden swing suspended from the ceiling of the front porch provided an ideal lure to keep Tommy occupied. He enjoyed sitting on Valentine's lap while she and I shoved the swing back and forth and chanted nursery rhymes. Most mornings he was content, but one morning he became unusually restless.

"Take me for a walk." He jumped down from Valentine's lap and tugged at her skirt.

"We might as well do it," she muttered. "He won't shut up until he gets his own way."

"Where will we walk?"

"Up the hill," Valentine suggested.

I resisted. "I don't want to walk up the hill toward Crazy Gurney's house. He might come out and see us."

"So what? He sees me here on the porch almost every day when he and his mother go into town and he doesn't pay any attention to me. Come on. Don't be such a fraidy cat."

Tommy whined and tugged harder at Valentine's skirt. "Come on. Let's go."

I surrendered.

My knees trembled when we reached the top of the hill and stood in front of Crazy Gurney's house. It looked secretive, threatening, as it crouched behind untrimmed bushes. A small rusty wagon with a missing tongue and a tricycle with a missing wheel lay in the tall grass in the front yard. I glanced furtively toward the silent house and pulled at Valentine's arm.

"Come on," I coaxed. "Let's go. I don't like it here."

"Shut up," Valentine whispered. "Somebody's looking

94

at us. The hairs are standing up on the back of my neck. Black says you can always tell when someone's staring at you by the way the hairs tickle the back of your neck."

I stood quiet, listening. Black's reputation for being a smart little bastard was verified again when the bushes by the side of the house suddenly parted and Crazy Gurney leaped out at us. In his hand he held a rusty sandbucket, which he waved wildly at Valentine.

"Pretty, pretty, pretty," he mumbled. Whether he spoke of the bucket or of Valentine, I couldn't tell.

Valentine took a firmer grasp on Tommy's hand and held her ground, whispering to me as Crazy advanced toward us.

"When he gets close enough, you kick him in the balls and I'll take Tommy and run like hell."

I didn't have to assume battle position. Crazy's mother materialized as suddenly as Crazy himself had appeared. I had not heard a door open or footsteps approach. It was as if she had sprung out of the earth to stand between us and her son. She shook a broken-handled broom at us.

"Shoo." She flicked a corner of her dirty apron at us as if we were chickens being chased out of the corn patch. "Shoo. Get out. Get back downhill where you belong."

She didn't have to tell us again. We each grabbed one of Tommy's arms and fled downhill, swinging him between us with his feet barely skimming the ground. When we reached the safety of the porch we collapsed on the swing to catch our breath.

"That scared the shit right out of me," Valentine admitted when she could speak.

"It scared the shit right out of me too," Tommy echoed.

"And it scared the shit right out of me." The dirty four-letter word rolled off my tongue with the speed of truth. Or, as Black would have said, as easily as pee sliding off a prick. Black would have been proud of me.

We had our second brush with Crazy Gurney later

that same morning when the iceman made his twice-weekly rounds. He parked his truck halfway between the two houses, pulled out a small block of ice, hoisted the ice-filled tongs over his shoulder, and went toward Kathy's house. Kathy left Mr. Grey and went across the gully. Valentine and I ran to the deserted ice truck to perpetuate the tradition that any chunks of ice small enough to be carried away by hand were within the public domain, to be claimed by whoever had the fists or the words to assert ownership. On Fourth Street there was no contest; the biggest pieces always went to Black. On Sycamore Lane, Valentine had no competition.

"Give me a boost," she ordered. I shoved her up to the tailgate and watched as she crawled back into the cold dark cave where the ice was stored. She grabbed three chunks and backed out of the truck, jumped to the ground, and gave Tommy and me a piece of ice and kept one for herself. We stood in the hot dust and ran our tongues over the ice and watched as it melted and dripped to the road, making funny designs in the dust.

Our pleasure was short-lived. The slap-slap of flopping shoe-soles running downhill made Valentine and me look at each other with big eyes. Crazy Gurney was loping toward us, getting close. Valentine's reaction was instinctive. She threw her hunk of ice at the grotesque figure.

"Scat," she shouted. "Get out of here. Go home."

Crazy skidded to a halt. He swooped the chunk of ice up from the dust and ran his tongue over it, not pausing to remove the sand that clung to its wet surface. As he licked the ice, he blubbered words that were garbled to me but made sense to Valentine.

"Ye gods," she groaned, "that dumb nut thinks I gave him the ice to be nice to him. He doesn't know I meant to hit him with it."

Hearing Valentine's comment, the old woman, who

had slowly been making her way downhill toward her son, touched his arm with an odd tenderness.

"Go home, son."

Crazy lumbered away, licking the ice. She watched him reach the crest of the hill and go into his house before she spoke, her voice heavy with warning.

"Don't mess around with my boy. If you know what's good for you, you'll leave him alone."

"You've got a screw loose somewhere if you think *I* was bothering *him*." Valentine put her hands on her hips and faced the old woman. "He's the one who was doing the bothering. Not us."

"That's a lie," the woman said. "You came up the hill this morning and got him all riled up. He ain't used to seeing people up where we live. I'm telling you again— leave my boy alone. Stay down where you belong."

She turned, walked uphill, and disappeared into the dark house.

8

The Fourth of July was the most exciting day of the year in Marietta. It was particularly rewarding for Big, who, as a member of the American Legion, was hired each year to take tickets at the fairgrounds where the carnival remained in full swing during the week of the Fourth.

Valentine promised that Big would let me sneak in free along with the Hart family. My mother wasn't overjoyed at the thought that I would be out after dark with Valentine and Black, but a poignant reminder from me that last year I had attended the carnival with my friends from Washington Street sent my mother scurrying for her pocketbook to give me a small amount of money to spend for rides. The few tickets Big was allowed wouldn't go far when they were divided among the Harts. Lacey generously kept only two tickets so she and Broken could ride the merry-go-round one time. She didn't think it prudent to get Broken too charged up—or too high up. One year when Lacey and Broken went on the Ferris wheel, Broken mewed "pee-pee" at the same instant that he put the word into action, and the woman in the chair below was soaked. Upon reaching solid ground, the wet woman had been so upset that she had foolishly yelled at Lacey that Lacey should have better sense than to take a half-witted kid on a Ferris wheel, and Lacey punched the woman in the nose. The fight that ensued was more exciting than the fireworks and drew a larger crowd.

"Lacey says you can have all but two of her free tickets," Valentine offered.

It sounded great to me. Valentine and I spent hours planning our day at the carnival. The anticipation brightened my lonely moments while Valentine was at work. We thought our plans were firm, but as usual they fell apart.

July was an unusual month in many respects.

The first day of the new month ushered in a week of crises in the Hart household. Black set fire to a woodshed up the alley and cheerfully confessed his crime. Lacey's big red X's on the calendar loomed bigger than ever when she was three days late, and she worried that she had been caught. Big's temporary job, which had lasted for three weeks, ended late in June and so far he had had no luck finding day work. Knowing that working at the carnival would bring in money for a week made his bad luck a bit easier to bear, but in the meantime he was temporarily unemployed. Those crises, as distressing as they seemed at the time, were but surface ripples that would soon be smoothed out and forgotten, as were most of the small annoyances and inconveniences that formed the backdrop of the Harts' family life. But underneath the surface ripples, a deep wave of trouble was churning.

It was during that hectic week that Lacey began to refer to Valentine as "Miss High-and-Mighty." I was present at Valentine's christening. I was in Lacey's flat, propped in the corner of the tired sofa, protectively holding myself steady on one elbow, and waiting for Valentine to come home from work so we could talk about our plans for the Fourth of July.

Big was sprawled on the dirty linoleum on the living room floor, staring at the ceiling and waiting for "Amos 'n' Andy" to come on the radio. As usual on hot summer evenings, Big was barefooted and barechested. Valentine too enjoyed "Amos 'n' Andy," and often listened to the program with Big and laughed as hard as he did.

But when she came home that evening, she didn't join Big on the floor. She stood over him and stared down at him. She pinched her nose and spoke through her fingers.

"You smell awful."

Big didn't answer.

Lacey answered for him.

"Knock it off, Miss High-and-Mighty. Big's had a bad day. He couldn't find any work, and Black set fire to the woodshed in the alley and admitted he did it and now Big has to pay for it. Don't make things worse than they already are."

"Why don't you make *Black* pay for the shed?" Fully aware of the answer, Valentine needled Lacey with the question.

"Don't ask dumb questions, Valentine," Black said. "You know there ain't nobody in this town stupid enough to give me a job."

"Then why in the heck did you burn the shed down? And why did you admit you did it? The least you could have done was not take the blame for it." Valentine gave Black a look as dirty as the floor.

"Nothing doing. No siree. If there's one thing I wouldn't lower myself to do, it's tell a lie. No siree. I burned the shed down and I told the truth about doing it," Black spoke proudly.

"I wish to hell you'd add lying to the rest of your bad habits," Big growled. "But Christ, no. Now I have to pay for your fun."

Big wearily pulled himself up from the floor and went into the hot kitchen. His broad shoulders shrunk as he reached beneath the sink and got out the coffee can. He tipped it up and emptied a few coins on the table, counted out half of them and gave them to Lacey.

"Hang on to this in case you need it, Lacey." He slid the remaining coins across the table toward Valentine. "Take the rest of the money over to that guy across the alley. Tell him it's all I can give him right now. I'll send over some more after I get paid for working at the fairgrounds next week."

"Nothing doing." Valentine shoved the coins back toward Big. "Let Black take it over. *He* set the fire."

"I'll take it over," Lacey intervened. "Black can't. The guy said he'd kick a new asshole in Black if he ever set foot on the place again."

Valentine stuck her nose up in the air and retreated to the bathroom, slamming the door behind her. Big sat down at the table and lowered his head to his crossed arms. Lacey stood behind him and stroked the back of his neck.

"I've got a swell idea, Big. Take this"—she held some coins out toward him—"and go buy yourself a beer. Heck, the money isn't ours now anyway. The minute I walk out of the flat with it, it'll go to the guy across the alley. So before you pay for *Black's* good time, have some fun for yourself. It's been weeks since you've had a beer with the guys. It'll do you good."

Big shook his head. "I can't do it, Lacey. I can't buy a beer when I know these kids ain't had a full glass of milk for a month."

"Yeah, Lacey." Black spoke accusingly from across the room where he had been quietly enjoying the trouble he'd stirred up. "What's the big idea, trying to get Big to spend money on beer when I ain't had an ice cream cone for a year? For three hundred and sixty-five whole days and nights, I ain't had an ice cream cone. You ought to be ashamed of yourself, Lacey, trying to talk Big into throwing that money away on beer. Taking the ice cream right out of your kid's mouth. What kind of mother are you anyway?"

"CRAP!" Big's shout brought Valentine out of the bathroom and Black off his chair. "I don't give a good goddamn if you never have another ice cream cone, you mean little bastard. You cost me more money and give me more trouble than the rest of this bunch put together. You need your ass beat, that's what you need."

Big's hands shook as he pulled a package of Bugler from his pocket and rolled a skinny cigarette, frugally putting in only half as much tobacco as usual, saving the rest of it for the next crisis, which arrived later that same evening.

Valentine and I were alone in Lacey's kitchen. Valentine was dripping Nestle's hair-setting lotion on my wet head and trying to give me a Claudette Colbert hair-do. We were quiet, intent upon translating the hair-do in Claudette's photograph to my own dripping head. Lacey's voice drifted easily into us from where she sat with Big in the living room.

"I think I got caught last month."

For a moment we heard nothing but silence, then Big groaned, "You got caught?"

"I think so. I'm three days late and you know I'm as regular as clockwork."

The flip-flop of Lacey's slippers hinted that she was on her way to the kitchen to consult the big grain and feed calendar that was suspended on one nail over the stove.

"Yep." She returned to the living room. "I'm three days overdue. Almost four. I reckon I got caught that night you and I laid on the floor and listened to the 'Grand Old

Opry.' We really had a swell time that night, didn't we, Big? I ain't surprised something took hold. You really gave it to me good that night, Big. Remember?"

"Yeh, I remember. But I wish to hell I didn't. What are you trying to do, Lacey? Send us all to the poorhouse? You know damned well we can't afford to feed another kid right now. For Christ's sake, I thought you said you'd be careful."

"Oh, did I say that? I thought you said you'd be careful, Big. I'm sorry. Really I am."

Lacey's voice held the sound of tears and Big softened, as he always did whenever Lacey felt bad. "Oh well, what the hell," he said in a gentler tone, "no use crying over spilled milk, Lacey. And like you said, we had one hell of a good time that night. One of the best."

I knew Lacey and Big well enough by then to know that even a casual reference to making love was enough to send them quickly to the nearest mattress. I was not surprised when Lacey stuck her head around the door a few minutes later and told us she and Big were going to turn in early. Nor was I surprised when the squeak of bedsprings came through the wall. It was my first exposure to the actual sounds of passion, and I hurried over to Lacey's cupboard and found a glass and put it flat against the wall so I could hear what was going on in the next room. Valentine looked disgusted.

"Why do you want to listen to that baloney?"

"You told me that it's fun to listen to them do it."

"Well, it isn't. It's awful. It's just plain disgusting. I hate to hear them. They sound like two big walruses grunting and flopping around. I wish they'd leave each other alone. And what's more, I think they're too old to carry on like that."

Valentine was changing.

I arose early the next day and walked to work with Valentine. We chattered about our plans for the Fourth.

The holiday was almost upon us, and we were giddy with anticipation. The last thing Valentine said to me when I left her was that we'd spend the entire day at the fairgrounds and not come home until midnight, after the fireworks were over.

I spent the day letting down the hem of the dirndl skirt I planned to wear to the carnival. I could have saved my energy and the thread. When Valentine came home she told me she would not be going to the fairgrounds on the Fourth of July.

"Mrs. Grey gets the day off and she asked me to go over and work with her. She wants to clean the house real good. She says with both of us working we'll get twice as much done, and she'll pay me extra. And Mr. Grey said why don't I plan to spend the night there. He says I can climb the sycamore in the backyard and see the fireworks real good. Sycamore Lane isn't far from the fairgrounds."

"But what about me?" I wailed. "What about our plans to go on the rides and see the sideshows and stay until midnight? What about all that?"

"You can go without me. Big will let you sneak in and you can have my free tickets." It was obvious that she didn't consider her generosity a sacrifice. I was wounded.

I cried myself to sleep that night.

Big shared my disappointment.

"The extra money don't mean that much," he told Valentine. "You'll probably only get half-a-buck, and I've already spent more than that on spit devils and sparklers and sky rockets for us to set off here after we get home from the fairgrounds."

Valentine was unmoved.

Black put an emphatic thumbs down on Valentine's proposal that Big could save his fireworks for the fifth of July when she'd be home in the evening.

"Hell, no," Black yelled. "Why should the rest of us miss out on our holiday just because you want to have your cake and eat it too? If you'd rather spend your day with Old Crip and a mop bucket that's your business, but it don't mean we have to sit around with a finger up our butt waiting for you. No siree. Nothing doing. Crap on that idea."

Lacey supported Black. "Black's right. Why should we make little Broken wait for his fireworks just because Valentine wants to have her own way? She doesn't have to sleep over there. She could work all day and then come home and go to the fairgrounds. Which is it going to be, Miss High-and-Mighty?"

Her direct challenge brought a direct answer. "I'm going to spend the day and the night on Sycamore Lane."

"Suit yourself, Miss High-and-Mighty. It ain't no skin off my nose," was Lacey's final philosophy.

Big didn't surrender so easily. As a last resort he appealed to Valentine's vague recollections of past holidays.

"Remember how much fun we had a couple of years ago, Valentine, when I was making good money at the factory and we bought that big box of sky rockets? And remember, we had sparklers, and you had me light them for you. Remember?"

Valentine picked up a movie magazine and leafed through it, acting as if she hadn't heard a word Big said.

I fidgeted, embarrassed that a strong man like Big sounded so humble and pleading. I pitied him, because I knew that Big had neither words nor memories powerful enough to lure Valentine away from Sycamore Lane. I was relieved when Lacey called Big back into the present.

"That was a long time ago, Big." Her usually strong voice gently chided him. "It don't do no good to chase after a yesterday. We can't catch a yesterday and bring it back no matter how hard we try. Yesterdays are like that cat Black torments. The more Black chases that cat, the faster it runs. Let Valentine do what she wants. If Miss High-and-Mighty don't want to spend the Fourth of July with us, we'll just have our own good time without her. A better time than she'll have, I bet. Her tail will be dragging by the time she spends a day with Mrs. Grey. That woman is a hard worker for a High-Muckety-Muck. I've watched her hurry around Monkey Ward's, and I can tell you, no grass grows under her feet. I hope she works the butt right off of you, Miss High-and-Mighty. And if she does, don't come home and complain about it to us. It'll serve you right for messing up everyone else's plans."

Valentine sniffed, stuck her nose up in the air, and marched out of the room. I followed her.

9

Two days passed before I was with Valentine again. When I told my mother that Valentine had canceled our holiday plans, she made a sharp comment about there being a certain class of people who had no regard for keeping promises. Though I was disappointed in Valentine, I found my mother's criticism of her unfairly hypocritical. I knew she was relieved that I wouldn't be spending the day at the fairgrounds with the Hart family. I wanted to cry, both at my mother's hypocrisy and my own frustration. I went into my bedroom and lay on the bed and contemplated the unfairness of life and adults.

My father joined me a few minutes later, and without mentioning my thwarted plans or my mother's attitude, he suggested that since both he and my mother had the day off, we could spend the Fourth on my aunt's farm. So I didn't fare too badly.

We left the evening before the holiday and returned home shortly before midnight on the Fourth. I was exhausted by the quick trip and by a day spent urging the old mare to get ready for a screen test. I slept late the next morning. Even the racket in Lacey's kitchen didn't awaken me. By the time I got up, Valentine was gone for the day. I waited impatiently for her return, and I met her on the stairs.

"Come outside, quick," she greeted me. "I want to tell you something and I don't want any of these big ears around this place tuning in to what I have to say."

We quickly left the building and walked to the big elm and sat on its thick trunk.

"What does the word *impotent* mean?" Valentine shot the question at me without preamble.

"Good grief, I don't know. I never heard it before. Maybe it means something like being important. Why?"

"Because that's what Mr. Grey says he is."

"Tell me why he said it, and maybe I can figure out what it means," I suggested.

Valentine told her story rapidly, determined to complete it before Black joined us or my mother summoned me in.

Lacey's prediction that Mrs. Grey would work Valentine's tail off had been accurate. By afternoon, Valentine was tired, and she slumped against the icebox to rest.

"If you need a break," Mrs. Grey said, "go in and clean out my dresser drawers. You can sit down while you do it. Sort out the hosiery that needs repair, and straighten out the drawers. Tommy was looking through them the other day and left everything scattered around."

Valentine emptied the drawers, relined them with clean paper, sorted the hosiery, then turned her attention to a pile of photographs, looking at each as she stacked them in a neat pile. Among them was a snapshot of a large beautiful house with a long curving driveway and a Pierce Arrow automobile. Mr. Grey stood beside the car; he was surrounded by several stylishly dressed men and women.

"The photograph was a little blurred," Valentine said, "but a light-haired woman stood out real clear. I thought at first it was a picture of Jean Harlow. The real Jean Harlow! But I took it over to the window to get a better look at it. The woman's face was turned to the side, and there were pretty curls hiding most of her face. She had her arm around Mr. Grey's waist. He was standing up tall and straight, looking down at the woman and laughing."

"*Was* it Jean Harlow?"

"No. Of course not. It was Mrs. Pain-in-the-Ass. She came in and saw me looking at it. I asked her who it was and she said it was a picture of her and she took it out of my hand and stood looking at it for a long time. And she did a funny thing while she looked at it. She smiled. Then she went over to the mirror and took the hairpins out of that bun on the back of her neck and she let her hair fall loose down around her shoulders. She looked a lot different with her hair down. And for the rest of the day she was real nice to me. About an hour after she looked at the snapshot she told me she thought we'd done enough work on a holiday, and she said we could have a picnic out in the backyard for supper. All evening long she kept talking to Mr. Grey about old times. Brought up names of people they used to know, talked about parties they'd given. She might as well have saved her breath. He wasn't buying any of that baloney. He didn't talk very much, but when he did, he talked about Gretchen and the weather and stuff like that. When she went in to put Tommy to bed, Mr. Grey said something real nice to me. He told me that my name fits me to a tee. He said that I remind him of one of those heart-shaped boxes of Whitman's chocolates that go on sale around Valentine's Day. He told me that I'm like that candy. Sweet and soft on the inside no matter how hard I pretend to be on the outside."

"Sort of like a sycamore ball," I said.

Valentine frowned. "That's dumb. There's nothing nice about a sycamore ball."

I quickly jumped to safer ground—I thought. "Maybe he's read some of those magazines Lacey reads. What he told you about being like a piece of candy sounds like some of the things the hero tells the heroine in Lacey's stories."

"That's dumb too. He wouldn't read that trash. But that's not what I called you out here to talk about. I want to tell you what happened later that night."

The hot summer night had been very quiet, she said, and Tommy was asleep beside her in his bed while she tossed restlessly from the heat. Voices drifted in from the other bedroom.

"Mrs. Pain-in-the-Ass made a real pest of herself. She said, 'For God's sake, Tom, don't you care anything about how I feel? Don't I mean anything to you?'

"Mr. Grey replied, 'It's late. Go to sleep.'

" 'I'm not sleepy. It's not sleep I need right now, Tom. It's you. I want to lie close to you.' "

Valentine heard the bedsprings squeak, and she knew Mrs. Grey was on her way to the other bed. Silence followed until the woman spoke again. "Can't you try, Tom? Can't you just try? You know I won't get angry if you can't do it, but at least try. Here, Tom. Put your hand here. Try, Tom. Please."

"When Mr. Grey answered her, he really sounded fed up," Valentine said. "He said, 'For God's sake leave me alone,' and he said it like he really meant it. And then he said that he's impotent, and he said it two or three times, like he wanted her to understand it real good. 'Impotent,' he said. Impotent.

"But she just kept on nagging at him. Wouldn't shut

up and leave him alone. She told him the doctors could have been wrong. Then she told him he hadn't touched her in months and she said she was starved for love. I had all I could do to keep from laughing out loud at that one. As mean as she is, she wouldn't know what to do with love if she did have it. Well, she sure as heck didn't get it from Mr. Grey. I heard her ask him to kiss her and that did it! He really told her off then. He told her to leave him alone and to get back in her own bed.

"He asked her why she was trying to talk herself and him into believing anything was any different that night than any other night, and she told him it was because of the photograph. She said it reminded her of how much in love they used to be. She said she wanted to forget and forgive the things that had made them grow so far apart. I heard her get out of his bed, and I peeked through the crack in the door to see what she was up to. She took the snapshot over to Mr. Grey and switched on the light and told him to look at it. He shut his eyes, but she still kept on pestering, and asking him to put his hand where she wanted it. I'm not sure where that was, but wherever it was, Mr. Grey wasn't interested. He really told her off. When she kept pestering him, he took it just so long and then he really told her what he thought of her. He told her she was like a bitch in heat and said for her to get out of his bed and leave him alone. And he told her that she'd reminded him every day and every night since his accident that he wasn't really a man, so why was she wasting her time now trying to get him to act like one. And then he said that word again. He told her it wasn't love she was after, it was sex. And he told her that was her problem, not his, because he's impotent. He told her sex is over for him and as for what she intended to do about it for herself, he didn't know and he didn't give a damn. She finally had enough sense to get out of his bed and leave him alone. He turned out the light and about an hour later I was still awake, trying to figure out what the word meant, when she came through Tommy's room and went into the bathroom. She thought I was asleep, but I wasn't. She was in there so long I took a chance and peeked through the keyhole and do you know what she was doing?"

"What?"

"She was naked as a jaybird, standing in front of the mirror, running her hands up and down her body like she was somebody else trying to find out what her body felt like. She had the snapshot propped up on the washbasin."

"Wow! If you ask me, we might as well get Black in on this and not waste time trying to figure it out ourselves. He's real smart. He'll know what it means."

Knowing that Black never did anything for free, Valentine and I scoured the neighborhood and found a few discarded soda bottles and returned them to the Clover Farm store. We approached Black with the deposit and with a proposition.

"I'll give you these pennies if you'll tell me what a certain word means." Valentine held out her palm. Black rapidly counted the coins. "Okay. What's the word?"

"Impotent."

"I never heard of it. I'll have to look it up in the library. Give me the money and I'll go find out."

"Nothing doing." Valentine closed her fingers over the pennies. "We're not dumb enough to pay you to do something we can do ourselves. We thought maybe you'd know right off the bat what it means. Forget it."

"Suits me. I got better things to do with my time than spend it in the library with old eagle-eye Sturgiss staring at me." Black turned and sauntered away.

I whispered to Valentine, "You'd better call Black back and make the deal with him. You know Mrs. Sturgiss watches you like a hawk ever since Broken wet on that book. She might not even let you use the big dictionary."

"She'll let you use it. You can look it up. She likes you."

"Nothing doing. I bet that word has something to do with men and women in bed together. Mrs. Sturgiss *does* like me—that's why I can't do it. She always wants to help me. I can't take the chance. She knows my mother, and if my mother ever finds out that I'm looking for a word that has to do with people in bed she'll have a fit. Call Black back before he disappears for the day. Make the deal. It'll be worth it. Black doesn't give a hoot what Mrs. Sturgiss thinks of him."

"BLACK," she shouted. "Come back here. We're ready to deal."

Black walked a few feet further to demonstrate his disinterest in our proposition before he reversed field and rejoined us.

"Okay," Valentine said. "Go look it up and then we'll pay you."

"No siree. Cash on the barrelhead, or no deal."

The pennies jingled in Black's pocket as he ran toward the library. He was back in ten minutes. It hadn't taken him long to find the word and select the definition he thought most interesting and scrawl it on a piece of notepad. Valentine read the words and frowned.

" 'Lack of ability to procreate . . .' " Valentine tore up the paper and threw it at Black. "Give me back my money. I don't even know what procreate means. I didn't get my money's worth."

"Not on your tintype, Miss High-and-Mighty. I'll tell you what the meaning means, and I'm keeping the money. Impotent means a guy can't get a hard-on. Can't fuck. Has a sick prick. Understand?"

Black had a gift for cutting through trivia and going directly to the heart of a matter.

After Black left, Valentine and I talked it over and decided the information was well worth its cost.

"It makes me feel good to know that Mr. Grey and Kathy love each other in a pure sort of way. If they don't fuck each other, there's nothing wrong with them being in love, even if they are married to somebody else. It was worth every cent we paid Black to know that a man can love a woman without sticking his thing in her all the time."

I didn't say so to Valentine, but personally I found Lacey's and Big's kind of love more exciting. I had slept over with Valentine a few times, hoping that Big and Lacey would couple and I could see them make their kind of love. I had just about decided that the discomfort of clinging to the edge of the narrow cot, sticking my fingers in my ears to block out Black's restless tossing and Broken's constant mewings, stepping cautiously over heaps of clothes on the bedroom floor, and fleeing the roaches in the bathroom wasn't worth it, when one night shortly after we learned that Mr. Grey and Kathy *couldn't* make love, Big and Lacey decided they *would*.

Valentine and I were sleeping on the floor in the living room when Big and Lacey started to romp in bed. I was lying awake, trying to capture any breeze that might drift in from the windows, when I heard furtive sounds of lovemaking. The door between the living room and bedroom was partially open, and by propping myself up on an elbow, in a telltale patch of moonlight I could see Big and Lacey blended into one huge lump beneath their light bedcover. I heard Lacey's breath quicken and Big's murmur become louder and more urgent. Again I would hear the sounds of love and this time witness it. I jabbed Valentine and put my mouth close to her ear.

"They're doing it, Valentine." I knew the moment I spoke that I should have kept quiet. The familiar expression of anger and disgust that Valentine had been wearing so frequently when she was in the flat told me that I'd spoken too soon.

Valentine jumped up and yelled, "You two sound like hogs rooting through a cornfield."

"Is that you, Valentine?" Valentine slammed the door on Lacey's call.

Black got into the act. "Who the hell do you think it is, Lacey . . . the Virgin Mary?"

I slipped on my sandals and ran after Valentine. Moments later Black followed me into the dark deserted street. We ran up to the elm and sat on its twisted trunk and felt the clean night air on our faces. For a brief time we shared a curious allegiance. On that summer midnight we were young fugitives fleeing from adult needs we did not understand.

Black picked at the tree and piled pieces of its bark together and struck a match on the brick sidewalk and tried to burn the bark, but the match went out before the bark ignited.

When we were again in the dark, he said, "Valentine, you ain't got the sense God gave a goose."

Valentine remained silent.

"Nope. You ain't got the sense God gave a goose. You sure did a dumb thing when you yelled and tore out of the flat. Big's really mad, and so is Lacey. After you butted in and spoiled their fun I heard old Lacey coaxing Big to try to give it to her again, but Big said no, he said you took all the starch right out of him. Lacey was mad enough to chew nails and spit rust. You'd better wise up, Valentine, and leave them alone when they're busy in bed. You're playing with fire when you butt in when Big and Lacey are trying to get a piece of ass."

"Oh, Black, shut up," Valentine growled. "You're as bad as they are. You're always talking dirty. Shut your filthy mouth."

"Oh, boy, listen to you, Miss High-and-Mighty. Since when did you think there was anything wrong with talking dirty? If you keep on acting so stuck up, you're going to find yourself out of a job. Big and Lacey are getting plenty

115

fed up with the way you've been treating them since you went to work for the High-Muckety-Mucks. Lacey will put up with a lot of crap from you about what's wrong with her housekeeping, and Big'll put up with a lot of baloney about how he looks and smells, but when you start butting in on them when they're screwing, you're just asking for trouble."

"Oh, yeh?" Valentine sneered. "And just why are you being so helpful all of a sudden and giving me all this advice? What's it to you?"

"Well, shit, you don't think I want you hanging around the flat all day, do you? The more you're gone, the better I like it."

Black's warning made sense to me, but it rolled off Valentine like water off a duck's back.

10

"Flint's home," Valentine told me a few days later. "It's a good thing Kathy was in her own yard. Flint came barreling up the road so fast she wouldn't have had time to get across the gully."

"What's he like?"

"Nearly as tall as Big. He has black curly hair and a dark beard. Looks like he hasn't shaved for a month. He's mean and loud and bossy. He yelled at Kathy all day. I don't like him and neither does Mr. Grey."

"Of course Mr. Grey wouldn't like him. He loves Kathy, so of course he wouldn't like her husband."

"It happens sometimes," Valentine insisted. "I saw a movie where a man fell in love with his best friend's wife and the men kept on being friends. In fact, the guy left town so he wouldn't be tempted to mess around with his friend's wife."

"Mr. Grey couldn't do that even if he wanted to."

"I know. All he can do is sit in that wheelchair and wait for Flint to leave. Mr. Grey says Flint never stays very long. It's a good thing too, because I don't think Mr. Grey could sit and listen to Flint yell and cuss at Kathy much longer. She never sasses him back. We didn't hear a word from her all day. By the middle of the afternoon, Flint was drunk. Mr. Grey was furious when Flint was yelling at Kathy, but the funny thing is, he got even madder when Flint quit yelling and everything got quiet next door."

"Maybe Mr. Grey thought Flint was in bed with Kathy."

Valentine was outraged. "That's disgusting. Kathy wouldn't let that big gorilla get in bed with her."

"She has to. She's his wife. When you're married, you have to let your husband do whatever he wants to in bed."

"You're dead wrong on that one," Valentine declared. "I'm going to ask Lacey about that."

"Do you think Lacey will tell you?"

"Sure. Why wouldn't she?"

"Because from what Black told us the other night, Lacey was really mad at you when you yelled at her and Big that they sounded like hogs rooting through a cornfield. Maybe she's still mad."

"Nope. Not Lacey. That's one thing I have to say for her. Old Lacey never carries a grudge for long. She gets fiery mad and gets it out of her system and then it's all over with. Unless someone says or does something to hurt Broken, and then she stays mad at them forever. But she's okay with me now. Come on. Let's go ask her."

She went to the kitchen and faced Lacey with a hypothetical question: "Lacey, does a woman have to let a man make love to her just because she's married to him? Can he *make* her let him fuck her?"

"Don't talk dirty." Lacey's reprimand was automatic; she went on to more important matters. "That's a dumb question, Valentine. Why would a man have to *make* a woman do it? For Pete's sake, if she didn't want to make love with a man, why would she marry him in the first place? It's all part of the bargain. That's what marriage is supposed to be—a bargain between two people who love each other. The man brings home the bacon, the woman fries it, and they both eat it."

Valentine looked disgusted. "That's a dumb answer, Lacey. Dumber than my question. What's bacon got to do with making love?"

"It's my way of telling you that when two people get married they promise to take care of each other. And men need a heck of a lot of taking care of in bed, Valentine. Remember that. If you marry a guy without wanting to make love with him, you're a cheater."

"I think Lacey's wrong," Valentine told me after we left the kitchen. "Just because she gets hot pants and Big gets a hard-on every time he sneaks a feel, Lacey thinks that's the way it is with everyone. I don't think Kathy Flint is like that. Not at all. When Flint leaves and I have a chance to talk to Kathy alone, I'm going to ask her."

"Can I come with you when you do? If I wait for my mother to tell me what I should or shouldn't do with my husband, I'll never find out."

We asked her two days later. No sooner had the dust settled from Flint's departing truck than Kathy slid down the gully and knelt again beside Mr. Grey.

"We'll leave them alone now so they can make up for the time they've been apart," Valentine said, "but as soon as Kathy goes home we'll go over and talk with her. I'll put Tommy to bed late for his nap so he won't be awake to pester us."

By late afternoon we were in Kathy's kitchen eating homemade bread spread thick with wild blackberry jam. While we ate, Valentine talked and I listened.

"You sure do have a nice kitchen, Kathy."

An empty Certo bottle stood beside the small glasses

of newly made jam. A tall red geranium in a brown clay pot brightened the center of the table. Bright yellow polka-dotted curtains framed the window over the sink.

"Yes." Kathy smiled. "I like my kitchen. It isn't fancy like the ones you see in magazines, but to me it looks real good. In fact, I like everything about my house. When I was a little kid, I wanted a dollhouse so bad I could taste it. I never got one then, but I have one now. A full-sized dollhouse with three rooms and a bath, and as long as Flint can pay the rent on it, I can play house."

"Do you like having Flint home?" Valentine's direct question brought a direct answer.

"No. But he isn't home very often."

"Lacey never seems to mind having Big hang around. In fact, she likes having him home."

I knew that Valentine was steering the conversation in a specific direction. I stayed quiet, intent on letting Valentine maneuver Kathy into answering the question we had come to ask.

"She must love him a lot." Kathy sounded wistful.

"Yeh. I guess so. Anyway, they're always fooling around with each other. Feeling each other up. Sometimes it's downright disgusting, the way they can't keep their hands off each other."

"Why do you think it's disgusting?" Kathy asked. "They like to touch each other because they love each other. There's nothing disgusting about that, Valentine. That's the way it should be."

Valentine had cleverly painted Kathy into a conversational corner.

"But if they *didn't* love each other, it would be disgusting, wouldn't it, Kathy? I mean, *you* wouldn't let someone *you* didn't love fool around with you, would you? You wouldn't let Flint mess around with you like Big messes with Lacey, would you, Kathy? If you're so happy to have Flint gone, you don't love him, and if you don't love him you wouldn't let him kiss you and mess around with you, would you, Kathy?"

Kathy attempted to sidestep the inquisition by emptying the ice pan. Valentine ate another piece of bread and jam and patiently waited for Kathy to put the ice pan back in place and join us at the table.

"You don't let Flint kiss you and mess around with you in bed, do you, Kathy?"

"He doesn't kiss me." Kathy's half-truth told the whole truth.

"He doesn't kiss you, but he fucks you. Is that what you mean?"

"Yes." Kathy was helpless against Valentine's tough, determined persistence.

"But you don't love him, do you?"

"No." Kathy's reply was quick, positive.

"Then doesn't it make you want to puke when he fucks you?"

"I just don't think about it while he's doing it," Kathy said. "It never lasts very long. It means nothing at all to me, and sometimes I'm not sure it means much to him. He never says nice things to me while he's doing it. He never kisses me. He just grabs me and does it and it's over with real quick. I knew when I married him that I'd have to put up with that sort of thing. It's the only way I have of paying my share of the rent on my dollhouse."

"Did you love Flint when you first married him?"

"I don't know. He was real good-looking. Still is, if you care for that kind of good looks. He paid a lot of attention to me at first. I grew up in the orphanage, spent most of my life there. When I was old enough I went out on my own and I got a job waitressing. I was awful at it. Spilled coffee on tablecloths, broke plates, couldn't make change. I was about to get my walking papers when Flint came in one day for a hamburger and he took a fancy to me and we started dating. I married him a month later. We got our license the same day I got my walking papers from my boss."

"Is that why you married Flint? Because you got fired?"

"Not entirely. He *is* good-looking, and he paid a lot of attention to me and he gave me rides in his truck. I'd never been out of Marietta before I met Flint, and when he took me for rides up to Lowell or down to Parkersburg, I thought I was really something, sitting way up there in the cab of his big truck. I felt like I amounted to something—for once I was looking down on the rest of the world. I know now that I was more in love with Flint's truck than with him. I was a terrible waitress. I would have been an awful saleswoman. I never learned how to type or take shorthand, so I couldn't work in an office. There weren't any jobs open anyway, The Depression had just started. So when Flint said let's get married, it seemed like a good idea at the time."

"Are you sorry now?"

"No. If I hadn't married Flint, I wouldn't be living on Sycamore Lane." All three of us knew that she meant if she hadn't married Flint, she wouldn't have met Mr. Grey.

After we left, Valentine and I tried to decide if Flint was really good-looking. We couldn't think of a movie star he resembled, so we decided he wasn't.

Flint returned unexpectedly the next week. Kathy had thought he would be gone for at least a month, but the unusually early ripening of the valley's tomato crop brought him back to town to transport the produce to the northern markets while it was still slightly green. I saw him arrive. I was interested that morning in a game Mr. Grey played with Gretchen. He threw sycamore balls into the air, whispered a command to Gretchen, and the dog leaped, caught the balls and delivered them intact to Mr. Grey.

"Why don't Gretchen's sharp teeth break the sycamore balls?" I asked.

"It's a matter of control. I have taught Gretchen not to bite the balls, just catch them."

"If you wanted to, could you teach her to bite them?"

"Of course. Gretchen is like most females. She'll do whatever she can to please people she loves."

The day was humid, the heat oppressive. The ice truck coming down the road offered a welcome oasis from the summer sun. I joined Valentine and Tommy on the porch, and we ran to the ice truck and grabbed small chunks of ice. Kathy had returned to her yard a moment earlier to let the iceman make his delivery. When Flint's truck roared around the corner, the scene was an innocent one. Two thirsty young girls and one little boy licking pieces of ice; Kathy in her kitchen paying the iceman; and a man in a wheelchair tossing sycamore balls to a dog.

Flint casually waved as he jumped from the cab of his truck. "Kathy, I'm home," he shouted and went into his house. No sound came from the house next door for several minutes. "Where in the hell is the booze?" The words exploded out of the window and across the gully. We heard Kathy's voice, but not her words.

"Don't be telling me what to do. I'll drink when I want to, and what I want to." Flint's shout was followed by the sound of flesh striking flesh.

Valentine jumped to her feet. Mr. Grey strained against the arms of his wheelchair; his veins were blue ridges. His face whitened, his shoulders stiffened, as he tried to hoist himself out of the chair. His helpless fury triggered Valentine into action. She ran to him and put her hands over his ears, pressed them tightly until color returned to his face. The house next door became quiet again.

I left for home. I fled to Lacey's flat and joined her in commiserating with "Mary Noble, Backstage Wife," and tried not to think about what might be happening on Sycamore Lane.

11

$\mathbb{B}$y late July, the bad luck that had pursued the Harts earlier in the month had reversed direction. Lacey was overjoyed when she got the curse that was really a blessing. She jubilantly informed Big that there would not be another mouth to feed. Big topped Lacey's good news by telling her that he had just been offered a full-time job. Not just an ordinary job, but the best job in Marietta, according to Valentine. Not in salary, but in power and prestige.

"Big's going to work full time at the Hippodrome. He'll take tickets and paint and work the lights, and he says he'll even scrape the chewing gum off the bottom of the seats if they tell him to. Big's been wanting that job as long as I can remember, and now he has it. And he can get free passes anytime except on bank nights and holidays."

I was a second-hand beneficiary of Big's good luck.

The first free passes went to Lacey, and a near-disaster followed when Lacey took Broken to see a Tom Mix serial and Broken got so excited that he wet his pants, the aisle, and the woman sitting in front of him. The woman was furious; so was the theater manager, who emphatically told Big that from that day on the free passes could be given only to persons eleven or older. Since Lacey refused to go anywhere without Broken, I inherited her passes. For a week or so, Black insisted on getting his share of the passes and was a noisy nuisance, hissing at the hero, cheering the villain, and making vulgar sounds during love scenes, and assuming a mask of complete innocence when the usher came down the aisle to locate the source of the disturbance. There was nothing Valentine could do about it; she didn't want to chance having Big's passes taken away if the manager learned that Black was the culprit. The best she could do was put up with Black while they were in the theater, then engage him in fisticuffs as soon as they were out. Black's role as movie critic ended abruptly one afternoon when he became bored with Nelson Eddy singing to Jeanette MacDonald. Announcing to us that he'd heard all the squawking he could take for one day, he left for the men's room where the shiny white tile inspired his most` creative decorations. Big strolled in and saw Black complete a favorite four-letter word. Big promptly picked Black up by the scruff of his neck and the seat of his pants and shoved him out the side exit of the theater with the warning that if Black ever showed his face around the Hippodrome again, Big would knock the holy shit out of him.

From that lucky day on, until we moved away from Fourth Street, Valentine and I spent our Sunday afternoons in the land of happy endings.

For Big, one of the fringe benefits of his new job was Valentine's increased respect. But now she turned her criticism toward Lacey. First she concentrated on Lacey's housekeeping.

One sticky hot night Valentine returned to the squalid flat and attacked Lacey. Hands on hips, she glared at Lacey who, as usual, was sitting with Broken and a magazine on her lap.

"I thought you said this morning that you were going to mop this cruddy kitchen today."

"Oh, did I say that?" Lacey was always nonchalant about neglected good intentions. "I forgot. I must have got busy with something else. Now, let me see. What did I do today?" As she reminisced, she opened her housecoat, lifted one huge tit, and pensively rubbed the soft, sweaty flesh beneath it. Valentine looked disgusted.

"Oh, yeah." Lacey yawned and let her tit drop back into place. "I remember. I read a story to Broken from a new *True Romance*."

"Oh, swell," Valentine jeered. "That's really just dandy. That's exactly what this dump needs—another one of those trashy magazines."

Lacey, usually a placid soul, took instant umbrage at Valentine's literary criticism. "Now look here, Miss High-and-Mighty, what I do all day is my business. You ain't running this joint. I am."

Valentine bit back. "Yeh? That's news to me. I would have bet a million bucks the garbage man was running it. Just look at that cruddy linoleum, Lacey. It's awful. You ought to mop it. Right now. It's a mess. It's disgusting."

Lacey settled back in her chair, reached into her wrapper, drew out her other tit, and gave it the same attention she had given its partner, lifting it and rubbing tiny pieces of dirt from beneath it.

"It sure beats heck how these nigger babies rub off a body on a hot day like this," she marveled, holding one of the little blots up and peering at it. "And speaking of hot days, Miss-High-and-Mighty, that's exactly why I didn't mop the kitchen today and it's exactly why I ain't going to mop it tonight. It's hotter than the hinges of hell. By the middle of the morning I was sweating like a nigger." Lacey ducked her nose toward her underarm and added, "Damned if I don't smell like one, too."

Valentine's nose turned up a little farther. "Don't say *nigger*, and don't say *sweat*. It's not nice to use those words."

"Yeh? Who says so?" Lacey sounded only mildly interested.

"Mr. Grey. That's who."

"Yeh? And what does Mr. Grey call a nigger?" Lacey's interest expanded.

"A Negro."

"Yeh? And what does Mr. Grey call *sweat*?"

"Perspiring."

Lacey made another exaggerated pass toward her underarms, elevated her eyebrows, and drawled, "Well, excuse me, Miss High-and-Mighty. I should have said, 'I smell like a Nee-gah-roe, and I'm perspiring like a Nee-gah-roe,' but I'll be damned if I'm going to work like a sweating nigger on a day like this. So put that in your pipe and smoke it. Here, honey," she hoisted Broken to her other knee. "Cuddle down here and listen to this story about an office wife. Boy, I sure am glad Big doesn't work in an office. God, the things those men and women do in those white-collar jobs you just wouldn't believe."

Remembering too late that my father wore a white collar to work, Lacey hastened to add, "But that doesn't mean that *all* men who work on a white-collar job mess around with the women in the office. Not even if they *are* married to a woman Who Wouldn't Say Shit if She Had a Mouthful."

I accepted her backhanded apology without comment, and she returned her attention to her magazine. Black disappeared into the night. Valentine, armed with paper and pencil, motioned to me to follow her into the kitchen. She sat at the table, spit on the end of the stubby pencil, and began to print.

"What are you doing?"

"I'm making signs to hang around this cruddy joint after Lacey's asleep tonight. I want you to be over here bright and early tomorrow morning to hear what she says when she reads them."

Valentine was well on her way to Sycamore Lane the next morning when Lacey and Big saw the signs tacked strategically throughout the flat. The sign over the sink cautioned Lacey not to comb her hair in the kitchen; the sign over the garbage can reminded Black to empty it. The sign over the washbowl in the bathroom ordered Big to shave. The sign atop the pyramid of dishes told Lacey to wash them. The sign on the kitchen floor repeated Valentine's suggestion that Lacey should mop it. Big and Lacey read all the signs—then roared. With laughter, not rage. They were so happy about Big's new job and Lacey's not getting caught that nothing as trivial as Valentine's bad humor could upset them. I blushed that evening when Valentine insisted that I repeat their comments.

"What did they say when they saw the signs? Come on, tell me word for word."

"They didn't really *say* anything at first; they just laughed. After they quit laughing Big said, 'The next thing you know I'll wake up and find a sign tied to my pecker telling me not to use it,' and Lacey, 'If you do, you can bet your sweet-patootie I wasn't the one who tied it there,' and they both laughed harder."

"Oh, crap," Valentine moaned, "I don't know why I don't just give up on those two."

"Neither do I, Valentine," I agreed. "They really aren't that bad. In fact, I like them a lot. And when I first met you, you all got along real well together."

"That was before I learned how people should *really* act," Valentine said.

Lacey laughed at Valentine's reminders, but she didn't ignore them completely. A week later she surrendered to the note that advised her to mop the kitchen floor. When Valentine and I returned to the flat on an unusually hot evening we found Lacey sprawled on the floor, her skirt pinned together between her knees with a wooden clothes-pin. She haphazardly swished a soggy rag over the worn linoleum while Broken crawled contentedly in her wake, his baggy pants dripping mop water. Lacey, glancing up and seeing Valentine in the doorway, settled back on her haunches and looked pious.

"See, Valentine, I said I'd mop the floor when it really needed it, and I'm keeping my word. It's crazy to work this hard in this heat but anything to shut you up for a while. So don't be nagging at me again."

Valentine let the tilt of her nose tell Lacey what she thought of Lacey's tardy effort to clean the linoleum.

"If you're going to do it at all, why in the heck don't you do it right?" Valentine pointed toward the icebox. "You didn't even move the icebox to clean under it. Look—there's that rubber ball Broken lost the day we moved into this dump."

Valentine nudged the ball out from beneath the icebox with the toe of her shoe and it rolled toward Broken. Eager to retrieve his plaything, Broken got to his feet and tried to run across the wet floor. He skidded and bumped into a chair that blocked his path. His mouth struck the chair and blood gushed from his cut lip. Lacey leaped up, screamed, grabbed Broken, carried him to the sink, and splashed cold water on his rapidly swelling lip. She worked with him frantically until his yelps quieted and the bleeding stopped, then she lifted the mop bucket, tipped the mop water into the sink, and threw the empty bucket across the room.

"SEE THERE, MISS-HIGH-AND-MIGHTY," she screamed. "See what you've done to Broken with your high-falutin' ways. I've told you time and again that no good comes of using too much water. Broken might have broken his little neck, all because you're getting too damn big for your britches. You'd better settle down, young lady, and get rid of those snotty ideas you've been dragging home. It'll be a cold day in hell the next time I let you nag me into doing things your way. There ain't a thing wrong with good healthy dirt. Too much water ain't good for anything, whether it's in a mop bucket or a bathtub. If you don't believe me, just look at Black. He only takes a bath when I run him down and throw him in the tub and he's as healthy as a horse. Kids are like carrots—they grow better in dirt than in water."

"Then we ought to grow like weeds around this stinking dump." Valentine turned to leave, thinking she had had the last word, but she didn't get out the door quickly enough. Lacey grabbed Valentine's arm, jerked her back into the kitchen, and plopped her down on the chair Broken had fallen against.

"You sit right there and listen to me, young lady. And don't you move your butt till I tell you to. I've got an earful for you and I should have given it to you sooner. But better late than never, so just shut up and listen. You've had your nose so far up in the air since you went to work for the High-Muckety-Mucks that you can't see straight. I gave you credit for having more sense than that. Just because a place or a person *looks* right doesn't mean it *is* right. It ain't what you see on the outside that counts, it's what you *know* on the inside. You've got yourself all mixed up this summer about what's important, and you'd better get yourself unmixed. Remember, young lady, there's as much dirt hidden beneath some of those High-Muckety-Mucks as there is showing on me or Big or Black or the kitchen floor. So the next time you make signs, make a couple for yourself. Print great big letters that say All That Glitters Is Not Gold and You Can't Tell a Book by Its Cover and hang them those words around your memory and take them out and read them while you're over there on the job. And remember, young lady, those High-Muckety-Mucks are worse off than me and Big. They came *down* in the world, and at least me and Big are holding our own. We ain't no worse nor no better off than we ever were, so maybe, just maybe, that puts us out ahead of the High-Muckety-Mucks. Now get your tail off that chair and scram out of here and don't let me hear one more word from you tonight."

Valentine scrammed.

12

Although Kathy had not expected Flint until mid-September, he returned in mid-August.

"Flint really beat up on Kathy today," Valentine reported to me one evening. "I wanted to go to the Clover Farm store and call the cops, but Mr. Grey wouldn't let me. He said it wouldn't do any good, that all the cops would do is put Flint in jail for a few days and then when Flint got out he'd take it out on Kathy. And Mr. Grey said that if Flint was in jail he couldn't deliver the produce to the markets on time and that could cost Flint his job. So we went inside and Mr. Grey played the piano and tried to drown out the sounds from next door. He hit the keys so hard I thought he'd break them. He didn't quit playing until Mrs. Pain-in-the-Ass came home. Flint was still carrying on. He was as drunk as a skunk."

"What did Mrs. Grey say?"

"Not much. Just that Flint is shanty Irish and has a brain like a flea so he has to roar like a lion. And she said something really dumb. She said that Kathy must not mind too much being slapped around or she wouldn't stay and take it. She said some women don't mind having a man get rough with them."

"Maybe she's right. Mae Clarke loved Jimmy Cagney even after he hit her in the face with a grapefruit."

Valentine reflected and partially agreed. "Maybe *some* women *don't* mind. In fact, I saw Big hit Lacey once."

"Big hit Lacey!"

"Yep. Popped her a good one because she voted for Hoover. A guy came through the neighborhood offering a box of chocolates to anyone who'd promise to vote for Hoover, and Lacey took him up on the deal. Boy, was Big mad! He said after the way the U.S. government shit on him and rubbed it in when he was on the Bonus March, he didn't want Lacey or anyone connected with him to ever again have anything to do with Uncle Sam. But a couple of minutes after he popped her, after she finished crying, they started feeling each other up just like nothing had happened!"

We visited Kathy the next morning as soon as Flint left. The oppressive heat made the sweater Kathy wore securely buttoned from waist to throat an obvious camouflage. As usual, Valentine wasted no time on polite preliminaries.

"Take off that sweater, Kathy."

Kathy studied her coffee, stirred it, pretended not to hear. Valentine persisted. "Take it off, Kathy."

"I'm chilly." Kathy wasn't a good liar. She blushed as she spoke.

"Yeh," Valentine mocked. "You're so chilly you're sweating. You can't fool me, Kathy. I know why you're wearing that sweater. Flint's been knocking you around again, hasn't he?"

133

Kathy's lips trembled and tears joined the sweat running down her cheeks. She crossed her arms and lowered her face to them. Her shoulders shook as she sobbed. Valentine and I sat and stared at each other until Kathy quit crying and looked up at us, then Valentine spoke again. "Now take off that silly sweater. It's really dumb of you, Kathy, to think you can fool me. Come on. Unbutton that sweater and let's see what the big gorilla did this time."

Kathy slowly unbuttoned the sweater and slipped it off. The small cotton halter she wore did little to hide the bruises on her back and shoulders. Her thin arms were black and blue and swollen. Valentine went to the sink and wet the dishtowel in cold water and pressed it against Kathy's back and arms.

Within minutes the tears and the sweat were gone from Kathy's face and she was ready to bounce back to happiness. "Flint's gone now and he won't be back for a couple of months. He's on his way to Iowa and the corn fields. The bruises won't last and neither will this beautiful summer morning. Let's go outside in the sunshine."

13

August turned into September, and summertime turned into schooltime. Autumn in the valley was spectacular that year; its brilliant colors brought out the poet in Valentine. She spent her spare moments composing a tribute to the new season, writing that the first frost had sneaked into the valley one night like a ghost army, leaving crimson, gold, and orange hostages, and taking captive the green of summer. I marveled that such beautiful words could come from someone my own age and from someone whose vocabulary ordinarily included more foul words than fair. Valentine's frequent criticisms of Lacey's words, deeds, and appearance had not inspired Valentine herself to turn over any new leaves. Her fingernails were still as dirty as her words, a fact that my mother often pointed out to me but that did not in the slightest affect my fondness for my Best Friend. I thought often of how dull my life had been before I met Valentine.

Her autumnal excitement was contagious. I shed my reserve and joined her in kicking the fallen leaves, scattering them, as Valentine wrote in another poem, into a fiery crazy quilt to cover the cooling earth.

Although I was busy that school year, Valentine was busier. She continued to work after school each afternoon and all day Saturdays. Weekdays, Tommy attended a day nursery run by the county for the benefit of working mothers. Mrs. Grey didn't like to leave him there until evening, so she arranged for him to go home in midafternoon. Valentine went directly to Sycamore Lane after school, carrying her schoolbooks with her. She did her homework while Tommy colored.

Our personal lives were in transition that autumn. Things were changing every day. Entering the seventh grade involved more than leaving the elementary school and moving into junior high school. It also meant more homework and less understanding from the teachers. Valentine was in only one of my classes, English Literature. I tried to persuade our teacher to read one of Valentine's poems to the class, but the teacher was dedicated to acquainting us with better-known poets. She had no interest in the poet sitting right in front of her.

True to his word, Flint did not return until mid-October. He stayed for only one night, and for once he didn't get drunk and beat Kathy. He slept, then left at daybreak the next morning.

"He's on his way to California," Kathy said. "He has a contract with a logging camp for the winter. He's headed West and won't be back for a long time."

For days we whistled "California, Here I Come."

As the afternoons grew chilly, Kathy huddled her thin shoulders beneath a moth-chewed chinchilla jacket that had been handed down to her from heaven-knew-where. Mr. Grey wore a shaggy coat sweater that was cut along good lines but had obviously seen many autumns. One day in early October, Mrs. Grey brought a new sweater home to him, and the old one was sent to the Salvation Army.

For weeks after my mother had stored away my ankle sox and laid out my long underwear, Kathy and Mr. Grey continued to meet in the yard, seemingly oblivious to the cooling temperatures. I wondered what they would do when the weather became really cold and the snow fell.

Kathy and the trees waged a daily battle that autumn which Kathy enjoyed losing. She loved to spend her days in the bright October sunshine, raking leaves into piles and burning them. Each afternoon the teasing leaf smoke signaled to us as we skipped up the road that Kathy had again spent the day raking while Mr. Grey watched. It was a mystery how she managed to gather the leaves, since her only tool was a rake that had been abandoned by previous tenants.

"The rake was toothless with age and ugly with rust, but she used it like a magic wand, to gather beauty, burn it, and return it to the earth," Valentine wrote in another poem.

We were intoxicated by the sparkling October, and like anyone who has drunk too much, we were boisterous, giddy, foolish. The brisk autumn air vibrated with Kathy's off-key whistle. She liked to whistle "You Are My Lucky Star" and the tune whisped skyward as she looked at Mr. Grey and pursed her lips. If I close my eyes and empty my mind of all else, to this day I can still see and hear us in that autumn of our glorious content—the last autumn we would ever know of untainted love and unsullied innocence.

Occasionally Mr. Grey worried that Kathy worked too hard in the yard. One chilly afternoon he cautioned, "You'll wear yourself out, Kathy. That rake is as big as you are. Put it down. Come sit beside me and rest for a while."

Kathy instantly dropped the rake, let it lay where it fell, and sat by his side.

That day was unusually full and crisp and golden. Its beauty seduced me into losing track of time. I was still on Sycamore Lane when Mrs. Grey arrived. Valentine and I were in the kitchen, preparing supper and studying for an Ohio History test when the sun went rapidly down and the shadows cooled. I'd have to rush to get home before my mother.

As I gathered my books and papers, Mrs. Grey's car turned into the yard. I saw her climb out and I watched her walk slowly toward the house. Her head was lowered, her shoulders bent. She looks worn out, I thought to myself. She looks lots more tired than Kathy did when Mr. Grey asked Kathy to put down the rake and rest. Would Mr. Grey notice how weary his wife looked? Would he ask her to rest for a moment before she changed into her housedress and slippers and helped Valentine with supper? Mrs. Grey came inside and sank down into the nearest chair and closed her eyes. Mr. Grey continued reading the newspaper; he didn't look at her.

Impulsively, I asked, "Would you like for me to make a cup of tea for you?" She opened her eyes and looked up at me and for just a moment I thought I saw her lip tremble, but I told myself it couldn't be—marble doesn't tremble.

"Thank you," she said. "I would like that very much."

After I fixed the tea, I went home. For some reason I couldn't explain even to myself, I wanted to cry.

I did not do well on the Ohio History test. In fact, all my grades slipped on the first report card of the new school year, and my mother instantly decided that I was spending too much time with Valentine and not enough time with my studies. She was right. No book could compete with Valentine.

"Until you bring your grades up, you're to come directly home after school and do your homework," my mother ordered. "You spend too much time on Sycamore Lane. You shouldn't go there so much. Valentine's getting paid for working, not for visiting with you. What's more, you're getting altogether too friendly with that bunch next door. If you aren't careful you'll end up just like them. Birds of a feather flock together, you know."

Pouting and making sad and frequent references to my previous friendships didn't move my mother. When it became clear that she would not rescind my sentence, I seriously applied myself to bringing my grades up so that my next report card would give me back my freedom.

Mine was not the only routine that changed. With the coming of cooler weather, Crazy Gurney and his mother added a second trip each day to their journeys to town. During the summer they passed the house only once a day, always a few minutes after noon. Their routine was so predictable we could have set the town clock by them. But according to Mr. Grey, when the days got cool their pattern changed. They passed the house at noon and again in the early evening. We were casually curious about the added trip.

The minor mystery was solved when Lacey dispatched Valentine to the Hippodrome to carry a sandwich to Big.

"Big has to work at Bank Night this evening. I didn't have a thing in the house to make him a sandwich, so this afternoon Broken and I went over to the Clover Farm store and talked the clerk into letting me have half a pound of baloney on the cuff. I want you to take a sandwich down to Big right now, Valentine, and don't let any grass grow under your feet. It's nearly seven o'clock and Big's stomach must think his throat's been cut."

"Oh, crap," Valentine snapped. "I just got in the house. Why can't Black run it down to him? I've already done a day's work and all Black's done is play hookey and chase that cat."

139

"You know darned well I can't trust Black to take a sandwich anywhere." Lacey thrust the brown paper bag out to Valentine. "He'd eat it the minute he got out of sight. So quit complaining and get your butt down there. If Big don't eat right he can't work right and if he don't work right he gets fired and if he gets fired you can say good-bye to getting into the movies free."

Valentine thumbed her nose at Lacey's back, but she grabbed the bag and ran. She had a strange story to tell me when she returned an hour later. On her way home from the theater, she took a shortcut through the alley behind the Red Lantern Café. As she rounded the corner into the alley, she collided with Crazy Gurney. He was taking food out of a garbage can and dropping it into a gunnysack. His mother was with him, and she too was fishing scraps of food from a can and dropping them into the gunnysack she carried.

"That's why they go to town twice a day. During the summer they had a small vegetable garden, but the frost killed it, so now they go get their supper. When they had the garden, they only had to go in for lunch."

"Ugh. I'd rather die than eat food that's been in a garbage can. Wouldn't you, Valentine?"

"I sure would. I sure would."

14

Progress marched up Sycamore Lane late in October when the PWA invaded the quiet country road, intent upon providing constructive work for the unemployed. Overnight our sanctuary became a beehive of daytime activity. Valentine was furious when we rounded the corner early one Saturday and saw several pieces of road equipment blocking our path, ready to attack the dusty lane early Monday morning. Her anger puzzled me.

"What are you so mad about? My father says it's a good idea to give men who are out of work a job with the PWA. He says it's a lot better than paying them for sitting around doing nothing."

Valentine stamped her foot. "I don't give a hoot what your father says." She gave me that look which, although I was a head taller than she, always dwarfed me. "I don't want a bunch of nosey strangers poking around here. Anyway, it's a dumb thing to do. The road doesn't go anywhere. Just up to Crazy Gurney's house. Why pave it?"

Mr. Grey explained the destiny of Sycamore Lane.

"The state plans to extend it over to join the highway west of town when they can afford to. Meanwhile we'll just have to put up with the confusion. It can't last forever. This road is too short for even the PWA to waste much time on it. It will soon be paved and we'll have it to ourselves again."

"Not soon enough to suit me," Valentine growled.

Kathy didn't like the construction any more than Valentine did. A lovely few days of Indian summer briefly opened Kathy's windows and the dust raised by the road crew drifted into her dollhouse. The only person on the road who enjoyed the intrusion was Crazy Gurney. The equipment fascinated him. He never passed the graders or the rollers without pausing to run his hands against them. One Saturday we saw him climb into the seat of a deserted grader and pretend to drive it. His mother stood patiently nearby and watched him play with his huge toys.

Indian summer didn't linger; it departed as quickly as it had arrived. The threat of an early and hard winter was in the air. Dusk usually covered Marietta before Valentine completed her chores and started home. One Friday evening, with a weekend ahead in which I could do my homework, my mother relented and gave permission for me to join Valentine on her walk home. It was still daylight when I left the flat, but when the sun went down it departed with a rush, and by the time I got to Sycamore Lane and waited for Valentine to clear up the kitchen, semidarkness had fallen.

An eerie half-light made it difficult to find a path through the heavy road equipment, which had been parked haphazardly and left unlighted for the weekend, the lane having been barricaded to traffic until the paving was completed. The gully on the east and the field of high damp weeds on the west forced us to weave in and out among the equipment. We enjoyed making our way through the obstacle course in the daylight, but in the dark, with fog sneaking in from the rivers and the few sycamore leaves that still clung to the trees whispering in the rising wind, the road was mysterious and threatening. We darted swiftly in and out among the rollers and graders, staying close to each other, moving as rapidly as we dared. We were within a few feet of the barricade at the beginning of the road when I knew we were not alone.

"Look!" I grabbed Valentine's arm and pointed toward a hunched figure crouched beside the grader. "Somebody's in the shadows over there."

Valentine, quick to draw on Black's wisdom when she needed it, said, "It's Crazy Gurney. Don't let him know you're scared. Black says don't ever run from something you're scared of because if you do, it'll chase you and get you for sure. We have to scare Crazy more than he scares us."

Her voice quavered but her shout was loud and clear. "I see you hiding there, Crazy Gurney. You'd better get home this minute or I'll go get your mother and she'll send you back to the nuthouse."

Crazy moved out of the shadows. He carried a gunnysack. He reached into it and took out a half-eaten apple and held it out to Valentine.

"Pretty, pretty, pretty," he said.

Valentine jerked the gunnysack from his hand and dumped its contents on the road. Crazy grunted and dropped to his knees and began to pick up the garbage, frantically stuffing it back into the bag. Valentine and I turned and ran and didn't stop running until we saw the streetlight on our corner.

We sat on the steps to catch our breath before we went in, and I warned Valentine, "That was a close call. If you

143

hadn't spilled the garbage out on the street, there's no telling what Crazy might have done. I think he's stuck on you. What if he decides to do to you what he did to that girl a long time ago? You've got to go in there right now and tell Big what happened tonight and let him handle it."

"Are you nuts?" she snapped. "You know darned well that they've just been looking for an excuse to make me quit my job. They'd jump at the chance to make me leave because of Crazy Gurney. I'm not going to say one word to Big and Lacey about what happened tonight, and if you do I'll never speak to you again."

Valentine was right about Big and Lacey looking for a good reason to make her quit her job. I had recently listened to Big and Lacey while they discussed Valentine's comment that Mr. Grey reminded her of Jesus without a beard.

Big snorted at the comparison. "It's time we straightened that kid out about a few things, Lacey. It's time to tell her that that guy sure as hell doesn't come close to being Jesus, with or without a beard. It's time to give her an earful about Grey."

My ears perked up; I had an eerie feeling that Big was about to put into words some half-formed thoughts that had been playing tag in my mind for some time. I sat very still on the kitchen stool and listened for an enlightenment that didn't come. Lacey disagreed with Big.

"Nah, Big. The best thing to do now is to keep our mouths shut when she starts laying on the lard about Grey. She says a lot of those things just to get our goat. It's a stage she's going through. I read about it in a magazine. Kids get to a certain age and the best fun they have is giving their parents a rough time. It's sort of like having baby teeth and adenoids. You wait long enough and it takes care of itself. She'll outgrow it."

"No," Big said. "It's more than just trying to get our goat, Lacey. I think she has a crush on the guy."

144

Lacey yawned. "So what? Kids her age always have a crush on someone. It's normal. A couple of months ago she was hung up on Richard Arlen. Next year it might be Clark Gable. Right now it's Grey. Anyway, who ever heard of anybody getting in trouble with Jesus, beard or no beard? Miss High-and-Mighty is just going through a case of puppy love. She'll get over it. It's a good thing she has it on Grey and not on some guy who could take advantage of her. After all, what harm can Grey do from a wheelchair?"

I had trouble concentrating on my homework the next evening. Fog was seeping in from the rivers, and the moan of the foghorn told me, as I waited for Valentine to come home, that she would not have an easy time finding her way through the mist. There were no street lights on Sycamore Lane to outline the heavy road equipment and pinpoint a danger lurking in the shadows.

I couldn't settle down. I wandered aimlessly around the living room, opening the curtains every few minutes to peer out at the night. I finally summoned enough courage to ask my mother if I could walk toward Sycamore Lane to meet Valentine halfway.

My mother looked out the window at the foggy night and gave a prompt, firm, and negative reply. "Absolutely not. This is no night to be out."

Her emphatic refusal relieved my conscience, but not my anxiety. I stared out the window at the streetlight on the corner. It was a fuzzy yellow haze, but when Valentine flitted out of the haze, I recognized her panic, even in the half-light. I ran downstairs to open the door. Valentine quickly jumped inside and slid the lock into place before she sobbed her story to me.

By the time she had gone to Sycamore Lane that afternoon, after spending a routine day at school, surrounded by the normalcy of classes and football fever—Valentine was trying out for cheerleader—Crazy's appearance on the road the night before seemed much less threatening. She mentioned the escapade to Mr. Grey, who applauded her quick thinking in dumping the gunnysack and agreed with Valentine that although the episode had been unpleasant, it was really no more important than the exchange between Crazy and Valentine during the summer.

"I truly don't think he meant any harm," Mr. Grey said. "The interesting thing to me is that his mother wasn't with him. The next time I see the two of them together, I'll speak to her about his being out without her. The best thing to do now is to put it out of your head. Be aware, but don't be frightened. The road equipment will be moved soon, and Crazy will probably lose interest in being out on the road."

His words comforted Valentine. She wasn't really frightened that night when she left to go home, even though the short dusk had ended and night had begun. She heard the foghorn on the Ohio River, warning that the night wasn't safe for travelers. She could see less than a foot in front of her as she made her way down the lane, using the deserted equipment as markers to keep from sliding into the gully.

Just in case Crazy should be in the shadows, she whistled as she moved along, hoping that the sound of bravado would impress him. When she neared the end of the lane and approached the barricade, she relaxed, thinking that Mr. Grey had been right; Crazy Gurney was not really a danger.

A streetlight, dimmed by the fog but still comforting, cast a thin light several feet beyond the barricade. Nearing its safety, Valentine stopped whistling, used her breath to run, zigzagging from one side of the road to the other. She had almost reached the barricade when Crazy jumped out of the shadows. His rough hand covered her mouth. His attack was so swift that she had no time to shout or fight back. Nor could she any longer talk herself into thinking that Crazy was harmless. She twisted and struggled and tried to scream, but he was too strong for her. Paralyzed by terror, she sank to the ground. She felt him pull at her underwear, and something hard and wet moved over her bare belly and down her thighs, seeking a way into her.

"I was afraid he was going to kill me if I fought back," she sobbed. "I just lay there and thought, let him do it and get it over with, just so he doesn't kill me."

I looked down at Valentine's skirt to see if there was blood on it; from things Valentine had explained to me about the kind of cherries that don't grow on trees, I feared there might be. Valentine saw me look at the skirt, and she knew what I was wanting to ask.

"No. He didn't get it in me. He tried to, and it was awful. Just awful. He slobbered on me while he tried to shove his thing in me. He almost did it, but Gretchen saved me. She was in the yard when I left, and she heard the commotion and began to bark. It scared Crazy. He loosened his hold on me and I drew up my knee and kicked him in the balls and rolled out from under him and ran."

"That settles it," I said. "You've got to tell someone. If you don't, I will. This can't go on. The next time Crazy catches you, you might not be so lucky. He might kill you. And if he doesn't kill you, he might put a baby inside you. Think of how terrible it would be to have Crazy Gurney's baby. You have to tell somebody."

"Okay. Come with me tomorrow after school and keep Tommy busy while I tell Mr. Grey. He'll think of something."

"You ought to tell Big. Let him handle Crazy Gurney. What can Mr. Grey do from a wheelchair?"

Valentine frowned; she was done with crying, she was ready to fight. "He can do a lot. And if you say one word about this to Big or Lacey, don't ever speak to me again. I mean it. So shut up and help me get in shape to go upstairs."

I tiptoed up to my bathroom and wet a washcloth and took it down to Valentine. She held it against her swollen eyes and slowly counted to fifty. I checked her clothes for any giveaway signs of a struggle. Her skirt was rumpled, and there was a small rip in it that hadn't been there when she left for school, but otherwise she looked no more unkempt than usual.

We went upstairs and quickly brushed past Big and Lacey, muttering a hello that wasn't returned. Their eyes and ears were pointed faithfully toward the blaring radio. We went to the bathroom and Valentine filled the tub, disregarding Lacey's perpetual high-water mark. As Valentine soaked in the water, we both stared at her body, seeing it with a new awareness carved by Crazy's hands.

"I'll never feel clean again," she said. "All the water in the world won't wash away that awful feeling of Crazy's thing against my body."

Always the practical one, I thought I offered good advice, "Then if the water isn't doing any good, you'd better hurry up and get out of that tub before Lacey comes in and sees how much of it you used."

For once, Valentine took my advice.

I went with her to Sycamore Lane the next day. Armed with a paper bag, scissors, paste, and an old Montgomery Ward catalog, I sat at the kitchen table and watched through the closed window while Valentine and Mr. Grey talked in the yard. Kathy had just gone home. I couldn't *hear* Valentine's words, but I could *guess* them as I watched Mr. Grey's fury build. I wasn't surprised when Valentine came in and whispered to me to keep Tommy busy in the kitchen.

"Mr. Grey wants me to push him up the hill."

I replenished Tommy's supply of crayons and paper and turned to the toy section of the catalog and put him to work with the promise that when he had cut out every one of the toys and pasted them on the paper bag, I would give him a big piece of chocolate cake. Then I hurried into the living room, opened the door, stepped out to the front porch, and watched uneasily as Valentine pushed Mr. Grey uphill. The road workers had gone for the day and the lane was quiet.

Mr. Grey set the brake on his wheelchair. I heard his shout toward the silent house, "You in there—come out here. I have something to tell you."

A nervous spume of smoke signaled from the crooked chimney that someone was inside, hidden behind rotting shutters. Mr. Grey shouted again, louder.

"I know you're in there. It won't do you any good to hide. I'm going to sit right here until you come out and hear what I have to say."

The front door creaked as the old woman shuffled out to the edge of the porch.

"What do you want?" Her voice was ancient and cracked and ugly, but she didn't sound angry.

"I want to tell you what your son has been doing."

She turned hard and defensive, like Lacey did whenever anyone dared criticize Broken.

"What about my boy?"

"He's been bothering this girl. Hiding in the shadows and jumping out at her. Last night he attacked her, tried to hurt her bad. You've got to put a stop to it. Make him leave her alone."

He gestured toward Valentine. The old woman's eyes, following his hand, grew hostile.

"Oh, that one," she sneered. "That little brat. I warned her to stay away from up here the first day she came snooping around. I told her to mind her own business, but no, she wouldn't listen to what I said. She had to come up here and tease my boy and get him all riled up."

"Don't be ridiculous. Valentine walked up here just one time. Your son has been down bothering her several times. He's the one who's making trouble, not Valentine. Ask him yourself. Call him out here right now and ask him to tell you what he tried to do to this girl last night. Call him out here. Face him with it."

"No need for that," the old woman growled. "I can handle this myself."

"Then you'd better handle it, and handle it quick, because if you don't, the police will. Your son should be sent back to Athens. Locked up and kept locked up. You know that as well as I do. He shouldn't have been turned loose after he attacked that other girl. He's dangerous, and you know it. You've known it for a long time. That's why you try to follow him around. But now you can't keep up with him anymore. He's too much for you to handle. You should turn him over to people who can."

The old woman drew herself into a long skinny pencil pointed at Mr. Grey. "If you know what's good for you you'll keep your nose out of my business. You take care of your house and let me take care of mine. Leave me and my boy alone. Get back downhill where you belong and don't come up here again."

Mr. Grey settled back in his chair and rested his hand on its brake.

"I'll get back downhill after you tell me exactly what you plan to do to make sure your son doesn't bother this girl again."

"I've got a chain, I'll chain him up if need be."

"She can't chain him if he doesn't want her to," Valentine spoke to Mr. Grey. "He's got arms like a gorilla. He's too much for her to handle. I know what I'm talking about. He nearly broke my back last night. She can't do a darned thing to him if he doesn't want her to. And Crazy sure isn't crazy enough to let her chain him up like a dog."

The old woman glared at Valentine. "Don't call my son crazy. Quit saying what I can and can't do. You've already caused enough trouble, flitting your tail around, making up to a poor boy who don't know what's what. You're a snotty little troublemaker, that's what you are."

Mr. Grey lowered his hand to the brake, preparing to release it and leave.

"I'm wasting my time trying to talk sense to you," he said. "You won't listen to the truth because you don't want to believe it. Valentine doesn't bother that poor fool of yours. He bothers her. She's right when she says you can't handle him. I'm going to report his attack to the police, as much for your good as for his. He's too much for you. Let the court send him away where he'll get proper care, and get some peace for yourself. He shouldn't have been turned loose in the first place. He should have been locked up and kept locked up, and this time he will be. I'll see to that." He released the brake and motioned to Valentine that he was ready to go back downhill. The old woman swiftly moved from the porch and blocked the path, placed herself in front of the wheelchair, and shook her fist.

"You try that. You just try that, and see who it hurts the most. Tell the police about my poor boy, and I'll tell them about your poor wife. I'll tell them and your wife too what got my boy stirred up in the first place. You ain't the only one that's got something to tell about what goes on around here. You ain't the only one."

"What are you talking about?"

"Don't play innocent with me." The old woman put her face closer to his, but she didn't lower her voice. "You know what I'm talking about. I'm talking about what you do with that little tramp next door. That's what's got my poor boy stirred up, makes him feel things he don't understand. He might not be real smart, but he ain't blind. He's watched you and that slut. He's seen what you do with her when you think nobody's watching. You ought to be ashamed of yourself, pawing that slut while your wife is out working, making money to keep you. You and those hussies you've messed around with all summer is what's got my boy all riled up, gave him wrong ideas, and I hate all of you for what you've done to him."

She spat; her spittle glistened on Mr. Grey's face, dripped onto his new sweater. "I hate you, do you understand?" she hissed. "My boy was doing all right, not bothering anyone, until he saw you with your bitches. That dog ain't the only bitch you've got. You and your bitches gave my boy ideas he never had before. And you ain't going to take my son away from me. He's all I have. I didn't spend my life taking care of him just to have him jerked away from me in my old age when I need him. There ain't nobody going to lock my boy up again. And you ain't going to say one word about my boy to anyone, because if you do, I'm going to give your wife an earful about what goes on while she's out working to support you. Your wife's a good woman, she is. Too good for the likes of you. Always has been. There's many a day I've had a good notion to go down there and tell your wife that you're up to your old tricks, but I kept my nose in my own business. I held my tongue, but I won't hold it any longer. If you tell the cops anything about my boy, I'll tell your wife about your whore. That Flint woman is as married as you are. She's two-timing her husband while he's out making money for her. She's a whore and you're a whoremaster."

Mr. Grey's reply was sharp, furious. "You hunk of garbage. Don't you ever say another word about Mrs. Flint. You aren't fit to speak her name."

The old woman's ugly cackle profaned the clear autumn air. "Oh, so now you call her Mrs. Flint, eh? That ain't what you call her when you think nobody's listening. And now you're worrying about her instead of the brat, eh? Or are you worried about both of them? Is that it? You don't want my poor boy to mess around with your bitches. I've seen what goes on in your yard, and I've got a good idea what goes on in your house when you and that brat are shut in there alone. You've got a young whore on the inside and an older one on the outside. Is that what's got you so fired up? You afraid my son will do the same thing to that brat that you've been doing? Are you playing dog in the manger with your two bitches?"

She spat again on Mr. Grey. "Now get out of here. If I hear another word from you, your wife will hear from me."

Her filthy garments swished as she turned and went into her house. Mr. Grey released the brake. With Valentine holding the back of the wheelchair to slow its downhill momentum, they came back to the house. It was dangerously close to the time for my mother to quit work. I had no time to wait and see what the next step would be in keeping Valentine safe on Sycamore Lane. I gave Tommy his piece of cake and ran through the darkening streets. When my mother arrived I was at my desk, studiously involved with my math homework. She was so impressed she didn't say a word when I joined Valentine as soon as I heard her footsteps on the stairs.

"What's going to happen now, Valentine?"

"Everything's taken care of. It's all going to be okay. Mr. Grey handled it just right. I knew he would."

"Oh? From what I heard, I thought Crazy's mother had the last word."

Valentine shrugged. "That stuff you heard didn't amount to a hill of beans. Mr. Grey has fixed things so I won't be on the road after dark from now on. He sweet-talked Mrs. Pain-in-the-Ass into letting me leave just as soon as she gets home. I bet if he wasn't stuck in a wheelchair he'd be in Hollywood. He did the best job of acting I've ever seen, even in the movies. When Mrs. Pain-in-the-Ass got home he spoke to her real nice. She looked like she couldn't believe her ears. He asked her what kind of a day she'd had. He told her she looked tired. Then he asked her if she'd mind sitting down and talking with him for a few minutes before she started supper. He said he was lonesome. Said he missed her. He gave her a song and dance about wishing they could have more time to be alone together, and he said he thought maybe it would be a good idea to let me leave the minute she got home from now on so they'd have more time alone with each other. He gave her a song and dance about wishing they could be like they used to be, and she fell for it hook, line, and sinker. I was listening from the kitchen and I had all I could do to keep from laughing out loud. She didn't start supper, and she didn't call for Tommy like she usually does. She went right over and sat with Mr. Grey."

"That reminds me of the day he talked Kathy into putting down her rake and sitting beside him."

"Don't be dumb. There's a big difference. He loves Kathy and he wants to take care of her. He can't stand Mrs. Pain-in-the-Ass. He was lying to her for my sake, to get me off the road before it gets real dark. He really put on a great act. He was as good as Leslie Howard. When I left he was playing the piano. He played 'Try a Little Tenderness,' and he told her the words made him think of her and of how hard she works and how much she has had to do without since his accident. When she called me in to tell me I could leave early, she had tears in her eyes. Isn't that a kick?"

So Valentine's job did not end that autumn. She was always safely off the road before dark. By mid-November the paving was completed and the heavy equipment was gone. Sycamore Lane lay clear and wide and unsecretive, with no dark shadows to hide Crazy. Snow whitewashed the trees and bushes and made the road as light and fearless by night as by day. Icy moonlit evenings and the clean cold smell of winter purified our memories, and soon Crazy's attack was no more real to us than the vague remembrance of any other transient nightmare.

15

On Thanksgiving evening, Valentine and I sat together at her kitchen table, which looked more festive than usual with a dish of bright red apples Lacey had splurged on for a holiday treat. There was one apple apiece, and with rare restraint, not one apple had as yet been eaten, not even by Black. They were admired in their place of honor in the middle of the cluttered table and hoarded for a bedtime snack.

Valentine was engrossed in making a Christmas list, a fantasy that most of us observed during the Depression, being aware in advance of its futility. Valentine had put aside a few cents each payday for the past several months in anticipation of turning her Christmas fantasies into reality.

As she wrote, she kept her hand over her paper so that Lacey, who sat opposite us as she leafed through her wish-book—Lacey's name for the Montgomery Ward catalog—couldn't read the items or names on Valentine's list. I watched from my vantage point at Valentine's elbow as she wrote "slingshot" beside Black's name, and then, in deference to the neighborhood cat, scratched out "slingshot" and substituted "dominoes."

Lacey spoke. "That's the tenth list you've made. You sure are having a hard time making up your mind. That money you saved must be burning a hole right through your pocket."

"Yeh." Valentine's reply was automatic. She wasn't really listening. The next name was Kathy's, and it merited Valentine's full attention.

"Lacey, look in the wish-book and see if you can find a pretty vanity case that I can afford."

Lacey spit on her finger, flipped to the index, and rapidly scanned the *v*'s. "I don't see any mentioned here. Maybe vanity cases are too small to be listed. Who are you planning to give one to?"

Valentine ignored Lacey's question. Lacey didn't know Kathy existed and Valentine intended to keep it that way.

Lacey tried again. "Who are you getting it for?"

Valentine avoided a straight answer. "I might not get one at all. I just wondered how much they cost."

Lacey looked coy. "Well now, if someone was planning to get *me* a vanity case, I sure hope it would be a round one with a pink powder puff. I like a round mirror. I have a round face, and a round mirror sort of frames it. By the way," she tried to sound nonchalant as she tossed a hint toward Valentine, "I saw a real beaut at the dime store yesterday. It sure did catch my eye. Funny you should mention a vanity case today when I saw that real pretty one just yesterday. It's probably still there on the cosmetic counter right inside the door. You can't miss it. It's got a cute little Cupid on its top."

Observing that Valentine wasn't listening, Lacey went

156

through the directions again. "I said, Valentine, that the vanity case I saw, the round one with a pink powder puff and a cute fat Cupid, is right inside the door at the dime store. At the cosmetic counter. I think it cost a quarter."

Big, overhearing the conversation, chimed in to reinforce Lacey's pointed message. "What do you want for Christmas, Lacey?"

Lacey was quick to repeat, "I'd love to have that round vanity case I saw at the dime store yesterday. It's right inside the door, on the cosmetic counter. It costs a quarter and it has a pink powder puff inside and a fat Cupid on the outside."

"Maybe Santa Claus will bring it to you." Big became as coy as Lacey as he glanced toward Valentine.

"Yeh. I bet the old boy's listening to every word I'm saying, right this minute." Lacey sounded smug. I knew from the vague look on Valentine's face that there was as much chance that she was hearing Lacey as there was that Santa Claus was listening.

Valentine scribbled "hankie" beside Big's name, then moved down to the last and most important name on her list.

"Lacey," she directed, "look in the wish-book and see what a man's belt with an initialed buckle costs."

"Yeah, Lacey, do that." Big sounded pleased as he jerked at the cracked belt that supported his trousers. "Those belts with initial buckles really look swell. The manager at the Hippodrome wears one and he's a snazzy dresser."

Valentine was impressed; she promptly wrote "belt with initial on buckle" opposite Mr. Grey's name.

The first really deep snow of the winter fell later that night. The day following Thanksgiving was a school holiday, and my mother gave me permission to spend it with Valentine. We planned to take Tommy downtown to see the Christmas parade and get a handout from Santa. The store windows in Marietta were traditionally unveiled for

157

the season on the day after Thanksgiving, and Valentine and I were determined to be first in line to see the gifts and decorations. By ruthless use of our elbows we efficiently shoved a path through the crowded sidewalks and hugged the store windows. It was a day filled with the magic of childhood. Rubber dolls wearing painted smiles of perpetual happiness slept in wicker baby buggies. Musical tops sat quietly in the windows, coaxing for someone to buy them and let them whirl and sing. Wooden horses waited for the starter's signal. Ice skates were reminders that soon the Muskingum and Ohio Rivers would turn hard and slick and shiny.

"We'll do our shopping after I take Tommy into Monkey Ward's," Valentine decided. "I promised Mrs. Pain-in-the-Ass I'd stop by with him."

That was the first and only time I ever saw Mrs. Grey away from Sycamore Lane. She looked, sounded, and acted different. When she smiled at a customer, she was pretty, and she looked soft, like Jean Harlow. When the customer turned away without making a purchase, Mrs. Grey spoke pleasantly, invited her to come back some other time. She smiled again as she bent down and flicked a spot of soot from Tommy's pink cheek and kissed him.

"Are you having fun?" she asked.

Tommy hugged her knees and pulled at her skirt. "Come see my sled." He was proud of the homemade sled Valentine had made for him by fastening a thick rope around a big washtub.

"I'd like to, but I can't. I'm the only clerk working the counter right now, and my boss won't want me to leave."

Tommy's lip trembled and she put her finger under his lowered chin and tipped his face up. "Don't cry. Please don't cry. If you cry, I'll cry, and then we might scare away a customer and my boss will really be mad at me." She reached into her skirt pocket and handed a fifty-cent piece

158

to Valentine. "You kids go to the dime store and buy your-selves a hot dog and a cup of hot chocolate."

"That's a lot of money," I said. "Can you spare it?"

"It won't hurt me to miss a couple of lunches," she said.

Valentine scolded me when we were outside. "Why did you ask her if she could afford to give us that half buck? She likes for people to feel sorry for her. I bet she has plenty to eat at lunch. And if she *can't* buy lunch, she can carry a baloney sandwich to work, like Big does."

While we sat on the stools at the lunch counter and munched hot dogs and blew on hot chocolate to cool it, Valentine reviewed her shopping list. By adding the two pennies she had left over from the fifty cents she had just given the girl behind the counter, she had seventeen cents apiece for each person on her list. She didn't need a pencil to figure that if she bought the vanity case for Kathy and the initialed belt for Mr. Grey, she would have very little money left for other gifts. She was frowning at the paper and puzzling over what to do about gifts for her family when a flurry of activity in the aisle behind us caught our attention. The price on the red and white boxes of choc-olate-covered cherries had just been reduced.

"Watch Tommy." Valentine jumped down from her stool and poked her elbows into the shoppers who had quickly surrounded the candy counter. She emerged from the crowd a few moments later, disheveled but triumphant, clutching a cellophane-wrapped box. She lifted Tommy from his stool. "Let's go get that vanity case and the belt."

"Who gets the candy?"

"My family. They can split it four ways. Broken loves chocolates and anything that makes him happy makes Lacey happy. And as long as Lacey is happy, Big is happy."

"What about Black?"

"He can go spit in his ear."

Pleased with her purchases, Valentine whistled Christmas carols as we pulled Tommy through the deepening twilight. The sun had gone down and the air was bitterly cold. As we turned up the path we saw footprints in the snow, leading from the porch to the gully. Winter had finally forced Mr. Grey and Kathy to retreat indoors. Valentine studied the telltale footprints. "I have a swell idea, Tommy. Let's make snow angels."

Tommy joined Valentine on the snowy ground. His small arms met hers and obliterated Kathy's footprints.

16

Big grumbled his way through the early winter of 1936, insisting at least twice a day that it was the worst he could recall. The snow that had begun Thanksgiving evening was refreshed nightly by new snow. Valentine and I loved it; the white blanket turned every street and lane in Marietta, even the shabbiest, into a Christmas card.

Lacey was on Big's side in the daily debate about the weather.

"You're as crazy as a bedbug," she told Valentine one frigid December morning as she watched Valentine scratch heavy frost from the kitchen window to make a peephole to see if another layer of snow had sneaked down overnight.

"Yep. You're as nutty as a fruitcake," Lacey added when Valentine squealed with delight that the snow on the outside was at least an inch deeper than it had been when we went to bed, and that more flakes were drifting down from the heavy sky.

"I don't know why you get such a kick from this lousy weather," Lacey growled. "You don't have any sense at all, Valentine. Your gloves are shot—there's not a whole finger left in either hand. And your boots barely go over your shoes anymore. One good pull and they'll split right up the side. But you run around like a gooney bird with the silly giggles every time it snows again."

"I like the snow." Valentine pressed her nose flat against the window to admire another flake. "Snow is pretty. It hides all the ugly stuff we have to look at the rest of the year. I like it."

"Well, you're the only one." Lacey plopped the coffeepot down on the back burner and glared at Valentine, who was prompt to challenge her.

"No I'm not, Mr. Grey says that snow makes Sycamore Lane look like a Currier and Ives print—whatever that is."

Big, who usually attempted to maintain verbal neutrality in Lacey-Valentine exchanges, snorted when he heard Mr. Grey mentioned. He poured hot weak coffee from a cracked cup into a chipped saucer and blew on it, managing to make his gesture reflect his opinion of Mr. Grey. Valentine shuddered and turned up her nose. When the coffee was cool, Big noisily slurped it, and Valentine stuck her fingers in her ears. Her disdainful motion infuriated Big. He abandoned his neutrality.

"I'd think the snow was swell too if I could sit inside a warm house all day on my dead ass and look out at it. But crap, I ain't that lucky. I walk ten blocks to work and back every day, morning and night, and by the time I get to work and home again my balls are frozen."

Valentine glared. The fingers in her ears hadn't kept her from hearing Big's crude remark. For Big to mention ass, balls, and Mr. Grey all in the same breath was too much for her to overlook. She removed her fingers from her ears and faced Big, elbows at half-angles, stub-nailed hands on her hips.

"That's not fair. It's not Mr. Grey's fault he can't work. He'd give anything to be able to go to work like you do."

"Yeh? Well, if he gives me enough, he can have my job and I'll stay home," Big growled. None of us believed that, not even Big himself.

"Give me your overshoes, Big." Lacey poured her cooled coffee into Big's empty saucer. "This is good drinking temperature. Drink it while I stuff some paper in your boots. Not that it will help much in snow this deep, but it might keep your feet a bit dryer. I can't do a thing about your balls, though. You'll have to handle that problem yourself."

Lacey winked, Black snorted, Valentine glowered, I blushed, and Big laughed and shoved his overshoes across the floor toward Lacey with the tip of his toe.

"Yeh Lacey. Paper will keep my toes from freezing. I'll take care of my feet today, and you can take care of my balls tonight."

Valentine indignantly turned her attention back to the window. Big put on his overshoes and kissed Lacey. "I'll be working outside most of the day. It's Bank Night and I have to shovel the sidewalk. There's always a crowd at Bank Night."

"What's playing?" Lacey asked.

"Something with Shirley Temple in it. It's called *Captain January*, or some fool thing like that. It doesn't make any difference what's playing on Bank Night. Nobody cares. They line up for a block even in this lousy weather, just to get a chance at winning something."

Valentine left the window, willing to make instant peace in exchange for a promise from Big. "I just love Shirley Temple. She's so cute, with those big dimples and little curls. Can you sneak me in, Big?"

Black entered the negotiations. "Don't do it, Big. Val-

163

entine don't deserve to get in free, not as mean as she is. She's just cozying up to you now because she wants to go see that phony midget pretend to be a kid. Valentine sure is dumb if she falls for that baloney. Anyone with half a brain knows old Shirley ain't a kid. She's at least twenty-five and she wears a wig. She gets those curls from a wig."

"You make me sick," Valentine snapped. "You think you're so darned smart. To hear you tell it, everything is fake. I bet you don't even believe Rin Tin Tin is a dog."

For once, Black was happy to agree with Valentine. "You're damned right I think everything is fake. And I mean *everything*. And the sooner you know it, Miss High-and-Mighty, the better off you'll be. You're so ignorant you swallow anything anyone tells you. I bet you think King Kong is a real gorilla."

"No, but I think *you* are," Valentine shouted. "I think you're a stupid-assed gorilla. That's exactly what I think you are."

Ignoring the philosophical disagreement flying around her, Lacey kissed Big, shoved him out the door, and put a magazine and Broken on her lap before she turned her attention toward the debaters.

"You're both a couple of gorillas, and I'm sick and tired of hearing you jaw at each other. Now get your tails out of here. You're going to be late for school."

"Not me," Black said. "I ain't going to be late because I ain't going at all. We'll no sooner get there than they'll send us back home. They just make us come for pure meanness and then send us right back out into the snow again. I ain't going to go. It don't make a damned bit of sense."

"Then go on outside and shovel the walk or build a snowman or chase a cat or do something," Lacey ordered. "Don't hang around here pestering me all day. Broken and me got things to do."

Black departed with suspicious eagerness. "Okay," he

called over his shoulder on the way out the door, "but remember, you sent me out. I was going to stay inside and behave myself, but you sent me out, Lacey. Out into the cold, cold world. If I get in trouble, it's all your fault."

Lacey ignored him. She propped her *True Confessions* magazine against the saucepan on the middle of the table and began to read.

"Here's a good one, Broken. It's called 'I Didn't Know My Husband Until Our Wedding Night.' It sounds real interesting, doesn't it?"

Broken made his usual mewing response, and Valentine assumed the role of literary critic.

"Oh, yeh," she scoffed. "It sounds just swell. Just swell. What a bunch of baloney. Why don't you read something decent for a change?" Valentine knew there was no quicker way to get under Lacey's skin than to ridicule Lacey's magazines.

She looked pleased with herself when Lacey bellowed, "YOU MIND YOUR OWN BUSINESS, YOUNG LADY. You have a fit if Black makes fun of the movies, but you think it's okay for you to make fun of my magazines. You're getting too big for your britches these days. Now get your tail out of here and go to school. You're going to be late, and I ain't going to write you an excuse."

Valentine retrieved her split overshoes from beneath the stove, tied a scarf over her head, and put on the coat that for the past two years had not kept pace with her growth. She stuffed a baloney sandwich in her pocket, picked up her books, and we left. As we walked to school, we stuck out our tongues to catch the snowflakes.

Black was right when he predicted that school would be dismissed early. No sooner had we shaken the snow from our coats, struggled out of our overshoes, and stored our wraps in the cloak room than the notice came over the loudspeaker that school would be closed within the hour. By noon we were back in our wet wraps and out again in

165

the snow, which swirled down with no hint of stopping. I took advantage of the early dismissal to walk to Sycamore Lane with Valentine.

Marietta was emptied of sound; motor traffic had been brought to a snowy halt. When we reached the lane, we again saw footprints leading from the gully to the porch. Inside the house we found Kathy sitting on the floor in the living room with her stockinged feet close to the gas heater. Mr. Grey's hand rested lightly on her head.

"The teacher is taking the class for a sleigh ride," Mr. Grey said. "Tommy won't be home until late this afternoon."

"Good." Valentine stretched out on the floor beside Kathy and put her feet close to the fire. "Now we can talk without him butting in."

Suddenly a clipped voice with an unfamiliar accent spoke clearly over the crackle of static that had been coming unheeded from the radio. "I never wanted to withhold anything . . ."

Kathy's eyes sparkled. She arose and turned the sound up on the radio. "That's the King of England. He's talking about that divorced woman he's been running around with. She's an American. Listen."

When the sad deep voice spoke of not being able to carry his heavy burden of responsibility without the help of the woman he loved, Kathy sighed. "He's giving up a kingdom for the woman he loves."

"Just like in the movies," Valentine said. "It makes me want to cry."

Mr. Grey's smile teased us. He reached for a small pencil sharpener on the table beside him. It was shaped like a globe with a map of the world painted around it.

"Here." He put the sharpener in Kathy's palm and squeezed her fingers around it. "I'm giving you more than a kingdom, Kathy. I'm giving you the world."

Valentine was ecstatic as we walked home. "Wasn't that

166

romantic? Wasn't it beautiful? Wasn't it the loveliest thing you ever heard in your whole life? Mr. Grey put the world in the palm of Kathy's hand."

"Yes. Mr. Grey made the King of England look like a cheapskate."

We became silent as we walked through the thickening dusk, the deepening snow. Our footsteps were going in the same direction, but our thoughts were traveling different routes.

Valentine spoke first. "I'll bet the King of England doesn't love that woman half as much as Mr. Grey loves Kathy. In fact, I bet nobody in the whole world loves anybody else the way Kathy and Mr. Grey love each other. What do you think?"

"I don't know. I wasn't thinking about people being in love. I was thinking about England—trying to remember exactly where it is. I know it's over in Europe somewhere, and I think it's an island. I remember seeing it on a map at school, but for the life of me I just can't recall exactly where it is."

"Good grief," Valentine scoffed. "Why in the heck are you wasting your time thinking about geography when you aren't even in school? Who gives a hoot where England is?"

17

It was my father's idea that we spend the Christmas of 1936 in the country with my aunt. My mother was a traditionalist and wanted to stay home for the holiday, but my father gently persuaded her that it would be less painful to share our first Christmas away from old friends with someone who loved us. Knowing I would be away, Valentine and I exchanged gifts early. She gave me a sample jar of hand cream that she had sent for from one of Lacey's magazines, and I gave her a framed photograph of Leslie Howard.

"You have such pretty hands." Valentine looked wistful as she watched me rub the cream into my hands. "Mine are ugly." I didn't reply; her hands with their ragged nails and callused palms were a mess. She made a New Year's resolution to let her nails grow, but before the first week of the new year was over, she broke the resolution.

My gift delighted her. She hung Leslie Howard in the kitchen beside Lacey's grain and feed calendar, and alternated between looking at Leslie with adoration and Big with disgust.

I bought a gift for Lacey with a quarter my father gave me. I asked my mother for money for Lacey's present, but she snapped, "Absolutely not. We don't have money to waste on a woman like Lacey Hart. Whatever you gave her would get lost in that hovel she lives in."

For one of the few times in my life, I actually disliked my mother.

My father interceded. "Christmas is a time for sharing with people less fortunate." He reached into his pocket and pulled out a quarter and gave it to me. I appreciated his generosity, but I didn't agree with the reasoning behind it. Personally I thought the Harts were fortunate in many ways. They were exuberant, courageous, exciting, and definitely had the determination and the ability to survive all sorts of crises.

I considered buying Lacey the vanity case with the fat Cupid on the cover, knowing very well that Valentine wouldn't, but decided instead to give Lacey a pick for her old guitar. The chords she strummed with the new pick were the most beautiful I'd ever heard, because I was part of them. I had helped Lacey Hart make music, in return for which Lacey Hart hugged me. She cuddled me tightly against her, and I understood precisely why Big loved to put his hands inside her robe. Her tits were warm, huge, loving.

A week before Christmas, Big hiked into the woods and searched out a tall pine tree and carried it home. Lacey propped it in a corner, and Black got a hammer and two nails and a piece of rope and secured the tree against a wall. Right after Thanksgiving, Big prudently began to save popcorn, sweeping it up from the floor of the theater and carrying it back to the flat. Valentine and I spent many frigid December evenings stringing the popcorn on bright red yarn. Black couldn't sit still long enough to help, and Broken's misshapen fingers were too uncoordinated to manage the needle. Black waited until the strings of popcorn were fastened to the tree before he nonchalantly stepped forward and added a store-made ornament—a beautiful shining red glass bell with a small gold clapper. He proudly positioned it on the top of the tree, balancing himself on the strongest chair in the flat, and we all sat back and admired it. Nobody questioned its source. We knew Black would tell the truth if we asked, and a moral judgment would have to be made. We accepted the shining red ornament in the spirit of the season. We hung the gaudy decorations to the rhythm of Lacey's new pick against the strings of her old guitar. When the trimming was complete, the tree looked slightly tipsy, as if it had drunk too much hot buttered rum. It was like Lacey's tits—flamboyant, beautifully promiscuous, haphazardly dressed.

My father had not tramped into the deep woods to find our tree; he had sensibly waited until two days before Christmas to offer the manager at the Clover Farm store a fair price for a small tree. It stood ramrod-straight on the round table in the living room, and it looked very sober and well-behaved. A string of electric lights outlined its symmetrical branches. My mother and I systematically fastened miniature angels, tiny reindeer, and jolly Santas on the tree with Wayne King's traditional carols playing softly on the radio. My tree was like my mother's breasts—disciplined, properly clothed, and definitely not exciting.

Valentine was waiting at the door to tell me about her Christmas when I returned home. There hadn't been many packages under the tipsy tree, but there had been some surprises. Big and Lacey had collaborated to create a crude dressing table from orange crates coaxed from the manager at the Clover Farm store. Lacey had stirred herself to unusual activity to sew fancy ruffles from an organdy hand-me-down dress into a pretty cover for the crates' splintery slats. I envied Valentine when I saw the home-made gift. My own staid oak dresser was dull compared to Valentine's ruffled crates. An ivory-colored hand mirror with small golden leaves around its rim lay on the dressing table. "It's a present from Mrs. Pain-in-the-Ass," Valentine said. "She left it at the Hippodrome for Big to bring home to me. He wasn't taking tickets at the time, thank God, so she didn't see him. He got up too late to shave that morning and he looked like a hobo."

I gazed at the lovely gift Big had made for Valentine, and something in me ached for him.

There were other gifts from Sycamore Lane. There was a beanbag from Tommy, and a finely polished heart-shaped piece of pine with Valentine's name carved in it. It was Mr. Grey's gift. Valentine reverently lifted the pin from its box and held it out to me. "You can look at it, but then I'm going to put it away and never wear it. I want to keep it forever, and I don't want to take a chance on losing it."

"Aren't you afraid Black might steal it?"

"No. He's a mean little bastard, but he isn't dumb. He knows if he ever touches that pin it will be the *last* thing he'll ever touch. Mr. Grey made Kathy a pin too."

"Did he make one for Mrs. Grey?"

"No."

"What *did* he give her?"

"Nothing. Why should he?"

"Good grief, Valentine, she's his wife."

"So what?"

"Husbands usually give their wives something for Christmas. My father gave my mother a purse, and we don't have much money this Christmas."

"It wasn't because Mr. Grey didn't have the money." Valentine was impatient with me again. "The pins didn't cost much. He could have made one for her if he'd wanted to. He didn't want to."

"I think he should have given her something."

I was surprised at my courage in speaking out against Mr. Grey. "It wasn't very nice of him not to give her some little thing."

I had pushed my luck too far. Valentine scowled. "Why should he give a present to somebody he doesn't even like? He's not two-faced. He gave Kathy a pin because he loves her."

"He gave you a pin. Does that mean he loves you?"

Valentine walked away. She went to the kitchen where Lacey was reading to Broken. "Okay if I listen in?"

Lacey looked pleasantly surprised at Valentine's sudden interest in stories she had scorned for the past several months.

"Sure."

My conversation had been brought to a forced halt.

Later in the evening Valentine showed me her other gifts. Black had been stirred by the holiday spirit; he gave Valentine a long narrow box, which she opened expecting to find a new pencil and instead found an Eversharp pen. Broken gave her a diary.

"Now we can write down everything we do," Valentine said.

"Great. We'll keep the diary in my flat where Black can't get at it."

"Good idea."

Relieved that Valentine and I had reestablished our friendship, I asked, "How did Kathy like the vanity case?"

"She loved it. She's never had one before."

"What did Mr. Grey think of the belt?"

"He was crazy about it. Said it was the best present he ever got."

"How did Black and Big and Broken and Lacey like the chocolate-covered cherries?"

Valentine avoided my eyes. "They didn't eat any of them. Lacey fed them all to Broken."

"Hmm. Did Mrs. Grey get any gifts at all?"

"She got a necklace from Tommy. He made it at the day nursery. He strung little balls of tinfoil on a string and put a fastener on it. She wore it on Christmas. The way she made over it when she showed it to me, you'd have thought the tinfoil was diamonds."

"Is that all she got? A tinfoil necklace?"

Valentine's eyes slithered away from mine again. "I gave her the plate of fudge I'd made for Kathy. I changed my mind at the last minute and gave it to Mrs. Pain-in-the-Ass."

"Why?"

"Darned if I know. The minute I gave it to her I wanted to take it back."

Kathy's gift for Valentine was a jar of blackberry jelly wrapped in gingham and tied with a dainty green rib bon.

"I told Lacey it was from Tommy," Valentine said. "The least old Lacey knows about Kathy, the better I like it."

"Did Mrs. Grey give Mr. Grey anything?"

"Yeh. She gave him a book about how to train a Doberman. I thought it was a silly thing to give him. Gretchen already does anything Mr. Grey wants her to. But he seemed to like it."

18

The snow remained white and fluffy long enough to usher the old year out, then turned to ugly slush. January of 1937 was unseasonably warm and rainy, and the Ohio and Muskingum Rivers reacted violently to the abrupt change in the weather.

"The river's up almost eight feet in Cincinnati, and it's over Front Street downtown." Big shook rain from his yellow slicker as he gave Lacey the current flood report. "By tomorrow night half of Marietta will be out of business. The Hippodrome closed at noon today and it won't open again until the water has gone down and the building's had a chance to dry out. We're going to have to tighten our belts, Lacey. I don't get paid when I don't work, and we can't run a movie with three feet of water on the floor."

Lacey tried to comfort Big with her own special philosophy. "There's a silver lining to every cloud, Big. Look at it this way. We were going to have a tough time paying the electric bill this month because of Christmas, and there's a good chance those bums at the electric company will be hollering for their money and turning off the lights if we don't give it to them. The last time we had a flood the electricity went off till the water went down. If it goes off this time, we'll just turn the tables on the electric company and tell them they owe us."

I found her logic fascinating, but it didn't seem to help Big, so Lacey turned to a tried-and-true remedy for Big's blues. She got out her old guitar and her new pick and sent him a musical message. She strummed and sang "Melancholy Baby."

> Come to me my melancholy baby,
> Cuddle up and don't be blue.
> All your tears are foolish fancies maybe,
> You know, dear, that I'm in love with you.
> Every cloud must have a silver lining,
> Wait until the sun shines through,
> Smile, my honey dear, as I kiss away each tear,
> Or else I will be melancholy too. . . .

And then she swung into a few chords of "Look for the Silver Lining" and Big relaxed and closed his eyes. Lacey put down the guitar and said, "See, Big, things ain't so bad. There's always a silver lining if you look for it hard enough."

Valentine arrived in time to hear Lacey's philosophy, and to add her own bad news to Big's. "Yeh, Lacey? See if you can make something good out of this. Monkey Ward's is flooded and Mrs. Grey can't go to work for a week or more. She sent me home and told me not to come back until she sends for me."

"Jesus," Black groaned, "does that mean you'll be hanging around the flat all day? That's worse than having a flood."

"Go drown yourself," Valentine yelled. Lacey stepped into the fray. "Both of you shut up. Big's got enough to worry about without you two jawing at each other. Now either shut up or get out."

Black and Valentine looked out the window at the cold rain dropping in sheets and shut up.

The rains continued for the next two days, falling so hard and steady that even Black didn't venture out of the flat. The enforced togetherness of five Harts led to many verbal and physical bouts. The blaring radio, kept at high volume to inform all the Harts about the weather no matter where they were in the flat, added to the general delirium. At times even I retreated temporarily to the silence of my own flat.

But I talked my mother into letting me sleep over at Valentine's one night during the flood. Valentine and I spread the covers from her bed on the living room floor and lay on them while she wrote in her diary and I read one of Lacey's magazines. The bedroom was dark and quiet long before Valentine and I turned off the lamp in the living room and settled down to go to sleep. I awoke in the middle of the night to the unusual sound of Lacey and Big arguing with each other. Their whispers got louder as they debated, and soon I could make out their words.

"Stop it, Big. I don't think we should take the chance." Lacey's reprimand to Big held a snap usually reserved for Black. "You ain't got any rubbers."

"No, and with the drugstore two feet under water chances are I won't have any for a week," Big growled. "You don't expect me to wait that long, do you? My God, I'll die."

"That's not true, Big. It won't kill you to wait."

"Yeh? Well, maybe it won't *kill* me, but it sure as hell will make me *wish* I was dead. You can feel it for yourself, Lacey. It's going to pop wide open if it ain't taken care of soon. Go on. Feel it for yourself."

176

A momentary silence was shattered by Lacey's, "WOW!"

"See. What'd I tell you?" Big sounded more urgent.

"You sure ain't lying. But I still don't think we ought to take the chance." Lacey's protest sounded weaker.

"Come on, baby. Feel it again." Big's voice was husky. Bedsprings squeaked; bodies shuffled under the bedcover.

"Will you promise to pull out in time?" Lacey sounded ready to compromise.

I nudged Valentine. I knew she was awake; in the dim light from the streetlamp I had seen her eyes open when sounds first began to come from the bedroom. "What does Lacey mean," I whispered, "when she asks Big to pull out in time? In time for what?"

Valentine didn't reopen her eyes; she ducked her head under the blanket and gathered it tightly over her ears. She was in no mood to explain Lacey's nocturnal request, nor was Big in the mood to grant it.

"I'll be damned if I'm going to promise you a thing like that, Lacey. The best I can do is promise that I'll *try* to pull out in time, but I ain't sure I can. My God, I'm laying here feeling like I'm going to explode and you're asking me to promise not to. That don't make sense. I might as well just thump it a good one and get it over with."

"That ain't the same thing, and you know it." Lacey sounded a bit panicky. "It ain't going to do *me* a bit of good if you just lay there and jack off. Come on now, Big, promise me you'll pull out in time and we'll go ahead and do it and both feel better."

"No!" Big's decision sounded final. "I'll be damned if I'm going to make you a promise I probably can't keep. I'm goddamned sick and tired of doing everything halfway. I eat half as much food as I want, I smoke half a cigarette, my overshoes are half gone, my belt is half worn out, I drink half a cup of coffee . . . everything I do, I do halfway. But I'll be goddamned if I'm going to stop screwing when I'm halfway through. If I was the kind of guy that could do that, I wouldn't be the kind of guy you'd want in bed with you. Now, are you going to turn over and give me what I need, or am I just going to turn you over and take it?"

The rhythmic vibrations of the bed told Lacey's answer. Several minutes later I heard them laughing and talking, and Big no longer sounded tense and Lacey no longer sounded angry. I, too, relaxed, happy that two people I cared for were having a good ending to a tough day. Valentine remained a tight, stiff, and silent little mound beneath the blanket. I didn't see her face until morning. Then I tackled her with the question she hadn't answered during the night.

"Did you hear Big and Lacey last night?"

"How could I help it? They made enough racket to wake the dead."

"What were they fighting about? What did Lacey mean when she asked Big to promise to pull out in time?"

"Go ask your mother," Valentine snapped. She didn't have the same reluctance, however, in tackling Lacey about Big's promise. She began her attack the minute Lacey appeared in the kitchen where Valentine and I were stirring milk into hot cornmeal mush. Valentine looked more thunderous than the threatening sky outside the window. Lacey made the error of verbally acknowledging Valentine's black mood.

"What's wrong with you?" Lacey yawned and sat down at the table.

"I'm disgusted. Just plain disgusted. That's what's wrong."

"What about this time?" Lacey yawned again and got up to pour a cup of coffee.

"About you and Big, that's what. We heard you messing around in there last night. Don't you think you're getting too old to mess around like that? I never heard anything so disgusting in my whole life, and when Big gets out here I'm going to give him an earful. A real earful."

Lacey flushed, but held her ground. "Listen here, Miss High-and-Mighty. We got enough trouble without you causing more. In the first place if you didn't always have your ears flapping in the wind trying to hear everything that goes on, you'd be better off. You're always snooping around sticking your nose in everybody else's business, and then when you hear what you've been trying to hear, you stick your nose up in the air. If you'd mind your own business you might not run around with a mad on so much of the time."

"Oh yeh? Well, if you and Big would act your age and stay on your own side of the bed, Big might not run around with a *hard-on* so much of the time. And you can bet your bottom dollar I'm going to tell Big just what I think of the whole disgusting mess the minute he gets up and gets out here. In fact, I think I'll go in and wake him up right now and set him straight."

Her path to the closed bedroom door was blocked by Lacey, angrier than I'd ever seen her.

"You ain't going to say one thing to Big about what you heard last night." She grabbed Valentine's elbow and lowered her face to stand eye-to-eye with her combatant. "That poor guy's worried to death about where his next dollar's coming from. He don't need a lecture from you."

"Oh yeh? It sounds to me like he needs someone to talk some sense to him. If he's so worried about where his next dollar's coming from, why's he messing around with you and taking a chance on you getting caught? And you're as bad as he is, Lacey. You're always hollering about not wanting another mouth to feed, but you haven't got enough sense to make Big stay on his own side of the bed. Both of you are disgusting."

Lacey shook Valentine, hard. "In the first place, Miss High-and-Mighty, it ain't a damned bit of your business what Big and I do in bed, and in the second place, if your ears hadn't been flapping in the wind you wouldn't have heard us in the first place, and in the third place, if Big and me hadn't messed around in bed thirteen years ago when we couldn't afford to feed another mouth, you wouldn't be sitting here now in the first place, complaining about what we did in the second place. So put that in your pipe and smoke it."

She released Valentine and returned to her cooling coffee. Valentine didn't retreat. She charged again.

"That was different. Thirteen years ago you and Big were young. You're old now and you ought to settle down and act your age."

"That just shows how ignorant you are, Miss High-and-Mighty." Lacey flushed, perspiring even in the damp, cold kitchen. I had a feeling that Valentine was about to lose a fight. "Do you want me to tell you exactly why I don't make Big stay on his side of the bed?"

"Don't bother," Valentine sneered.

She stood up to leave, but Lacey grabbed her and shook her again.

"You started this argument, young lady, but I'm going to finish it. Settle down and listen or I'll shake the pure shit right out of you. I don't make Big stay on his side of the bed because after a week like we've just had, there ain't a hell of a lot I can do for him. And there ain't a hell of a lot he can do for me. He don't have a dime for a glass of beer, I don't have a nickel for a candy bar. I ain't got money enough to buy a decent dress, and Big's feet are half-frozen from wearing worn-out shoes. I ain't got money to buy milk for Broken. In the daytime, Big and I ain't got a damned thing to give each other. Nothing. Nothing at all. You kids aren't much better off than Big and me. In the daytime, you ain't got anything much either. But at night, at least you kids can dream of better days to come. But like you just pointed out, Valentine, Big and me ain't kids any longer. Our dreams at night ain't a hell of a lot better than what we see in the daytime. If anything, they're uglier in the dark. The only good thing about nighttime is that Big and me can wrap around each other and know that I've got him and he has me. And sometimes, Miss High-and-Mighty, we ain't even doing what you're yelling about. We ain't being what you call disgusting. We're just holding each other close, real tight, because it's the only way we can keep ourselves and each other from falling apart before morning. Now shut your mouth and get out of my sight. I'm fed up with you."

She released Valentine and we went over to my flat, emptied for the day. The flood waters hadn't drowned out my parents' jobs.

"Lacey makes sense," I told Valentine from the safety of my kitchen. "All she and Big *do* have is each other. And they *do* love each other."

Valentine didn't see it my way. "So they love each other. So what? They can love each other without jumping on top of each other every night. Mr. Grey and Kathy love each other just as much as Big and Lacey do, and they don't mess around."

"Mr. Grey can't," I reminded her. "You remember that word Black found out about, Mr. Grey *can't* mess around with Kathy. It's impossible."

"He wouldn't even if he could," Valentine insisted. "He's too clean. I know what I'm talking about. When Crazy Gurney got me down and ran his thing all over me, it felt awful. Just awful. Disgusting. Dirty. No woman with any sense would *want* to have one of those things shoved in them, and no man who really loved a woman would want to shove it in her."

"You didn't think so when I first met you. Before you went to work on Sycamore Lane you told me it was fun to listen to Big and Lacey make love."

Valentine stamped her foot. "That was before I understood a damn thing about love and what it should be like. That was when I was real dumb. Before I met Mr. Grey. I'm lots smarter now."

I dropped my defense of Big and Lacey. For all I knew, Valentine could be right. She had learned from Crazy Gurney what a man's thing felt like. I didn't even know for sure what a man's thing *looked* like, other than the sketch Valentine made when she gave me my first lesson in sex.

Black didn't hang around the flat after the rains finally stopped. He became a family hero for a few hours—at least in Lacey's eyes—by volunteering to help the local fire department as they moved through Marietta in the wake of the receding flood waters and cleaned up the debris.

"Black's doing it for free," Lacey boasted, proud that after so many years of having nothing but trouble from Black, she now had something good to say. "He went down to the fire department the minute he heard they were looking for volunteers and he offered to go into the stores and mop up. That takes a lot of nerve. There are rats and snakes in flood water."

Valentine and Big looked dubious. They knew Black was up to something besides helping his fellow man; it was merely a matter of time, their faces predicted, before the real reason for Black's sacrifice came to light. It was not long in coming. The disclosure came the first evening Black returned home, sank into a kitchen chair, and motioned to Lacey to help him take off the big hip boots provided for the clean-up crew by the fire department.

Lacey, who ordinarily would have told Black to take his boots off himself, was still hypnotized by Black's unusual public spirit, so she obediently sat down on the floor in front of him and pulled. When the boots came off, a shower of objects cascaded out of them and spread over the kitchen linoleum. We stared, speechless, while Black picked them up one by one and triumphantly held them up for us to admire.

He handed a Junior G-man badge to Broken. The cardboard around it was damp, but the badge was bright and shiny and Broken cooed over it. Black again dived to the floor and surfaced with a Brownie camera, which he held up to the kitchen light and focused critically before placing it squarely in the middle of the kitchen table. He waved a slightly wet but still readable *Tarzan* comic toward Big, and a *Big Little Book* toward Broken. Broken grabbed the book and promptly began to chew its soggy, soiled cover.

We were a speechless, fascinated audience, as Black dug down deep into the left boot, and with an exaggerated pretense of nonchalance, brought out a compact. A round compact with a fat Cupid on the cover. "Here." He held it out to Lacey. She reached for it gingerly, as if she was reaching for a mirage. She ran her eager fingers over the fat coy Cupid, as if she was trying to make sure it really existed.

"Open it," Black ordered. Lacey opened it. A pink powder puff looked up at her. Lacey's lips trembled, and she laid her head down on the kitchen table and cried.

Pretending to be blind to Lacey's tears and deaf to her sobs, Black reached inside the right boot. Making the suspense last as long as possible, he very slowly pulled out a long leather belt. A belt with an initialed buckle. Black held the buckle, a big brass *H*, out to Big. Big said, "Jesus Christ," and stroked the belt from one end to the other, then went into the bedroom, keeping his face turned away from us on the way out of the room. When he returned, the belt rested proudly around his waist, and his eyes were red.

"You stole that stuff," Valentine accused Black.

"So what?" Black sounded more weary than angry.

"It's wrong to steal. That's what."

183

"Who says so? Who says it's wrong to take stuff that was just getting ruined anyway? I worked damned hard today, Miss High-and-Mighty. A lot harder than you ever did. You spend your day playing with a kid and fetching things for a cripple. I spent my day wading though water a foot deep, full of rats and snakes. I spent my day scraping mud that looked and smelled like shit off floors and walls. I was wet and cold all day, and right now I'm dead tired. I didn't get one red cent for doing that work, so I paid myself."

"You pilfered. You did what Mr. Grey says is one of the very worst things anyone can do. You pilfered from people who are down on their luck. You pilfered from those poor store owners."

"Oh shit." Black was too weary and disgusted to defend himself vigorously. Valentine assumed her usual battle position—hands on hips. She moved closer to him, pressed her nose against his.

"You pilfered," she repeated. "You stole those things. Shame on you."

Black moved away from her and sat down by the kitchen table and reached for a piece of cornbread.

"Shit, yes," he agreed, "I stole those things. Of course I stole them. Did you think Santa Claus dropped that stuff down my boots? Of course I stole them. I ain't Daddy Warbucks and I ain't the tooth fairy. If I hadn't stole them, we wouldn't have them."

"You're disgusting." Valentine was red with indignation. "If you'd been caught stealing your name would have been in the newspaper and everyone in town would know that I have a brother who steals things."

"Oh shit, Valentine, knock it off," Black sneered. "You know damned well you don't really care what anyone in town thinks—anyone except Old Crip. That's what's bugging you, and you know it. You're afraid Old Crip will

184

hear about it and find out you ain't as hoity-toity as you try to make him think you are."

Black leaned back on two legs of his chair and peered at Valentine through eyes that were more closed than opened. His scornful look brought Valentine to full fury. She turned from him and attacked Big and Lacey.

"Are you two going to let him get away with stealing that stuff? Shame on you, Lacey, and you too, Big. Lacey, you know that vanity case doesn't really belong to you. It belongs on the counter at the five-and-dime store. And Big, you know that belt isn't yours. It came from the rack at Stetson's Men's Store. Lacey, you don't even have a right to look in the mirror inside that vanity case. You don't have a right to touch that powder puff. Big, you don't have a right to hold your pants up with that belt—not even if it does have your initial on it. Both of you know it's wrong. Dead wrong. You ought to make Black take that stuff right back to where he got it from, this minute. You're as bad as he is if you let him give you those things."

Lacey's eyes sought Big's; she caressed the compact as if she was bidding it good-bye. Big reluctantly began to unbuckle the belt, and turned to go into the bedroom. But the compact stayed in Lacey's hand, and the belt remained around Big's waist.

Black spoke, and not with his usual sneer. He sounded older, determined, strong, and his words were not weakened by false bravado.

"You're going to keep that compact, Lacey, and you're going to keep that belt, Big." He turned to Valentine. "And you're going to keep your big mouth shut. SHUT. You hear me? SHUT. Don't preach me no sermons about what's right and what's wrong, Valentine. And don't be preaching to Big and Lacey the minute I turn my back, either. The next time you feel like yelling about what I carried home today in my boots, just stop and think back to Christmas

185

morning. Think back to what Lacey and Big felt like when they thought you were buying them the things they wanted the most, and instead the only thing you gave all of us was one lousy box of chocolate-covered cherries. I should have snitched those things before Christmas, and I would have, but I really thought you were going to buy Lacey her compact and get Big his belt. They thought so too. Boy, were we wrong! You didn't give a shit about what Big and Lacey wanted for Christmas. You were too busy thinking about the High-Muckety-Mucks to think about us. So shut up, kiddo. And I mean SHUT UP! I ain't taking those things back and if you know what's good for you, you ain't ever going to say another word about it. Not to me or Lacey or Big. Pass me the cornbread, Lacey."

Lacey did better than merely *pass* the cornbread; she arose, cut a big piece, drowned it in homemade sugar syrup and proudly carried the plate to Black. Valentine never again said a word about the compact with the cupid on its top or the belt with the initialed buckle. Not even to me.

The Ohio and Muskingum Rivers had returned to their banks, the mirror had loosened on Lacey's compact, the brass had tarnished on Big's buckle, and a hard winter had surrendered to an early spring before Flint again appeared on Sycamore Lane. He returned late in March, unsteadily gunning his truck over the new pavement, screeching to a halt. His three-day visit was mercifully short and mercilessly brutal. He was drunk when he arrived, while he was there, and when he drove away. Unusually warm afternoons called for open windows, and Mr. Grey and Valentine heard and shared Kathy's pain.

"It's awful," Valentine told me, "just awful. We haven't seen or heard Kathy since Flint got home. All we hear is him yelling and cussing and slapping Kathy around. I asked Mr. Grey again to let me call the cops but he said it wouldn't do any good, that all the cops would do is lock Flint up until he's sober and then he'll be meaner than ever to Kathy when he gets out. Mr. Grey says all we can do is wait and hope that Flint leaves soon."

Flint departed as suddenly as he had arrived. When the echo of his truck faded, Valentine scrambled across the gully to see how Kathy had survived the latest homecoming. Her lip was swollen, but otherwise she was the same accepting, complacent Kathy, ready to take what Flint had to give—paying her share of the rent on her dollhouse—and eager to forget about Flint the minute he was out of sight. She was even willing to make excuses for what he had done to her.

"It's the booze that makes him act like that. He doesn't know what he's doing when he's drunk."

"Then why in the heck doesn't he stop drinking?" Valentine asked.

"I don't know. Maybe he needs the stuff. Maybe inside he's scared and the whiskey makes him feel brave. I don't know why he gets drunk, and I don't want to think about it anymore. He's gone now, so let's forget about him."

Forget him we did. Flint was not laughter and sunshine and love; Flint was not part of Sycamore Lane.

19

Early in April, I packed away my long underwear and stepped into the bare-legged freedom of ankle sox. My mother stored my heavy skirts and sweaters in mothballs and got out last summer's dresses. They were too short and too tight. She widened seams and lowered hems and told me I'd have to make them do for one more summer. I did get one new piece of clothing— a brassiere. I needed it. Every morning before I dressed I stood in front of my mirror and admired my sideview and knew that before another spring, I would have tits.

As genetically unlikely as it seemed, Valentine appeared doomed—physically at least—to belong to the world of the breasts. Her bust was still flat and childlike. Her legs, however, did show improvement when they emerged from long underwear. They were quite shapely. Her knees no longer sought each other as they had the summer before.

What Valentine lacked that spring in bust development, Lacey more than made up for. Lacey's tits, always large and luminous, assumed even more majestic proportions with every passing day. Although she had often been mistaken in her predictions that she had "been caught," she was not wrong in late winter when she consulted the red Xs on her feed and grain calendar. This time there was no doubt about it—there definitely would be another mouth to feed within the next nine months.

"Well, that's what you get for messing around," was Valentine's smug comment when she learned of Lacey's pregnancy. "I told you to make Big stay on his side of the bed, but no, you wouldn't listen to me. Serves you right, Lacey."

"Oh, shut up," was the best Lacey could come up with against Valentine's tactless but true reminder.

In mid-April, Valentine and I began our countdown to summer vacation. When Mrs. Grey asked Valentine to work full time as soon as school ended, Valentine was quick to agree. The long spring days lengthened Valentine's work hours; she frequently remained on Sycamore Lane after dusk to straighten the kitchen. The sweet talk Mr. Grey had used so effectively in the autumn about wanting more time alone with his wife had long since been forgotten, and Crazy's attack on Valentine was only dimly remembered.

Neither Crazy nor his mother had shown any interest in us during the long winter months. Occasionally, from inside the warm house, we watched the two of them struggle downhill toward town to get their wintertime meals from the Red Lantern's garbage cans. The newly paved road was forsaken by the county as soon as the paving was completed. It was not plowed in the winter, making walking treacherous. Crazy and his mother never looked up from the snowy path as they lifted high first one leg, then the other. Crazy's boots were split; they had lost their fasteners and flopped loosely around his thick ankles. The old woman's feet were swathed in a mysterious combination of paper and cloth. When the snow turned to slush and the slush dried and pavement again surfaced, the two weird figures continued to ignore us. The bitter confrontation between the old woman and Mr. Grey had ended in a draw; both were content to let the matter rest.

Valentine's theme song that spring came from a movie. One Sunday afternoon we were entranced by Sylvia Sidney in *The Trail of the Lonesome Pine*. We tried unsuccessfully to convince ourselves that Mr. Grey resembled Fred MacMurray, having already agreed that Kathy resembled Sylvia Sidney. We finally had to concede that Fred MacMurray and Mr. Grey actually had little in common, so we promptly sat down and wrote to MGM suggesting that they make a movie starring Leslie Howard and Sylvia Sidney. We never did hear from MGM but comforted ourselves with the thought that since we could watch the real thing, we could do without the movie.

Valentine constantly warbled the sentimental love song from the movie that spring. Her singing was dreadfully off-key, but her sentiments were right on target. To Valentine, love was indeed everywhere, since to her *everywhere* meant Sycamore Lane, the only world she chose to accept.

I was with Valentine when her dream world became a nightmare. It was the day of our first severe springtime thunderstorm. Kathy had gone home. Tommy was spending the night with a friend. The sky was blackening; the clouds rolling rapidly toward Sycamore Lane were dark, menacing. A vicious wind tossed leaves and branches and leftover balls from the sycamore trees, agitating Gretchen and making her nervous. She pranced restlessly around the yard until Mr. Grey called her to his side and held her collar and patted her head.

"The storm looks like a bad one," he told Valentine and me. "I want you girls to go home now. Don't stay to fix supper. If you hurry, you can get home before the storm breaks. Go on, now. Scoot."

We scooted. We ran through the house and closed the windows and then left for home. Heavy black clouds swallowed the remaining slivers of daylight; the sycamores bordering the lane danced a weird ballet to the eerie beat of the wind. Before we were halfway down the road, the late afternoon had turned as dark as evening. Valentine gallantly tried to whistle, but the wind blew her whistle away as quickly as it left her unsteady lips and it was lost in the dusk. We moved as rapidly as we could, but with the wind fighting us and blowing us back step for step, our progress was slow and erratic. We were blinded by hair blowing in our eyes and dust billowing up from the road.

Neither of us saw Crazy Gurney until he sprang out of a shadow and grabbed Valentine. Even then I did not see him clearly, but Valentine's scream, trembling on the edge of her raw nerves, was spontaneous and piercing and it rose above the cry of the wind.

"RUN!" she shouted. "RUN!"

I ran—I ran back toward Mr. Grey. He had shut Gretchen inside, but he was still in the backyard. I was frantic, incoherent, but my jumbled words were unnecessary. He guessed what was happening to Valentine.

"Push me," he ordered. "Fast!" I grabbed the wheelchair and propelled it out of the yard. He seized the old leaf rake leaning against the gate and held it across his lap. "Faster," he urged. "Faster!"

The wheels of the chair creaked and protested as they gained momentum and spun downhill toward the figures

191

struggling in the middle of the road. Crazy had forced Valentine to the ground; she was fighting, but her strength was no match for his. By the time we reached them, she was down in the dust, and Crazy was straddling her, fumbling at her skirt, pulling at the front of his trousers.

"Hit him with the chair," Mr. Grey shouted. I crashed the wheelchair into Crazy. Mr. Grey grasped the rake and flailed Crazy with it, striking his arched back again and again. Valentine rolled aside and I ran to her and crouched down beside her in the dust. Crazy cowered and whimpered and held out his hands to fend away the rake, but Mr. Grey showed no mercy. He struck until the handle of the rake snapped, then threw the rusty tines at Crazy's face. They slashed his cheek and left cuts like scratches made by giant fingernails.

His fury spent, his weapon useless, his battle won, Mr. Grey turned away from Crazy and moved toward Valentine. Crazy struggled to his feet and ran uphill, rubbing blood from his cheek and bleating for his mother.

"Are you all right, Valentine?"

Through her sobs, Valentine said, "Yes, but I wouldn't be if you hadn't come when you did. He was going to hurt me real bad. He might have killed me."

Huge drops of rain splattered down on us.

"Take me back to the house," Mr. Grey said. We pushed the wheelchair uphill, struggling against the wind and the rain. We were soaked through when we got into the kitchen, but our wet clothes went unnoticed.

"What are we going to do?" I was the first to put words to the unspoken question. How were we to deal with the old woman's fury when she saw the deep gashes on her son's face? And if we *could* handle the woman, could we handle Crazy? It was obvious now that the old woman could no longer control him. Valentine was not safe on Sycamore Lane. We could no longer pretend that if we ignored things and people we didn't like, they wouldn't exist. Something must be done—but what?

"What are we going to do?" I asked again.

"I have to think." Mr. Grey leaned his head back and closed his eyes. Valentine and I were very quiet; only the wind outside and the clock on the wall broke the silence. Minutes passed before Mr. Grey opened his eyes and looked directly at Valentine.

"It's too bad they have a house to live in. If they didn't have a roof over their heads, they'd move away. They would definitely leave Sycamore Lane, and they might even leave town. They'd be out of our lives forever."

I waited for Valentine's response. It did not come. Only her face spoke; she no longer looked frightened. She looked determined. I had come to know so well the look that signaled Valentine had made up her mind about something and that neither hell nor high water could change it. I was puzzled. I had the eerie sensation that although I had heard every word spoken by Mr. Grey, I had missed a message Valentine had received.

The storm passed as quickly as it had come, and the night sky was clear again when I finally understood. Just before midnight, when the fire truck sped past the flat, lights flashing and siren wailing, I instinctively knew where it was going. I jumped from bed and joined the neighbors who had been awakened by the sirens and had gathered on the street to share the excitement.

Lacey was leaning out a window. Big was on the sidewalk, conjecturing as to the truck's destination. "It looks like it's headed out toward the fairgrounds."

"Yeh," someone agreed, "but the only thing out that way is a couple of old shanties on a little side road. If that's where it's going, it had better get there quick. Those shacks are so rotten they'll go up like smoke."

"That's right." Black spoke from behind me where he

was standing unusually close to Valentine—a rare occurrence for two people who most of the time got within arm's reach only to exchange blows.

"They can't get there fast enough. There ain't going to be anything left but ashes in a couple of minutes." The pride in Black's voice and the grin on Valentine's face told me the story. Our eyes met. We looked at each other, sharing a secret nobody else in town suspected.

"Okay, Valentine, it's time to pay up." Black's eyes shifted from my face down to my body, studying me from head to feet, slowly, carefully scrutinizing me. Suddenly I wished I had tossed my light summer robe over my thin pajamas before I left my bedroom.

"Can't you wait until tomorrow?" Valentine hedged.

"No. Not on your tintype, Valentine. We made a deal and I kept my part of it and you'd better keep your part or I'll call Big over here and I'll tell him the whole story. Quit trying to shinny out of a bargain. A deal's a deal. Now get out in the alley and pay up. I'm going to count to ten— fast—and if you ain't in the alley by the time I finish, I'm going to give Big and Lacey and everyone else in earshot an earful."

Before he said *three*, Valentine grabbed my hand and pulled me toward the alley. Black stayed close behind. He didn't stop counting until we were in the dark deserted alley, away from the people still standing on the sidewalk waiting for news about the fire.

Black looked at me. "Okay. Take it off."

I stared at Valentine. "What's he talking about?"

She squirmed. "He wants you to take off your pajama top."

"What?" I wondered if I was dreaming. The scene had no meaning for me, no reality.

"She said I want you to take off your pajama top," Black answered for Valentine.

"Why?"

194

"Why do you think? So I can see what's under it."

"There's nothing under it. All I have on is this pair of pajamas."

Valentine interceded. "He means he wants to see what your tits look like."

"What in the world makes him think I'd let him do that?" I gasped, but I was slowly beginning to understand.

Valentine's determination, Mr. Grey's obscure message, Black's pride when he spoke of the fire, and his threat to tell something to Big and Lacey if Valentine didn't keep her part of a bargain all began to come together. "What kind of a deal did you make with Black?"

"She promised me you'd let me see your tits if I burned Crazy Gurney's house down," Black said.

Valentine hissed at him. "Shut up, Black. Let me handle this." She moved close to me and whispered, "It's the only way I could get him to set the fire. And the only way we could get rid of Crazy and his mother was to burn them out. You know what Crazy was trying to do to me. You know what he *will* do to me sooner or later if we don't get rid of him. I didn't have a chance to tell you about the deal. I had to wait until Big and Lacey were asleep to talk to Black about what he'd take to burn down the shack and the only deal he'd make was for you to take off your pajama top and let him see what he can see."

"Quit yapping, Valentine," Black growled. "Let's get this thing over with before Big or Lacey yell for us to come back inside. I've waited long enough. It's put-up or shut-up time."

"If all you want to do is find out what a woman's bare chest looks like, why don't you look at Lacey's?" I asked Black. "It's no trouble at all to see hers."

"It ain't no trouble, and it ain't no fun either. I ain't a damn bit interested in what a woman as old as Lacey looks like."

195

"Then let Valentine show you hers. She made the deal, I didn't. Look at hers."

Black laughed. "Hell, there ain't nothing to see on Valentine. She's flat as a pancake that's been stepped on. Now take off that pajama top and pay up or I swear to God I'll go out there and tell the whole damn town just who set that fire and why."

I looked at Valentine. She was no help. "Just take your top off for a minute. All I promised him was a look. It can be a real fast look. If he tries to feel you, I'll kick him right in his balls."

"Valentine, Black, where are you?" Lacey's call drifted from the upstairs window and into the alley.

"See, what did I tell you?" Black was angry—and we both knew what Black's anger could lead to. "You've fooled around so long that Lacey's wondering where we are. The hell with it. I'm going out there right now and blow the whistle on the whole deal." He turned toward the sidewalk, but Valentine quickly drew him back.

"I'll go calm Lacey down. You two stay here. Take off your pajama top," she told me. "All Black gets to do is take one quick look. If he touches you, scream, and I'll come running and kick the shit out of him and he can tell Big and Lacey anything he wants to." She shouted, "I'm coming, Lacey," and ran out of the alley.

Black and I were alone.

We stared at each other for a moment. When Black spoke his voice was strangely soft, not at all like the Black I thought I knew.

"Please take it off." It was the first time I had ever heard him say please.

The night was clear; the moon was bright and beautiful as it crept down the alley. I no longer heard the tumult on the sidewalk; I heard my heart. It was beating fast, and somewhere deep in my body I felt the same stirring I had known the first time I watched Big and Lacey reach for each other. I remembered how I had wished that night that I could make that feeling return, linger, become stronger.

"Please take it off," Black whispered.

I slowly unbuttoned the three buttons on my pajama top and slid it off, watching Black's face, then looking down at myself. Black and I both studied my body for a few seconds, and in those few seconds I knew for sure that someday I would be a woman who would be able to feel the things Lacey felt with the man she loved.

"You are so clean." Black's voice was gentle. He moved his hand toward me and then jerked it back and put it in his pocket. I moved closer to him, deeper into the shadows.

"Do you want to feel them?" I whispered.

"Yes."

He reached out and gingerly ran his hands over my tits, touching them gently, cupping them. My body stirred again, stronger, and I felt it moving toward his, just as Lacey's had moved toward Big's.

"Touch my nipples," I whispered. He touched them, and my nipples came alive. His fingers brought them to a point. They stood up, reached out, begged to be tasted. My body was ready to give pleasure, to receive love.

I reached down and slipped off my pajama bottoms and kicked them aside and stood naked. I moved out of the shadows and into the bright moonlight and Black and I looked down again at my body, and I realized for the first time that the fine curly dark hairs that had been appearing on my body for the past year were not an embarrassment, as I had once thought, but were a lovely dark contrast to my soft white skin.

"Do you want to touch me down there, Black?"

Black shook his head. "I want to, but I'm not going to. Maybe sometime, but not tonight. Put your pajamas back on." His voice was rough, but not mean.

"Not yet." I reached for his hands and pulled them

toward my tits again. I put his fingers around my nipples, and while they came to a point, I came to a climax. I didn't know at the time what it was, but I knew I wanted it to last forever, and I knew why Lacey didn't make Big stay on his own side of the bed. My body moved. Without my willing it, my body moved, and I could no more have stopped its movement than I could have turned off the moonlight. I was Lacey. I was Eve.

"Sweet Jesus Christ," Black groaned. When my body stopped moving and stood still and stationary and forever changed, he removed his fingers from my nipples and stooped over and picked up my pajamas.

"Put them on." He held the top while I stepped into the bottom. By the time Valentine returned to the alley with the assurance that Lacey was pacified, Black and I looked the same as when she left us, but he and I both knew that I would never again *be* the same.

It was the only secret I ever kept from Valentine.

20

The fire was the talk of the town the next day, and the talk of Lacey's supper table that evening. She read the newspaper article to Big and Broken, milking every drop of drama from it.

"It's a wonder the old woman wasn't burned to death. The paper says if it hadn't been for the storm wetting down the shack earlier in the day, she wouldn't have had time to get out before the house went up like a match. But she not only got herself out, she got her son out too. Saved his life."

She looked up from the newspaper at Valentine who was listening noncommittally.

"I never knew Crazy Gurney lived out there," Lacey said. "It's a good thing I didn't know it when you first got that job, or I'd never have let you take it, Valentine. I know it was quite a few years ago that he did whatever he did to that little girl, but a leopard never changes his spots and that goes for a nut like Crazy Gurney too. Did he ever bother you, Valentine?"

"Good grief, no, Lacey. Never paid a bit of attention to me."

Lacey returned to the newspaper and began to reread the story. Her second reading was interrupted by Black. Behind Lacey's bent head he winked at Valentine. Valentine ignored him.

"I wonder what started the fire?"

Big made a guess. "The old woman probably left something on the stove. Hot grease, maybe. More than likely she brought the whole thing on herself."

"She sure did," Valentine muttered, just loud enough for me to hear.

"I wonder where they'll live now?" Lacey mused. "They sure can't live out on Sycamore Lane."

"They sure can't," Valentine agreed.

"They'll probably hit the road," Big said. "There's lots of people not living anywhere special these days. Maybe they'll hole up in a Hooverville somewhere."

Lacey laid down the newspaper and picked up her inevitable thread of silver lining to weave into the story. "Maybe it's all for the best. Lord knows I wouldn't wish a thing like that on anybody, not even my worst enemy, but now they'll leave town and no one in Marietta will have to worry about Crazy Gurney messing around with some innocent little girl. There's always a silver lining to every cloud."

"That's right, Lacey. Nobody in Marietta will have to worry about those two again." Valentine sounded smug.

"Yeh, Lacey, like you say, there's always a silver lining to every cloud." Black spoke softly and looked at me.

We saw Crazy Gurney and his mother one more time before they left Marietta forever. A few days after the fire, when the ashes had cooled enough to be sifted, the two of

them shuffled uphill to search through the charred re-
mains, seeking any of their belongings that might have
miraculously survived the flames. We watched them from
behind motionless living room curtains as they made their
last journey down Sycamore Lane. They remained with
the ashes for a short time, then came back downhill, their
eyes lowered. The unwashed cuts on Crazy's face were
crusted with dark dried blood. He carried the eternal in-
signia of the vagabond over his stooped shoulder; all that
was left of their possessions was tied in a bandana fastened
to the end of a bent tomato stake. They were on their way
out of our lives.

"Do you think we'll ever see them again?" Valentine
asked.

"No. They're gone now. So let's forget about them.
Let's pretend they never existed."

21

Flint arrived a few days after Crazy and his mother left. His visit was unexpected and violent. He was well on his way toward being drunk when he drove up the road, his truck swerving from one side of the lane to the other, narrowly missing Kathy's mailbox when it screeched to a stop. He wavered as he walked up the path; the words he shouted across the gully were as unsteady as his gait.

"Looks like there was some excitement out here." He gestured uphill toward the ashes. "House burned down, huh?"

Mr. Grey nodded.

"Good thing it did," Flint decided. "Got rid of that halfwit and his old lady."

No answer from Mr. Grey. Flint stumbled up the steps

and went into his house. We didn't see him or Kathy again until he drove away four days later.

"What's that thing he's wearing around his neck?" Valentine asked.

"It's a St. Christopher's medal," Mr. Grey told her. "Flint's a Catholic. In his religion, St. Christopher is the patron saint of travelers. He's supposed to keep them safe while they're on the road."

"Maybe Kathy could sneak it off his neck and throw it away," Valentine suggested, "and Flint would have an accident and die."

Mr. Grey smiled. "Small chance of that. It would take a guillotine to separate Flint's neck from that medal. He's worn it as long as I've known him."

"Lacey doesn't like Catholics," Valentine told me as we strolled home that evening. "She says all kinds of things go on between the nuns and the priests. Most of the time, I don't think Lacey knows shit from Shinola, but she must be right about the Catholics. A religion that puts a saint in charge of keeping a drunk like Flint safe has to be bad."

When Flint left and Kathy reappeared, her freckles dimmed the bruises on her cheeks, but her brief halter and shorts did little to hide the marks on her arms and legs. Kathy had again paid her share of the rent the hard way. She refused our sympathy, turned it aside. She was in high spirits. The bruises would fade and her bad days would soon be forgotten. She had good news to tell.

"Flint won't be back again until late summer. I know it for a fact because I saw the contract he signed to haul produce in Oregon. It will be months before we see him again, so let's not waste a summer thinking about him."

We were quick to agree. Crazy and his mother and Flint were gone. Fate smiled on us, and we smiled back. We drank joyfully of the heady wine of freedom from fear.

The anticipation of a carefree summer went to Kathy's

head. Often she would still be with Mr. Grey when the town clock struck, reminding us that although Flint was off in faraway Oregon, Mrs. Grey was right in town. Heeding the clock's warning, Kathy would scurry like a field mouse down, across, and up the gully to her own yard. Breathless from haste and giddy with happiness, she would climax her pantomimed departure by lying on the grass and laughing at herself, while from our side of the gully we laughed with her.

Life was going in the right direction for me, too. My grades had remarkably improved, and with Valentine's increased attention to using soap and water on herself as well as cleaning up her language, my mother became more tolerant.

"You've been a good influence on that peculiar girl next door," she said. I accepted her praise, but I knew it was not I who was responsible for Valentine's new leaf; I was her model, but Mr. Grey was her inspiration.

Since my mother chose to ignore Black, she had no opportunity to observe that Black too was making some adjustments. Not many, it was true. He still tormented the cat, cursed like a sailor and continued to be a mean little bastard—to everyone but me. Although he and I never discussed the episode we had shared in the alley, we saw each other through different eyes. To Black, I was no longer Valentine's tag-along echo. I had stepped out of that role when I stood with him in the moonlight and stepped out of my pajamas. I was now a special person, one who had not scorned his touch, but had invited it, responded to it. To me, Black was no longer merely Valentine's unwelcome twin, someone to be either insulted or avoided. He was the first person to bring my body fully awake, and he and I both knew that if he'd not had his own code of honor, he could have gone much farther with the awakening than he did.

With the improvement in my grades and in Valentine's

appearance, it was a rare day when my mother did not let me go to Sycamore Lane after school. I spent almost as much time there as Valentine. My role was similar to Gretchen's; neither the dog nor I were points of the triangle formed by Mr. Grey and Kathy and Valentine. We were content to stay on the sidelines, just as long as we could be included.

I became quite good that spring at playing games with Gretchen. One of our favorites was for me to toss a sycamore ball high in the air and tell Gretchen to catch it; she caught the balls and brought them back to me without biting through them and scattering their fluffy insides.

22

Happiness on Sycamore Lane died on a day unsuited to death—a mid-May day, full of color and life. Yellow dandelions garnished the greening grass; purple violets nestled in the damp moss beneath the sycamores. Robins hopped boldly past Gretchen and paused to tug reluctant worms from the earth. The sky was cloudless—a solid blue canvas painted by an artist with only one color on his palette. The breeze was light and teasing; it rearranged Kathy's short brown curls and gently rippled the bed sheet on her clothesline.

I stayed in the backyard and played the sycamore ball game with Gretchen while Valentine pushed the Bissell over the cabbage roses in the living room and entertained Tommy. It was an afternoon much like most of our afternoons—tranquil, enjoyable, until it turned treacherous.

I had gone into the kitchen to join Tommy and Valentine when a car turned into the driveway and a door slammed. The familiar click, click of high heels sounded on the porch. Mrs. Grey was in the kitchen before Valentine could warn Kathy to go home. She sailed past us, not pausing to speak. Tommy ran after her and pulled at her skirt; she jerked open the door with him clinging to her like Broken clung to Lacey, not bringing her to a halt, but mercifully delaying her, giving Kathy time to leap to her feet and disappear across the gully.

Valentine ran to the window; I was by her side in seconds. Mr. Grey reached down and picked up the newspaper from where it had fallen beside his chair. He slowly unfolded it and pretended to read it. Only his sudden pallor said that he was aware of the angry woman crossing the yard toward him.

When she reached him, her arm shot out, and I flinched, thinking she was going to hit him, but her hand stopped short of his face. She shook a dirty envelope at him.

"Do you want to read a letter I got today?"

"No." Mr. Grey did not look at her, did not look interested.

"Maybe you don't have to read it. Maybe you already know what it says."

"I don't know and I don't care."

Mrs. Grey's hand moved, swift as a snake's tongue, and struck his face, leaving a red mark on his cheek. He was as disdainful of the blow as of her words. He ignored her and kept his eyes turned to the newspaper. Her hand shot out again, jerked the newspaper from him, ripped it, and tossed the torn pages to the grass. Robbed of his prop, Mr. Grey retreated behind closed eyelids. His face was impassive.

"Read this." She tossed the envelope on his lap. "Read it. Tell me what you think of it." Strangely, her voice was less angry than her appearance. She sounded as if she was pleading with him to read the letter and assure her that it told a foolish lie. "Read it," she repeated. "Read it."

"I'm not interested in that piece of trash." Mr. Grey leaned back in his chair, eyes still closed. "For God's sake, leave me alone."

She stared at him, willing him to open his eyes, to look at her, to read the letter and deny it. He didn't move, didn't speak.

The only sound came from Tommy as he whined and tugged at his mother's skirt and demanded attention she was not ready to give.

"Valentine," she called, "come get Tommy and take him inside."

"What'll I do?" Valentine muttered.

"What can you do? You have to do what she said. Get Tommy and bring him in here. There's nothing else you can do."

Valentine shook her head. "No, I won't ever do another thing for her. Not after she hit Mr. Grey."

"Then I'll do it." I went out to the yard and knelt beside Tommy and unclasped his fingers from her skirt. I don't think she knew or cared that it was I, not Valentine, who took Tommy into the house and locked the screen door.

She left the wheelchair and walked over to the gully. "Kathy," she shouted.

Mr. Grey came out from behind his closed lids. "What do you want with Kathy?"

"What did *you* want with her?" The anger in her voice told the story. Crazy Gurney's mother had had the last word—it was in the dirty envelope that lay in the grass.

"Leave Kathy alone. She's done nothing to you."

"Nothing? She's done nothing to me? Then let her come out here and say so. Kathy," she raised her voice, "come out right now, or I'll come over there and drag you out."

Accustomed to obeying strength, Kathy opened the screen door and stood on the porch, her thin arms wrapped around the rail.

"Leave Kathy out of this. If you have something to say, say it to me." Mr. Grey's voice was harsh.

"It's a little late for that, isn't it? How dare you tell *me* to leave her out of it? *You* got her into it. *I* didn't." She shouted again, "KATHY, COME OVER HERE! COME READ THIS LETTER I GOT TODAY. IT'S ABOUT YOU."

She swooped down and picked up the envelope and waved it at Kathy. "Here it is. Come and get it. Don't you want to know what it says?"

"No." Kathy's voice trembled. "I don't want to read it."

"You aren't interested in what people think of a married woman who plays around with another woman's husband? You don't want to read about the good time you've been having together? Read it, Kathy. Take your medicine. If you can't stand the heat, you shouldn't have moved into my kitchen. Come read it. Now!"

Kathy left the porch and walked slowly down the steps, but Mr. Grey stopped her before she reached the gully.

"Get back in your house, Kathy. Go. And don't come out again, no matter what she says. Go."

Kathy turned and fled.

Mrs. Grey carried the envelope over to the wheelchair and dropped it in Mr. Grey's lap. It fluttered to the grass. He ran the wheels of his chair back and forth over it, pressing it into the ground.

"That's what I think of that piece of trash. It belongs in the dirt, like the filth it is. Leave it there and go into the house and shut up. You're making a fool of yourself."

"It's too late for me to make a fool of myself. You did that to me a long time ago, and you've done it to me too many times. I should have known you couldn't change. I should have learned my lesson. I've been a fool all right.

209

I honest-to-God thought things were different now." Mrs. Grey made no effort to salvage the letter. It no longer mattered; something much uglier and more lasting than an old woman's spite was in the yard.

"I'm not listening to any more of this nonsense." Mr. Grey rolled his chair toward the house. "I'm going in, and if you have any pride at all, you'll stop playing the fool in front of the girls and Tommy. You're hysterical. Hysterical and ridiculous."

"No, I'm not hysterical. Ridiculous, yes. Ridiculous to think you could ever change. And I'm curious too, Tom. Very curious. Just tell me one thing. Why in the name of God did you do this to me? Haven't I had enough grief? Haven't you had enough women? Why did you have to add that poor little fool to your collection? What can you possibly see in her? Just tell me, Tom, what can you possibly see in Kathy Flint?"

"Things you know nothing about," he said. "Gentleness, joy, kindness. And love. Lots of love."

23

So the innocent little backyard love affair ended, but it did not die gently. Its death throes were savage. After she killed the romance, Mrs. Grey did not let it rest in peace. She kicked the corpse every waking moment, reminding Mr. Grey that once it had lived but now it was dead. The dirge began each evening as soon as she arrived, and continued beyond the time Valentine left. Occasionally I was there to listen to it.

"She's really terrible," I said one evening as Valentine and I listened to the woman's sarcastic reference to a wheelchair Romeo. "I don't know how Mr. Grey puts up with it."

"I don't think he even hears her. It's as if he has a knob inside that he can turn off so he doesn't hear a word she says. He tunes her out."

"I wish I had a knob like that. I don't know how to act when she says those things."

"Do what Mr. Grey does. Ignore her. That's what I do. I just get busy and think about something else. So she really ends up talking just to herself."

I tried to take her advice, but it didn't help. I was apprehensive and embarrassed during the evening attacks. I didn't know where to turn my eyes, and I couldn't direct my thoughts in other directions. I didn't share Valentine's talent for blanking out things I didn't want to see or hear. Nor did I share her courage, which let her vent her resentment by thumbing her nose at Mrs. Grey's back.

"If she ever turns around and catches you doing that, you'll be out of a job," I warned.

Valentine wasn't impressed. "She won't catch me. There's not a chance of a snowball in hell that she can turn around fast enough to catch me. Even Lacey can't catch me, and she *knows* I do it to her. Don't worry about Mrs. Pain-in-the-Ass firing me. She won't. She thinks I'm on her side."

"Why?"

"Because after she got that letter she made me promise I'd keep an eye on Mr. Grey and tell her if he ever speaks to Kathy again."

"You made a promise like that?"

"Sure. I don't mind at all making a promise I don't plan to keep. I'm not Black. It doesn't bother me to tell a lie. Especially to a pain-in-the-ass."

"How does she know Kathy won't come over here while you're in school?"

"She doesn't know for sure, but she says that until school ends and I'm here all day she'll have to take it for granted that Kathy has learned a lesson about playing in her own backyard."

If Mrs. Grey had a false accomplice in Valentine, she had a very real one in Tommy. There had never been any warmth or closeness between Tommy and his father, and Mrs. Grey mercilessly exploited that. Each evening she reminded Tommy, "Your daddy is bad." The first time she said it, the afternoon when she rushed home with the letter, Tommy asked, "What did Daddy do?" and Mrs. Grey answered, "Your daddy played with someone else's toy."

"That's not so bad," Tommy said, "I do that sometimes."

"But your daddy took another boy's toy and did bad things to it. You wouldn't do that, would you?"

"Oh, no." The child's self-righteous reaction marked the beginning of a parody of the relationship between the man and the boy. Tommy enjoyed his moral superiority over the man who had always been neutral toward him— the man who could listen to tantrums, look at tears, witness pouts, and remain totally unmoved, completely disinterested.

"Daddy's bad, Daddy's bad," Tommy chanted one day as he sat astride a shortened broomstick and galloped around the wheelchair. As always, Mr. Grey's eyes closed against the taunts thrown at him that miserable summer. The stirring of Kathy's kitchen curtains on the breezeless afternoon told us that Kathy was hearing Tommy's insults, seeing Mr. Grey's withdrawal.

Day nursery ended two weeks earlier than school; with Tommy home all day, his mother ruthlessly manipulated him.

"I want you to watch Daddy every minute, and tell me if he and Mrs. Flint speak to each other. Will you do that for Mommy?"

His eager assent earned him hugs and kisses and praise . . . and cold hard cash. Mrs. Grey brought home a china piggy bank one evening and gave it to Tommy. The two of them sat on the living room rug and ceremoniously rubbed pennies against the cabbage roses until the copper gleamed, then she showed him how to drop the coins through the slot in the pig's painted head.

"I hate that pig. I'd like to break it into a thousand pieces," Valentine muttered one day, but a few days later she herself dropped two pennies through the slot, feeding the pig to bribe Tommy. It was her penalty for losing her temper when Mr. Grey ordered Tommy to quit throwing rocks at Gretchen, and Tommy impudently told his father, "Shut up. You can't tell me what to do. You're a bad daddy." To prove his point, Tommy threw another rock, missing Gretchen by several feet, but hitting Valentine. Valentine grabbed Tommy and shook him. She pried another rock out of his clenched fist and threw it in the gully. Tommy wailed. He threw himself facedown on the grass and kicked and screamed.

"You're in for it now, Valentine," I predicted. "When he tells his mother that you shook him, you're done for around here."

"Yeh. You're right. I'd better see what I can do about shutting the little brat up." Valentine knelt beside Tommy, wiped the tears from his cheeks, and promised him a walk every afternoon and the biggest piece of ice the next time the ice truck rolled around. Tommy accepted all the bribes and held out for more. Before negotiations were complete, Valentine had promised to feed the pig. That night she sneaked into Big's coffee can, and the next day she and Tommy rubbed the pennies on the cabbage roses and he fed them to the painted pig. He kept his part of the bargain and didn't tell his mother that Valentine had made him cry. Valentine learned a lesson in endurance. Bad or good, Tommy's behavior from that time on was insignificant.

"I don't care what the little brat says or does," Valentine declared. "I have to keep my temper so I can stay with Mr. Grey. I'm all he has now, just me and Gretchen."

When her taunts of "parasite" and "cripple" and "wheelchair Romeo" seemed not to bother Mr. Grey, the

214

woman turned to other methods to hurt him. She discontinued delivery of the daily newspaper. She removed a tube from the radio and carried it to work with her, ensuring that he would have no diversion, no link to the world outside Sycamore Lane. If she wanted to listen to the radio, which she rarely did, she reinserted the tube and sat close by the set, her ear against the speaker, the volume low. The absent radio tube hurt Valentine more than Mr. Grey. She could no longer listen to make-believe miseries while suffering real ones. She refused to seek Lacey's help in keeping up with the soap operas. She wouldn't give Lacey the satisfaction of knowing there was trouble on Sycamore Lane.

Big suffered vicariously from Mrs. Grey's newest form of revenge. When Valentine returned to the flat one sticky-hot June evening, she stumbled over Big who lay sprawled on the living room floor. He held a rare bottle of beer in his hand. His chest was bare; his chin rough and blue-stubbed. He was completely relaxed, at peace with his world, listening to "Amos 'n' Andy." His placid contentment in the midst of the early heat wave, which had lasted for more than a week and had added physical discomfort to Valentine's emotional anguish, brought out the worst in her.

"Why are you sprawled there with your undershirt off?"

Determined not to let Valentine get under his skin, Big ignored her. He propped himself up on his elbows, tipped back his head, and gulped the cold beer. "Damn, that sure tasted good," he said and settled back down on the floor.

"You smell bad." Valentine stood at Big's feet, wrinkled her nose, pinched it, and glared at him.

Big stretched, yawned, reached for the bottle and tipped it again. "Yeh. I sure do. I worked hard today. Painted the ticket booth. Did a damn good job of it, too, if I do say so myself."

Valentine renewed her attack. "The radio's too loud. I heard it clear up to the corner."

"Yeh. It is sort of loud. Lacey's trying to hear it out in the kitchen. This is the night Madame Queen and The Kingfish are finally really going to square off. Lacey and I don't want to miss a word of it."

He returned his stare to the Crosley.

Frustrated by her failure to transfer her own misery to somebody else, Valentine stepped over Big and turned the knob on the Crosley, cutting off The Kingfish's encounter with Madame Queen before it began.

"What's wrong with the radio?" Lacey popped her head around the door and broke the sudden silence.

"For Christ's sake!" Big leaped to his feet, bumping his elbow against the beer bottle and leaving a foamy island on the dirty floor. "What's the big idea, Valentine? I told you Lacey and I want to hear this program. What the hell do you think you're doing?" He turned to Lacey. "Instead of asking what's wrong with the radio, you'd better ask what's wrong with this crazy kid. She tore in here and jumped all over me and gave me hell for stuff that's none of her damned business, and then for just plain goddamned meanness she turned off 'Amos 'n' Andy.' She knew damned well she'd get my goat. What's the big idea, Valentine?"

She couldn't tell him the truth. How could she say she loved Mr. Grey and hated Mrs. Grey and that she missed Kathy and was furious with Tommy?

"That's a lousy program. It makes fun of colored people."

"What the hell are you talking about? They ain't making fun of colored people—they *are* colored. Amos and Andy *are* niggers. They sure as hell ain't making fun of themselves. That's the way niggers act. That's the way niggers talk. Where do you get those screwball ideas?" Big roared.

Valentine turned to what she knew from past experience would be a sure way to get under Big's skin.

"Mr. Grey says Amos and Andy are white men pretending to be colored just to make money."

"CRAP!" Big's fist thudded against the dusty table. "Crap from a crip, that's what that kind of talk is. What the hell does Grey know about making money? He sits on his dead ass and looks down his nose at working people while his wife keeps him. What the hell does Grey know about work or niggers or money or anything but how to sit on his butt and let a woman take care of him?"

I knew there was real trouble ahead. Big's angry words echoed Mrs. Grey's. Valentine could not fight the woman, but she could fight Big.

"Don't you ever say a word about Mr. Grey AGAIN!" she screamed. "Don't you ever say another mean word about him. If you do, I'll run away from this hog pen and you'll never see me again as long as I live. NEVER! Not if I live for a hundred years."

She ran from the flat. I followed her, but she was halfway up the block before I got to the bottom of the stairs. Dusk was closing in, and I didn't dare go after her. My mother's rule about not leaving Fourth Street after dark was very strict.

I returned to the flat and sat on the steps and waited for Valentine. A couple of times Lacey came to the landing and tried to sound casual when she asked if I happened to know where Valentine had gone and when she would come back. Once Big came out and walked to the corner and looked up and down the street. He didn't say anything to me, nor I to him. Valentine had not returned when my mother called me in and made me go to bed. I couldn't go to sleep, but I didn't want my mother to know Valentine had run away, so I went to bed and lay awake listening for news from the flat next door. Shortly after the town clock struck midnight, I heard the creak of the downstairs door and Valentine crept up the stairs. I rolled from my bed and tiptoed to the landing.

"Where have you been?" I whispered.

"I went to the movies. The ticket taker recognized me and let me in free."

"What did you see?"

"*The Bride Comes Home.* Claudette Colbert was in it."

"Was it good?"

"It was okay, I guess." Her lukewarm response told me that to Valentine nothing was good anymore, not even the movies.

"Valentine." Lacey's voice called from inside the flat, "Is that you? Are you all right?"

"Yes."

We waited for Lacey to scold Valentine, but Lacey went back to bed without saying another word.

"You're going to win a rabbit at the matinee at the Hippodrome next week," Black told Valentine the next morning.

"How do you know?" Valentine was skeptical.

"I heard Big and Lacey talking after you tore out of the flat last night. It sure beats me, Valentine, how you get away with things. If I'd pitched a fit like you did last night, Big would have flattened my ass. But when you pitched a fit, he just sat around and stewed about how to get back on the good side of you. It sure beats me."

"Oh, make sense," Valentine interrupted. "They draw the lucky name at the Saturday matinee. How do you know I'll win the rabbit?"

"Big and the stage manager are in cahoots. Big says he can fix it for your name to be pulled out of the hat."

"Why are Big and Lacey letting me have a rabbit? They never let me have a dog or a cat."

"Because you scared the shit out of them. They thought you'd run away for good last night. They wanted to call the cops to look for you, but I talked them out of it. Hell, I knew you'd come back. You're stupid, but you ain't so stupid you'd take off with no place to go. You ain't got the guts for that. I have, but you ain't."

Valentine stopped walking and sat on the curb. She didn't want Black to come to Sycamore Lane, but she did want to hear the rest of his story.

"Big thought you might quit being so shitty if you had a pet. Lacey said what she always says—that they can't afford to feed another mouth. Then Big said, what about a rabbit? Big says a rabbit eats clover and grass and carrot tops and stuff like that, things we can get for free, and that's when Big comes up with the idea of fixing it so you can win the rabbit. Big says he can bring home the pen they keep it in at the Hippodrome."

Valentine asked no more questions. She jumped to her feet and skipped up the road. For the first time in weeks she whistled. I followed in the wake of "Don't Give Up the Ship."

It was Broken who finally named Rabbit. All the Harts offered suggestions, Big preferring to christen it Henry, after the cooperative stage manager. Lacey objected, saying that Henry wasn't in line with the rest of the family nicknames. She thought Lettuce Hart would be appropriate. That idea was promptly hooted down by the rest of the group.

"We could name it Sweet," Lacey said, "but if the new baby is a girl, I'd sort of like to nickname her Sweet. It would be too confusing to have two Sweets in the house. Maybe we should name it something rabbity, like Peter."

"Too common," Valentine objected.

Black wanted to call it Shotgun, in honor of the constant trail it left behind it as it hopped through the flat, but Valentine turned nose up and thumbs down on that idea.

Broken settled the question by pointing to the animal and saying, without stuttering, lisping, or mewing, "Rabbit."

Broken's unexpected break through the language barrier delighted all the Harts so much that a sign was immediately penciled and tacked to the crate. RABBIT, the board proclaimed. The box was placed beneath the kitchen stove where its proximity to the table kept Rabbit well supplied with small and frequent sacrifices. Along with bits and pieces from family meals, Rabbit's diet included red clover and green plantain, which Valentine and Tommy gathered from among the weeds along Sycamore Lane. Black donated a fresh carrot each day. The carrots always had dirt clinging to them, but nobody asked Black if they had been recently requisitioned from somebody's garden. Again, Black's reputation for telling the truth spared him questions.

Lacey made her contribution to Rabbit's well-being by offering to clean his cage daily, and actually cleaning it once a week.

Rabbit was impartial with his affections, wiggling his pink nose at all his admirers with equal friendliness. He was a peacemaker, bringing a temporary armistice to the war waging between Valentine and the other Harts.

24

When school ended in June, Valentine was on Sycamore Lane from early morning until early evening. It was then that she offered to carry the newspapers to Mr. Grey.

"I can bring yesterday's paper with me every morning, Lacey just uses them to wrap the garbage in after she reads them."

"No." Mr. Grey patted Valentine's hand. "Newspapers don't mean that much to me. If it gives Tina some sort of sick pleasure to think that she's depriving me of something I want, let her do it. I don't care anymore."

"I don't think it gives her a darned bit of pleasure," Valentine mused. "She gets meaner every day, so she must not be feeling any better."

"Yes. She hurts herself more than she could ever hurt me. She doesn't have the power to hurt me. She doesn't mean anything to me. She can't make me feel good, so she can't make me feel bad. She can't make me happy, so she can't make me sad. Nothing she can do or say can make the slightest difference to me, and she knows it. She'll wear out this sick jealousy sooner or later and until she does, all we can do is grin and bear it. Or at least bear it. She absolutely cannot hurt me, Valentine, so don't worry your pretty little head about it."

He was dead wrong. She did find a way to make him open his eyes, listen to her, ask for an armistice, beg for a compromise. I don't know why she hadn't found it sooner, and why we ourselves hadn't anticipated it. Perhaps it was because Kathy was no longer one of us. Occasionally we saw her walk down the path on her way to the grocery store or hang laundry on the clothesline or weed her small garden. She never looked our way, never waved, never smiled. Her only callers were the insurance man who stopped once a week to collect a small premium, and the iceman who stopped twice a week. Kathy was alone, more isolated than we were. She had only empty days and nights, and the guilty knowledge that her short-lived happiness had brought days and nights of unhappiness to the man she loved. Kathy was removed from the battle between a man and his wife—until Mrs. Grey drew her back into it.

I was in the kitchen with Valentine, drying the dishes as she washed them, when Mrs. Grey came in.

She spoke loudly. "Valentine, do you know when Flint will be home again?" The question asked in the kitchen was obviously intended to be heard in the bedroom where Mr. Grey had retreated for the evening.

"No," Valentine muttered.

Mrs. Grey shrugged. "No matter. The point is, he definitely *will* be home sometime. When he gets here, I'll have news for him. No hurry, though. The news will keep. It kept for a year, so a few more weeks or months won't change anything. It will still be news to Flint, whenever he hears it. Bad news."

She hummed with a false happiness as she brushed crumbs from the oilcloth.

In his haste to reach her, to reason with her, Mr. Grey bumped his wheelchair against the door as he left the bedroom and entered the kitchen. Triumph was on the woman's face, but her voice was composed. "Run along home, girls. I'll finish the dishes. It seems my husband has a sudden desire to be with me."

Valentine untied her apron and left the house without speaking. I followed. We stopped at the edge of the yard and crouched in the shadows to listen to the conversation that came from the open window.

"Do anything you want to, to me, but for God's sake leave Kathy alone. She's had enough trouble."

Mrs. Grey's laugh was harsh, as unreal as her humming.

"Kathy Flint doesn't even know the meaning of the word yet. But she will. Believe me, she will. She'll learn it when Flint comes home and I have a talk with him. I won't rush right over with my news. I'll wait until he's drunk. Then I'll pay a neighborly call on Mr. and Mrs. Flint, and young Mrs. Flint will learn a good lesson about how to stay out of trouble."

"You can't do that. You know he might kill her. You've heard him when he's drunk. You've heard him beat her."

"Yes. I've heard him, and so have you. You've heard him more than I. But it didn't matter, did it? You knew all along what kind of man Flint is. You knew it since the day we moved here. But you didn't let that stop you when you needed a woman as a sop to your vanity. You had to be worshiped, and all your other worshipers forgot you the minute you landed in that wheelchair."

"My God, Tina, isn't there any pity in you?"

"Yes, there is. Believe it or not, I pity that little fool next door. I'm sorry for her that she had the misfortune to be the only woman available for you to try out your charm on. To see if you still have what it takes to make a woman make a fool of herself over you. Yes, I pity her. You're the one who didn't. But maybe you will when Flint comes home."

"Do you want that on your conscience?"

"On *my* conscience? On *my* conscience? You have the nerve to talk about *my* conscience? You started this thing. I'm going to finish it. I'm going to teach you a lesson you won't forget. For once in your life you're going to have to face up to what you've done."

"Don't do it, Tina. Don't do it. I'm begging you not to do it. I haven't seen or spoken to Kathy since that filthy letter came. I swear to you I will never speak to her again. Isn't that enough to satisfy you?"

"Not nearly enough. Not nearly."

"Then I'll promise more. I'll promise to try to work things out between us, Tina. We've had disagreements before, and we've worked them out. Why can't we put this whole thing behind us and start all over again?"

His voice was soft, seductive, reminding me of how he sounded on the morning he gave Valentine the four-leaf clover and the afternoon he gave Kathy the world on a small painted pencil sharpener.

Evening had turned into night. Valentine and I crept closer to the window.

"Maybe the doctors were wrong. Maybe it isn't too late to try to be what we used to be with each other." His words were intimate, suggestive.

"That'll do the trick," Valentine whispered. "She'll fall for that. That's all she wanted in the first place—a piece of ass from him. They'll make up now. Just wait and see."

We tiptoed across the wet grass and crouched below

224

the window, not wanting to miss a word of the woman's surrender.

"You really think it's that simple, don't you, Tom? You really are that vain, that sure of yourself and of me, to think that after all the times I've lowered myself to beg you to touch me, humiliated myself to coax you to hold me, to love me in any way you can, and you've turned your back on me, you really think now that all you have to do is speak to me in a soft voice and make useless promises and I'll fall into your arms like a lovesick schoolgirl. It's too late, Tom. Too late. You've made a fool of me once too often. There's nothing you can do or say now that will change anything. When Flint comes home, he'll hear straight from my mouth the words I read in that obscene letter. Then he can do whatever he wants to about it. And you know what that will be. He's a stupid Irishman, but he's a *man*—he won't hurt *you*. He won't hit a cripple. You're protected, Tom. Your weakness is your strength. You know who will pay for your selfish ego. You know."

Valentine pulled me back toward the path, away from the window. "Let's get out of here. I can't stand any more of this." No words followed us as we left. Obviously everything had been said.

Mr. Grey sent Valentine over to talk to Kathy the next morning. "Go before Tommy wakes up. Ask Kathy when Flint will be home."

Kathy opened the door before Valentine tapped on it. "I saw you coming across the gully. Something's wrong, isn't it?" Kathy held a summer skirt in her hand; thread dangled from the side seam, which she was deepening.

"When is Flint coming home again, Kathy?"

Kathy paled. "As far as I know, he'll be here right after Labor Day. He's in Colorado now, working the early fruit crop. Why?"

"She's going to tell him about the letter. She's going

225

to give him time to get drunk and then she's going to come over and tell him what the old woman said about you. She wants Flint to beat up on you, and she wants Mr. Grey to hear him do it. She's trying to hurt him by having Flint hurt you."

"I was afraid she'd do that," Kathy said. "That's why I haven't spoken or waved to any of you. I hoped she'd leave me out of it if I never had any more to do with Tom. But I knew all along that sooner or later she'd tell Flint."

"What are you going to do, Kathy?"

"I don't know. There's not much I can do, except hope she's just making threats she won't keep. Maybe she's just saying it to torment Tom."

"Flint will be home around Labor Day," Valentine reported to Mr. Grey. "Kathy's really scared. She says she doesn't know what to do."

"There's only one thing she can do. Go over there right now and tell her she has to leave town. Tell her I said if she loves me at all she'll run away as fast and as far as she can. Make her promise to leave today. Don't stop talking until she agrees to get out of Marietta. Tell her Flint might kill her if she stays. Tell her."

Valentine turned to me. "Go stand by Tommy's bedroom door. If he wakes up, go in and read him a story. Don't let him get out of bed."

"Okay." I went in and watched Tommy sleep.

Within minutes Valentine had delivered the message and had returned with Kathy's reply. "I might as well have saved my breath. Kathy says she won't leave town. She says she can't make a promise she can't keep. She says she can't afford to go anywhere else to live. She can't get a job because she doesn't know how to do anything, and anyway, she says, there aren't any jobs even for people who do know how to do something. But she says the main reason she won't leave is because now she can at least look out of her window and see you. And she says that even if she did want to go, she can't. She doesn't have any money. Just enough to buy food for this week. Flint sends the rent to the landlord each month and then sends Kathy just enough to get by on from week to week. She says Flint can't hurt her any more than she's already hurting. She says even if he kills her, it doesn't matter. She says nobody can kill a corpse, and she says she's already dead inside. She won't leave, Mr. Grey. That's all there is to it. Kathy won't leave. What are we going to do?"

"Let me think," he said. "I need time to think."

Valentine did some thinking of her own that evening as we leaned against the elm, keeping a wary eye out to be sure Black wasn't sneaking up on us.

"Kathy should sue for a divorce," Valentine said. "Tomorrow morning I'm going over there and tell her that if she won't leave town, she has to leave Flint. I think that's a swell idea. I'm surprised none of us thought of it before. Divorce works out real well for lots of Lacey's friends. I hear them talk about it. Lacey says she herself doesn't believe in divorcing a man unless he's brought home a case of clap but she says she doesn't hold it against women who have got a divorce. And she knows lots of them. Most of them make out real well too, Lacey says. They get alimony and they don't have to put up with having a man underfoot. Yes, that's what Kathy will have to do. Divorce Flint. Then he'll have to send her money and he won't be allowed to pester her. I'll tell her first thing in the morning."

"What did Kathy say?"

I ran up the block to meet Valentine the next evening, to ask the question that had been on my mind all day.

"She says it won't work. She says it takes money and time to get a divorce and she doesn't have either. And she says that even if Flint finds out about her and Mr. Grey, *he* won't get a divorce, and he would never let her get one. She says Flint is a Catholic, and Catholics just don't ever get divorced, no matter what happens, or they'll get kicked out of the church and live in hell forever. And she says that Flint never pays much attention to religion most of the time, but he's superstitious about some of the things Catholics believe in. Like wearing that St. Christopher's medal to keep him safe. She says we might as well quit thinking about a way out for her. She says she'll just have to take her medicine when Flint gets home and get it over with."

"Do you think Kathy knows what she's talking about? Maybe she's wrong. Maybe some Catholics *do* believe in divorce."

"Yeh. I'll ask Lacey. Lacey doesn't know a heck of a lot about some things, but every once in a while she knows what she's talking about. Let's go ask her."

We went back to the flat and tried to look nonchalant as we ambled into the kitchen and sat down at the table with Lacey, who was stirring her coffee and studying the *True Confessions* magazine propped against the cornmeal mush pan.

"Lacey," Valentine said, "what do you know about the Catholic religion?"

Lacey glanced up from her story. She looked slightly surprised at the question and even more surprised at Valentine's friendly attitude. They hadn't been getting along well together for several weeks, since most of Valentine's conversational approaches to Lacey began with criticism, progressed to insults, and terminated in shouts and slammed doors.

"Oh, I know a lot about the Catholic religion," Lacey said. "What do you want to know?"

"Anything you can tell me. I'm just wondering why the Catholic kids go to a different school than we do and why their teachers wear those black outfits. . . . Just tell me anything you know about Catholics."

Lacey, happy to be recognized at last by Valentine as a credible authority on at least one thing, closed the *True*

Confessions magazine after marking her place with a sticky fork and sat back to enlighten Valentine.

"Well, the blackbirds—that's what I call the nuns, but the Catholics call them sisters—anyway, the blackbirds wear those funny outfits because they don't have any hair on their heads. They shave it all off, quick as it grows on. Yep, they're as bald as a bean under those hats. And Catholic kids go to their own schools because they're mean little devils and the priests and blackbirds can keep an eye on them at a Catholic school and make them go confess their sins every so often. And Catholic women get caught a lot because they ain't allowed to do anything to keep from getting caught. Catholics are taught that the only reason they should ever make love is to make babies. Yeh, the Catholics really believe in making babies. In fact, I happen to know for a fact that that's why the blackbirds always live right next door to the priests. Makes it easier to get together. . . . They're always making babies and sending them off to places where there ain't many Catholics so when the babies grow up they can make more Catholic babies. The Catholics have a real thing going with babies. They want to fill up the whole world with mackerel snappers. Anything else you want to know?"

"What do they think about getting a divorce?"

Lacey was an authority on that subject too. "Dead set against it. No way in God's world would a Catholic get a divorce. No way. Which just shows how dumb they are. Anything else you want to know?"

Valentine wrinkled her forehead. "Suppose for some reason a Catholic did get divorced. What happens? Do they get kicked out of the church?"

"Oh, it's lots worse than that, Valentine. If a mackerel snapper doesn't do what the priest tells him to do, he'll go straight down to hell and stay there until a bunch of other Catholics go to church and pay lots of money to burn candles to get him out of hell."

229

"You mean if they burn enough candles he'll get up to heaven?"

"Well, I don't really think so myself. I think the mackerel snappers are headed for hell no matter how many candles they burn, but it does make a lot of money for the church. And who knows"—Lacey was big-hearted about the infidels and their odd practices—"who knows . . . maybe the candles do help get some of the Catholics up off the hot seat. Probably some Catholics are worse than others. Just like some regular people are worse than others. Anything else you want to know, Valentine?"

"Yeh, as a matter of fact, there is. Why do people call Catholics mackerel snappers?"

"Because if they don't eat fish every Friday they'll go to a place hotter than the oil they fry the fish in and they'll fry there for a long, long time. Anything else you want to know about Catholics, Valentine?"

Valentine rose and stretched.

"No, not tonight. If I think of any other questions about Catholics, I'll come and ask. Thanks, Lacey."

"That's okay, Valentine." Lacey returned to her *True Confessions*.

After hearing Lacey's learned dissertation about Catholicism, I viewed the Catholic church, which was a few blocks away from the flat, with a new interest. Its activities sounded much more exciting than the Sunday afternoon dinner-on-the-grounds so popular with the Presbyterian congregation.

Mr. Grey dispatched another message to Kathy the next day.

"Tell her when she finds out definitely when Flint will be home, she's to send us a signal. Then you go over and find out when he's expected. Until then, I think it's best to stay away from Kathy."

Valentine crossed the gully and returned in moments with the signal.

"Kathy says she'll whistle 'Smoke Gets in Your Eyes.' "

"Why did she choose such a pretty song to whistle for such an ugly reason?" I asked.

"She said it reminds her of last autumn when she and Mr. Grey were so happy."

I lay awake that night and thought about love, tried to understand why last autumn's love affair had been innocent and tender until dirty words stuffed into a filthy envelope turned it into something indecent, threatening. I was perplexed, and when I tried to talk about it with Valentine the next day, she turned away, pretended not to hear my questions. For once, not even Valentine had the answers.

25

Valentine didn't work on the Fourth of July. Big's dream of a family holiday came true a year late. "I've got free passes for all of us," he said, "so come early and stay late." We left the flat promptly after breakfast and hurried out to the fairgrounds, with Lacey carrying Broken on her hip while Valentine and I skipped along beside her and Black ran ahead of us. We felt quite affluent that day. Coins jingled in our pockets. Valentine contributed a quarter from her wages, Black added another quarter from bottle refunds, my mother donated several dimes, and Lacey again lightened Big's coffee can.

When we reached the midway, Valentine and I stood beside the merry-go-round and watched Lacey and Broken bob up and down on the gaudy horses. Black stood nearby for reasons of his own. "If Broken pees on anyone, I want to see what happens," he said. Broken didn't, so Lacey stayed on the horse with him until she ran out of nickels. Black ran off to his own pursuits, and Valentine and I rode the Ferris wheel. Our only concern that day was how to keep our dirndl skirts clutched tightly between our knees as we rose up in the air and swooped back toward the earth.

When all our coins were spent, we turned to free entertainment. We strolled over to the livestock exhibit and tried to ignore Black's vulgarities about the bulls and the stallions. We elbowed our way through the crowd gathered in front of the freak show platform and listened, fascinated, to the description of the peculiar creature hidden backstage behind the tent curtains.

"Step right up, ladies and gentlemen," the barker invited. "Step right up and get your ticket now. See the only half-man, half-woman in captivity."

"Do kids get in free?" Black yelled up at the barker, who scowled down at Black and said, "Dry up, sonny. You ain't even dry behind the ears yet. This is a show for grown-ups. Not for snot-nosed kids."

"What did you say you've got behind that curtain?" Black asked innocently, and the barker fell right into Black's trap.

"Step right up, ladies and gentlemen," he lifted his megaphone and shouted again to the crowd, "and get your ticket now. See the only half-man, half-woman in captivity."

"Ah, tell it to go fuck itself," Black yelled, and the crowd roared.

Our holiday ended in a blaze of glory at midnight when, tired but content, we strolled back to the flat and Big nailed a huge pinwheel to the trunk of the elm tree on the corner.

"Here, Valentine." Big gave Valentine a box of farmer matches and stood aside. "Light the fuse."

The fuse caught fire and the pinwheel twirled and

whirled and painted the clouds with the only sunshine Valentine saw that summer. The day had been a lovely escape from the ugliness of reality. Valentine held Big's hand on the way up the stairs, and Big beamed.

Holidays end; reality endures.

One morning in mid-July we watched the mailman give a postcard to Kathy, and we heard her whistle "Smoke Gets in Your Eyes," as she read the card and walked slowly into her house.

"She knows when Flint's coming home," Valentine whispered to me over Tommy's head. I sat with Tommy later that day while he napped and Valentine crossed the gully and returned with a message.

"Flint won't be home until Labor Day," she told Mr. Grey. "That's almost two months from now. Two months is a long time."

"Sometimes two months can be an eternity," Mr. Grey said, "but other times it can be as brief as a snap of the fingers."

"But at least we know Kathy's safe for the rest of the summer."

"Yes. She's had a reprieve, Valentine. But not a pardon. And Labor Day will come just as surely as tomorrow. I have to think. I have to think." He sounded desperate.

While Tommy napped the next day, Mr. Grey sent Valentine up the narrow steep stairs to the small attic over the kitchen.

"Bring down the rifle that's standing in the corner. It's not loaded, but handle it carefully anyway. Hold it with the barrel pointed up."

Valentine gingerly carried the rifle down the stairs and gave it to Mr. Grey. He checked it to be sure it was not loaded, then balanced it on his shoulder and aimed it around the living room, squinting down its length, getting the feel of it again.

"There's a small kit in my top dresser drawer," he

said. "A metal box. Bring it to me, Valentine, and bring me one of my undershirts."

The closest Valentine and I had ever been to a gun was in a front-row seat at the Hippodrome watching Ken Maynard and Hoot Gibson skillfully twirl their Colt .45's. We watched, hypnotized by the unfamiliar closeness of a deadly weapon, while Mr. Grey cleaned the gun and polished its butt.

"Are you going to shoot Flint?"

Mr. Grey laughed at Valentine's question. "Heavens, no. Can you really imagine me shooting anyone?"

Valentine squirmed and looked uncomfortable while she considered the possibility. Then she relaxed and smiled. "No, not really."

None of us heard Tommy get up from his nap. His bare feet were noiseless as he padded into the living room. He was on his way to the gun before we could head him off or stop him. When he reached up to touch it, Valentine took his arm. "Let's go outside and swing." I took his other arm and the three of us left the room. When we returned, the gun was gone.

"What happened after I left?" I had been jittery for the rest of the day after I went home. I waited restlessly for Valentine to arrive so we could discuss the gun and its purpose.

"Mrs. Pain-in-the-Ass found the gun. Mr. Grey hid it under the cushions on the couch. The first thing the little brat said when his mother asked him what his father had done that day was, 'He cleaned a gun.' She went through the house hunting the gun and when she found it she gave Tommy a nickel to feed to his pig."

"Was she mad at you? She must have known you got it down for Mr. Grey."

"Yeh. I couldn't lie my way out of that one. When she asked me why I got it for him, I just looked dumb and said because he told me to. And he told her that was right,

I did what he told me to. And then she told me not to take any more orders from him, and I said okay, I wouldn't. Then she began to make fun of Mr. Grey. Thanked him for cleaning the gun. Said she'd forgotten they had it, and now that he'd been good enough to remind her and to get it all shined and polished up, she'd take it to the pawn shop right away and see what she could get for it. And she called him Buck Jones in a wheelchair. Laughed at him. She laughed until she cried and she kept making fun of him, calling him a dime store hero. They had a real battle. He told her she was sick, and she said yes, she was, but she'd be better after Kathy Flint took her medicine, and got what was coming to her. And then she asked him if fooling around with that skinny little tramp next door was worth what he was going through now and he said yes, it was, and rolled himself into the bedroom. She was still yelling when I left. It was awful. She gets meaner every day."

It was true that with each day that passed, Mrs. Grey's acts of revenge were pettier, more degrading. One morning she ordered Valentine not to launder Mr. Grey's shirts.

"He doesn't need a clean shirt every day. He's not going anywhere."

"I hate her," Valentine said. "I think I hate her even more than Mr. Grey does."

When Valentine returned to the flat that evening and found Big bare-chested, she attacked. "You look like a bum. The hoboes down at the freight yard look better than you."

"Shut up, Miss High-and-Mighty," Lacey shot back. "It's none of your business how Big looks."

"Oh yeh? Well, maybe it matters to his boss. If Big doesn't start taking better care of how he looks, he just might find himself out of work again."

"Oh, shut up." Big echoed Lacey. "As long as I do my job right, my boss doesn't give a good goddamn how I look. I ain't appearing on the screen. Anyway, Miss High-and-Mighty, if you're rubbing it into me again that I don't look as good as that High Muckety-Muck you work for, just remember this: I pay my way. Nobody keeps me. And that's more than you can say for Mr. High-Muckety-Muck."

Valentine stamped her foot and shouted, "THAT'S NOT FAIR! Mr. Grey would work if he could. It's not his fault he's stuck in a wheelchair. It would serve you right if some day you found out what it's like not to be able to work."

The next day, Big fell from a ladder while he was painting the theater marquee and sprained his ankle. When Valentine returned home and saw Big's right foot wrapped in bandages much whiter than any Lacey could have provided, she knew without asking that Big had been treated by a doctor—a rare occurrence in the Hart household, where Lacey acted as doctor, nurse, and all-around medical expert when ordinary physical crises developed. Only a disaster could have forced Lacey to pay a real doctor.

"What happened to you?" Valentine stared at Big's foot.

Big shifted his weight, seeking comfort. "I fell off the ladder at work today. Sprained my ankle. The doc says I'll have to stay off it for a while."

"We'll have to tighten our belts," Lacey said. "Big don't get paid when he don't work."

Valentine frowned. She knew too well from past experience what Lacey meant when she said they'd have to tighten their belts. Even worse than the thought of tightening the belt, though, was the fear that the free passes to the movies would no longer be coming her way. I read the question on Valentine's face, and I hoped she'd be smart enough not to put words to it. But, as usual, she rushed headlong into trouble.

"Do I still get into the movies free?"

Lacey stopped plumping out the pillow beneath Big's

leg and spoke sharply. "For Pete's sake, Valentine, is that all you've got to say about Big being hurt? He's in pain. And all you care about is whether you're going to get a free pass to the movies. The answer is no. No, you won't. Not until Big gets back on the job again."

Valentine's frown deepened. "Serves him right," she declared. "He's always poking fun at other people who can't work. Now he knows what it feels like. It's good enough for him. He had it coming."

Lacey swung away from Big and whipped her flat open palm hard across Valentine's face, then looked as amazed by her action as Valentine. Valentine flinched and glared at Lacey, waiting for an apology that did not come.

"That's all I want to hear from you, young lady," Lacey snapped. "You're so high-and-mighty now, let's see what you're like after Big misses a few paydays. Passes to the movies will be the least of your worries. Big's been laid off before, sure, but he's never been laid up. So put this in your pipe and smoke it—you ain't never had it as bad as you're going to have it while Big's foot is propped up on this chair."

Lacey was dead right. While Big was laid up, I learned from visiting the Harts' flat that there are stages of poverty. The first stage wasn't so bad: dishing your own servings of food, just as long as you were sure not to let your eyes get bigger than your stomach. Being hard-up was inconvenient, but if you concentrated on the things you *had*, rather than on the things you *wanted*, the first stage of poverty was bearable.

The second stage added embarrassment to inconvenience. It was the slight knock of the meter man, and his red-faced apology that he hated like hell to do it, but he had his orders. It was waiting for Lacey to serve the food in carefully measured portions. It was pretending not to notice the grocer's frown when he was asked to add a few more items to the already overdue bill. If your hide had been thickened enough by living, the second stage of poverty could be borne.

But the third stage was something altogether different. It was one small meal a day of soup beans without the beans. It was watching a cupboard that had never been completely filled become completely emptied. It was watching Black go out to look for work that he already knew nobody would give him. It was short rations, rumbling stomachs.

Rabbit was the only creature in the Harts' flat who did not go to sleep hungry. The plaintain and clover that Valentine carried home daily kept Rabbit satisfied and plump.

Big had been laid up for two weeks when Valentine was laid off. "I'm taking an unpaid vacation next week," Mrs. Grey told her. "I hate to lose the money, but I need a week at home before Tommy starts school. I can't afford to pay you for the week, so you will have it off too."

Valentine hadn't realized how much the meals on Sycamore Lane meant until they were taken away. By the time she'd been off work for two days her stomach constantly growled at her. I did what I could to help the Harts, but the small bit of food I could forage from my icebox didn't go far toward feeding five people. One day my mother sent a meat loaf over; she put it on a paper plate and sent the charitable offering out with the uncharitable comment that she wasn't going to take a chance on losing a good plate. I was disappointed by my father's response when I turned to him for help for the Harts. He usually was inclined to defend them against my mother's sharp barbs, but when it came to feeding a family, my father put the burden directly on Big's shoulders.

"There are agencies to help hungry people," he said, "and Big Hart shouldn't be too proud to contact them. We all have to compromise with our pride during these hard times."

Big and Lacey never got around to contacting those

agencies; they built their hopes on Big's rapid recovery and quick return to work.

Occasionally I'd heard Big mention a sister who lived on a farm in the next county. One day I asked Valentine why Big didn't ask his sister for food, and again earned one of Valentine's scornful looks.

"We thought of that, but we don't have a phone and her car's broke down and her chickens aren't trained to fly fifty miles to let us eat them and her cow just isn't in the mood to walk over here and give us milk."

Hunger made each of the Harts react differently. Big never discussed food; he sat and flexed his toes and looked pensive, and when he spoke it was to predict that soon he would be back on his feet again. Lacey, usually the serene philosopher, was huge in her pregnancy and uncomfortable. She became difficult, depressed. If size was any indication, it seemed probable that she would have to think of a second name to go with Sweet. She cried at the drop of a word, and hit back at everything anyone said.

Black rose to heights of heroism unsurpassed since earlier in the year when he had volunteered to help the flood victims. We watched with amazement as he poured most of his weak soup into Broken's chipped bowl one day; another time, Black poured half of his watered milk into Broken's glass when Broken whined and tipped his empty glass to coax another swallow from it.

Valentine's reaction to hunger mirrored Lacey's. She cried, complained, attacked. With Valentine and Lacey sharing despair, numerous confrontations between them were inevitable.

One afternoon I took a walk with Valentine, and I shuddered when she stooped down to pick up a peach from the gutter. The fruit was half-eaten, and Valentine eagerly ate the other half. Later that day she went up to the flat and came back downstairs with a paper bag in her hand. Without speaking, she began to walk toward town, obviously with a specific destination in mind. I ran to catch up with her.

"Where are you going?"

"Down to the Red Lantern to get some food. Like Crazy Gurney and his mother did last winter. I'm hungry."

"That's terrible," I gasped. "I don't know how you can do that, Valentine. The very thought of it makes me want to puke."

"Then you aren't very hungry." Valentine didn't waste time arguing. She walked to the Red Lantern, but she got there too late. The lids were off the garbage cans, and only paper remained in the stinking containers. Obviously there were other hungry people in town.

"Oh, hell," Valentine moaned. "Let's go home."

When we got back to the flat, the Harts had gathered for their one meal a day. There was only one item on the table—a jar of home-canned tomatoes. Valentine pointed to the jar and scowled at Lacey. "Is that all we get to eat today?"

Lacey tried to stay calm. "That's it. That's all there is, there ain't no more." She scrupulously divided the tomatoes equally into each of the five bowls.

Valentine watched scornfully. When the jar was emptied she charged into Lacey again. "Do you mean to tell me there's no bread, no milk, no cornmeal mush, not a thing but these tomatoes?"

Lacey clanked the spoon against the oilcloth and sat down. "You've got it. That's all there is, there ain't no more. I'm sorry, but I forgot to tell the chauffeur to bring home some caviar and steak."

"You don't need to be sarcastic," Valentine snapped. "All I did was ask a simple question."

"You're a good one to call somebody else sarcastic," Lacey bit back at Valentine. "You haven't said a decent word to anyone around here for a year, so don't get smart with me. I'd like to have a good meal too. I've got a gut, same as you have, Miss High-and-Mighty, and it gets hungry, same as yours. And what's more, I'm eating for two. So put that in your pipe and smoke it."

"That's not my fault," Valentine gibed. "I told you to make Big stay on his side of the bed, but no, you wouldn't listen. It's not my fault you didn't have enough sense to make him leave you alone."

"Oh, shut up." Lacey turned to her bowl of tomatoes and began to eat.

Valentine stared at her dish, stubbornly refusing to taste the tomatoes until she had made one more point.

"You make me sick, Lacey. Every time I open my mouth around this dump you jump all over me. I'm the only one here that's bringing home any money, and what do I get for it? Nothing. Nothing but a lot of lip. Rabbit eats better than I do, and I'm the one that feeds him, too, while the rest of you sit on your butts."

Lacey's eyes filled with tears. Big saw them and spoke sharply. "That's enough, Valentine. Leave Lacey alone. Here, take my tomatoes. I don't want them. I'm not hungry."

He shoved his bowl across the table toward Valentine, who immediately aimed it back toward Big, pushing it hard. Before Big could stop its rapid slide across the oilcloth, the bowl slid past his hand and tottered for a second on the edge of the table, then crashed to the floor and broke. The tomatoes, scorned a moment earlier, but precious now, splashed over the linoleum and soaked into its cracks. Valentine was the first to break the momentary silence. In shame and self-defense, she attacked Big.

"Why did you let it fall?"

Big didn't answer; Lacey spoke for him.

"All right, Miss High-and-Mighty. That settles it. You've ridden your high horse long enough. Tomorrow I'm going to do what I should have done a week ago."

"I don't give a hoot what you do tomorrow," Valentine sneered. "I'll be back to work tomorrow. I'll be out of this dump. And for all I care, you and everything in this place can dry up and blow away."

"Just remember you said that," was Lacey's cryptic warning.

I strolled over toward Sycamore Lane the next evening, wondering whether to tell Valentine what had taken place that day in the flat or let her find out for herself. She chattered when she joined me and we walked home together; she talked about the big juicy hamburger she had had for lunch. "I'm not going to tell Lacey that I had a good meal. Just let old Lacey think I'm still hungry. It serves her right."

When we reached the door of the flat, an appetizing aroma drifted down the stairs to meet us. Valentine wrinkled her nose and sniffed. "Something sure smells good. Is your mother cooking something special?"

I didn't answer. I followed Valentine into her kitchen and watched her begin her routine. As she did every evening, she went directly to Rabbit's box to give him some red clover. Rabbit's box was gone. I saw her face change as she looked around the kitchen, seeking Rabbit. Lacey and Big had retreated to the living room when they heard us on the stairs. I was alone with Valentine when she realized what smelled so good, what was in the Dutch oven that gurgled on the back burner.

Big returned to work the following week, even though his ankle still pained him. He borrowed against his coming week's salary and bread and milk again appeared on the table. Lacey even seemed pleased with a bar of Fels Naphtha and I was surprised to hear her say that doing dishes wasn't quite as bad as she had recalled it to be. Other good things happened when Big returned to work. The meter man became congenial and agreed to a compromise. Lights

243

flashed on and soap operas were heard again throughout the flat. And, most wonderful of all, the Sunday matinees were again invaded by a haughty Valentine, whose upturned nose told the theater manager that she held him and Big equally responsible for depriving her of the movies for three long weeks.

26

Early in August, Kathy's uneven whistle again quivered in the morning breeze, signaling that she had heard from Flint. Valentine relayed the postcard's message to Mr. Grey during Tommy's afternoon nap. "Flint's getting closer. The postcard was mailed from Iowa. He'll be out there hauling corn for the rest of the month, but then he'll be on his way home."

"That gives us five weeks." Mr. Grey studied the calendar on the wall.

"Five weeks to do what?" Valentine asked.

"Five weeks to convince Kathy to leave town, to get away before Flint comes home. You can do a lot of talking in five weeks, Valentine. You must start tomorrow morning before Tommy gets up."

"Okay, but it won't do any good. She won't leave. Not while you're still here."

Valentine was right. Kathy remained adamant.

"I won't do it," she told Valentine each morning that week. "I just won't do it. I can't do it. I have nowhere to go, and no money to take me there even if I did."

On the last day of that week, Kathy asked Valentine to discontinue her visits.

"If Tommy wakes up and sees you over here, you won't be on Sycamore Lane any longer than it takes him to tell his mother about it," she said. "Then Tom will be all alone. Don't come over again. It will make things worse for all of us if she finds out you've been here."

"She's right, Valentine," I said. "You remember when Tommy caught Mr. Grey with the gun, he told his mother about it the minute she got home. It's too risky. You can't change Kathy's mind anyway, no matter how hard you try."

Mr. Grey said, "You tried, Valentine. You did the best you could. I'll have to think of something else."

"The 'something else' he thought of didn't work either," Valentine reported to me that evening. "He told me to stay in the kitchen and keep Tommy busy when Mrs. Pain-in-the-Ass came home, and then he stayed out in the yard and when she went out to tell him off like she does every time she comes home, he asked her to give him her word that she wouldn't say anything to Flint about Kathy. I heard every word he said. He told her he wasn't *begging* her, he was *asking* her, and she just laughed at him. Told him to save his breath. Said she'd already made too many promises to him and she'd never make another one. Told him to quit whining and take his medicine and let Kathy take hers. He was quiet for a few minutes and then he told her he'd never again ask her for anything. Then he wheeled himself into the bedroom and I came home."

I spent the next morning with Valentine. Kathy made one of her infrequent appearances in the yard. She did not look toward us while she did trivial tasks. She picked a ripe tomato from a scrawny plant. She hung a solitary, threadbare sheet on the clothesline. She walked across the lane and picked sunflowers and ragged robins and crowded them into a pint milk bottle and sat it in her kitchen window. She was thin to the point of being skinny. Her shoulders were bent, as if the thin halter she wore were heavy. Mr. Grey watched her but didn't speak. Later that morning he told Valentine that he wanted to take her up on her earlier offer to bring him Lacey's old newspapers.

"I miss reading the news," he said.

"I'll bring you some papers too," I volunteered. "My mother brings the *Columbus Dispatch* home from the office almost every day."

"Great," he said. "The more the merrier. And after I read them, I'll use them to play catch with Gretchen."

Valentine left every morning with her arms filled with newspapers to be delivered to Sycamore Lane. She prudently hid the papers behind a sycamore at the entrance to the lane until Mrs. Grey was safely away. Mr. Grey caught up on the news and occasionally rolled a paper and tossed it to Gretchen and she caught it like she caught the sycamore balls and brought it back to him. After the reading and the game were ended, Valentine carried the papers to the ditch at the side of the road and set fire to them and scattered the ashes while Tommy napped.

A week later he made another request. "Bring me all the tinfoil you can find."

"Tinfoil? Why?"

"While I was playing catch-the-newspaper with Gretchen the other day I thought of a trick I'd like to teach her."

"What's the trick?" Valentine asked.

Mr. Grey laughed. "I don't want to tell you. I want to teach it to her first and then let you see it for yourself. And by the way, don't burn the newspapers anymore. I'll do that myself when I'm done with them. And there's another thing you can do for me. Convince Tommy that he wants to go to the park each morning. I need time alone with Gretchen to teach her the trick, and with Tommy running around in the yard, I won't have her complete concentration."

It wasn't difficult to talk Tommy into wanting to spend his mornings at the playground in the park. We walked over to the park with him one afternoon and let him play in the sandbox and on the sliding board and the swing. When Mrs. Grey came home that evening, Tommy—with a little private urging from Valentine—whined and nagged at his mother to let Valentine take him to the park the next day.

"You may go for an hour," she said, and Tommy's morning hour in the park became an established routine. Valentine and I exerted ourselves to be sure he had a good time and would want to return each day. Most of our hot, dry August mornings were spent in the playground. Valentine and I browned our bare legs as we stretched out in the grass beside the sandbox and watched Tommy fill and empty his tin sandbucket. He loved every minute and each evening chattered to Mrs. Grey about what a good time he had had and whined to return the next day.

Mr. Grey was pleased with the arrangement and thanked us for doing our part in helping Gretchen learn the trick.

"An intense hour of instruction goes a long way when it's uninterrupted," he said.

"When do we get to see the trick?" Valentine asked.

"In due time, Valentine. In due time."

One morning we left the house without Tommy's sandbucket. When we reached the sandbox, Tommy insisted that one of us go home after it.

"I'll go," Valentine volunteered. "Keep an eye on Tommy."

She was gone much longer than I expected. When she

248

returned with the sandbucket, I asked, "What took you so long?"

"I watched Mr. Grey and Gretchen for a few minutes. I peeked at them through the kitchen window. He didn't know I was there."

"What's the trick?"

"He made a doll out of the papers. He tossed it and said something to Gretchen—I didn't hear the word—and she caught it and tore it up."

"What's so great about that? She already knows how to catch sycamore balls without crushing them. Isn't that more of a trick than catching a newspaper and tearing it up? I don't get it."

"Neither do I," Valentine admitted. "But I figure there's more to the trick than I saw. I was only there a couple of minutes. When Mr. Grey's ready, he'll show us the whole thing. Until then, let's not tell him we have any idea what it is. He wants to surprise us."

"Okay. But tomorrow morning it's my turn to sneak back and get a look."

"Sure," Valentine agreed, "as long as you don't let him know you're there and spoil his surprise."

The next morning my tennis shoes were as silent as Valentine's bare feet had been the day before. From inside the kitchen I watched Mr. Grey toss the tied newspapers and saw Gretchen respond to a command I could not hear. She leaped and caught the papers. Her teeth ripped the bundle, shredded the papers. The pieces fluttered to the ground while Gretchen trotted back to Mr. Grey with the object she had caught in her teeth—a bright shiny necklace made of tiny tinfoil balls. It gleamed in the sunlight as she laid it on his knee. He patted her head and said, "Good girl, Gretchen, good girl," and she settled down beside him, happy with his praise.

"Did Gretchen carry a tinfoil necklace back to Mr.

Grey when you watched the trick yesterday?" I asked Valentine when I returned to the playground.

"No. She just ripped the newspaper. There wasn't any tinfoil necklace."

"There is now. Go see for yourself tomorrow morning."

She did.

I remained in the park with Tommy while Valentine returned to Sycamore Lane. She was gone a long time. When she rejoined us at the sandbox she was very quiet. Her face was pale beneath her freckles.

"What's wrong with you?" I asked.

"I don't want to talk about it" was her curt answer.

Every morning that week she returned to the lane while Tommy and I remained at the playground. Each morning when she came back to us she was withdrawn, distant, unusually silent. My questions about what was bothering her went unanswered. I finally quit asking them.

27

Unfortunately for Valentine's continued employment, her reticence with me that week did not carry over to Big and Lacey. Unable to do anything with her anger toward Mrs. Grey and her worry for Kathy, Valentine transferred her frustration to Lacey. I was on the scene when Valentine and Lacey had their most ferocious battle, and Big ordered Valentine to quit her job.

As usual, Valentine asked for the trouble she got. She had not noticed, as I had, that since her unsympathetic reaction to Big's sprained ankle and his weeks of being out of work, Big no longer treated her as somebody special. Big saw her through disillusioned eyes; he kept a distance between himself and Valentine. He didn't invite her to play Chinese checkers with him. He didn't volunteer information about the movies scheduled to come to the Hippodrome. He continued to bring home the free passes, but he no longer handed them personally to Valentine; he simply tossed them on the kitchen table without a care as to whether they got lost in a maze of food and dirty dishes and Lacey's magazines. Valentine's ultimate downfall came from assuming that she could get away with saying anything she wanted to to Lacey.

As with many historical military engagements, Lacey's and Valentine's last big battle was triggered by a triviality— by Mrs. Grey's curtain stretchers, in fact, which were a painful mystery to Valentine, since Lacey's various households rarely boasted a curtain. On a stifling mid-August evening, I sat with Valentine at the table and watched her suck her sore fingertips, which she had repeatedly pricked that day, attempting to stretch Mrs. Grey's curtains. Lacey, watching Valentine run her tongue over her sore fingertips, offered her own form of sympathy.

"It's just plain crazy to stretch curtains. It doesn't even make much sense to *wash* them, let alone *stretch* them. All it takes is a good hard shake to get the dust out of them. You don't even have to take them off the rods. Curtains don't really get dirty. You don't walk on them or lay on them or sit on them, so how can they be dirty enough to go through all the trouble to take them down and wash them and stick them on all those little tacks? It's crazy, that's what."

Valentine was in no mood to appreciate Lacey's housekeeping philosophies. "A lot you know about keeping things clean," she growled. "To hear you tell it, Lacey, *nothing* ever needs to be washed. Just look at that rag you're wearing. It sure could use soap and water. A lot of it. It looks like a bowl of dried soup. It's disgusting."

Lacey glanced down at her huge smock and agreed, "Yeh. My belly's so big I can't keep food off it. But after Little Sweet is born and I get my shape back I'm going to take better care of how I look. I'm going to scrape out some money for a new dress and get me a fancy hairdo. I owe it to Big to get gussied up every now and then. Big let me and Broken sneak into a Mae West movie last night, and I got a real eyeful. Mae sure is some hunk of woman. She makes those skinny movie stars look sick. She's all woman, Mae is. Yes sirree. And Big says I look a lot like her. What do you think, Valentine?"

"I think Big needs glasses," Valentine snapped. "I think you look more like W. C. Fields."

Lacey ignored the insult, but through the open doorway I saw Big's eyes turn away from the radio and toward the kitchen. Something about the firm set of his broad shoulders told me that Valentine had best leave Lacey alone. I tried to signal to Valentine, but I couldn't catch her eye. Lacey looked down at her swollen body and patted the huge bump that protruded in front of her and kept her from getting close to the table.

"Yep," she sounded proud, "I sure am big. This kid must weigh a ton. Say, wouldn't it be funny if there was more than one kid in there? Wouldn't it be a kick if I had five kids all at once, like that woman up in Canada did?"

"Oh, yeh," Valentine scoffed, "that would be a kick, all right. I'd die laughing. You can't even take care of the kids you got now. Things would really be a mess around here if you had five more."

"Oh, no, Valentine. If I had quintuplets, our troubles would be over." Lacey settled back to indulge in a lovely new daydream. "We'd get rich quick, if I had quintuplets. When that Canadian woman had five kids all at once, people gave her lots of money and sent her presents, and now the whole family is on Easy Street. It's only when you have kids one or two at a time that nobody gives a darn how you get along."

"The chances of having five kids at a time are about one in a billion." Valentine put a quick and cutting end to Lacey's happy fantasy. "And with our luck, if you did have quintuplets they'd probably all be as halfwitted as Broken."

I saw Big get up and move toward the door and I thought, You've gone too far this time, Valentine. Too far.

Lacey put her hands over Broken's misshapen ears and spoke sharply. "Don't talk like that in front of Broken," she scolded, "not when he's listening."

"Oh, come on, Lacey." Valentine's lips curled. "You know it doesn't matter what anyone says in front of Broken. He doesn't know shit from Shinola, and you darned well know it."

Broken remained passively unaffected by Valentine's criticism, but Lacey's lip trembled, and Black, watching as I was, Big's slow but steady approach toward the kitchen, warned, "Knock it off, Valentine."

Valentine ignored him and resumed her attack. "It's just too bad, Lacey, that you didn't finish the job when you ran that coat hanger up your ass. But leave it to you, Lacey. You can't even get rid of a kid without making a mess out of it."

None of us saw Big move that time. One moment he was standing in the doorway, and the next he was seated on a kitchen chair with Valentine slung over his knees and his huge hairy hand slapping hard against her thin cotton shorts. When he finished, he set her off his knees and thudded her firmly back to her feet. Black cheered, Broken stared, and Lacey simply said, "Thanks, Big."

Valentine turned to run for the door, to escape before she let her tears fall or her pride take a tumble, but Big reached out and grabbed her arm and gripped it, stooping over and drawing her up higher, off the floor, so that his nose met hers and their eyes faced squarely into each other's. The head-on collision that Valentine had precipitated for the past year was in Big's hands and everyone in the room knew it.

"You've really cooked your goose this time." Big's voice

was under control, firm and steady, and much more impressive than his futile shouts of the past months. "You tell those High-Muckety-Mucks that when school starts, your job stops. All you've given us since the first day you went to work for them is lip and trouble. You've been as useless as windshield wipers on a duck's ass for the last year, and it's going to end right now. And I mean RIGHT NOW. I don't want to hear one more word from you tonight or tomorrow or the next day or the next. You get your tail over there tomorrow morning and tell them you won't be back again after school starts. If you don't tell them, I'll go there myself and give them a big earful. I'll fill them in on how you treat us and I'll tell them how you talk to Lacey and then we'll see how high-and-mighty you are. And there's no ifs, ands, or buts about it. Do you understand?"

Valentine nodded. Big lowered her to the floor, released her, then gently wiped the tears from Lacey's cheeks and patted Broken on the head. Black slid off his stool, went over to Big, and stuck out his hand.

"Put it there, Big."

I followed Valentine's escape route and found her sitting alone on the twisted roots of the elm, her face turned toward the trunk, hiding her tears against its rough bark.

"You brought it on yourself, Valentine," I said. "You shouldn't have said those things to Lacey about Broken. You know how much she loves him."

She didn't reply. I sat beside her and reflected about love, and the complicated role it had played in Valentine's life for the past year. Valentine's love for Mr. Grey, and Mr. Grey's love for Kathy, had somehow gotten all mixed up with Big's love for Lacey and Lacey's love for Broken, and had lessened Valentine's love for Big, and Big's love for Valentine. Love was much too confusing for me to handle that night, too complex for me to understand, too mysterious for me to discuss. When Valentine stopped crying, I gave her a clean handkerchief from my skirt pocket and she blotted her tear-streaked face.

"Maybe if you go back in there right now and apologize to Lacey for what you said about Broken, Big will let you keep on working after school starts."

"No," she shook her head. "I wouldn't go back in there for all the tea in China and lick Big's boots. No way. That's the first time in my life that Big ever hit me and I'd cut my tongue out before I'd tell him I'm sorry. And what I said to Lacey about Broken is the truth. It would have been better if she'd gotten rid of him. Someday he'll end up like Crazy Gurney and Lacey will be like Crazy's mother— following him all over town to be sure he doesn't hurt someone. If it wasn't for Crazy Gurney and his mother, this whole mess wouldn't be happening. Kathy and Mr. Grey would be together, and things would be like they were last summer."

"You don't have to mean it," I told her. "You can cross your fingers when you say you're sorry. You don't have to mean it—just say it, so Big won't make you quit your job."

"No. That's not what I cried about. I planned to quit anyway when school starts. It's time for me to leave. I'll tell Mrs. Pain-in-the-Ass tomorrow morning that I won't be back after Labor Day. I would have quit even if Big hadn't made me."

"I know how you feel," I said, "and I don't blame you. I wouldn't want to be there either to hear Flint beat up on Kathy when Mrs. Grey does her dirty work. I'm glad you're leaving, Valentine. It's not fun to go to Sycamore Lane anymore."

28

Valentine gave Mrs. Grey notice the next morning, along with reasons that were logical and not altogether false. It was true that Big was again working full time and had been given a raise; his three-week absence had reinforced his importance. It was true that the eighth grade would be more difficult than other school years. It made good sense that with another Hart on the way, Lacey needed another pair of hands to help around the flat.

"Not that I really intend to help Lacey," Valentine told me, "but it makes a good story to feed to Mrs. Pain-in-the-Ass. In fact, I'm not going to do one darned thing to help Lacey; if she wants to live like a hog in a pigpen I'll just shut my eyes to the slop and stay away from the flat as much as I can until I'm old enough to quit school and get a job and then Big and Lacey will never see me again. *Never.*"

"What did Mrs. Grey say when you gave notice?"

"She said she understood, and she thought it was right for me to spend more time with my studies and with helping Lacey. She says she'll arrange for Tommy to stay in the day nursery until she picks him up after work."

"What did Mr. Grey say?"

"Something strange. He said it's time for me to leave. He said he'd planned to ask me himself to quit before Labor Day."

I went to work with Valentine each day during the following week. Every morning of that week she left me at the playground with Tommy while she sped back to Sycamore Lane. When she rejoined us she was reserved, uncommunicative. Each evening she became more taciturn, more withdrawn. Big and Lacey attributed Valentine's unusual reticence to Big's slaps on Valentine's rump, but I knew better. Her stillness had nothing to do with repentance. It was related to her solitary visits to Sycamore Lane. One morning, curious and a bit miffed that she was preoccupied with thoughts she would not share with me, I suggested that she remain at the playground and I would check on the progress of the trick.

"No."

"Why not?"

"Because there's nothing to see. The trick didn't work. Mr. Grey gave up on it."

"That doesn't make sense, Valentine. If he gave up on teaching Gretchen the trick, why do you keep going back there every morning to watch it?"

She looked down and kicked at the dirt. "I don't want to talk about it. And if you want to keep on being my friend, you'll shut up about it. Forget it."

I couldn't *forget* it, but I did stop questioning her. I knew that tone in Valentine's voice, and I backed off. . . .

During Valentine's final week on the job, Mrs. Grey brought home a soft pink wool cardigan sweater set for Valentine, one that Valentine had admired when we leafed through the newly arrived fall and winter Montgomery Ward catalog.

"She must have heard you say how much you liked it," I suggested, but Valentine disagreed. "No. She never cares about what anyone likes. All she cares about is getting what *she* wants."

"It's real pretty and it fits you perfectly."

"Yes. At first I was going to tell her I didn't want it, but then I thought, what the heck, she probably got it at a discount. I hate to take favors from her, so I took the sweaters and told her I wanted to do some extra work to make up for them. She said okay, I could give her bedroom a good cleaning."

Valentine refused my offer of help. "No. I don't want you to come with me again until my last day on the job. Then you can come over and say good-bye to Mr. Grey and Kathy and Gretchen."

Her brusque refusal hurt me. The curt response was typical of most of our conversations that week. I could feel our friendship dying—not ending quickly as had the fickle friendships in my old neighborhood, but painfully deteriorating. Valentine was pushing me away, shoving me out of her life.

Evenings, she deliberately sought Black, supposedly to instigate half-hearted arguments, which even Black scorned as being unworthy of his participation. I knew that her search for Black was inspired more by her determination not to be alone with me than by her hope to start a fight with Black. Throughout that last week of August, I found myself turning more and more toward Lacey, seeking conversation and comfort. One day I spoke to her about Valentine.

"I don't understand what I've done to make her treat

me this way. I don't know why she doesn't want to be with me."

Lacey was quick to close her magazine and open her heart, to dispense philosophy and advice. "Don't let Valentine bug you. Her nose is out of joint because Big finally put his foot down and let her know who's boss around here. When she gets away from those High-Muckety-Mucks who've been putting those high-falutin' ideas in her head, she'll settle down. She'll be darned glad to have you to talk with when she gets back here where she belongs. Wait and see."

"I hope you're right, Lacey, but I'm afraid you're not. I don't think the way she's treating me now has anything to do with her job. I'm afraid she doesn't like me anymore, and I don't know why."

Lacey had an answer for that too. "It's because you let her push you around. Ever since you two have become friends, she's bullied you. Tells you what to think, how to act, what to do. Valentine's smart. Almost as smart as Black. She knew how lonesome you were when you moved next door, and she took advantage of your lonesomeness. Valentine never had a real friend until she met you. Maybe because we live different from most people. Or maybe because we move around so much. Or maybe because she just hadn't met any girl she wanted for a friend until you came along. But she's a smart kid, like I said, and she wrapped you right around her finger the first time she saw that lonesomeness in your eyes. I know what I'm talking about. Remember, I've known Valentine a heck of a lot longer than you have."

I couldn't dispute that.

"Try telling her where to get off one of these days," Lacey suggested. "You might be surprised at what happens. Sometimes that's just what a bully needs—someone to bully right back at them. Like I said, Valentine's a smart kid, almost as smart as Black, and in her own way she's as mean as Black. Meaner, maybe. Black only does mean things to cats and to people who have done something to make him mad. But Valentine does mean things to the people who treat her the best. Look at how she's treated Big and me for the past year. And look at how she's treating you right now. Take my advice, honey, and either tell her off the next time she throws her weight around, or punch her right in the nose. If she's really your friend, that will straighten things out between you. If she isn't, who needs her? I'll tell you this much, since Big walloped Valentine's ass, Big and I sure have felt one heck of a lot better."

That was true. There was no debating the fact that Big's physical reaction to Valentine's verbal bullying had released both Lacey and himself from emotional bondage. Valentine's attack on Lacey and Broken had cut whatever umbilical ties remained between Lacey and Valentine, and Lacey fanned her way through the dog days of August without a care in the world as to what Valentine thought about anything or anybody. Serenity settled over Lacey like a huge warm comforter. Each day as her belly grew larger and she awkwardly transported her little unborn Hart from kitchen table to living room couch to crowded bedroom, she hummed and plucked lullabies on her old guitar and chattered to Broken about the little sister who would soon be there to play with him. Big, seeing Lacey content and happy and no longer vulnerable to Valentine's attacks, became his own boisterous self again and reached for his razor only occasionally, sprawled on the floor nightly, guffawed at Madame Queen's exchanges with The King-fish, and gulped cold beer without apology.

Valentine, true to her word, stayed out of the flat as much as possible.

The only combatants who fully functioned throughout that late summer month were Black and the cat, and their engagements usually ended in a draw. The cessation of hostilities between Valentine and Big and Lacey was not an armistice. It was the end of a year-long battle that had been called off by both armies due to lack of interest. The wounded feelings and dead relationships that remained were not worthy of burial or eulogy. They were out in the open, left to decay.

I tried to take Lacey's advice. When Valentine came home that evening, I followed her as she began to track Black around the neighborhood.

"Why are you mad at me?" I asked.

"Who says I am?"

"I can tell. You don't talk to me anymore."

"I'm talking to you right now."

"You know what I mean, Valentine. We don't talk like we used to. You never want to be alone with me anymore. Right now you're running around *looking* for Black, and it used to be that you tried to stay away from him. You act like you're mad at me."

"That's crazy," she said, not looking at me. "Why would I be mad at you?"

"I don't know. But I wish you'd tell me. I thought you were my Best Friend and now you treat me like you treat Lacey and Black and Big."

"Well, if you don't like it you can lump it," she snapped.

So much for Lacey's advice.

Instead of following it any further, I followed Valentine around until we found Black.

There was an armed truce between Valentine and me for the rest of the week. I stayed away from Sycamore Lane in the daytime, and each evening I went over to the Harts' flat and sat on the stool while Valentine ate supper, and then followed her outside to chase fireflies and Black.

29

I went to Sycamore Lane on the Saturday before Labor Day. Valentine's final day on the job was a sad day—a busy day. She had triumphed over the curtain stretchers that had precipitated her losing battle with Big, and she spent the morning laundering and stretching the lace curtains from Mrs. Grey's bedroom.

Our talk was small as we worked. Would Claudette Colbert write to us if we wrote to her? Would we be in any classes together in the eighth grade? Would my mother let me start using light pink lipstick? We spoke of important trivia—suitable to keep us from talking about the thing we were thinking about. Would Flint come home on Labor Day? What would happen to Kathy?

We took the stretched curtains inside moments before a brief but heavy afternoon thundershower soaked the backyard, forcing Mr. Grey into the house. I held the curtain rods while Valentine slipped the curtains over them and we rehung the stiff curtains in the brightly polished bedroom windows.

"Come out here and let me play some of your favorites for you," Mr. Grey called to Valentine.

"I'll be there in a minute."

Valentine adjusted a tie on a curtain, then took a cigar box from the dresser drawer. She opened it and took out a photograph, which she furtively slipped into the pocket of her shorts.

"What did you just put in your pocket?" I asked.

"A snapshot of Mr. Grey. Mrs. Pain-in-the-Ass is in it too, but I'll cut her out when I get home."

"Why did you sneak it? Mr. Grey would let you have it if you asked for it."

"I know. But I don't want to ask. It's the snapshot I told you about a long time ago. The one with him standing beside the fancy automobile. It was taken before he had his accident. I don't want to remind him that there was a time when he could stand and walk."

"Is it the same snapshot Mrs. Grey tried to get him to look at when you slept here last Fourth of July?"

"Yes. It's the one she looked at and unpinned her hair. It's the one she propped in front of her when she was naked in the bathroom. But she won't be in that snapshot any longer than it takes me to find Lacey's scissors."

We joined Mr. Grey in the living room and sat on the sofa and listened to the raindrops bounce against the tin roof while Mr. Grey played "Painting the Clouds with Sunshine" and "The Sunny Side of the Street." When the raindrops ceased and the sun shone again, he ended his recital with "I'm Always Chasing Rainbows." Appropriate choices for a day filled with laughter and tears, sunshine and raindrops.

The hot rays of the returned sun quickly dried the wet grass.

"I'm going to go outside," Mr. Grey said. "It's nearing time for you to leave, and I want to tell you good-bye out in the open, where we've had such good times together."

He was resting in the late afternoon sunshine when Mrs. Grey came home and Valentine prepared to leave. The house was spotless. The red and white checkered oilcloth was wiped clean and shiny; the cups were on their hooks beneath the small cupboard. The ice pan was empty. The cabbage roses on the carpet were pink and pretty and free of footprints. The veneered tables gleamed, and the beaded lamp shades sat straight and proper on the polished brass floor lamps. Everything was in good order in Mrs. Grey's house. Valentine left it exactly as she had found it many months earlier. The only thing changed was Valentine herself, and she was ready to leave.

Our good-byes to Mrs. Grey were brief. She wished us luck in the coming school year and thanked Valentine for the good job she had done with the house and with Tommy and promised her a reference should she ever need one. Tommy reached up and Valentine stooped down. He hugged her and she hugged him.

"Will you come back to play with me sometime?" he asked.

She didn't reply. She unfastened his arms from her neck and left the house, went to the backyard to say her most important good-bye. I followed her. At the kitchen door I turned to look at Mrs. Grey. She was seated in the easy chair in the living room, her eyes closed and her head tilted back. She held Tommy close against her, snuggled to her side. I never saw either of them again.

The backyard farewell was also brief. Mr. Grey shook my hand. I walked over to pat Gretchen and tell her good-bye while Mr. Grey had his last conversation with Valentine.

"You'll never know what you've meant to me, Valentine," he said. Her lip trembled. She didn't try to speak.

"You've done a lot for me, and now I must ask you to do one more thing. It means more to me than anything else I've ever asked of you—more than anything else you've ever given me. I want you to give me your word you won't come to Sycamore Lane again. Ever. Give me your word, Valentine."

I stopped patting Gretchen. I listened, waited, wondered.

"I promise," Valentine whispered. "I promise."

"Thank you. Thank you. Now it's time for you to go."

She put her hand out; he took it and slowly unclenched her fingers. He drew her open hand close and pretended to read the lines on her palm.

"I see a long and happy life ahead of you, Valentine. It's time to start living it. The minute you leave here."

"I have awful ugly hands," Valentine said. Her voice trembled.

"There is nothing ugly about you, Valentine Hart. You are beautiful. Beautiful. And don't you ever forget it."

He lifted her hand to his lips and kissed it. "Now go," he ordered.

Valentine turned to leave.

"Aren't you going to tell Gretchen good-bye?" I asked.

She didn't reply; she moved quickly toward the gully, toward Kathy's house. I followed her.

When we were on Kathy's side of the gully, Mr. Grey called out, "Everything's going to be all right, Valentine."

She hesitated, looked as if she were thinking about returning to him.

"Don't come back," he said. "Don't ever come back."

"I won't."

"Everything's going to be all right," he said again. "Believe me, Valentine. Everything's going to be all right."

"I know it," she said. "I know it."

He turned and wheeled himself into the house. We

266

walked up to Kathy's back porch, neither knowing nor caring if we were being watched from the house next door.

Valentine tapped on the screen door. We could see Kathy in the shadowy kitchen, sitting at the table. Her head was bowed, her forehead pressed against her palms. She looked up and motioned for us to enter. She tried to smile, but her trembling lips twisted the smile into a grimace.

"We came over to say good-bye," Valentine said.

"Is this your last day over there?"

"Yes. Lacey's due any time now and she needs me at home. And Big got a raise so they don't need my wages. And the eighth grade is supposed to be harder than the seventh. So I'm leaving."

Such logical reasons; the same logic she had presented to Mr. Grey—to Mrs. Grey—to me. Logic that, illogically, I did not believe, any more than I believed that Big's order, reinforced by his hand against Valentine's butt, was her real reason for leaving Sycamore Lane. Had she not already made up her mind to leave, nothing Big or Lacey could do or say would have made her surrender so easily. She was lying to all of us.

Kathy, more innocent and trusting than I, didn't question Valentine.

"I'll miss you," she said, "even though we didn't get to visit much this summer, it was good to know you were over there. It made me feel better to know Tom had somebody with him. He's all alone with her now. It'll be rough for him. You know, I really hope Flint gets home this weekend. Then he can do whatever he has to do to me, and maybe she'll leave Tom alone. I'd rather have Flint beat me and get it over with than sit over here day after day, night after night, and listen to her tongue-lash Tom."

"Aren't you afraid Flint will kill you?" I asked Kathy.

"I know that he *might*, but as for whether I'm *afraid*, I can't truthfully say. Like I told Valentine, when I had to stop seeing Tom, I died inside. I've already been through one kind of death. I don't know how another kind can be any worse."

"You aren't going to die, Kathy," Valentine said. "Everything's going to be all right. Believe me, everything's going to be all right."

The same words Mr. Grey had spoken across the gully to Valentine—the very same words. Comforting words— why did they make me uneasy, apprehensive? Why was I unable to accept them? Kathy could.

"You're right, Valentine," Kathy agreed. "Everything will be all right just as soon as she gets her meanness out of her system by telling Flint, and Flint gets his out by beating me. Everything *will* be all right. But now"—Kathy held out a hand to me and one to Valentine—"I want you two girls to sit down with me for a minute. There's something I want to say before you leave. You two girls walked into a situation that had nothing to do with you. Tom and I had been in love for more than a year before you met us. We didn't see each other often, but we knew we were in love. Then, when you came to work on Sycamore Lane, Valentine, we were able to be together almost every day. You understood that we had to be together. You helped us be together. You've been part of our love for each other. That's why I want to talk with you now, about love and marriage. Some day, sooner than you realize, you girls will be grown up and ready to get married. And maybe then you'll think about me and Tom, and remember how we met in the yard and sat by the fire and loved each other, and when you grow up and meet the right man, you might wonder if we were wrong in what we did—wrong to fall in love when we were each married to somebody else. If you love your man a lot, you might decide that we were unfaithful to our marriages, and you might begin to believe untrue things. No matter how anyone tries to make it dirty, our love was clean. All Tom and I ever did was hold hands

268

on summer afternoons and talk while we watched leaves burn in the autumn and laugh together by a gas fire in the winter while the snow fell. Tom didn't make love to me—not the kind that that dirty letter talked about—because he couldn't. But if he had been able to give me that kind of love, I would have gladly taken it. I love him completely. He's the only man I've ever loved. I'm the only woman he's ever loved—he's told me so a thousand times. That's the truth about what you girls have been part of, and I want you to remember it when you grow up and think back on these years and try to sort things out."

Kathy opened the screen door and waved us out into the deepening twilight. "Now run along home," she said. "It's getting late. It will be dark soon."

30

I knew our summer had ended as we walked away from Sycamore Lane. I saw its death in the deepening shadows, felt it in the chilly breeze. Valentine and I didn't speak on the way home. When we got to the flat, we found it vibrating with activity. Relatives from the country would be in town for the holiday weekend, and Lacey was in high gear, getting ready for them and the treats she predicted they would bring.

"We'll be eating high on the hog for the next few days," Lacey promised. "Big's sister always brings a chicken or two already cut up and milk fresh from old Bossy and thick country butter. That's one good thing about farmers—they might go to bed with the chickens, but they eat like hogs."

The impending arrival of Big's sister and the anticipation of a refurbished larder stirred Lacey to unusual activity. Armed with a new yellow bar of Fels Naphtha and an old undershirt, she tackled the kitchen linoleum again, puffing and groaning and attempting to secure her loose skirt between her knees to keep it dry as she scrubbed. She pointed out to Valentine the moment we entered the flat that it was a good thing she hadn't mopped the floor earlier in the summer when Valentine nagged her about it, since had she done so, she would have to repeat the task now that company was coming. Valentine didn't reply; she didn't seem remotely interested in whether Lacey and the floor and the rest of the flat were clean or dirty.

Inspired by Lacey's rare devotion to domesticity, Big pitched in to help when he got home. He lugged the overflowing garbage can down to the alley and rinsed it before dragging it back upstairs. When Lacey ordered Valentine to cull out silverware that might have resisted Lacey's indifferent dishwashings, Valentine, who a week earlier would have snapped at Lacey to do it herself, did not argue. She obediently began to sort through the utensils, and spoke as she sorted.

"Lacey, didn't you tell me once that when a Catholic dies, if he's done something bad, people can go to church and buy candles and light them and pay his way out of hell?"

Lacey, always delighted to be an authority on any subject, plopped the wet undershirt down, leaned back on her heels, rubbed her swollen belly, and gave Valentine the benefit of her theological knowledge.

"Yep. That's right, Valentine. In fact, that's the only way a bad Catholic *can* get out of hell. It takes money and candles for a mackerel snapper to get out of the hot place. I'm not real sure they go on up to heaven, like real Christians do. In fact, I don't think the Baptists hold out much hope for the mackerel snappers to ever get through those pearly gates, but at least they get off the hot seat. Why do you want to know?"

Valentine cleverly evaded answering Lacey's question by asking another of her own.

"How much money do you think it would take to buy a bad Catholic's way out of hell?"

Lacey wrinkled her brow, scratched her head, and then admitted she wasn't really sure of the exact price of redemption, but she suspected it was based on how much money a person could afford to spend on candles.

"God's pretty reasonable about most things," she reflected, "so I don't think he'd expect anyone—not even a mackerel snapper—to spend more money than he could afford. Dealing with the Lord is probably sort of like dealing with the manager of the Clover Farm store. The manager would like for me and Big to pay the whole amount we owe him, but he'll settle for what he can get."

Valentine returned to the silverware, Lacey returned to her mop rag, and I sat back and reflected. Small pieces of conversations, bits of questions, scraps of comments—in themselves trivial, unimportant, puzzling—were starting to meld, to form a thought, a vague knowledge. The pieces of the jigsaw puzzle were all there—waiting for me to force Valentine to tell me how they fit together.

Lacey and Big went to bed unusually early, but not to make love. Lacey's expanding pregnancy had put a temporary halt to passion and had inspired Big to express his love in gentler ways. As Lacey's belly expanded, Big's nighttime attention to her lush body changed direction—centered on rubbing her back with witch hazel, stroking her swollen ankles. Throughout late August, Lacey paid more attention to her tits than Big did. He still slipped his hands inside her wrapper whenever it gaped open, but he handled her tits carefully, humbly, as if they were filled with gold instead of milk.

"What's wrong, Big," Black chided Big one morning, watching Big's reverent reaction to Lacey's open wrapper, "are you afraid Little Sweet will have to drink buttermilk if you shake old Lacey up?"

"Shut up, Black," Lacey answered for Big. Her own daily tribute to her pendulous milk-factory was more vigorous; she briskly rubbed her tits with cocoa butter each afternoon as she sat and read her *True Confessions* magazine to Broken.

"Keeps them from getting blue lines," she explained to me as I watched, mesmerized by the jiggle-jiggle of the huge mounds.

Before dusk turned to darkness on that end-of-summer evening, the lights were out in the Harts' bedroom and Big and Lacey were sound asleep, wrapped around each other, restoring their strength, getting ready to reap tomorrow's harvest.

There was a lot of evening left after the bedroom was darkened, and I knew too well what Valentine's next move would be. She would do as she had done every evening for the past two weeks—she would search for Black and keep him as a conversational buffer between herself and me. Knowing her pattern so well by then, I also knew how to change it. Before Valentine reached the bottom of the stairs, I reached Valentine. When she tried to scoot past me, out the door, I blocked her path. When she demanded, "Let me out," I said, "No."

It was the first time I ever refused to do what she ordered; my unexpected rebellion brought her to a halt. She stopped trying to get past me.

"What?" Her eyes said they didn't believe what her ears heard.

"I said no," I repeated, "and that's exactly what I mean."

"You'd better get out of my way," she threatened, "or I'll punch you right in the gut."

I grabbed her arm and twisted it, hard, then twisted

it again, forcing myself to fight the way I knew Valentine would fight. When she yelped, I twisted it again.

"You aren't getting out of this door, Valentine Hart, until you tell me why you're mad at me."

"I'm not mad at you. Let me go." She tried to squirm out of my grasp, and I gave another vicious twist to her arm.

"Don't lie to me. You're mad at me about something and I want to know what. I've done things for you that I would never have done for anyone else, Valentine. I've lied and I've stolen money and I even let Black look at my bare tits, just because I thought you were my Best Friend. But you aren't treating me like a friend. For the last two weeks you've treated me worse than you treat Big and Lacey and Black. And I won't put up with it."

She looked down at the floor, avoiding my eyes, trying to evade my question. "Oh yeh," she muttered, "what do you think you can do about it?"

I had my answer; I had had it on the tip of my tongue all evening, and I was eager to spit it out. "I know darned well what I'll do about it. I'll yell for Black and when he comes I'll tell him everything that's been going on for the past year. I'll tell him about Crazy Gurney and his mother and Kathy and the letter and everything else I can think of. I'll spill the beans all over the place, and you can bet your bottom dollar Black won't waste any time giving Big and Lacey an earful. And you know what will happen then. Big will be out on Sycamore Lane first thing tomorrow morning to tell Mr. Grey what he thinks of him for not calling the police the first time Crazy jumped on you. I'm going to count to ten, Valentine, and if you haven't started talking by the time I get there, I'll yell for Black. I mean it." I started the countdown. Before I got to three, I knew I had won. I felt my victory in the weakening of Valentine's body as she slumped to the bottom step and hid her face in her hands. I heard my triumph in her sobs. I was a ruthless conqueror, determined not to let Valentine's weakness undermine my strength. While she sobbed, I counted. When I said "ten" and she hadn't spoken, I turned and opened the door and stepped out into the night.

"Black," I shouted. "Hey, Black, where are you?"

She jerked my arm, pulled me back into the stairway. "I'll tell you." There was panic in her voice. "I'll tell you. But I can't let Black hear. You're the only person in the world that I can tell this to. We've got to go where we're alone. Where nobody can hear us."

"Okay." I released her arm. "But don't try to fool me, Valentine. You can't do it. I know you too well by now. I might not *talk* as tough as you but I can *be* just as tough. Remember that."

"I won't fool you," she whispered. "I *want* to tell you, but we've got to be sure Black isn't around."

We surveyed the shadows as we walked to the corner and sat with our backs against the elm. The September moon was full and brighter than the dim streetlight above us. It illuminated Valentine's face and let me see her as she spoke.

"Mr. Grey is going to kill Flint," she said. "He's going to kill him before Flint hears about the letter."

I gasped. For a moment I was angry, furious at the thought that Valentine was trying to outmaneuver me, telling me an impossible story, thinking that I would believe it.

"You're crazy to say such a thing, and even crazier to think I'd swallow it. You know darned well Mr. Grey can't hurt Flint."

"He's going to kill him," she repeated. I studied her face. Her eyes were huge, haunted, and I knew that even if *I* didn't accept her weird story, she did.

"How? Mr. Grey doesn't have a gun. He can't fight Flint. He doesn't have anything to use against him."

"Yes, he does," Valentine said. "He has Gretchen. He's

already worked for a month teaching her to be a killer dog. She knows how to catch a newspaper, how to rip it."

"You aren't making sense. How is ripping a newspaper going to kill Flint?"

"Mr. Grey puts a tinfoil necklace around the paper. He's trained Gretchen to grab the necklace and bring it to him. She can't grab the necklace without getting her teeth in the paper. She rips the paper to get the necklace. She'll rip Flint's throat the same way she rips the paper."

"Flint doesn't wear a necklace."

"No, but he wears a St. Christopher's medal around his neck all the time. You know that. Kathy told us so. We've seen it ourselves. He's never without it. He'll be sure to have it on when he gets home. Mr. Grey will call him over, make up a reason to get him in the yard, and then he'll give the signal to Gretchen and she'll jump for the necklace and rip into Flint's throat."

I almost laughed. Almost, but not quite. Valentine's story was ridiculous, macabre, unbelievable . . . but she believed it. I saw belief in her eyes, heard it in her voice. She was totally convinced. Frighteningly sure.

"I know the signal," she said. "I know the word Mr. Grey says to make Gretchen jump for the necklace. I've overheard it twice. I just caught part of the word, but I could guess the rest. He says 'Chris' so I know he plans to say something to Flint about the medal, and when Flint reaches up to touch it and the sunshine sparkles on it Gretchen will leap for the medal and she'll rip open Flint's throat."

"I don't believe it," I said. "There's too much that can go wrong, Valentine. What if the sun isn't shining? What if Flint doesn't come across the gully? What if Mrs. Grey gets to Flint before Mr. Grey does? What if Gretchen is so good at the trick that she jerks the medal off without touching Flint? It doesn't make sense, Valentine."

"It's the only thing that *does* make sense. It's the only way Mr. Grey can save Kathy. He won't just sit there and let Flint beat her. You know that. He loves Kathy. And like you say, he can't fight Flint. I know now that he would shoot Flint if he'd been able to keep his gun. But the gun is gone, so he had to think of some other way to help Kathy. You heard him tell me that everything would be all right when we told him good-bye today. He told me two times that everything would be all right. He doesn't know that I've seen the trick, but he wants me to know that Kathy will be safe."

"But what if it doesn't work? What if it just doesn't work?"

"What has he got to lose? Nobody can prove anything. Nobody knows about the trick but you and me. Even Kathy doesn't know. He works with Gretchen in the far end of the yard, out of sight of Kathy's kitchen window. If Gretchen doesn't jump, then that's that. If she *does* jump and gets the medal but doesn't get Flint's throat, then Mr. Grey can just scold Gretchen and give the medal back to Flint. And Flint will never know how close he came to getting killed. But it *will* work. It *has* to. Wait and see."

"If you really believe what you're saying, we have to tell somebody, Valentine. You're talking about murder. You're helping commit a murder. We can still stop it. We can run over to Sycamore Lane right now and tell Mr. Grey we know what he's planning. He won't do it if he knows we know. Come on."

I got to my feet and reached down to give Valentine my hand, to get her on her way before it was too late.

"No." She drew back. "No. We *have* to let him try it. Maybe you're right. Maybe it won't work. But we can't stop it. We have to keep our mouths shut. You know Flint will kill Kathy when Mrs. Pain-in-the-Ass tells him her lies. Kathy can't fight back. Mr. Grey has to fight for her. If we stop him, we're helping to get Kathy killed. If somebody has to die because of that dirty letter, it should be Flint. Not Kathy. She never did anything to hurt anyone."

"But it's wrong, Valentine. Murder is wrong."

"Lots of things are wrong, but they happen. And I've figured out a way to make up for it if Flint is killed. I've saved my pennies and the minute I hear for sure that Flint is dead and I know he's in hell, I'll run right down to the Catholic church and buy candles until I'm flat broke, and I'll burn them for Flint. Lacey says God is reasonable, and I think she's probably right. I'll pay Flint's way out of hell, just as soon as I'm sure that he's down there."

My only salvation lay in denial. If I didn't believe Valentine's story, I didn't have to reveal it. If I didn't believe it, I would not be forced to make a decision between right and wrong. If I didn't believe it, I would not have to choose between my friend and my conscience.

Through denial I cleansed my conscience and kept my friend. "I don't believe a word you're saying, Valentine. I think you're imagining things. So I'm not going to tell anyone what you told me."

"Promise?"

"I promise."

We went back to the flat.

31

I hung around the fringes of the activity in the Harts' flat the next morning. As Lacey had predicted, Big's sister arrived early and dispatched box after box up the stairs. I watched Lacey put the freshly killed chicken on ice, and I helped Valentine portage a basket of newly picked ears of corn and a couple of sacks filled with bright red tomatoes up the stairs. Black carried two boxes of eggs from the car to the kitchen without breaking a shell, which promptly earned him a large slice of pink watermelon.

Big's visiting sister was much like Big himself; she was huge and hearty, and the presence of one more neighborhood kid didn't inhibit her one bit. She patted Lacey's swollen belly, jabbed her elbow in Big's ribs, and made ribald comparisons between Big and the stud horse back on her farm. Big beamed and looked proud, Black snickered, and I listened more intently. Valentine sat quietly by the open window, head cocked to one side, waiting to hear something more important than the jokes and laughter filling the flat.

We heard the wail of the ambulance at the same moment, and when our eyes met, hers said, "I told you so." The ambulance was heading west—toward Sycamore Lane. I knew then that a bloody ending had been written for the innocent love story I had watched for so long. I knew it before I heard the excited comments drifting up from the sidewalk. I knew it before the local radio station interrupted the network program with a special report. I knew it before Lacey moved over to the radio, which had been contributing background noises to the general confusion in the flat, and turned the knob and sent the announcement loud and clear through the room.

"A woman is dead on Sycamore Lane . . . killed by a dog. More details to follow. Stay tuned."

"A woman? A WOMAN?" Valentine's whisper became a moan, and the moan became a scream that would not stop.

"We have just received word," the radio voice continued, "that Mrs. Thomas Grey, who at one time was very active in Marietta's social circles, is dead. Mrs. Grey was attacked and killed by the family dog in the yard of her home on Sycamore Lane. Stay tuned for further details."

Valentine's voice became a whisper again. "Mrs. Grey."

Somewhere worlds away I heard Lacey say, "Good grief, I didn't think Valentine would take it that hard. I didn't even think she liked Mrs. Grey very much."

I sat beside Valentine's rumpled cot. The shades were pulled down against the golden September morning; the conversation from Lacey's kitchen was subdued. Big and Lacey had never before seen anyone faint, and they were uneasy in the face of the unfamiliar. They were glad to leave the bedroom when Valentine opened her eyes and said she wanted everyone but me to go away and leave her alone.

When the bedroom emptied, she whispered, "Get me the snapshot. It's in the pocket of the shorts I wore yesterday."

I rummaged through the pile of clothes lying on the bedroom floor. I found the snapshot and took it to the window and studied the woman with the golden curls and the happy smile and the soft cheeks and the eyes filled with love and the long, slender throat. . . . A woman who looked up with worshiping eyes at the man who stood straight and tall and looked down at her with the same look in his eyes that Kathy and Valentine had seen so often when he looked at them.

"Turn it over," Valentine whispered from the cot. I turned it over.

"Is there something written on the back?" I nodded. "Read it."

"You don't know what it says, Valentine?"

"No. I never looked at the back. Read it."

I read aloud the words which I would see forever. Words written a long time ago in Mrs. Grey's round, clear handwriting: "Tom and me on our wedding day, May 30, 1929, leaving for our honeymoon." And beneath the woman's words, a message written by another hand: "You'll always be my one and only love. With you by my side, Christina, my whole life will be a honeymoon."

Valentine and I could no longer deceive ourselves. The truth was brutally clear. I spoke it.

"It was her he meant to kill, Valentine! Not Flint. When he taught Gretchen to jump when he said *Chris*, he wasn't talking about the medal around Flint's neck. He was saying Mrs. Grey's real name. Tina was just her nickname. He meant to kill her all along, Valentine. From the day he first asked us to get him the tinfoil and the newspapers.

Maybe even from the day he asked you to get the gun down from the attic. He probably called out her name—Christina—after he had Tommy put the tinfoil necklace around her neck. He called Christina and she turned toward him and the sun caught the shine of the tinfoil . . . just like he planned it would."

"Yes." Valentine's voice was hard and flat. "I had it figured all wrong."

"What would you have done if you'd known it was Mrs. Grey, not Flint? Would it have made a difference, Valentine? Would you have told him you knew? Would you have tried to stop him?"

"I don't know," she said. "I'll never know."

32

We left the flat; fled from the innocents in Lacey's kitchen—from good people who knew nothing of murder, hatred, revenge. We left the flat—but the story followed us. It was being told and retold all over town, on every street we traveled.

"Grey shot the animal himself. The chief offered to do it, but Grey said no. Said it was his job. Borrowed the chief's pistol and drilled the dog right through the heart. Killed it with the first bullet. Killed it dead. Dead."

"Shooting was too good for the damned brute. Grey should have clubbed it to death with a ball bat. Should have made it suffer before it died."

"They say it happened real quick. The woman died instantly. Never knew what hit her. Those dogs move like greased lightning."

"Mrs. Grey was a good woman. A real good woman.

Nice to me every time I stopped to get hosiery. Took a lot of time with me. Was polite whether I bought anything or not."

"The poor woman sure had her share of grief. Once she had everything any woman could want. Then Grey had his accident and they lost the house and everything else."

"Yeh. And she spent all the money her family had left her. Spent it on Grey, trying to get him fixed up so he could walk again. But it didn't do her any good. He's still in the wheelchair. Always will be."

"She must have loved him a lot."

"Yes. A lot."

"I heard that she was wearing a tinfoil necklace the little kid made for her and put around her neck that morning. Folks say the sun shining on the tinfoil might have triggered the dog to jump on her."

"They say the little boy saw the whole thing. They say he couldn't stop screaming. Poor little tyke. He'll never get over it. Never."

"It was a hell of a way to die. It just doesn't make sense."

Walking brought no escape. The story followed us. We left the streets and sought refuge in the theater, but the Hippodrome was no longer a haven. We crept in and stared at the screen without seeing it; we could no longer expect a happy ending.

We returned to the flat and the darkened bedroom. Valentine lay back down on the cot and I sat beside her. There was nowhere to go, nothing to do, nothing to say.

"Are you going to go to the funeral?" Lacey asked.

Valentine shook her head, and Lacey reached into Big's coffee can and again lightened his dream. She took Broken's hand, left the flat, and lumbered over the uneven brick sidewalks and made her way into town. She stopped at the five-and-dime and bought a sympathy card, signed her name and Big's to it, and dropped it off at the post office. Then she walked over to the florist shop and searched out the fifty cents she had taken from Big's coffee can and chose a small spray to be sent to the funeral home. She put Valentine's name on the tag. By the time Lacey got back to the flat she was exhausted. She puffed and panted as she climbed the stairs and sank into her kitchen chair. "Little Sweet is kicking the be-Jesus out of me," she groaned. "I don't think she enjoyed the walk downtown."

"Can you really feel the baby move around inside you?" I asked.

"Sure," Lacey said. "Here—feel it for yourself." She took my hand and placed it on her swollen belly, and for the first time I felt life inside a woman's body. It made me feel oddly comforted to know that life was replenishing itself, that birth was as constant and as mysterious as death.

Lacey fussed at Valentine a week later when Valentine still had not gone to Sycamore Lane. "You've got to get over there and pay your proper respects," Lacey scolded. "Do you want Mr. Grey to think you haven't been taught any manners? It's not right that you haven't gone over to tell him how sorry you are about what happened. You're trying to pretend that what happened to that poor woman didn't really happen, and that's not right, Valentine. I know it ain't fun to go where somebody you like died, but you have to do it. Everybody dies sooner or later, and the sooner you put that in your pipe and smoke it, the better off you'll be. Nobody lives forever. Even Little Sweet, that ain't even born yet, is going to grow up and die someday. There's no getting around it, Valentine. Everybody dies sooner or later. Some day Big and Black and me will die, and even little Broken will go to heaven sooner or later, and that's that. There's no getting around it. The trouble with you is you see too many movies. You've got the notion from sitting in the Hippodrome that everything *always* turns out okay, and then when it don't happen in real life like it does in the movies, you get all mixed up. Now get your tail over there and say something nice to that poor man. You want him to think you ain't been raised right?"

To silence Lacey, Valentine walked toward Sycamore Lane. I went with her. We stopped at the curve of the road and sat down in the grass for a few minutes—long enough to make Lacey believe we had paid our proper respects—and then we turned around and walked back to the flat. After that, Lacey quit nagging about Sycamore Lane and began instead, as Lacey was eternally inclined to do, to look for a silver lining.

"It's a good thing you quit your job before poor Mrs. Grey died," Lacey observed to Valentine over breakfast one bright October morning. "Yep, it's a good thing you gave notice when you did. Otherwise I wouldn't have had the heart to make you quit and you'd still be over there taking care of the cripple and the kid. We're doing just fine now without your wages, and I'll say this much—you sure are a lot easier to get along with now that you're away from the High-Muckety-Mucks."

Valentine did not reply; she stirred the oatmeal and stared at it, and only I knew what she was really seeing.

The new little Hart made her appearance right on schedule and with the minimum of inconvenience. Lacey stayed in bed one morning in late October when we left for school and was still in bed when we returned home that afternoon, but she was not alone. A funny-looking little red bundle yawned and gaped and sucked at Lacey's tit and Lacey formally introduced us to Mae West Hart, then promptly told us that from that moment on, the name Mae would be used only for matters of legality, and the squirming little new Hart would thereafter be known as Little Sweet.

The name suited the baby. Little Sweet was a happy, contented, lumpy piece of humanity, and she joined the Harts' family circle without displacing any of the existing members. Broken looked at the baby noncommittally and let Lacey move him to one side of her lap while she supported Little Sweet against her big bare milky tit and let the baby noisily suck her meals. Little Sweet's frequent and enthusiastic visits to Lacey's big tits provided Lacey with another reason for believing in silver linings.

"Like I always say, Valentine, most things work out for the best." Lacey shoved her big brown nipple further into Little Sweet's eager mouth one morning and settled back, complacent, serene, and happy in her world, with Broken clinging to her leg and Little Sweet clinging to her bosom, and gave Valentine the benefit of her philosophy.

"Like I said, most things work out for the best. For instance, if you were still over there with the High-Muckety-Mucks, with your nose up in the air like it was for so long, you'd have a conniption fit every time I pulled my tit out to feed Little Sweet, and then I'd get upset from the way you acted, and Little Sweet would get a bellyache from my milk. Yes, everything works out for the best, if you just wait long enough."

I saw Valentine's spoon become motionless in the cornmeal, and I knew she was not hearing Lacey's words—she was hearing music from another world—a world forever lost.

Big agreed with Lacey and said so. "That's the truth. Valentine don't even nag me to keep my undershirt on, now that she's off her high horse and away from Grey."

Black laid down the punchboard he had been peddling at school and set Big straight. "Crap, that ain't because she's not working for Old Crip anymore. It's because she's stuck on that guy Gable—the one with the elephant ears. She saw him in a movie once without his undershirt on and anything anyone does in those dumb movies is okay with Valentine. I don't think Old Crip has a thing to do with your undershirt."

"Nah, Black," Lacey added her two cents' worth. "I

don't think you or Big either one understands why Valentine doesn't nag Big anymore. It ain't because she *does* see the *movies*, and it ain't because she *doesn't* see the *High-Muckety-Mucks*. It's because Valentine has finally realized that we're her family, and that we're all okay. Isn't that it, Valentine?"

"Yes." Valentine got up and left the table. I followed her.

On the way out we heard Big say to Lacey, "I sure am glad Valentine's back to being her old self again. I don't care what did it, I'm just glad it happened. She's the same old Valentine, just like she was before she went over there with the High-Muckety-Mucks. The same old Valentine."

33

She wasn't, of course, the same old Valentine, nor would she ever be. She and I were not the same together. We were quiet, we did not laugh as quickly, nor cry as easily. We were not sure of anything, nor of anyone, only of each other. We clung together, isolated from the rest of the world, which knew nothing of intrigue and murder and guilt.

Valentine did not speak of Sycamore Lane for a long time. Not until another Thanksgiving had passed and another Christmas season had come and gone and another spring flood had risen and receded.

One morning she asked, "Lacey, have you heard anything about how Mr. Grey and Tommy are getting along?"

Lacey's arm paused in midair; she looked beyond herself in the mirror and stopped brushing her hair for a moment. Watching Valentine's reflection instead of her own, she said softly, "That's the first time you've mentioned him since his wife died."

"I know. I just didn't feel like talking about it."

"Yeah. I don't blame you. It was a terrible thing. I still get shivers up and down my spine when I think of that poor woman having her throat ripped open by a dog. She sure did have more than her share of trouble."

"So did Mr. Grey," Valentine said. "He had a lot of trouble, too. With his accident, and not being able to walk."

"Yeah." Lacey laid her brush down on the sinkboard and scooped Little Sweet up from the dirty linoleum and nestled her nose in the baby's soft, sweaty neck. "You sure smell good," she said and then spoke again to Valentine. "Yeh, he had his share of trouble. But he brought a lot of it on himself."

Valentine was silent for a moment, and when she did speak I knew she was forcing herself to ask a question she did not want answered. "What do you mean—he brought it on himself?"

"Well, his accident, for instance. The car accident that crippled him. He was messing around with a married woman at the time—and it wasn't his wife. I've forgotten all the details, but it was quite a story around town for a while. They were out joyriding in his big fancy car, maybe fooling around a little, I don't know. Anyway, the car went around a curve too fast and turned over. Killed the woman and put Grey in a wheelchair."

"Was he in love with the woman?" Valentine pushed the question at Lacey and closed her eyes, waiting for Lacey's answer.

"I doubt it," Lacey said. "I don't know for sure, but I do know that he had a string of women before that happened. He was a real woman chaser. Gave his wife a bad time more than once."

"How do you know?" Valentine's question was hard

and flat and uncompromising. She opened her eyes and looked for the truth.

"Good grief, Valentine, everybody in town knew. Those High-Muckety-Mucks don't get away with much, even if they think they do. People Just Like Us usually have a handle on what the High-Muckety-Mucks are up to. We might not have much money, but we sure have eyes and ears. And mouths. Like I say, it was the talk of the town for a few years, the way Grey two-timed his wife."

"Why didn't she leave him?"

"I don't know. Maybe because of the little boy. Maybe she didn't want to break up the kid's home."

"Maybe Mr. Grey had money," I suggested. "Maybe she stayed with him for his money."

Lacey had the facts on that subject too.

"Nope. She's the one that had the bucks. Grey came from a good family—fairly well off. He inherited enough from his parents to keep him and Mrs. Grey on Easy Street if he'd managed it right, but he liked living high on the hog and he ran through their money fast. Then he started spending hers. Her family had money, his family had name, so it was a fair enough match. From what I hear, she was head over heels in love with him. No matter how often he two-timed her, she stuck with him. Kept her head high and her mouth shut. And in the end, I guess it paid off."

"How can you say that?" Valentine asked. "How can you say it paid off for her in the end?"

"Well, look at it this way: after his accident he couldn't two-time her anymore. She had him all to herself for a couple of years before she died. He was hers and hers alone. She didn't have to wonder if he was running around on her, and she didn't have to share him with any other woman. It was terrible the way she died, but at least she died happy. Yep, Mrs. Grey's dark cloud had a silver lining for a while, at least."

Valentine grew silent again. When she spoke, her voice was sick with despair. "Why didn't you tell me about him sooner? Why didn't you tell me what he was like? Why didn't you tell me about his other women?"

"Good grief, Valentine, we tried to talk to you about him a couple of times, but you pitched a fit every time we mentioned his name. You beat the holy shit out of Black that morning after you first started to work on Sycamore Lane when Black tried to give you an earful. Anyway, there wasn't a heck of a lot to tell, except that Grey had a reputation for being a woman chaser. Lots of men have a roving eye. Probably more do than don't. It ain't every couple that have the kind of marriage Big and me have. There's lots of skirt-chasers around. It ain't as if Grey was a thief or a murderer. And me and Big didn't worry about Grey messing around with you. He chased women, not kids. Anyway, all crippled up like he was, he couldn't have messed around with you if he'd wanted to. What harm could he do from a wheelchair?"

EPILOGUE

Valentine and I told each other good-bye on a snowy late-winter day, much like the day we had met two years earlier. Ironically, it was not one of Lacey's planned escapes from a frustrated landlord that separated us. It was I who moved out of Valentine's world.

I was not unique in my transition that year. Life was changing focus for many people. The thunder of heavy boots storming through the Rhineland, the ominous rumble of impersonal tanks traveling the autobahns of the Third Reich, the portentous rattling of Fascist swords, and the war clouds that were rapidly darkening Europe were beginning to paint an economic rainbow on the still peaceful side of the Atlantic. Industries that had been paralyzed by the Depression were stirring to new life. Men were looking each other in the eye again. Women were remembering how to smile. Children were no longer going to sleep hungry.

The economic renaissance resulted in the opening of a new branch bank in Columbus, and my exodus from the land of the tits soon followed. As a reward for having tamely entered a teller's cage in the Marietta bank and performing his menial duties without growling or clawing, my father was made manager of the new branch bank.

When he was officially notified that he was to be released from captivity and given the privilege of roaming free in the plush office of the new bank, he hired Black to wash and polish our old car and tipped the clean-up boy at the barber shop to shine his shoes—the first professional attention they had enjoyed since his demotion. Even seated, he looked taller as he left for Columbus with a luster to the car, a shine on his shoes, and a glow on his face. My mother stood in the doorway and waved joyfully until he was out of sight, on his way to reenter his proper orbit, and to return my mother to hers.

He remained in Columbus for a week, then drove triumphantly home to give my mother the best news she'd had in years—he had rented a spacious house in suburban Columbus and we could move in immediately. It was a fine house, he told us, with a yard and three bedrooms and a working fireplace. Before he had completed his description of our future home my mother had already started to wrap our cups and saucers in newspapers.

"Good," she said. "I'll start packing right now. The sooner we get out of this place, the better. I don't know how we put up with it as long as we did." She and my father stayed up all night packing, and neither of them looked a bit weary the next day. They were rejuvenated, reborn, given a second chance at life. In two days we were packed and ready to leave.

My good-bye to Valentine was brief, subdued. There were no tears—no laughter. No promises to write to each other, no pledges to keep in touch. No last-minute vows of everlasting friendship. We had no need of tears and laughter and promises and pledges; we were as bound together as Siamese twins—coupled by spilled blood and torn tissue.

I could not speak as I stood in the hallway and looked at Valentine, nor could she. We could not give quick, easy, casual words to our thoughts. My mother, as usual, misinterpreted my silence; I overheard her tell my father that it appeared I had finally outgrown my ridiculous attachment to that peculiar girl next door, and didn't seem at all sorry to be ending the friendship.

It was Lacey, of course, who knew and understood what Valentine and I were feeling. It was Lacey who shed the tears Valentine and I could not shed. Warm and loving, and not ashamed to show it, Lacey put her round white arms around me and gathered me close to her soft, comforting tits.

She patted me and said, "I know how you feel, honey. It's tough to leave a good friend. I've said a lot of good-byes in my time, and I know it isn't easy. Good-byes leave a hole in your heart. I don't care how many of them you say, it never gets any easier. We'll miss you just as much as you'll miss us, honey, and don't you ever forget it." Then, paying me her greatest tribute, she said, "You're welcome here any time, honey. You've always been People Just Like Us, from the first time you stuck your head in our kitchen."

Big extended his huge hairy hand and shook mine, then squeezed it. "Thanks for being our friend." His voice was rough.

To give myself a chance to swallow the lump in my throat before it became a sob, I reached down and lifted Little Sweet off the dusty floor and nuzzled my nose in her soft, spongy neck. She gurgled and pulled at my hair ribbon, and the lump in my throat went away.

Black came out to the hallway, and I saw that his hair was combed neat and flat, and he had washed his face—and the lump returned to my throat. I had never before seen Black with his hair combed and his face spotless. He stood in the shadows, as he had done so often. I went over to him, joined him in the shadows, and said, "Good-bye, Black. Don't forget me."

"I won't. I'll always remember you." Only Black and I knew that he was promising me that he would always remember me as I looked when I stood naked in a dirty alley on a clean summer midnight—a girl foreign to his world. A girl who was immaculate, untouched—and his for the asking, but not for the taking.

I turned to go down the stairs. My mother and father were already in the car, impatient to escape, to flee from the flat. I went down one step—then went back up one step—back to the landing. I knelt and I hugged Broken and I kissed the top of his misshapen head. I took a Tootsie Roll from my coat pocket and put it in his twisted hand. Broken didn't appear to notice or care about the hug or the kiss or the Tootsie Roll, but Lacey did. Tears flowed from Lacey's beautiful blue eyes and cascaded down her soft pink cheeks as she unwrapped the Tootsie Roll and put it in Broken's lopsided mouth.

I turned to leave and Lacey reached out and drew me to her one more time—gave me one last squeeze against her lovely tits, and I turned and left.

By the time the first pale crocus emerged from beneath the late springtime snow of 1938, my life had gone full circle. Again I lived on a quiet, tree-lined street and walked to school with girls like myself. Our tams were set at the same jaunty angle, and our midlength skirts swirled in unison a few inches above our white, rolled ankle sox and brown and white oxfords. Our sloppy-joe sweaters were universal and not a bit sloppy. We were girls whose hair was styled like Bonita Granville's and bounced around our shoulders and flirted wildly with the wind as we reached up to smooth it and flirt tamely with the boys.

Again I was with girls who rarely used profanity, and, should an occasional oath escape from our Tangee'd lips, we followed the mild oath with a deprecatory giggle to indicate that profanity did not roll easily off our tongues. Again I was with People Who Wouldn't Say Shit if They Had a Mouthful.

My friends and I talked confidently of going to college, then sensibly took a few business courses, just in case the funds for college did not materialize. We attended all the home economics courses, knowing that our ultimate goal when our days of games and studies were over would be to marry and play house.

We were paper dolls—all cut from the same bland parchment.

I was a senior in high school on Pearl Harbor Sunday. My friends and I had gone home from school on a Friday evening as sure of ourselves and our destinies as any persons not yet dead could be; we returned to our classrooms on Monday morning hushed, bewildered, no longer sure of anything but that our dreams of romance, early marriage, and comfortable domesticity had gone down, for at least a time, with the ships and the men lying submerged in Pearl Harbor.

The next four years were filled with war, emptied by deaths. Deaths that bestowed a bitter reality to those once-vague shapes in my sixth grade geography. I knew precisely where England was when I listened to Edward R. Murrow bid us good-bye and good luck from London. I had no trouble finding Anzio and Normandy on the huge wall map my father kept by his radio. The first boy I ever kissed remained on an Anzio beach; our high school quarterback never completed his run through the hedgerows of Normandy.

The war was persistent, pervasive, had a life of its own,

monopolized everybody's thoughts, affected everybody's actions. I was no longer interested in going to college. I was eager to participate immediately in whatever life remained for my generation. The typing course I had taken as a sideline in high school became my lifeline to Washington, D.C., where again I was regimented to walk in lockstep with the times.

I became quite sophisticated during the war. I learned to drink Scotch, to swirl my swizzle stick, stir the ice, make a couple of drinks last throughout an evening. Occasionally, when the war news was especially grim, I feared that the war would never end, and I drank the Scotch rapidly, letting it flow through my body, to warm me and make me believe for an hour or so that the world would soon be cozy and safe again, and that I would have many good tomorrows. The Scotch gave me courage; made me brave. At such times I shared a strange rapport with my memories of Flint who also sought comfort and strength from a bottle. My intoxicants were more sophisticated than his, and my intoxications briefer and more civilized, but my motives were not so different.

During the war the capital was filled with many transient young men, eager to live before they died. One of them became very important to me, and it was with him that I finally completed what I had begun in an alleyway with Black Hart so many years earlier. It was with him that I learned what had held Lacey and Big together through so many long nights and short rations. He and I spent countless hours in his room and lay naked on his bed while he looked at my tits and ran his fingers around my nipples and lowered his head to taste them.

"My God," he whispered one night as he stroked my body, "you have lovely breasts."

"No," I corrected him. "I don't have lovely *breasts*. I have lovely *tits*."

Although at times I feared the war would never end,

it did, and my life resumed its peacetime pace. I moved back to Columbus, found a job typing for a large insurance company, and made friends with young women whose days and nights were much like mine. Again I walked in lockstep with People Who Wouldn't Say Shit if They Had a Mouthful.

Throughout those busy years I rarely thought about the Harts. The times that I had thought I would remember forever grew hazy, indistinct, mercifully neutralized. Throughout the decade away from Valentine, memories of happiness as well as of horror dimmed, almost disappeared, and the thought of returning to Marietta held neither anticipation nor dread. When my mother asked me one mid-October day to drive down to Marietta with her while she visited an old friend, I told her yes without hesitation.

The drive through the valley was breathtaking; autumn was at its most glorious. Leaves drifted across the highway and brushed against the windshield. We were in Marietta by midday; I dropped my mother at her friend's house with the promise that I would return for her early in the evening, then drove downtown. I parked my car and walked over the same brick sidewalks Valentine and I had so often traveled.

As I passed the Hippodrome I saw on its marquee that Loretta Young was appearing in *The Farmer's Daughter*. The theater was smaller than I had recalled from those Sunday afternoons when Valentine and I so reverently approached our house of dreams.

I strolled down to Front Street and saw that the Red Lantern Café was still offering cheap lunches. The battered garbage cans that overflowed into the alley behind the café looked amazingly like those that a decade earlier had provided meals for Crazy Gurney and his mother but had not been so generous to Valentine when she was hungry. I walked over to the park and sat on a bench and watched a tug push a barge down the Muskingum, and my thoughts drifted back to the first day of our summer vacation when Valentine and I stood on the riverbank and wondered where a tug was going. The day we made summer plans that we didn't get to keep.

I was alone in the park but for a workman who was cleaning pigeon droppings from the World War I doughboy who stood with his gun eternally at the ready. A second monument that had not been there when I lived in Marietta loomed beside the doughboy. I read the dozen or more names engraved on it, and saw only one that I recognized.

I heard the town clock strike twelve times; hours remained before it would be time to rejoin my mother. On an impulse, I walked toward Fourth Street. I stumbled over a loose moss-covered brick, and I remembered Lacey—could almost see her again, with Broken clinging to her leg as she journeyed to town to get her love stories and newspapers. The distance from town to the flat was shorter than I had recalled, just as the Hippodrome had been smaller than I remembered.

If I was subconsciously seeking nostalgia, I did not find it on Fourth Street. The vertical, freshly painted façade of the flat gave it the fashionable mien of townhouses I had seen in Baltimore. Flowerboxes filled with bronze mums and fallen red leaves lined the windows from which Lacey had so often viewed her world. As I passed by, a woman emerged from the doorway. She wore a neat, broad-shouldered suit. A little boy trotted out behind her; he looked healthy, alert. The flat and Lacey and Broken were gone—replaced by a smartly dressed woman, a normal little boy, a dignified dwelling.

I felt a sudden, unexpected sense of loss, and I turned quickly and looked down the street, fashioning in my memory the sight of Big coming over the horizon, and of

Valentine flying down the street to greet him. Big's Valentine—his gift of love from Lacey.

Big was not there.

I wandered up to the corner and studied the giant elm. It had not changed. It looked no older, no smaller. The roots that had so often served as a seat for Valentine and me were still thick, twisted, rough. The tree that had listened to our secrets and had helped keep them safe from Black was eternal, comforting. I touched the elm, ran my hand over its trunk, took a small piece of its bark and put it in my skirt pocket and rubbed it between my fingers as I walked back to town. It had not taken me very long to retrace my childhood.

As I reached town I heard the courthouse clock strike one time, and I wondered what to do with the rest of the day. I stood on a curb and waited for a traffic light to change and casually looked at the people on the street and wondered how many of them were people I had once known. They were impossible to recognize; they were as altered as I by time and events.

The light changed and I stepped off the curb. Suddenly I looked up and I saw a young woman with bright shining red hair striding up the street in front of me. It was Lacey's hair. I knew it. *It had to be Lacey Hart's hair.* There was no other hair like Lacey's in the entire world. But the girl beneath the glorious head of hair was slim; her shirtwaist blouse was white and crisp. The striped scarf that drifted back over her shoulder and rested against her cardigan was spotless. The seams in her nylons were straight as they ran from her flared plaid skirt to her black patent high-heeled pumps. The smart handbag that swung from her shoulder was fresh off the pages of the Montgomery Ward catalog.

It was the set of her shoulders that told me who was striding ahead of me, wearing Lacey Hart's lovely red hair.

There was only one person in the world with shoulders so straight, so determined, so fearless—daring the world to challenge her right to be in it.

"Valentine," I shouted. "Valentine Hart!"

She paused, turned, and she knew me.

She was beautiful. Really beautiful. Even more beautiful than Lacey. As I saw her for the first time as a young woman, I heard again Mr. Grey's words the day she told him good-bye.

"You are beautiful, Valentine," he had said, "and don't you ever forget it."

We hugged each other. For the first time we hugged each other, neither seeing nor caring about the passersby who had to detour around where we stood in the middle of the sidewalk. The moment I saw that red hair and recognized the set of those shoulders, I knew what I would do with the rest of the afternoon. Valentine knew it too.

"Wait right here," she said, and as usual, I did what Valentine told me to do. I waited in the middle of the sidewalk, ignored the bodies walking impatiently past me. I saw Valentine go to a telephone booth and search through her handbag to find a coin. She dropped the coin in the box and spoke a brief message; she was back by my side in moments.

"I called my boss and told him I ate something for lunch that made me sick and wouldn't be back to work today."

"Terrific, Valentine. Do you think he believed you?"

"Sure. Have you forgotten what a good liar I can be? I was always great at telling lies when I had a good reason to. And I'm a lot better at it now than when we were kids. I've had more time to practice."

We laughed and began to walk, aimlessly at first. We moved in perfect unison, in harmony, and suddenly I knew that all those other locksteps I had taken with so many People Who Wouldn't Say Shit if They Had a Mouthful throughout my years away from Valentine had been mockeries. They had been false steps, going nowhere. At last my step was back where it belonged, marching to the beat of my very special and different drummer.

We chattered as we walked, talked about unimportant things. I told her about my years in Washington, my apartment and my job in Columbus. She told me that she was a telephone operator for Ohio Bell, and that she was attending college at nights, taking courses to become a librarian.

"It might take me forever," she said, "but sooner or later I will work in a library, and when I do, I'll let every dirty little kid that comes in the door steal as many books as she wants to."

She told me about her small apartment. "It's over in your old neighborhood. In one of the big houses on Washington Street. It's real pretty. I have a checkered tablecloth in the kitchen and matching curtains on the windows and a geranium in the middle of the table. I have lace curtains in the living room and a flowered carpet and my very own Bissell carpet sweeper."

"You're playing house again, Valentine."

"Yes. Playing house."

We became silent, visiting other kitchens, playing in other houses. Kitchens now gone, houses now decayed. When we spoke again we spoke of trivial things, using those trivialities as skates to whirl us over to Sycamore Lane, to keep us from really speaking to each other until we reached the only place where we could speak the truth.

Our chatter was inconsequential, serving only to fill time as we journeyed back through time, knowing that sooner or later we would be ready to speak of life and death.

We kicked the fallen leaves as we walked. Occasionally we paused to lean against a tree or each other, to take off our shiny high-heeled pumps and shake small leaves from them. We turned our faces up to the blue and white October sky and wrinkled our noses as milkweed drifted by. The brisk autumn breeze lifted my pageboy bob and tossed Valentine's red curls. Our words tumbled over and atop each other as constantly and as wildly as the leaves falling in our path. We were sophisticated young women in mid-calf skirts and high-heeled pumps and broad-shouldered cardigans.

We were children, playing in the leaves.

We chattered until we turned into Sycamore Lane and then we really began to talk.

"This is the first time I've been back here since that day Lacey made me come out to pay my respects," Valentine said.

"Then you kept your promise to Mr. Grey never to set foot on Sycamore Lane again."

"Yes. I've never been back. Till now. I never wanted to come back. But I think somewhere in my mind I always knew that someday you and I would come back here together."

We were silent. We took off our cardigans and spread them on a rock and sat on them. A DEAD END sign nailed to a post at the beginning of the road verified that Valentine had been right and Mr. Grey wrong in their predictions about the fate of Sycamore Lane. It stopped at the rise where Crazy Gurney's house once stood; it did not run over to join the highway west of town. The pavement Valentine and I had seen born so many autumns earlier we now saw buried in big brown sycamore leaves and hard prickly sycamore balls. Only wooden skeletons of two houses remained, partially collapsed, emptied of everything but ghosts.

Valentine spoke, softly. "Black's dead. He died on Guadalcanal."

"Yes, I know. I saw his name on the new monument in the park. Rudolph Valentino Hart, it says."

"Yes. Lacey's real proud of that. Every once in a while she takes Broken to town and lets him run his fingers over Black's name. Big's real proud, too. Proud of Black, at last. You should have seen him the day Black came home in his Marine uniform. Big and Black both got roaring drunk that night and went out and tried to catch the cat. Lucky for the cat it was sober, so it got away."

"I'll bet Black was a good Marine."

"Yes. And I *know* he was a good fighter. I helped make him one. He probably learned more from fighting with me than he learned from his drill sergeant."

We both laughed—small, gentle laughs. I fleetingly considered telling Valentine about standing naked in the alley and telling Black he could touch me, but I didn't. My silence was my salute to Black, the mean little bastard who was now an equal with all those others listed on the marble slab. Just as good, just as bad, just as dead.

"What's Big doing?"

"Working two jobs, as usual. Works at the Hippo-drome daytimes and graveyard shift at Remington Rand five nights a week."

"Does he still get free passes for you?"

"Yes. But I don't keep them. I pass them on to some kids I know. I can pay my own way now."

"What about Lacey? How is she?"

"She's the same old Lacey. Still reads her love stories, but now she reads them to herself because Broken can't sit still long enough to listen to them."

"How is Broken?"

"About the same, only bigger. He's on the move most of the time, and Lacey follows around after him—keeps an eye on him."

Valentine put words to my unspoken thought. "Sort of like Crazy Gurney and his mother."

"What about Little Sweet?"

Valentine laughed. "She's still sweet, but she's not little. She's fat and funny and Big loves her almost as much as he used to love me. And Lacey thinks the sun rises and sets on her. She adores Lacey's love stories, and she's nice to Broken and sticks up for him when Lacey's not around to do it. She doesn't do too well in school, but she gets along great with all the kids. She's not at all like I was at her age."

"Is Lacey still keeping one hop ahead of a landlord?"

"No need to now. She and Big used the money from Black's service insurance to buy a house outside of town. When Broken got older and bigger, people in town didn't like having him around, so Big and Lacey moved. Nobody believed Lacey when she told them Broken wouldn't hurt a fly. They bought a shack on the outskirts and nobody bothers them there. Lacey keeps saying it will look real good when she gets it in shape."

"The same old Lacey." I laughed. "Thank God, she's the same old Lacey. But what about you, Valentine? Let's talk about you. Have you ever been in love? Are you in love now?"

"No. I thought I was once, during the war. With the guy who worked on the assembly line with me. He was 4-F. Had a punctured eardrum. I liked him a lot. We dated and kissed, and I didn't mind him kissing me. But when he tried to make serious love, I just couldn't let him. We got as far as taking our clothes off and getting in bed together, but when he started to put his thing in me I started screaming and I couldn't stop. All I could think about was how it felt when Crazy Gurney got me down and rubbed his thing over my belly. I screamed so hard I scared the guy and he jumped into his clothes and ran out the door and never asked me for another date. What about you? Have you made love?"

"Yes. Several times. It hurt the first time, and I didn't get much out of it, but then we did it again an hour or so later, and it was terrific. Each time I do it, it gets better. I think making love is a lot like telling lies—the more you do it, the better you get at it. I understand now why Big and Lacey did it so often. When your body is ready for love, Valentine, there's nothing you can do but give in to it. And it's wonderful, Valentine. Really it is. It isn't a bit like that thing that Crazy Gurney tried to do to you. Maybe it isn't really because of Crazy that you're afraid to make love."

"What do you mean?"

"Maybe when you think you're remembering Crazy, you're really remembering Mr. Grey. Maybe he hurt you more than Crazy did. Maybe it's love that has you scared, Valentine, not sex. Maybe you aren't really sure yet how he felt about Kathy—about love."

"Are you so sure, then?"

"No. Not at all. But I am sure of one thing, Valentine. When the right man puts his thing in you—like we used to say—the right way, and your bodies come together, it's just like Lacey's *True Confessions* stories say it is. I hope someday you'll find out for yourself."

A cloud scuttled in front of the sun. The deserted road was shadow filled. Big brown leaves whirled downward from the sycamores. Tree branches whined, and somewhere in the distance a dog howled. I shivered and got up and brushed the leaves from my skirt.

"It's time to go," I said.

"Yes."

We didn't talk on the way back to town. We walked slowly, pensively, heard the leaves crunch beneath our high heels. Dusk came quickly, overtook us. Lights flashed on in the houses we passed; we saw people inside those houses, under the lights, out of the darkness Valentine and I shared.

When we reached the downtown streets, the shop lights were lit, and the mannequins in the windows looked very smug, very haughty, very sure of their positions. Very dead.

We paused beside my car and Valentine watched while

307

I fumbled through my purse, seeking my car keys. When I found them, I opened the car door, then turned to Valentine, and we hugged each other for the second time.

"I love you, Valentine," I said.

"And I love you," she whispered.

I never saw Valentine Hart again.